Amanda's Story

Praise for Brian O'Grady's national bestseller, *Hybrid*:

"I thoroughly loved reading *Hybrid* by Dr. Brian O' Grady! This well written suspenseful thrilling novel will keep you on your toes waiting for what happens next. Move over Michael Crichton there is another medical thriller novelist on the block!"
– Gather

"This novel grabbed me from the first page and I just couldn't stop reading. It is terrifying and intriguing and I was drawn to the author's use of modern technology to give the plot a sense of realism."
– Simply Stacie

"*Hybrid* is a slick, tight thriller which when you step back and think about it, is scarily possible. I couldn't put this book down… If you like Michael Crichton or Dean Koontz, this is the book for you!"
– The Bibliophilic Book Blog

"This book is both exciting and suspenseful. It is the type of book that keeps you on the edge of your seat and makes you want to keep reading from the beginning to the end."
– Dad of Divas

"From the first page, I was hooked and could NOT put it down until the ending forced me to…. *Hybrid* is AWESOME! Any fiction you read this year has to include this mind-blowing book from Brian O'Grady."
– True Crime Book Reviews

"This book is absolutely fantastic…. You do not want to miss this book. Make room on your book shelf, your night stand, your coffee table or your Kindle… and get this book! It's worth every penny spent and every second of your time."
– Outnumbered 3 to 1

Amanda's Story

Brian O'Grady

The Story Plant
The Aronica-Miller Publishing Project, LLC
P.O. Box 4331
Stamford, CT 06907

Jacket design by Barbara Aronica Buck

Print ISBN-13: 978-1-61188-047-2
E-book ISBN-13: 978-1-61188-048-9

Visit our website at www.thestoryplant.com

For information, address The Story Plant.

First Story Plant Printing: November 2012

To Margaret, as always.

Acknowledgments

I would like to thank Dan Howard my new editor who taught me that being a little pedantic is sometimes a good thing.

I would also like to thank my publisher Lou Aronica for the opportunity of giving my imagination a voice.

CHAPTER 1

"It is a cold night, my friend," Khalib said as a greeting, his sandals scraping along the dusty path. "It is always cold at night in the desert." He hefted his bulk onto a rock next to Ahmed's. "Hot in the day and cold in the night," he continued the mindless banter while securing his Kalashnikov rifle between them. Khalib spoke only Punjabi, which limited his overall utility and his conversation partners. "It is late, and you were not in your tent."

"So you were sent to find me," Ahmed said, staring at the cloudless night sky.

"They feel that it is important to know where everyone is, especially your kind." Khalib wore a thick camouflage jacket and he pulled it tight around his huge frame. The Pakistani was close to 150 kilograms and more than two meters tall; in another world he would have been a star in American football. Despite his size, he was agile and quick, qualities that made him perfect for his sentry duties.

"You mean our kind," Ahmed answered.

"Your kind, my kind, their kind; it's all the same out here."

"Is that what the Sheik believes, or just says?" Their isolation freed Ahmed's tongue.

"Let the Arabs have their fantasies of superiority; in the end it will not matter. They will be rewarded or punished based upon what they have done, not on what they think they are entitled to." Khalib ran his fingers through his thick black beard.

"Does your simple wisdom keep you comfortable at night sleeping in a fly infested tent while they sleep inside in warm beds?"

"One day the scales will be balanced, and that knowledge keeps me warm," he said.

"I wish I had your faith," Ahmed confessed.

"I am a simple man with only my heart to guide me. You are an educated man burdened with a mind that leads you astray."

"You are not as simple as you pretend, Khalib."

"How goes your work?"

"Are you testing me?" Ahmed asked, suddenly suspicious of the abrupt change in topic.

"What good are secrets so far out in the desert? You work underground, building your bombs and weapons, while we run around in the sun pretending to be simple terrorists for the American satellites. I wish only to know if we are actually accomplishing something worthy of the sacrifice."

"I don't think we will need to be here much longer," Ahmed said, without offering anything more.

"That is good. I have been here nine months. That is a long time to be away from the mountains, and a longer time to be away from my wife and children. I will take the money that the Arabs give me, buy a farm, and never leave it again." The Pakistani reached for his weapon and slowly climbed to his feet. "I will tell them that I found you up here praying. I believe that will give you a little more time for your heart and mind to wrestle." The big man dipped his head in a pious gesture and trudged back down the dusty trail to the camp below.

Ahmed would need more than a little time to resolve the conflict between his heart and mind. Once again he found himself alone, not just physically but in every respect. All his life he had felt like an outsider. Growing up in the Ja'amal region of Turkmenistan he was the lesser of two sons born to the great-nephew of Ja'amal himself. Before deciding to settle down, Ja'amal and his ancestors had been nothing more than bandits. A lawless tribe that roamed the southern mountains of the former Soviet Union, robbing, killing, and raping at will. Fifty years earlier, the invading Russians had tried to secure their southern borders by attempting to subdue Ja'amal. Within six weeks, having lost more than a hundred men and more weapons than they could spare, the Russians limped home after making a deal with Ja'amal—on his terms. It was into this environment that the slightly built, cerebral Ahmed Ja'amal had been born. His older brother bore more resemblance to Khalib than to Ahmed and was received with great deference by their father and the rest of the clan. After winning a national tournament for memorization of the Qur'an, and a degree of acceptance previously unknown to him, Ahmed knew that his path in life would be in the greater world.

At the age of seventeen, Ahmed left for Oxford. England could very well have been on a different planet. It was loud and crowded; no one carried guns, and life was not dictated by violence or the local Imam. There were women everywhere in various stages of undress, and morality was just a word in the dictionary. It was both wonderful and terrifying at the same time. Despite the traditionally tolerant English society, his fellow classmates viewed him with a degree of suspicion, accepting him scholastically but not socially. He found a mosque in a working class suburb but was viewed with even more suspicion for existing beyond the world of Islam. After eight years of living in a no-man's land, he returned home with a PhD in molecular biology and found that in his absence very little had changed. He was still an outsider in his own family. His brother, who was only marginally literate, was resentful that Ahmed got to come and go as he pleased without the responsibility of carrying on the family business of extortion, drugs, and prostitution. His father branded him a heretic after learning the aims of molecular biology, this despite the fact that the older Ja'amal was completely non-religious. Two weeks after returning home he accepted a university position in Paris and moved to France, intending never to return.

Six years later he sat on a rock in the cold Libyan Desert on the cusp of destroying the world. *Two hundred meters from here are the bodies of seven men.* Ahmed looked at his watch and corrected himself. *Probably eight men now. They were once your colleagues, Khalib, your countrymen.* Each had received a "vaccination" the day before; Ahmed himself had given each man the shot that he hoped would lead to a horrific death. It was the culmination of two years of round-the-clock work and was an achievement unmatched in the history of science. They had created a new life form. Technically still a virus, in reality it was so much more. They had merged the genetic material of Ebola, a primitive RNA virus, with the more complex Herpes Simplex virus, a double-stranded DNA virus, to form an entity that had all the properties of both. The greatest laboratories the world over had failed to achieve what they had accomplished in a poorly equipped underground lab in an empty desert. It was a scientific breakthrough worthy of the Nobel Prize, and a quantum leap in weapons technology. A leap that rivaled the creation of the nuclear bomb, and Ahmed sat on his rock wondering if Robert Oppenheimer had had similar emotions as he watched the mushroom cloud form over the New Mexican desert.

This new virus could be aerosolized or converted into a powder; even its mutations could be directed. It was, without question, the most lethal pathogen on Earth, and in the coming days he would direct the formation of nearly twenty-three pounds of it—more than enough to directly infect every person on earth.

Only Ahmed and his mentor, Jaime Avanti, understood what had been achieved. Others within their group of sixteen suspected that a breakthrough had occurred, but the work had been so compartmentalized that none of them had a working knowledge. Within a day, maybe two, all that would change. There would be no going back; the genie would be once and forever out of the bottle.

He would have to dissect the eight bodies to discover this new weapon's true potential, and then they would have to safely dispose of them. After that they would need more, many more "volunteers." The virus refused to infect anything other than living human tissue. In time a substitute might be found, but for now, more men like Khalib would have to die.

Even if he could live with the idea of sacrificing more volunteers, Ahmed wondered if he could live with the thought that his work would be directly responsible for the destruction of whole civilizations. Is this really what Allah wanted? He had been raised as a Muslim in name only, and perhaps that's why—after finding himself alone in France, searching for an identity—he gravitated to the Islamists.

Ahmed's mind drifted back three years to a particular sunny Paris afternoon. He and his cabal of academics were sipping tea in a bistro passionately debating how best to defend the purity of Islam against the creeping infestation of modernism. Was there a place for radio, television, or the internet for the average Muslim? Could they be trusted to see through the bright lights and commercialism to the corruption beneath? Ahmed listened quietly and realized that this little knot of intellectuals would never be moved to action. They were happy to define the eradication of Western influence on Muslim societies as a noble, holy mission, and the responsibility of every true Muslim, so long as someone else was doing the heavy lifting. Their hypocrisy offended him, and the long suppressed genes of his grandfather finally asserted themselves. He cursed their inaction; apostates, he called them. They had substituted intellectualism for true faith which required resolute action, and not fancy discussions in street side cafes. He punctuated his point by staining their snow-white thobes with his tea. The memory of their shocked and surprised faces had sustained and propelled him down the dark road of extremism.

What would they think of me now? he asked himself. Would they view his accomplishments as noble or holy? Could they justify genocide as a legitimate method in the defense of Islam during one of their Sunday afternoon debates? He doubted it. They would accuse him of hijacking their peaceful religion and label him an apostate for substituting true faith with his vision of hate and intolerance.

Years earlier, when the fires of religious fervor burned brightly in his soul he would view their label of heretic as a badge of honor. Any derision by such feckless men was surely something to be cherished. Except now, after the fires had long since burned themselves out and the reality of what he had done became manifest in the death throes of eight innocent men, with millions more to follow, he felt the weight of his mistake. Even at the height of his religious rapture his intent had never been genocide. His work was aimed at creating a weapon that leveled the playing field, offsetting the enormous military advantage of the non-believers. A modern version of mutual assured destruction.

"MAD," he said in English and smiled. It had worked for the Soviets and Americans during the Cold War, but he knew the Arabs lacked similar restraint. Under the guise of religious righteousness, they would use the virus to spread their will and power just as the Crusaders had done. History had come full-circle.

He accepted the hypocrisy of his thoughts. When he began the work he knew that it would lead to the deaths of others, but rationalized it with the belief that in the end it would be for the benefit of infinitely more. Only now, at the completion of his work, the reality was something very different. This was not a weapon that could be controlled, or entrusted to man; their success had turned his initial intent on its head. A few would benefit and infinitely more would die. His virus was an abomination before Allah and he had a responsibility to destroy it.

"Khalib," he called loudly, and the large man, backlit by the lights in the camp below, turned.

"So, you are done wrestling?" He slung the automatic weapon over his shoulder. "Come, I will protect you from the wild animals and the dark night."

"A question first. I saw Dr. Avanti leave the laboratories earlier this evening. Do you happen to know where he went?"

"Not precisely. I do know that he took one of the Range Rovers and headed north, with his little Arab boy." Khalib sneered the last part. He had no proof, but it was widely rumored that Avanti shared more than just a tent with the young man.

"Strange," Ahmed said, thinking that Avanti was still somewhere in the camp. The nearest settlement to the north was almost a day's drive, something that Avanti would never undertake at night. "Normally, if he was going to be gone for any length of time he would have told me. Did he say anything to anyone?"

Khalib stared at the smaller man, hesitating to answer.

"It's all right, Khalib, I don't want you to betray any confidences. We are at a critical point in our research, and it's an odd time for the Director to disappear." A sliver of fear stole through Ahmed. Avanti himself had told him that parts of the research were being stored offsite, and it was possible he was simply inspecting the secret cache, but instinct told Ahmed something else. "Come, my friend, I have to get back to work." The pair hurried down the hill, stopping at the entrance to the underground facility.

"I am going to Tar'uq tomorrow, so don't go wandering off. There will be no one to find you," Khalib said as both a joke and a warning. Once again he gave a slight bow and shuffled off to the small city of dusty brown tents.

Ahmed typed in his pass code at the keypad, and the recessed glass door silently slid into the rock face that disguised the facility. He waited for the outer door to close and for the pressure to equilibrate before the inner door opened with a muted hiss. Two uniformed guards checked his ID before they allowed him to pass down the glistening stainless steel stairwell. It was a perfunctory step—Ahmed Ja'amal was the Assistant Director, and with Avanti gone he was in charge. His face was well known to everyone.

A minute later he reached his lab. For months it had been filled with screaming, stinking monkeys of every variety, until Avanti and Ahmed concluded that only the human primate could carry their new creation. He had become so frustrated with the monkeys that he couldn't spare any emotion over their ultimate fates; he was simply grateful for the clean air and the quiet. He turned on his computer and his heart dropped as he checked the logs. Avanti had accessed the files three hours earlier—all the files. Ahmed randomly selected a folder and opened it.

"Folder Empty," the computer returned. He sat straighter in his chair and selected a second file, then a third file. Each time, the computer beeped and informed him that the contents had been deleted. He worked his way down the directory and found his personal password-protected files. Hours before, they had contained the detailed observations of his eight volunteers and their agonizing last 24 hours. Only he and Avanti had access to these very special files.

"Folder Empty." The screen blinked. Two years of work was gone; his boss and mentor had deleted everything. A thrill of hope rushed through Ahmed; perhaps Avanti had succumbed to the same reservations that assailed him, but Ahmed knew the man too well and his heart sank. Avanti had his own agenda, and morality.

He quickly stood; a sudden thought and fear propelled him towards the freezer. A thumb print was required for access, and only his thumb or Avanti's would work. A moment later he found six empty slots in the orderly arrangement of twenty-four frozen vials. Avanti had it all—the research and the virus. The genie was out of the bottle.

He returned to his computer desk and slumped into his chair. Six vials were likely all Avanti could carry without raising suspicion, and by themselves posed little risk. Combined with the computer sabotage, however, it was clear what Avanti had intended. The virus and the computer files were all he needed to begin work elsewhere, away from the prying eyes and greedy hands of their Arab paymasters. Avanti's resentment of the Saudis far exceeded Ahmed's, and he had always suspected that the large, hirsute Ukrainian had ulterior motives. There was an airstrip, more just a straight strip of compressed sand, only a few miles from here, and it was likely that at this very moment Avanti was somewhere in the air, flying to freedom with their research and an insulated box that carried the six frozen vials.

The enormity of the situation paralyzed Ahmed. He knew that he should do something, tell someone that they had been betrayed, but to what end? Avanti was a clever and careful man; he would have planned his escape down to the final detail. The chances of him being caught, with the research and the vials being recovered, were nil, even with the long arms of the Arabs.

Still, I have to try, he told himself, and reached for the phone. The instant he touched the plastic he had a vision of his body, along with the remaining research team, being thrown into a shallow grave next to a pile of stinking monkeys. There was no way the Arabs would allow him or anyone else to live once they had learned of Avanti's deception. Even if they believed that Avanti had acted alone, Ahmed and his team would still be viewed as unacceptable risks—risks that were easily eliminated. He pulled his arm back and stared at the phone. He was a dead man. Jaime Avanti, his friend, perhaps his best friend, had engineered his death. A few hours from now Avanti's disappearance would be discovered, then the theft of the computer files, and finally the missing vials of Hybrid virus. He could disguise the theft of the vials, but he could never reconstruct the hundreds of missing computer files. Avanti's final insult to the Arabs was to deprive them of not only their prize, but also of the data they had paid so much for, and in doing so had signed the death warrants of Ahmed and the rest of the research team.

His head dropped to the table and he began to weep. He didn't want to die, especially a meaningless death. The bravado and conviction about stopping the Hybrid virus was suddenly lost in the fear of his own mortality. He accepted that he wasn't a brave man, and hadn't been born with physical courage, but he had always believed that he had the courage of his convictions. But at this moment, the only thing that was important was the desire to live. He was filled with an overwhelming imperative to run, and his head quickly came off of the desk. His pupils dilated and his heart raced.

Where? he asked himself.

Nowhere, his mind answered. They were a hundred miles from anything that resembled civilization and safety; the camp had been placed here for this very reason. He could steal a vehicle, but it would need fuel, and that was kept at the opposite end of the compound for security purposes. There was no way he could commandeer a vehicle without alerting the soldiers placed there to protect them, drive across the compound, fuel the vehicle after subduing or subverting those soldiers, drive through the compound's main gate—once again through a phalanx of armed terrorists—and disappear into the desert.

"I see you have returned to work," said a voice, in French.

Ahmed literally jumped in his chair, and wasn't completely certain but thought that he may have let out a small cry as well. Turning, he found the last person in the world he wanted to see.

Klaus Reisch was tall, thin, and rather sinister looking. He had an aura perfect for the compound's chief of security. "I see that Khalib reported back to you," Ahmed said, after taking a moment to regain what little composure remained to him.

"Khalib reports to his superior, who reports to me." Reisch walked arrogantly into the lab, pulled a nearby chair from beneath a table, and sat directly in front of Ahmed.

"You are not authorized to be in here," Ahmed said, unconsciously leaning away from the German. Reisch looked like a lion studying a young gazelle, wondering if he should eat it now or later.

"Ordinarily that is true, but we have a problem, don't we, Professor?" Reisch reached for the keyboard, and after a few moments of rapid typing he turned back to Ahmed. "Do you see what I mean?"

The screen had a title written in English that read "Culture Results: Day 23;" the page that should have been full was completely blank. "I've only just discovered this," Ahmed confessed weakly.

"I believe you," Reisch said unexpectedly. "Where did Dr. Avanti go?"

"I have no idea." Ahmed felt a line of sweat roll down his back.

"Do you know if anything else is missing?" Reisch leaned in towards the small man and used his size and eyes to hold him in place.

Almost as if the German had willed it, Ahmed's eyes darted to the freezer and back. He knew that the German had seen the unconscious admission and the only option open to him was the truth. "Six vials of the latest specimen are missing."

"Is this the specimen that is responsible for the eight bodies downstairs?"

If Satan had a voice, it would be Reisch's, Ahmed thought. "Yes." His voice was becoming both softer and higher in pitch.

"Can you think of any legitimate reason why the Director of Research would copy all the computer files, delete them from the hard drive, and then leave the compound without permission with six vials of a lethal virus in his possession?" Reisch inched just a little closer. Ahmed tried to retreat but his chair hit the wall.

"None. If he were taking the samples and files for safekeeping he would not have deleted them here."

"Those were my thoughts precisely." Reisch slowly pushed back and then rose to his unnatural height. "I think it is best that you come with me. We need to keep you and the rest of your team safe." He stepped aside and two men dressed all in black, from their berets to their combat fatigues and automatic weapons, advanced on Ahmed.

"What about the rest of the samples?" Ahmed's voice was as high as a little girl's.

"We will secure them," Reisch said as both of his soldiers lightly steered Ahmed from the laboratory.

CHAPTER 2

"Does it make any of you angry that a little less than a year has gone by and very few Americans remember what happened?" Mindy McCoy, super-model turned talk show host, asked the four women that surrounded her. She shifted her long legs and casually inclined towards the pale, blonde woman to her left, just as the voice in her ear had instructed.

For a moment Amanda met the gaze of her host, but she became distracted by movement just beyond the glare of the stage lights. Three large television cameras prowled the permimeter of their group, and she could almost feel them focusing in on her face. She had said very little during the fifteen minute interview, and it was becoming uncomfortably obvious. Heather Waylens shifted her legs as well, just not as casually as Mindy, Reflexively, Amanda glanced across the stage at the older woman's stony glare. It communicated one message to Amanda: "Do your part." A weak, joyless smile crossed Amanda's face as she stared into the cameras. She took a long breath as the panel, the audience, and the TV world waited. "At this point in my life it takes almost everything I have to get out of bed in the morning. I simply don't have the luxury of being mad at anyone."

Mindy McCoy and the rest of the world waited for more, but Amanda's gaze had returned to the floor. The moment began to stretch, and just as everyone began to shift rather uncomfortably, Heather and one of the other panelists jumped into the void. At first their comments stepped over each other's, but it was Heather's voice that prevailed. "The American mindset is always looking forward. It is a requisite for progress and one of the reasons that America leads the world in so many ways. Of course, the cost of that is a short memory. We have to guard against the mistakes of the past being forgotten so that we as a people can incorporate those lessons as we work to fulfill our great destiny …" Heather continued for a full two minutes before yielding the floor back to their host, who immediately took them to a commercial break.

The stage quickly filled with show personnel. Despite the attention of her make-up artist, Mindy whispered to Amanda: "Honey, we need a bit more from you." Her careful and practiced elocution had been replaced by a more natural drawl.

"Hold still or you won't be beautiful," the make-up artist scolded Mindy.

"Amanda," Heather called, but the frenetic activity gave Amanda a convenient excuse to ignore her summons. "You need to tell your story, for everyone's sake," Heather pleaded, with a tone that was much too close to a demand.

"Especially yours," Amanda whispered to herself. Everyone was trying to turn her grief to their advantage, particularly Congresswoman Heather Waylens. Her husband, the previous Representative of Kansas' Third District, had died along with 202 others, including Amanda's husband and their two-year-old son, when Delta flight 894 crashed into an Iowa cornfield. The governor of Kansas appointed Heather to serve out her late husband's term, but she had every intention of holding onto that seat well beyond the remaining sixteen months, and perhaps other seats as well. She used her loss and the pain of others to further her ambition, and right now Amanda hated her. She had never hated anything or anyone in her entire 24 years, but she was certain that at this instant she hated the Congresswoman from Kansas. It was a good hate, a righteous hate that for a moment burned brightly in the confines of her hollow soul, and then, just as quickly as it had flared, it began to fade, depriving Amanda of its heat and energy, leaving her drained from the emotional effort.

A figure suddenly blocked the bright lights, and Amanda found a young, slight man scanning her face. "Just checking for shiny spots," he said, leaning in close and inspecting her forehead. "Sweetheart, you were made for TV," he sang while straightening, and playfully patted her nose with his powder-puff.

"Coming out in thirty seconds," a voice screamed, and the flurry of activity that surrounded the group spun even faster. Something touched Amanda's hand and she turned to find Mindy's face inches from hers.

"I know that this makes you uncomfortable, and it's more than a little intimidating, but try and forget all this." Her arm swept across the stage. "Ignore the lights, the cameras, even the Congresswoman, and just talk to me as if we were in your kitchen; just us two girls, no one else." Mindy's eyes sparkled, her smile was natural and infectious, and Amanda realized that Mindy had more going for her than just a singular beauty, a perfect figure, millions of dollars, her own TV show, and uncounted adoring fans.

"I'll try," Amanda answered.

"People want to hear what you have to say. They should hear it and, between you and me, I would prefer that it come from you rather than a politician." Her head gave a quick jerk towards Heather.

"It's difficult for me to care about what other people need." Amanda paused as the stage lights came up. "That didn't come out right." She smiled. "I probably should be angry— maybe at the mechanic who didn't fix the door correctly, or Delta Airlines for not ensuring that he was properly trained or, as Heather would like people to believe, the Transportation Board and the government for allowing Delta to perform their own inspections. Maybe I should take it all the way up to God, who gave me something wonderful and then snatched it back. But what does it matter; in the end they're still gone, and their absence is all I can feel."

"You're trapped," Mindy said.

"I'm stuck; that's what everyone tells me. It's why I'm here, to get 'unstuck.'" Amanda briefly smiled, but then her head sagged as she began to examine a spot on the stage a few feet in front of her shoes.

"But you don't want to get unstuck, because as long as you still feel their absence, in some way they're still with you," Mindy said softly, with a tone that revealed more than understanding. "Getting unstuck means taking a step away from their memory and is an acknowledgement that they are never coming back, that things will never be as they were."

Amanda looked up from the studio floor and found Mindy's eyes glistening with unshed tears.

"My parents, when I was thirteen," Mindy said, answering Amanda's look. "The details aren't important; what is important is that I know what it means to be stuck. I know what it's like to have others tell you that you need to do this or that, feel this way for this amount of time, and then move on to this next stage. But they really don't understand what being stuck means. In some ways it's an acknowledgement of the people that we've lost, how their passing has torn out a large part of you, and that 'moving on' means filling that void with something other than them. In some ways it's a violation of their memory."

Amanda stared into Mindy's flawless face and realized that someone else in the world understood—that she really wasn't alone. Since the accident, she had met with more than a dozen other "survivors" of Flight 894, and each of them had managed to either move past their grief or controlled it well enough to put on a brave face, which only increased Amanda's isolation. "But you survived," Amanda managed to say with only a slight waver.

"For a long time that's all I could manage." Mindy's perpetual smile had a painful edge as her hand slipped into Amanda's and they shared a private moment on national television. "My director is having a fit upstairs because we are so far off topic and I'm starting to sound more like Dr. Phil than an empty-headed talk show host. I think he's afraid that if I show more than one dimension I'll demand more money." The studio audience erupted in a mixture of laughter and applause. "Well, I think we are right on topic." Mindy let go of Amanda's hand and half-rose from her seat. She faced the camera and had to shout over the audience, who began to cheer. "A year ago two hundred and three people died in what some say was a plane crash that should never have happened, but the human toll was far greater than that, and these four ladies, along with hundreds of others, will have to deal with their loss every day for the rest of their lives. My next two guests will hopefully try and explain why. Coming up after this short video salute to the victims of flight 894 are Kevin Tilits of the National Transportation Authority, and Dennis Hastings, president of Delta Airlines." The audience cheered louder and the stage lights dimmed.

A stagehand appeared at Amanda's side and began to unclip the microphone attached to the collar of her blouse. "Please follow me," he told Amanda rather curtly the moment she was free.

"Can you give me just a moment?" she asked the young man. "Thanks, Mindy," she said, reaching for her host's arm.

"Can you stay until we're done here?" she asked Amanda, who nodded. "Good. Will you please escort Mrs. Flynn to my dressing room?" she ordered the stagehand as much as asked him, and then returned to the argument she was having with her director.

Amanda followed the irritated and stressed man offstage; apparently Mindy's dismissive attitude towards the crew was not entirely unusual, and Amanda felt obliged to apologize for his help.

"Don't worry about it; she always gets this way when the boss man is riding her."

"I think she's in trouble because of me," Amanda said as they navigated through a maze of cables, wires, and video equipment.

"Are you kidding me? That was great TV. It'll be all over the entertainment channels in an hour, and tomorrow our share will be up by at least ten points. If she keeps this up she won't have to ask for more money, they'll be throwing it at her." He opened a door for Amanda, and as she walked through she felt his eyes follow her into the room. "Do you have anyone here with you? I could bring them up while you wait."

"That would be nice, but I don't want to impose."

"You're not imposing; it's my job."

"My mother-in-law, Lisa Flynn, is in the yellow room. She's about five-five, short brown hair …"

"It's OK; I think I can find her. I'll be back in a moment." He shut the door and the latch closed with a muted click.

Mindy's dressing room was sparse. She had a table covered with a variety of cosmetics; above it was the obligatory mirror rimmed with bright lights, and aside from a small sofa and a recliner, the only other thing in Mindy's room was a television, which was tuned to her show. Amanda quickly turned the TV off, as the video showing the remains of Flight 894 focused on an undamaged teddy bear lying on its side. Behind it was a shattered airplane seat. This particular frame had become the symbol of the tragedy, and it pierced Amanda to the core. It was the main reason that she had been invited here. The bear's name was Fred T. Bear, and Amanda had bought it for her son's second birthday, a month before he died. She had no idea whether the seat behind Fred belonged to her son, her husband, or someone else. It didn't really matter, they were gone; only Fred had survived, and he was safely wrapped in plastic somewhere in her in-laws' home.

CHAPTER 3

Khalib watched the security team escort Dr. Ja'amal to his tent with little surprise. The small man had been much too willing to share his feelings about the powers beyond his station. He shook his head and returned to his rounds. He would walk the perimeter of the compound until the sun came up, protecting his nearly one-hundred colleagues as they slept. He didn't mind his sentry duties as much as the religious indoctrination that would follow. Like every other morning, he would pretend to listen as the Imam droned on about duty and jihad, nodding his head at all the appropriate points and praising Allah for his beneficence. Khalib believed himself a good Muslim, but to his mind that did not require him to be martyred, or to kill those who did not share his belief. He was here to play a part, nothing more. All the activity above ground was a ruse to deceive the Americans into believing that this was a small, inconsequential training camp, not worth much attention, and certainly not a biologic weapons laboratory. So they ran around in the desert, pretending to shoot and blow things up as ineptly as possible every time a satellite passed overhead. Khalib smiled with the thought that there were only a handful of real weapons in the entire compound, and most of them were carried by the security force that remained hidden.

He rounded a corner and decided that he needed to sit for a while and perhaps get something to drink. He had an uncomfortable buzzing sensation in his head and was uncharacteristically fatigued, both certainly due to dehydration. The water in his canteen had a funny salty taste, and each time he took a sip of it his mouth tingled. Hours earlier he had poured what remained of his daily ration into the sand. It wasn't unusual to have problems with their water, and for the last week they had been using a small tanker truck for their supply. The bitter and salty aftertaste was an indication that they were getting down to the last of it, and he hoped that some tea would mask it. He turned back the flap of the mess tent and was greeted by silence. Normally at least half a dozen men would be busy preparing breakfast for the compound. Khalib glanced at his watch, found that his estimation of the time was correct, and after a moment of confusion walked through the tent and into what passed for a dining hall in the middle of the Libyan Desert. A large central aisle was framed by six rows of long metal tables arranged along both sides of the pavilion. A figure with his back to Khalib sat at the second table; he watched the figure struggle with something and then recognized his grunting.

"Good morning, Habib," he greeted his countryman and tent mate. Habib did not respond, but continued to struggle until he finally screamed and frantically stripped off his tunic. By the time Khalib had reached his friend he was on the ground scouring his chest with sand and rocks. Within moments his skin was raw and bleeding. "Habib, what are you doing?" Khalib grabbed the smaller man's hands and restrained him.

"It burns," he screamed in full voice. "It burns, it burns …" he continued, and Khalib wrapped his arms around his friend and forced him back up to one of the benches. Habib's right arm came loose and he started to tear at his face, all the while screaming. Khalib noticed blisters and deep scratches on the back of Habib's hands and arms as he pried his friend's fingers out of his face.

"I need some help," Khalib called; he was a big man, but so was Habib. "Have you burned yourself?" he asked his friend, who had begun to wail and thrash inside his grasp. "Somebody help me," Khalib yelled even louder. Flashlights and then dark figures began to appear, but none of them approached the pair of struggling Pakistanis. "Come, somebody, grab his arm," he yelled, and despite the fact that most would not understand his language, his need was evident. "What's wrong with you dogs?" Khalib demanded, and then followed the beams of their flashlights to the bloodstained sand just outside the tent. Another man lay on the ground, his head almost severed from his body, an expression of horror frozen on his upturned face. The figures began chattering away in some foreign language, and then, first one, and then all of them, fled, leaving Khalib alone with the struggling Habib. "What have you done, my friend?" He asked the wailing man, noticing more blood and at least two more corpses.

Habib suddenly stopped struggling, and his insane gaze was replaced with terror. "Khalib," he said plaintively, "you have to help me."

"Tell me how, my friend." Khalib relaxed his grip on Habib's wrist.

"You have to kill me. The desert demons have found me. They're inside of me," Habib finally said, with a tortured but clear voice, and the blood in Khalib's veins froze.

When Khalib was a small boy, his grandfather and uncles took great joy in terrifying him with stories of demons in the desert who could devour a man's soul in the blink of an eye. It took Khalib years to realize that his family was using him only for sport, but the fear had taken root. He tried to exorcise it by sharing some of the stories with Habib and their three other tent mates on dark quiet nights, but instead of dissipating, the fear seemed to strengthen with each tale.

Unconsciously, he relaxed his grip even further and Habib sprung from his grasp, running and screaming into the darkness. Khalib stood but did not follow his friend, who was clearly beyond any assistance he could render. He began to pray as a short burst of gunfire came from the opposite side of the camp, and then a second salvo much closer. He heard feet running towards him, and suddenly lights were flashing on all over the compound. He squatted down below a bench and worked his way back to the empty supply tent. It was clear that they were being overrun by something, and as he wedged himself between the tent wall and some crates he tried to convince himself that it wasn't demons.

Demons are a child's fear. A man killed those men, and it couldn't have been Habib, he told himself without conviction. It was possible that Habib had been out looking for something to drink, just as he had, and witnessed someone killing the kitchen staff, the violence unhinging the mind of the gentle Habib. Now the murderers were running through the camp, slaughtering anyone they found. Khalib reached for his weapon and pulled it between his knees, using it for support as he squatted. He was one of the few who were armed and could offer a degree of protection.

Nine months you have walked in the desert and have never found a trace of demons. Get up, you coward! he demanded of himself, but his heart prevented his legs from responding. He knew—as well as he knew the love of

Allah—that it wasn't invaders that were killing his comrades; it was something that couldn't be stopped by bullets.

More gunfire, closer still, followed by screams of joy and insanity, told Khalib that it was time to move. It wouldn't be long before they found him and either made him into one of their own or into one of their victims. He had to make his way to the desert, at least until the sun came up; demons respected the dawn and feared the sun. He kicked his leg out to stand but found that his balance was off. He slowly climbed the stack of crates, using his arms more than his wobbly legs, until he was safely on his feet. He waited a second more, and when his balance had fully returned he quietly slipped out of the tent into the cool night air. The buzzing in his head was louder, and a sudden thought riveted him to the ground. Demons can pass from person to person through a simple touch, and he had certainly touched Habib. Could he be possessed already? After a moment's consideration, he rejected the idea; his thoughts were his own and his intentions were to flee, not to kill and destroy. Perhaps the demon was too busy controlling Habib to pass through to him. It was a lucky break, and one that was unlikely to be repeated.

He retreated into the shadows of a nearby tent, resolving to shoot anyone who got near him. Most of the compound's lights were on, but there were enough dark spots to get him into the desert and safety. He plotted his course, and just before sprinting to the next dark spot he saw a phantom float effortlessly through the air directly in front of him. It was nearly translucent, but Khalib could still make out a body draped in a fine silk robe that rippled behind the specter, blood-stained arms with sharp talons, and a head covered in long, flowing black hair. It had the snout of a dog, its teeth sharp and exposed, its tongue black and lolling to one side. The eyes bright red and alert as it scanned the path ahead. If only his long dead grandfather could see this, Khalib thought, pressing himself into the canvas. *Then he would be the one scared.*

He waited a full minute before sprinting to the edge of the next tent. Twice more he did this before reaching the tents fronting the fence. He watched as another demon floated in from the desert, not even pausing as it flowed through the tall chain-link. He was close to the small hill where earlier he had seen Dr. Ja'amal and reasoned that this would be a good place to hole up until sunrise. His grandfather had taught him that demons didn't like heights, which was one of the reasons they preferred the long, flat deserts. If Khalib could reach the top of the hill unseen it was unlikely that any would search there.

He slid along the back of the tent in total darkness until he reached the end of the canvas. He risked a peek around the corner and came face to face with one of the Security Force. The man jumped back into his colleague and for a moment all three regarded each other. Khalib was first to recover. It was clear that these two had the same idea that he had, and the mere fact that they were raising their small automatic weapons meant that they were unwilling to share the refuge. He grabbed the smaller man by the neck and pushed him into the next man. All three weapons began to fire at once, and in less than a second they were dead and Khalib was bleeding from his arm and hip. He stepped away from them and back into the shadows just as two demons rounded the corner, drawn by the smell of blood and death. They let loose screams of delight that paralyzed Khalib, and then began savaging the bodies. He tried not to listen to their slurping sounds or to the crack of breaking bones. He dared not move or even breathe until they had had their fill; it felt like an eternity before the gorging stopped and the demons glided away, almost certainly looking for flesh to feed upon, or to inhabit.

Khalib waited a full minute before running to the next tent and then another minute before reaching the final tent. All the demons had moved to the center of the camp, and he had a clear path to safety when the door to the underground lab slid open. The head of security, a man as tall as Khalib but not nearly as broad, stepped cautiously out into the darkness. His weapon was already raised as he surveyed the area. A small ray of light from the doorway fell on the man's exposed arms, and Khalib saw the same blisters that had afflicted Habib.

The sign of the demon! He aimed his weapon at the man/demon, but before he could fire the thing ran off into the darkness. Khalib waited a moment longer as safety beckoned him, and then he sprinted up the hill completely unseen.

In seconds he reached the tallest rock and slipped behind it. The buzzing in his head had become relentless, intensified by the physical exertion and fear. A powerful wave of nausea struck him and he fought the need to vomit. His heart was racing and his breaths were coming in gasps as he fought for control of his normally reliable body. He began to silently pray, and slowly his body responded. The rushing, uncontrolled thoughts of panic began to be replaced by reason and instinct. He surveyed his surroundings in the dim light, and despite the safety that came with height he still felt exposed. He worked to wedge himself deeper into the rocks; twisting his broad back, he found a gap just large enough to admit him and he disappeared into the blackness of the night. After several moments of complete quiet he began to feel as if he had escaped Death itself. Relief washed over him and he closed his eyes, his mind shutting out the horrors that had been visited upon his comrades. He floated away to the western mountains of Pakistan; a warm and inviting campfire beckoned to him and he found himself sitting in a circle with his family. His wife, her black hair reflecting the fire, stared at him with love and devotion, his children arranged by his feet, comfortable and safe. A sense of peace and contentment enveloped his small family as the fire crackled. He watched the sparks spiral up into the night sky and with a start found his grandfather standing over him.

"Demon," he hissed over the fire, his frail arm rising in accusation.

"No," he answered with the voice of a small child pleading for reality to be only a bad dream. He felt his wife's hand leave his and he turned to find her face covered in blisters, her eyes rolling upward in death. He felt the small bodies of his children fall against his crossed legs. He tried to jump to his feet but his head hit something more solid than his skull and he awoke to find himself alone in the cold desert.

He began to weep silently. Surely the demons would sense or smell his misery if he didn't control it, but he couldn't master his emotions. The weeping became crying and soon he was wailing as much as Habib had been earlier. A part of his mind pleaded with him to stop, but he was powerless against the fear. Images of his wife and four children raced through his mind, memories of his father warning him about leaving them for money, his grandfather's face illuminated by firelight, telling him about the malevolence of the desert demons. He wiped the tears from his eyes and in the dim light saw blood on the backs of his hands. He touched both eyes and found that they were oozing blood. A drop fell from his jaw to his shoulder; he was bleeding from his ears as well. He wiped more blood from his eyes with his dirty sleeve and noticed the blisters covering his forearms. He had been marked as well. He screamed and pulled at his sleeves, finding even more blisters, some of which were filled with his blood. He scrambled from his cover and started to run but pulled up short when he realized that the small stone circle was now filled with demons.

Their fetid breath infected every breath he took, and his mind collapsed. He started firing his weapon, but the bullets passed through them, striking the surrounding rocks and pelting him with splinters. He kept firing until his clip was empty, and then he threw the rifle at the nearest demon just before they smothered him. The last sound he heard was the crack of bones breaking and the slurping of demons as they ate him alive.

***

It had been quiet for hours, and the midday sun was boiling Ahmed inside his tent. He was still lucid, or at least thought he was lucid. His eyes had filled with blood and his vision was reduced to only shadows. The skin on his face, torso, and arms had peeled away, and he left a trail of blood and plasma as he staggered towards the tent's opening. He refused to die like this. He pushed open the tent flap and the heat of the sun seared the exposed nerves in his denuded skin. He cried aloud and sunk to his knees, but even this afforded him no relief. He started to crawl through the dust towards his laboratory, each meter an exercise in agony. A lifetime later he reached the entrance, which was mercifully already open. A body blocked the closure of the glass doors, and he slowly crawled over the liquefied remains of a human being he had probably known, and finally reached the shade. The inner door was sealed, aside from a series of bullet holes that stitched their way across the left panel. With a modest amount of force, Ahmed reasoned, he could shatter the remains of the pane and retreat further into the structure.

"What's the point?" he asked no one. Painfully, he propped himself against the cool glass and surveyed his work. Nothing moved; the Hybrid virus that he had helped to create had served Jaime Avanti's purpose well. The Ukrainian had probably emptied a vial of the virus in the air purifiers and another into the water before escaping. Ahmed thought that he would have preferred a bullet in the head over this, and that thought took root. He scanned the immediate area for a weapon, but only the corpses of the professional staff were within reach, and the most lethal weapon any of them carried would have been a clipboard.

Something moved just beyond the first tent, and Ahmed strained to see. The brilliant sunlight and the blood in his eyes made it difficult, but after watching for several minutes he realized that it was a vulture feeding on a body. He was filled with revulsion but didn't have the energy to vomit.

As his eyes began to adjust he found more of the large birds doing what came naturally to them.

"Birds," he said through bleeding lips. They had never tried birds, and although it no longer mattered to him, Ahmed was somehow certain that they could have used birds to study the virus instead of humans. Of course, then the eight men he himself had killed two days earlier would either be dead or dying at this point anyway. He smiled; Avanti had managed to absolve Ahmed of murdering the "volunteers."

He watched the process of life and death, refusing to close his eyes for the last time. The Imams taught that true faith required an acceptance of one's fate, as all things are the will of Allah, but his mind, with all its complexities, refused. In a moment of clarity, he realized that his faith had always been hollow. He had never really believed that a golden palace and seventy-two virgins awaited him in paradise, or that it was the will of Allah that drove him ultimately to a painful death. Islam was more his identity than his religion. Something he had used to fill a void created by an indifferent family and society, something that offered him no peace in his ultimate time of need.

"The decisions I made were my own," he declared to the uninterested birds. He knew that this was the ultimate heresy, and he accepted it. In the moments that preceded his death he would not wail and plead for Allah's mercy. He would stand on his own two feet, at least metaphorically, and accept the consequences of his actions.

His mind was slowing, but it dawned on him that the carrion birds, if capable of carrying the virus, would spread it before Avanti could. It was possible that in time Avanti himself would become infected by a progeny of the very virus that had killed Ahmed. He tried to smile and, with his life literally draining away, he found enough peace to finally close his eyes.

CHAPTER 4

"She's right, you know," Lisa Flynn finally said.

Amanda had been braced for her mother-in-law's comments since the two left the television studio. "I know," she said quietly, watching but not really seeing downtown Chicago fly by their taxi's window. Like Amanda, Mindy McCoy had forever changed with the death of her parents. The once gregarious, active youth was replaced by a reclusive, apathetic teenager, and the transformation had nothing to do with hormones. It took her years to find her way back to herself.

They rode in silence for several more minutes when Lisa impulsively sat up. "Excuse me, driver, could you drop us just up here?" She pointed at the corner of State and Lake and turned to Amanda. "Let's get something to eat," she said, a smile lighting up her face.

Amanda responded with a weak smile that conveyed only resignation. Lisa was a force of nature that could not be denied. The taxi stopped and Amanda followed Lisa out into the street.

"Come on," Lisa encouraged. "The sun is out, the air is warm, and the water is blue. It's time to live." She practically skipped across a busy intersection with Amanda in tow. She found a spot along a rail that overlooked the Chicago River and started excitedly pointing out all the sites: Marina Towers, the Wrigley buildings, even Lake Michigan off in the distance; all the while talking a mile a minute. A large boat filled with tourists passed beneath them; Lisa began waving and elbowed Amanda into joining in. Several cameras flashed in their direction and Lisa began to pose.

On any other day a part of Amanda would have resented Lisa's freedom, but the morning had emotionally drained her. "You're like a little kid seeing the circus for the first time," she said, and her smile finally conveyed something more than resignation.

"Oh look!" Lisa had spotted some restaurants sitting just above the water's edge. "We have to go there," she said, grabbing Amanda's wrist and practically dragging her across the bridge. They made their way down the steps and found a table outside.

"I must be living right," a man in his mid-twenties said, startling both ladies as they settled in. He dropped linen napkins onto their laps and boldly pulled up a chair and sat across from them. With a good deal of flourish he propped his elbows onto the table, dropped his chin into his hands, and appraised his two guests. "My name is Richard, but you can call me Ricardo." He rolled the "R." "I will be your waiter this afternoon, and with a single 'yes' I can be so much more this evening." His eyebrows danced provocatively as he wore an exaggerated leer, waiting for their response.

Lisa's face immediately flushed and she began to hide behind a menu.

"I can tell that you are new to our fair establishment." He scooted his chair next to the red-faced Lisa. "Perhaps I can help you." He reached for her menu and opened it to the first page. "We reserve the right to insult any of our customers," he read loudly. "Of course it is only a legal disclaimer. To insult either of you would surely be a crime against nature herself." His arm shot into the air.

"Well, Ricardo," she said, rolling the "R" twice as long as he had. "What would you recommend for two out-of-town ladies who sadly have no escort?"

"I would recommend starting with the Oysters Rockefeller, followed by a night of aamoraa …"—it took him almost five seconds to finish his last word. He focused on Lisa, but then quickly turned to Amanda, whose mouth was agog, and winked. He leaned back into his chair, raised his eyebrows a couple of more times, turned his head slightly to the side, and resumed his leer.

Ricardo alternated his gaze between the two ladies and then decided to examine his finger nails. "You may sit here all day, basking in my aura, if you wish." His accent was over-the-top Italian. "But I warn you, there are people here who are extremely jealous of my ways with the women." His W's had become V's. "And after a minute or two of staring, they will probably start charging you." He hadn't taken his eyes off of his fingernails.

"Well, in that case, I believe that we will both have an iced tea," Lisa said, as a crowd had started to gather.

"Very well," he proclaimed loudly. "If I cannot entice you to try something tall, dark, and handsome I shall leave. But know this …" He jumped to his feet and shot an arm into the air. "One day soon I shall return, and when I do,"—his hand clutched his chest—"I shall bring you iced tea." He took a dramatic step away and then turned back. "Think of me while I am gone, because the image of both of you has been burned into my heart." He sauntered away to a smattering of applause.

"That was fantastic," Lisa said, leaning toward Amanda and clasping her hand.

"It was," Amanda answered, and despite the fact that she had enjoyed Ricardo's performance, Lisa seemed unhappy with her response. "What?" she asked.

Lisa took a moment and her smile slowly faded to an expression of mild discomfort. "This used to be your life, sweetheart. Not long ago you probably would have ended up dancing with that guy. It breaks my heart to see you this way; it's as if a light has gone out of the world." Lisa dropped Amanda's gaze and fiddled with her napkin. "I should not have said that; it was stupid of me."

"No, you're right, and Mindy was right. I have a choice to make. I either accept my life as it is, or I change it. Only I doubt I am going to get a modeling contract and become the mega-star she did."

"You don't need a modeling contract, or to be a mega-star. And for the record, I think you are far more attractive than Mindy," Lisa said.

"Not a chance," Amanda answered, discreetly putting her hands in front of her breasts. "I'm a couple sizes short."

"Even still, you're different from Mindy. She's Raquel Welch to your Gwyneth Paltrow; she's sexy to your elegance."

"Elegant, huh," Amanda smiled, and for the first time in a long time it wasn't so difficult.

"I have returned, and I hope my absence was not too painful," Ricardo said, twirling around the two ladies as he served the iced teas. "You must know that I live to serve. Please tell me, what can I bring you to make your life complete?" Once again he slid into the chair opposite them.

"I believe that I will get a Cobb salad," Lisa answered, after consulting the menu.

"I would like a turkey club on wheat bread," Amanda followed.

Ricardo stood and put a forearm over his eyes and then a fist to his mouth. "Please excuse me for a moment," he said, in a voice choked with emotion. "Setting aside the fact that you are my first guests of the day, that is the most perfect order I have had since yesterday. I must leave now before your beauty breaks my heart." And Ricardo was gone in a dramatic rush.

"It's hard to have a conversation with Ricardo around," Lisa said.

"Actually, he makes it a little easier." Amanda sipped her tea. "What do you think about me going back to work?"

"I think it's a big step, but one in the right direction," Lisa said, after a pause prompted in equal parts by the sudden shift in the conversation and the sudden shift in Amanda's attitude.

"You weren't expecting that, were you?" Amanda said almost playfully.

"Well, after this morning ... It didn't sound like you were ready."

"I wasn't, but now that this interview is behind me, plus the fact that I don't have to deal with Heather Waylens any more ... it feels as if ..." Amanda paused. "Mindy mentioned that there was a moment ..." Amanda struggled and her face darkened, sudden and uncontrolled emotions welling up. It was almost two minutes before she continued. "Ever since the accident I have had this tiny voice in my head. It's Jacob, and he's saying that thing ..."

"I hurt me self," Lisa filled in, and both ladies started to tear.

"For a long time, every time I heard it in my head I just wanted to die. No matter where I was or what I was doing, if I heard his sweet little voice I ..."

Lisa listened quietly.

"Michael was always the strong one. He made all the decisions; he protected me. I still wake up feeling his arms around me. Sometimes I'm not completely awake and I feel so safe, and then I remember. It's like losing them all over again." Her tears were falling freely now.

A painful silence, filled with loss, followed. Finally, Amanda began to dry her eyes with a napkin. "For the last week or so when I hear Jacob ... it doesn't ... affect me the way it did." She looked up into Lisa's eyes and held them for a long moment. "I hurt me self," she said. The tears started again but Amanda didn't break the connection. "I think maybe this is my moment. I know I have to move on."

Lisa smiled and silently took both of Amanda's hands.

"I know that I'll never be the person I was, but I think I'd like to try and find her," Amanda said while squeezing her mother-in-law's hands.

"I'm so happy," Lisa said quietly.

"I'm sorry for doing this here; I know you wanted to have a good time." Amanda turned in her chair and began to look around, embarrassed by her public display. "Where is our Casanova?"

"Where were you thinking of working?" Lisa asked.

"The Lieber Institute. An old classmate called a month ago and asked if I had any interest."

"Not a hospital?" Lisa looked confused.

"No. I think I need something different. The Lieber Institute coordinates public health at the state and international level. They also contract with the International Red Cross for disaster relief. It would mean a lot of traveling."

"Well, I know we'll miss having you around all the time, but it sounds like an interesting opportunity. Are they based in Colorado Springs?"

"Now comes the hard part." Amanda paused. "They're in Dallas."

Ricardo swooped in and served them with a muted "Bon Appetite" as he disappeared.

"Dallas?" Lisa's voice had dropped.

"I still don't have all the details; I may not even have to move there. It's possible that I could do most of it over the internet."

"That doesn't sound likely." Lisa began to stir her salad aggressively. "What would you actually be doing?"

"A lot of logistics. Coordinating vaccinations in schools here in the States and in Central America."

"That part doesn't sound all that stimulating. Why wouldn't they want a public health nurse for that?" Lisa answered quickly.

"They just need an RN. All the protocols are in place, and all that's needed is someone to coordinate them. Besides, that's just the day job. What they really want is someone willing to coordinate disaster response. I would be assigned to a team, and at first assist the senior coordinator with logistics. Sometime down the road, after I've gained enough experience, I would be assigned my own team."

"Sounds like you've looked into this quite a bit." Lisa's voice dropped another notch as Amanda watched her study the Cobb salad.

"Not really. Martha, my old classmate, sent me all the promotional material. She called me just before we left to make sure that I got everything, but I put her off and promised to read it while I was here."

"Is this what you want, Amanda?"

"I don't know. I haven't lived outside of Colorado for a very long time, and the prospect of moving away from you and Greg terrifies me. On the other hand, I could use a fresh start. No reminders." Her last sentence was only a whisper. "What do you think?"

"Well, you sound excited, and you haven't sounded excited about anything in a long time." She looked up at Amanda and then quickly looked away "It scares me, you all alone in Dallas." Lisa abruptly cut herself off and returned to picking out the black olives from her salad. "Who puts olives in a Cobb salad?"

"I'm not even sure it means a move. I'm not even sure this is what I want." Amanda's voice began to drop as she watched her mother-in-law dissect her meal. "Maybe we should talk about this later." She retreated into her club sandwich. The two ladies sat in silence for a long uncomfortable minute, conflicting emotions left unsaid.

"No, we should talk about this now," Lisa said suddenly. "I was being selfish. A part of me wants to tell you that this is a terrible idea, so you'll stay with us and allow us to watch over you, but you don't need that. You don't need anybody." Lisa took Amanda's hand. "We will always be here for you, but you need to do this for yourself. If the Lieber Institute or Dallas isn't right, then find something else that makes you feel happy."

Amanda looked up to find Ricardo standing over Lisa, a guilty look on his face after inadvertently overhearing a part of their conversation.

"Sorry for interrupting." Ricardo had reverted back to Richard. "I see that you are not a fan of olives," he observed.

"Not in a Cobb salad." Lisa smiled back at the waiter.

"Is there something else that I can bring you?" he asked Lisa. Amanda turned in response to the sudden change in persona, and he gave her a smile in return.

"No, I'm fine," Lisa answered.

"I'm good," Amanda said as he turned to her.

"You are so much better than good, mi amore." Ricardo had returned. He dragged his fingertips along her bare shoulder, batted his eyebrows lasciviously, and sashayed away to another table, where he announced his presence by yelling: "What the hell do you want?"

"If disaster management doesn't work out, maybe I could come and work here," Amanda said as she craned her neck watching their waiter's third persona.

CHAPTER 5

14 days later

It wasn't unusual for Larry Ryan to work around armed men. Despite being a civilian, he still worked for the military, but to have a platoon of heavily armed soldiers—all dressed in the same isolation suits—watching his every move was unnerving.

"Have any of you ever read *1984*?" No response.

"I figured," he answered himself. "Well if we're not going to discuss literature, can someone please tell me something about these bodies?" Two body bags, both currently occupied, lay in shallow tubs beneath bright theater lights.

"I'm sorry, Doctor, but you have already been told everything that we can tell you." A disembodied voice answered him from a wall speaker.

"Well, Colonel, good evening. I thought you had gone and left us. Although I'm not sure where you would go," Dr. Ryan said to himself. Medical Facility 104 was somewhere in the deserts of Nevada; at least that's what he surmised. He had never actually seen the facility from the outside. Each time he received that very special phone call or tap on the shoulder that told him that he had 30 minutes to drop what he was doing and disappear for the next several days, it had been at night. Then, just to be absolutely certain, he was flown in a plane without windows that taxied directly into the facility—a facility that as far as he knew consisted only of a single changing room, a single small bedroom, a single pathology laboratory, and a single autopsy room. Even his meals had been brought to him.

"While I appreciate the need for secrecy and security, don't you think you're taking it a little too far? I am seventy-one years old and walk with a cane, and I'm sure neither of these two fellows is going anywhere."

He unzipped the first bag and recoiled. "Okay, seriously, what the hell is this?" The body was a putrid, liquefied mess, and any jocularity Ryan had had was lost.

"Colonel, I'm going to need a good deal more information before I do anything, and that is non-negotiable." He was the former Chairman of Forensic Pathology at the Armed Forces Institute of Pathology, which carried a civilian rank equal to a two-star general and a security clearance beyond Top-Secret. Those facts alone should have insulated him from taking orders from a mere colonel and working in the dark, especially in a situation as unusual as this. He adjusted the overhead light and examined what was left of the face closely and then zipped the bag closed.

"Did you hear me, Colonel?" He walked to the far corner of the autopsy theater and looked up into the observation room above. Colonel Nerring had his back to the glass and a phone to his ear. Ryan pulled up a rolling stool and carefully sat down. He was recovering from hip surgery, and the last thing he needed was to fall in this cumbersome and slippery isolation suit.

"I charge by the hour," he said after several minutes.

"Doctor," Colonel Nerring's voice finally echoed through the sterile room. "General Kane has asked me to relay a message. He would view this as a personal favor if you could examine the bodies, take tissue samples, and determine cause of death without any more information that could possibly color your findings. Once you are done he will personally answer any questions that you may have."

Ryan pondered this for a moment and then stood. "Two things. First, he's going to owe me a case of double malt scotch, and second, I need an honest answer from you. What is the risk?"

"Extreme," Nerring answered immediately.

"At least you're being honest. I suppose that's why I have no lab assistants?" He walked to the second body and unzipped the bag completely. The condition of this corpse was only slightly better than the first. "I'm going to leave them in the bags for now. This will reduce the possibility of contamination. He pulled an overhanging microphone close, dictated his name and date, and then began to work.

It took him nearly two hours to finish with the first body, but less than an hour with the second. He zipped what was left of the two men back into the black bags, which would serve as the only coffins they would ever know. "Okay, fellas, let's go," he said to the platoon of soldiers who had silently watched him dissect two bodies. He opened the door to the airlock and began the cumbersome process of extricating himself from the contaminated isolation suit.

He emerged into the cool air of the control room to find both Colonel Nerring and one of his oldest friends, Major General Ralph Kane. Ryan nodded to his friend and said, "I need a drink."

"Come with me; I know just the place," Kane said. He led them through a maze of corridors, none of which Ryan had never seen.

"So Ralph, can you confirm or deny the existence of Area 51, because by my reckoning this could be the very place." Ryan hobbled after the two soldiers, who had politely matched his speed.

"Come on Larry, you know that if I told you the truth Colonel Nerring would shoot us both. Isn't that right, Colonel?" Kane had led the trio into a small conference room.

"Without hesitation, sir." Nerring retrieved three plastic bottles of water from a small refrigerator and passed them to the two older men.

"Not the drink I had in mind, but for now it will do." Ryan took a quick gulp and turned to Kane. "Okay, I did what you asked, now fill me in. Something nasty happened to those two poor bastards."

"What was it?" Kane asked as all three men found a seat.

"Definitely a viral pathogen, but a whole lot worse than anything I've seen before. This is something new and something that most definitely needs to be contained." Ryan drained the last of his water. "Looks like some form of Ebola or another hemorrhagic fever, only far more aggressive. I didn't think that was possible, but there it is. Like I said, nothing I've ever seen before, and I've seen them all. Both men were Middle Eastern, judging from the dental and medical work; both were healthy and in excellent shape, at least before they had their little run-in. The first body died of three bullet wounds to the chest, and the second from …" For a moment he was at a loss for words. "The best that I can say is that he was dissolved. His lungs, heart, kidneys, brain, everything was in an advanced state of dissolution. Whatever did this attacked virtually every cell type and caused massive and relatively sudden cellular damage. This guy lived maybe several hours after being exposed, no more."

"But the first man was shot?" Nerring questioned.

"Three to the chest. Probably bled out in under a minute; he had a big hole in his left ventricle." Ryan held up his pinky finger. "No bullets recovered, but they were from a high caliber assault rifle."

"So this Ebola-thing wasn't the cause of his death?" General Kane phrased it as a question.

"The bullets made it a cleaner, quicker death, but this guy was just as infected as the other guy. In fact, that's what makes this so nasty. Death at a cellular level takes hours, and despite this guy being clinically dead, the virus, or whatever it is, was still active, at least until there were no more viable cells. I'm guessing that he was infected shortly before he ran into those bullets, but our happy little pathogen continued to do its thing. Nothing I've ever heard of does that."

"We recovered the bodies from a camp in the Libyan Desert. They had disguised an underground research facility as a small terrorist training camp. When they first showed up on satellite, we watched their fighters train for a little while, but they seemed relatively harmless and ineffectual, so we pretty much forgot them. Which unfortunately is exactly what they wanted, but a couple months ago we received some intel that made us take a fresh look. A few years back they bought some medical equipment—things like incubators, centrifuges, isolation equipment, nothing very alarming. At least until they purchased 20 squirrel monkeys." Kane waited for Ryan's reaction.

"Oh, shit," the pathologist said, and then tried to take a sip from his empty water bottle.

"Yeah, that sent up red flags all over and their little ruse began to unravel. Three days ago we raided the place. We found these two guys along with about a hundred others, all dead." General Kane swirled his plastic bottle of water nervously.

"So the working assumption is that they were sophisticated enough to create this thing but not contain it? Sounds a little incongruous."

"We don't really know what happened. Some are speculating that it was sabotage. There was a lot of gunfire; the three-in-the-chest guy wasn't alone."

"The good news is that this thing kills so fast that it won't make much of a weapon beyond creating a local hot spot." He paused as implications beyond the creation of a small cluster of infection began to tickle his mind. "I'm impressed and a little worried that they could do this in some lab hidden in a desert. I hate to think what they could do in a real facility. Any idea who was behind this?"

"Nothing definitive," Nerring answered.

"You probably wouldn't tell me if you knew." Ryan smiled and neither of the two officers responded. "Well, I would strongly recommend that you find this guy and put a net over him. With a little more work this little pet of his could become a giant problem for us." He slowly, painfully got to his feet. "It's hell being old, but it beats the alternative. Okay, I have to get back to work. One of you is going to have to show me back to the lab. I don't want to accidentally walk in on any alien autopsies."

CHAPTER 6

After a week of policy and procedure classes, Amanda's excitement over starting a new life and job had given way to boredom. As her mind drifted away from the lecture detailing legal responsibilities in foreign countries, she was happy to be bored. One of the inherent properties of boredom was a desire to be doing something else. After a year of despondency and paralysis, with no desires, wants, or needs to be here or anywhere else, a little boredom was a refreshing improvement. A part of her still guarded against a relapse, but on the whole she felt as if she was adjusting well to her new circumstances. "Are there any questions?" The lights had come up and Amanda, along with the six other new members of the Lieber Institute, began to stretch and yawn. The lecturer waited a discrete interval, thanked them for their attention, gathered his notes and awkwardly left the small classroom without another word.

"Well, that was exciting," the only male in the class said after the door closed. He turned in his seat and casually glanced around the room, waiting for the next lecture. Amanda felt his gaze linger on her a little longer than a casual glance allowed. She was sure that he was about to say something when the door opened and all attention returned to the front of the room as Bernice Scott, their orientation proctor, walked into the room.

"Well, I see everybody is awake now. Sorry about that, but by law we are required to inform you of your legal position when you're working out of the country. As you've probably guessed, you do not need to have a personality to work for the State Department." The class gave her a small chorus of laughter. "Okay, we are going to break for lunch now. Your next lecture will start at 1:30; see you then." Everyone began to stand. "Amanda, can I have a word?"

"Sure," Amanda answered, pulling on her coat.

Bernice was in her early sixties, and rumor had it that she was a relative of Dr. Martin Luther King Jr. "So how is it going?" Bernice asked as Amanda walked to the lectern.

"Fine." Amanda was confused by the sudden personal attention. Over the past week she had talked with Mrs. Scott several times, but it had always been as a part of a group and strictly professional. "A lot of new things." She smiled, trying to remain positive despite the spate of dull lectures.

"Most of which you won't need," Bernice smiled back. "You have been assigned to my team."

"Good. Great!" Amanda truly was excited. Bernice had proven personable and professional throughout the week, and Amanda was confident that she could lean on the older women as she learned "the ropes."

"Before you get too excited, I have some good news and bad news. The good news is that you don't have to attend any more lectures; the bad news is that we are leaving for Honduras in just about three hours."

At first Amanda stared blankly back at her new boss, but in less than a moment realization hit her. "The hurricane in the Caribbean. I was wondering if we were going to be involved."

"Despite the fact that we have had people down there for a week, preparing for this very moment, we still have to wait for official permission. The wheels of bureaucracy definitely need some air. Nervous?" Bernice smiled broadly, excitement lighting up her face.

"Nervous, overwhelmed, excited, unsure—you name it. I'm not even sure what I'm supposed to do," Amanda answered, a distantly familiar thrill of anticipation racing through her.

"Whatever I tell you. For the next two weeks you are my Girl-Friday."

"Why me?" It was a question Amanda had meant to ask herself, but somehow it gained a voice. Of the seven in her orientation class, six were being assigned to disaster response teams, and Amanda was the youngest by at least a decade.

"Do you want me to answer that objectively or subjectively?"

"Both, of course," and for an instant Amanda was worried that she was coming off as a shallow, teen-age girl.

"Objectively, it is policy that the least experienced assistant be paired with the most experienced coordinator, and that just happens to be me." She nodded her head in a muted salute. "Subjectively, Martha Salazar, a woman I trust, speaks very highly of you, but more importantly, my instincts tell me to snatch you up before anyone else does. So, consider yourself snatched-up."

"Okay," Amanda said simply, finally starting to feel as if she were a part of something beyond a support group. "All right, I need to get back to my hotel, pack, and then get back here ASAP." Her mind began to race through logistics, both personal and professional. "I'll need my emergency medical supplies, and …"

"Slow down. Everything has already been taken care of. I'll drive you to the hotel and then we'll catch a ride to the airport."

Four hours later Amanda and Bernice were stuck on a Dallas runway, more than an hour past their scheduled departure, waiting for the weather to clear. The pair shared a row of three in an otherwise full flight. "How did we get so lucky?" Amanda asked Bernice after the main cabin door was finally shut.

"Luck had nothing to do with it. I always buy an extra seat, so don't think we're going to share it." She then awkwardly sprawled across both seats. "This is the way I sleep." She continued to contort herself until she was bent into the shape of an "L," with both legs draped over Amanda's lap. "I hope you don't mind."

Amanda laughed and ignored the stares of their fellow passengers as they gawked at the animated middle-aged woman. "Yes, I can see that you must be very comfortable."

"Don't laugh. One day soon everyone of note will travel like this. I plan to …" Her explanation was interrupted by the flight attendant.

"Ma'am, if I could ask you to put at least one foot on the floor before takeoff."

Bernice obediently disentangled herself and then flopped noisily back into her seat. "For the record, all the great minds in history encountered resistance."

"Along those lines, can I ask you a personal question?"

"He was my great uncle," Bernice answered automatically as she straightened her blouse.

"I guess you get asked that a lot, but I had something else in mind."

"Really? So you don't want my opinion on civil rights, or the Viet Nam war, or whether or not Martin Luther King Jr. was influenced by the Communists? How refreshing. It seems as if everyone wants to know if I have any secret insights into the man, or where I stand on social issues, as if by being born into a famous family makes my opinion more relevant." A serious, almost bitter tone filled Bernice's voice.

Amanda crossed her arms and pulled back into her seat, uncomfortable with Bernice's sudden change in temperament.

Bernice stopped playing with her seat belt and seemed to realize that she had made her traveling companion uncomfortable. "Oh child, you're going to need a thicker skin than that if you're going to survive around me. Let's get this straight from the beginning—most of what I say should bounce right off of you. You'll know when I want something to stick." She stared into Amanda's eyes and winked. Her face stretched into her usual broad smile. "Now, what did you really want to know?"

"I want to know how you let things bounce off of you? You've survived thirty years in this job, dealing with disasters and human tragedy on an almost daily basis, and it doesn't seem to have affected you. You're a lot like my mother-in-law: both of you truly live in the moment. You're naturally spontaneous, almost impulsive, but when the moment requires it you become completely serious and professional."

"Good question; much better than the one I answered. Have you ever asked your mother-in-law?"

"No."

"Some questions are better asked to a stranger than a family member. But if you did ask her I would bet, if I wasn't a good Christian woman, that she would tell you that she has a clear understanding of what is and what is not important, and everything else is not worth fussing over. Once you learn that, freedom is your reward." She undid her seat belt and retrieved her large, overflowing purse from beneath the seat in front of her. "My carry-on luggage," she said, answering Amanda's quizzical look. "It contains all the wisdom of the world, including the accumulated files of Amanda Flynn." She withdrew a thin manila folder. "All right, maybe more of a summary of all the accumulated files of Amanda Flynn." They both stared at the folder as the air around them somehow became still. "We all know what's happened to you this past year; I won't insult you by saying that I understand, because I don't." Her voice dropped to just above ambient level. "I can guess what was important to you a year ago. Do you know what's important to you now?"

Amanda looked out of the window. "Survival," she finally said.

"You've set the bar pretty low."

"Not from where I sit."

"Okay, I think I understand. You're still lost, but at least you're moving in the right direction."

"Can you please fasten your seat belt and stow your purse under the seat in front of you?" The stewardess had reappeared, and shot Bernice a tired, reproachful glare.

"I think that woman has it out for me," Bernice said and winked at Amanda.

CHAPTER 7

Luis Munoz walked along the waterfront, surveying the damage wrought by a Category Four hurricane on his small barrier island. The sky was finally clear, and the wind had calmed to just a warm breeze. Despite being on the leeward side of the island, the storm had ravaged their wooden dock; fortunately, the majority of the fishing boats had left for the mainland days earlier, where they were pulled from the water and sent far inland. Within days they would be back at work, and maybe within a week they would return home and life would resume, at least until the next storm. Hurricanes were an unpleasant but ever-present fact of life. The same tropical heat that warmed the waters, which drew the fish and American tourist dollars, also spawned the storms, and Luis and his people had learned to live with them.

He jumped from the concrete seawall to the sugar-white sandy beach below. They had been fortunate not to lose it. Docks could be rebuilt quickly, but the loss of a beach to the scouring winds would have been ruinous to the tourist trade, and therefore to his village. Already he could see a handful of workers using rakes to comb the sand free of the storm's debris. It would take the morning, and dozens of other workers, but by midday the beach would be clean enough for digital pictures. He would then post them on the internet to reassure the world that Isla Maderas had not only survived Hurricane Michael, it was open for business. He turned and faced the jungle and found the sun was just rising above his island's small mountain. He snapped several pictures, taking care to exclude the battered village. Most of the brightly-colored shops and restaurants faced the water and the mainland, situated both out of convenience and to take advantage of some of the greatest sunset views in the world. The sunsets would remain, but every structure in the center of town would need at least some degree of repair, and at least two of their restaurants would need to be rebuilt completely. Their two marquee hotels were more modern, built with cement blocks and hurricane shutters. Their biggest problem would be cleaning up the grounds and the swimming pools.

Luis walked a hundred yards down the beach and idly swept sand off a buried beach chair. To his surprise, he found it mostly intact. He flipped it over, tested its stability, and finally sat in it. There were drenched palm leaves all around him, but from this viewpoint they were the only indications that hours earlier a maelstrom had visited this very spot. A voice called to him from the road and he turned to find a man waving. He was too far for Luis's poor eyes to make out, but the camera flash identified him as Raul Alvarez, the editor of their local newspaper. He waved back, hoping that Raul was also posting his pictures on the internet.

"Mayor Munoz enjoys the beach hours after Hurricane Michael," he laughed to himself, the anxiety over the massive storm melting away into the glorious morning. His island, city, and people had survived virtually unscathed a storm that would be talked about for decades. He began to mentally catalogue all the things they would need to be up and running. The biggest impediment would be the damaged dock. They had an artificial floating dock that could be used for small boats, but they couldn't use it for the ferries that shuttled tourists from the mainland and the other Bay Islands. Plus, it was no good for the fishermen. They were going to lose at least a week's worth of income. He was weighing the possibilities of proposing a temporary tax on sport fishing and diving when he caught sight of a boat's wake. He fumbled for the set of binoculars beneath his bright peach shirt and found his son's 25-foot runabout powering through the flat water. Normally the eight-mile channel between Isla Maderas and the mainland would be busy with fishing boats, dive boats, and sailboats, but only Jorge's powered catamaran was visible today. Jorge had ridden out the storm with his father in the basement of the Catholic Church, while his boat sheltered in their concrete garage. He had left for Tela, the nearest mainland city, more than four hours earlier with the island's only nurse practitioner and a very pregnant Mayan woman. She had stumbled into the church with her family hours after the winds had started and nearly a day after she should have evacuated.

Jorge angled his boat for the dock, and after scouting it from the water turned the catamaran towards his father, who was now at the water's edge. Luis raised his hands in confusion when he saw that Jorge was still accompanied by the nurse, the pregnant woman, and her husband.

"What happened?" Luis screamed over the revving engines. Jorge was too busy to respond and briefly held up one finger, telling his father to wait. He raised the props until they were just beneath the water line, pointed the boat directly at his father, and gunned the engines. The catamaran lifted its bow and gently slid across the sand, beaching itself. "What happened?" Luis repeated.

"What happened is that I helped to deliver a baby," Jorge said as he pivoted himself off the boat and into the ankle-deep surf. The nurse handed down a small package, wrapped in a blanket. "Look, it's a little girl." He carefully walked through the sand as mother, father, and nurse watched.

"Jorge," Alanis, their nurse, called. "You think you could give us a little help?" The new father didn't wait; he silently slid off the back of the boat, reached for his wife, and carried her through the water to a proud Jorge and their child.

"Never mind." There was a splash, and an irritated Alanis joined the group. "Always the gentlemen, aren't we?" She elbowed Jorge.

"Just as we got to the dock some guy started screaming at us. He wasn't making much sense. We told him that she was in labor, and that's when he started throwing things down at us. He actually hit Alanis in the head with a piece of wood." Jorge pointed at an ugly knot on Alanis' forehead. "I tied us up, and then he comes running down the stairs when someone shoots him in the back. Just blew this guy away right in front of us. After that we just took off. I tried the beach but there was way too much debris, we never would have made it, and then she starts to scream, and we have a baby." He lifted the bundled baby as if she were a prize. Her mother gasped. Jorge said, "Oh, sorry," and passed the baby over to her mother.

"I'll take them up to the clinic and check them out." Alanis stepped between Jorge and the new parents. "I don't know what happened back there, but I'm not going back to Tela. I think that you need to contact the military," she said to Luis, and then led the family up the beach.

"The military? Over one man being shot?" Luis asked his son.

"It was more than one. We got close enough to the beach to see maybe ten bodies. I didn't get a chance to look real well, but I think there were more down the beach."

"Drugs? Rebels?" For the most part, Honduras had been spared the bloody civil and drug wars that wracked some of its neighbors. Even the constitutional crisis that led to a coup d'état in 2009 had been largely peaceful. "After a hurricane?" It didn't make sense. "Let's push the boat back in the water. I want to survey the dock and then maybe run over to Tela and see this for myself."

Three hours later Jorge was guiding the catamaran along the eerily quiet coastline. Luis directed him toward Tela's long, tall dock, which had managed to survive the winds and storm surge. Through his binoculars he could see the body of the man who had attacked Jorge, as well as a second victim, sprawled face first down the stairs. A dark stain of what had to be blood surrounded the head and reached almost to the lower dock. "This doesn't make any sense," he said to himself.

"There are more bodies on the beach. It's like they were brought here to die."

"Tela had a mandatory evacuation. There should only be military and rescue personnel in the entire town." After Hurricane Mitch destroyed nearly half the country in 1998, Hondurans developed a near-religious zeal for hurricane preparedness. "I can't believe that there are more than a few hundred left in town." Luis scanned the shoreline with his binoculars.

"Dad," Jorge said, a moment before a sharp crack. "Dad, get down!" Both men dropped into the well of the boat as something pinged off of the boat's tower. A second sharp crack followed almost immediately. A third was almost lost to the sound of the two engines as Jorge steered the boat from under cover out into the open ocean. After two minutes with the throttle wide open, he slowed the boat and hazarded a quick look. "Okay, we're out of range." He was breathless from the excitement. "I'm going to try the marine radio. Maybe the Tela harbormaster knows what's going on." He flipped open the watertight console and turned up the volume. He was greeted with static.

"What's wrong?" Luis asked.

"Nothing. I was tuned to the Maderas harbormaster, and I have to find the correct channel for Tela." He slowly turned the dial, resisting for the moment tuning directly to the emergency channel. "This is *Whale Shark*

One out of Isla Maderas trying to reach Tela harbormaster." He repeated the message three times on three different channels.

"Are you sure Tela has a harbormaster? They really don't have much of a harbor." Luis knew next to nothing about boats, fishing, or harbormasters. He was strictly a landlubber. Jorge, on the other hand, ran a successful dive and fishing charter service and was on the water almost every day.

"He's not really a harbormaster; he manages the dock and relays search and rescue messages. I met the guy a few times and he takes his job very seriously. I doubt this guy would have evacuated, voluntarily or not." He tried a fourth and then a fifth channel before a voice answered.

"Have you come to rescue us?" asked the voice of a frightened woman.

"I am trying to reach the harbormaster," Jorge answered. He turned to his father and they shared a look of confusion.

"Are you here to rescue us?" Her scream was so angry and wretched that Jorge answered without thinking.

"Yes, we can rescue you. Where are you?"

"I'm in my house." Frustration caused each of her words to become successively louder.

"We are trying to reach the harbormaster. Do you know where he is?" Jorge asked, hoping for a more lucid response.

"He's DEAD!" She screamed. "He had to go out and now he's dead." Her wailing was cut short by Jorge.

"Okay, calm down." He waited for her to stop crying, but it took several seconds and two more reassurances from Jorge that they were here to help before she allowed him to continue. "All right, can you tell us what's happening?"

"What's happening is that my husband is dead and there are people outside with guns shooting everything that moves." She was back to screaming now, and her words were starting to slur together. Both Jorge and Luis needed a moment to understand exactly what she had said.

"Are the police there, or the military?"

"They're the ones with the guns." She began to curse him for his lack of intelligence and breeding. Jorge and his father listened quietly, waiting for an opening.

Luis took the microphone from his son's hand. "Can you get to the dock?"

"Yes," she said after a long second, her anger now exhausted. "I think so. What should I bring?"

The two men shared a confused look. "Nothing. How long will it take you?"

"I'll have to wait for the bus." The next word—another curse—was cut off. "Sorry, I don't know what I was saying. I can be there in five minutes."

"All right, five minutes. Now go," Luis ordered, and he replaced the microphone.

"We aren't seriously going back in there?" Jorge asked his father.

"We can't just leave."

"If you say so, but you're paying for any bullet holes in me or my boat." Jorge swung the boat around, away from shore, and steered east, then turned south once they had passed the long pier. "Here we go," he said, turning west and then north back towards shore. After closing the distance by half, he pulled the throttles back and let the boat coast to a stop. "It's probably best if we stay out here until we see her."

"Good idea. I am officially making you the admiral of Isla Madres' navy. Congratulations."

Jorge laughed humorlessly at his father's attempt to break the tension. Five minutes passed slowly, and then another a little faster. "How long do we give her?" Jorge asked after another five minutes.

"I don't know, but we can't leave her."

"We could contact the military with the satellite phone."

"Look," Luis said suddenly. They both scanned the dock with their binoculars. A frail woman had just stepped onto the long pier. "What's that she's dragging?"

"I don't know," Jorge said after scrutinizing the woman for several seconds. She was pulling a large black object, about half her size, behind her. When she was three-quarters to the end he dropped his binoculars and gave the two marine engines a little gas. They purred quietly and the boat glided towards the dock at the end of the long pier.

Luis continued to watch the woman with his binoculars. She was struggling under the weight of her mysterious burden. "I think, as crazy as this sounds, it's a vacuum cleaner." His mind had been trying to fit any known item into the puzzle of the black object, and an old-fashion vacuum cleaner was as good a fit as he could come up with.

"Well, she needs to drop it and move her ass," Jorge whispered needlessly, because they were close enough to hear her swearing at both her burden and the bodies that lay in her path.

"Jesus, what is that smell?" Luis asked, watching the woman finally reach the stairs to the dock. He checked the last two bodies that she would have to negotiate, and then panned upward. He saw her bare feet, then her legs; she turned her back to him and began to drag the black object over the first body, and Luis finally got a clear look at it. "Oh my God," he screamed. "It's some kind of bird." It was hideous, huge, and very dead. Jorge had retrieved his binoculars. "What is that?" Luis asked again.

"Dad, I think that's a vulture. Look at its bald head and legs." He adjusted the zoom on the lens. "Vultures aren't that big." Having negotiated the last body, the woman turned and faced them.

"Jesus, Mary, and Joseph," Munoz senior said and quickly made the sign of the cross.

"Oh, fuck!" Jorge said. Her face and arms were covered in sores that ran red with blood and pus. He looked lower and found the blisters covering her legs as well. "We can't let her in, Dad," he said flatly.

"Let's get out of here," Luis said. Jorge turned the boat on its keel and sped out to sea.

CHAPTER 8

"Tela is a city of thirty-two thousand. It has been mostly evacuated, but the military estimates that there are at least two hundred citizens that remained along with military and police personnel." Bernice was virtually screaming. The only space that could be found for their group was a corner in a military hangar. The collective voices of hundreds of soldiers, along with jet engines in the distance and helicopter engines in the foreground, echoed throughout the massive structure. "Unfortunately, the only road connecting Tela with the rest of the world was washed away last night. As a result, we need to pare down our supplies to the bare essentials because we are catching a ride with the Honduran air force. Who's ridden in a helicopter before?" Bernice excitedly raised her arm, but only two others in the group of fourteen joined her.

Amanda's heart sank. For obvious reasons she was not a big fan of flying, and now she would have to fly in something without wings.

"We are going to have to scale back our goals, at least until we can re-establish reliable transportation."

"So you're saying that helicopters are not reliable?" It was one of the two physicians who now asked the very question that had popped into Amanda's head.

"For those of you who do not know Dr. Greenburg's history, he started out as a standup comedian, but turned to medicine after nearly starving." Everyone laughed at the not-so-inside joke. Dr. Greenburg easily tipped the scales at three hundred pounds.

"Now, as I was saying, we're going to have to make do with less for a while, but we still have critical objectives. First and foremost is communications. Next is medical. The two-hundred-plus estimate may be wildly inaccurate—and remember, that's just for Tela; it doesn't include the surrounding villages. Triage will be critical. Review your manuals, and if in doubt, ask someone." Bernice's gaze casually wandered Amanda's way. "Does everyone have their PDAs?" Half the group waved their devices in the air. "Good. I've updated everyone's responsibility for the next three days." She turned to Dr. Greenburg. "I figure that's how long it will take before the trucks and all the rest of our equipment will take to reach us. Oh, one more thing before I turn it over to the general. There is word that the hospital ship *Mercy* will be on site in two days, so we may get resupplied directly from the Navy. Now let me introduce General Regara of the Honduran Air Force."

"Good afternoon, and welcome to my country. I want to thank each one of you for assisting us in this time of need." General Regara was a small, compact man with the same thick dark mustache that adorned every Honduran soldier. "We plan to use six helicopters, two for personnel, two for supplies, and a final pair for a security escort. I know that this is not something we discussed …" He directed his last comment to Bernice Scott. "But we are getting some confusing reports from the area about possible looting. It is my responsibility to ensure your safety. These men will also be available to assist you with setting up your camp and crowd control if it is needed. They are not authorized to direct or impede your movements, within the confines of our law. They will also carry additional communication equipment and can help with the local dialects." The general paused, waiting for questions or comments.

"Well, I for one think it's a great idea. Now I have someone to do all my heavy lifting," Dr. Greenburg joked.

"Please don't expect to be carried, Doctor; we don't need a bunch of soldiers with hernias," Bernice answered, and even General Regara chuckled.

"We plan to land at the airport if it is at all possible. Unfortunately, the airport in Tela is fairly close to the sea, and we expect at least a moderate degree of damage. We have chosen a backup landing site located approximately two kilometers from town if the airport is unsafe. This may mean that you will have to walk to Tela on your own. Perhaps we can find a good strong burro for the Doctor." The group began to loosen up, and their laughter was a bit more natural. "Logistically, the airport is probably the best location for you to set up camp, but as I said, we expect some storm damage and you may find no habitable structures." He paused for a response to this unexpected inconvenience.

"It's all right, Colonel; all of us have slept outside before," Bernice answered for the group.

"Excellent. We will be shuttling in supplies for you once a base camp has been set up, and I believe the second trip will include additional tents and cots. You may not be completely comfortable, but at least you'll be off the ground and dry." He received a confirmatory nod from one of his staff and then continued his briefing. "We had hoped for two more disaster teams to be deployed in the area, but as it will take most of our airlift capability to position your team, I'm afraid until a stable ground corridor can be established you will be on your own in that respect. That may change if the airport and local roads can be cleared quickly. The trip will take approximately seventy-five minutes, and we hope to leave as soon as possible to give you enough time to walk into Tela and set up your base camp before sunset."

"Can you update us on the conditions of the local utilities?" asked one of the male volunteers.

"All the power lines were above ground and we must assume that they are gone. Cell phone towers are down, and all telephone service has been cut off."

"So in short, all we have is radio communication."

"For now," the general answered.

"What about emergency medical flights out?" Doctor Jorgenson, the second of the two physicians on the team, asked.

"For now we have only minimal capacity to deal with emergencies, both from a transport capability and a medical capability. Even here in El Progresso, we are overwhelmed." His pained expression made it obvious that he was uncomfortable discussing his country's limitations. "I am sorry to say but the care that you deliver is probably the best care available."

"Well, at least we know that we're working without a safety net," the doctor observed.

"What is the condition of the town itself?" another volunteer asked.

"We have had no radio contact with the local garrison, so the only information comes from a handful of civilian broadcasts and a single reconnaissance overflight. It appears as if all multi-story structures have sustained damage as far as a kilometer inland, and the roads appear to be impassable."

"Could be worse—could be raining," the second volunteer quipped in his best Marty Feldman impersonation.

"Okay, let's get loaded and let's get started. If it's nothing else, it will be exciting." Bernice jumped to her feet and vigorously pumped the general's hand while Amanda and the rest of the team began to gather their personal effects and move them to the flight line.

"I've done this for eight years and I can't remember ever going into a situation with so little backup," Mary Ecklers, the team's senior nurse, said as she came alongside Amanda. She was a dour, overweight woman in her fifties, and she struggled with an enormous rucksack.

Amanda slung her smaller backpack over her shoulder and began to help Mary stabilize her cumbersome load. "What do you have in here?" Amanda asked, feeling its weight.

"As much of my bedroom and bathroom as I could carry," Mary said, finally getting her arms through the straps. "Thanks. So this is your first time. I would have recommended somewhere else. This one is shaping up to be a real corker."

"How so?" The impending helicopter flight and having only a vague understanding of her responsibilities were already beginning to take a toll on Amanda's nerves. Mary's trepidation added to Amanda's growing discomfort.

"No trucks means that we take in only a fraction of the supplies that we depend on. They'll ferry some of the lighter things in by chopper, but with the coastal mountains between here and Tela they're not going to risk overloading one of these little birds with our big generators, or sterilizers, or a half dozen other things that make our lives and jobs easier." She motioned Amanda towards a ridiculously small helicopter.

"That's what we're taking? It looks more like a traffic helicopter than a transport."

"Welcome to the third world." They had reached the flight line and two soldiers reached for Amanda's smaller backpack, leaving Mary to struggle alone. "Ahem," she said loudly to their backs, but before they had turned a third soldier lifted her rucksack from her shoulders and very nearly took her as well. She turned to find a huge man in an ill-fitting, sweat-stained uniform. He smiled down at her and she mumbled, "Gracias."

"If it rains I'm going to stand under him," Amanda said as the large man one-handed the heavy bag over to the nearest helicopter.

"Not on your life. You can have your two little caballeros, but that one's mine. What's Spanish for bear?" She asked Amanda, but one of the soldiers had overheard.

"Oso," he said, with Amanda's backpack around his arm. "But oso also means 'the fool,' so I would not suggest calling Miguel 'oso.'" He smiled.

Both the ladies blushed. "Okay, that was dumb of us. Do you all speak English?" Mary asked.

"Everyone in our unit speaks English, Spanish, and at least some Mayan." He was having fun with their embarrassment. "You better hurry. Your helicopter is going to leave without you." He pointed at a second helicopter and turned away.

Within minutes the pair, along with four others, were being strapped into the small helicopter. They each had been given a pair of headphones that had more than a passing similarity to a pair of coffee cups on end. "How do we communicate?" Amanda asked the copilot after he finished checking her harness. He smiled and apologetically shook his head. He climbed into the front seat and the engine began to whine. She scrambled to put on the bulky headphones as the pitch started to become uncomfortable and realized with near panic that no one had closed the cabin's door. She had been the last to board the craft and had the seat closest to the now gaping exit. She tried to reach for the pilot but was firmly held by the harness. She tried screaming, but not even Mary, who sat next to her, responded. The helicopter took off at an impossible angle and Amanda clutched the arm strap above and the seat cushion below, not daring to look outside as the military base and the city of El Progresso passed beneath them. The wind buffeted her face and her short hair whirled madly.

Mary tapped Amanda's hand and she opened her eyes. The older woman was yelling something, but it wasn't until Amanda took off her headphones that she understood. "Next time force your way into the back seat." She made spinning motions with her hands as the air swirled around them.

Amanda nodded and pointed at the yawning maw of the open sliding door.

"Typical," Mary yelled, as if the omission held no threat.

It took almost an hour of flying before Amanda was comfortable enough to ease her numb hand out of the leather strap that hung from the metal ceiling. She braved a look out the cabin door and found that they had descended below the low clouds. The dark green of the jungle seemed to extend all the way to the blue of the sea, and she began to gauge their progress with the approaching shoreline. When the sea seemed so close that Amanda was certain that they had missed their landing site, the pilot leveled off just above the tree tops of the dark green jungle. She watched as the thick canopy began to thin and finally gave out altogether as open fields that once were farms slipped beneath them. She surveyed the storm's damage and after several minutes hadn't found a single upright structure. They swung inland slightly and passed over the smashed airport. The tower and the antennas were scattered in ruin across the single runway, and shards of glass reflected the brilliant afternoon sun. Mary was leaning into Amanda and yelled that there was no chance of landing here. The pilot had reached the same conclusion and banked sharply to the left. It was now Amanda in Mary's lap as both women scrambled for their ceiling straps.

They doubled back into the jungle and found a clearing big enough for three of their six helicopters. Just before touching down, Amanda spotted a soccer goal high in one of the trees. The landing was surprisingly soft, and the copilot was unstrapping Amanda before the rotors had even slowed. He helped her out of the helicopter a little too aggressively and she landed on her knees in wind-whipped, waist-high grass. She scrambled out of the way as the rest of the passengers made less than graceful exits from the helicopter. Doctor Greenburg was the last out, and he nearly fell face first into the grass after his foot caught on the door railing. The copilot helped the man to his feet and then forcefully directed him to follow the other passengers to the far end of the disused soccer field. Seconds after the doctor had cleared the rotors, the helicopter took off at a thirty degree angle; it was quickly replaced by a helicopter packed to the ceiling with supplies.

"That pilot has watched too many Viet Nam movies," Greenburg said as he neared the small band. He turned along with the rest of the team to watch the platoon of soldiers quickly empty the helicopter of its supplies and then execute the same emergency take-off. "What's their hurry?" he asked.

"Sunset is two hours away. I'm guessing they don't get too many hours flying over the mountains at night," a voice from the group answered. Amanda thought it came from one of the four volunteers.

"What about the second trip, and our additional supplies?" asked another voice Amanda didn't recognize.

"Get used to disappointment. You will be told a lot of things down here, but only a few of them will actually be true," Doctor Greenburg added sourly as he flopped his mass into the tall grass. "Somebody wake me when things get organized."

"So how was it?" Bernice Scott suddenly appeared at Amanda's side.

"They left the cabin door open."

"They do that sometimes," she answered, watching as the team's supplies were stacked in untidy piles. "They generally strap you in fairly well."

"So if the pilot suddenly decided to turn right and my straps weren't quite tight enough?"

"Then something unfortunate would have happened." Bernice smiled and winked. "Don't worry, I doubt you'll have to take another helicopter. I think we're here for the duration. Or at least until the roads open up." Without another word she sprinted over to the soldiers as two of them awkwardly carried a large wooden crate. "Be careful," Amanda heard her scream.

Twenty minutes later the team of fourteen and platoon of seventeen stared at a mountain of crates, boxes, and plastic as the echo of retreating helicopters faded into the living sound of the jungle. "All right, if I could get everyone's attention!" Bernice was in her take-charge mode. "We had hoped to use the airport, but Lieutenant Garcia"—she paused and pointed with an open hand at the cleanest of the seventeen soldiers— "tells me that the security situation is still uncertain. So for tonight it is probably better if we just set up here."

"I like the sound of that," said the muffled voice of Doctor Greenburg, who was still reclining in the grass.

"It will give us all," she emphasized the last word, "a chance to organize our supplies."

"I hope you are not including me. I was promised a tropical vacation in a seaside resort," he answered.

"Well, you are in the tropics, and there's the sea," Bernice retorted.

"I want a Margarita. Did we pack a Margarita maker?" Greenburg continued.

"Doctor!" Bernice now flipped into her disciplinarian mode. "We have less than two hours to create some semblance of order out of this mess. I appreciate the attempt to lighten the mood, but it's time to work." Her voice reverberated through the clearing.

Greenburg sat up and whispered a chastened "sorry."

Order restored, Bernice rapidly handed out assignments. "Finally, I am going with the lieutenant and some of his men into town to make contact with the security force, and hopefully get us some wheels. Maybe even con some of the residents to come and help set things up." She crossed the fingers of both her hands.

"Bernice, is that wise? You just told us that the security situation was uncertain." Doctor Jorgenson had politely worked his way to the front of the group so he could face Bernice directly.

"That's true, but we have some local help. A number of the soldiers grew up in Tela." Several soldiers subtly responded. "I'll be fine, David. I know what I'm doing." Bernice smiled, but by the expression on Jorgenson's face he clearly remained unconvinced.

***

Amanda marveled at nature's destructive power, but also at its resilience. Parts of the jungle had been completely flattened, as if a giant boot had stomped the trees and vines. She had been warned to expect this; tornadic winds—giant eddies in the usual straight line currents—were common in powerful storms. What was unexpected was their focal nature.

"This is amazing," Bernice remarked as they approached a clearing half as large their landing site. Stumps of trees that only days earlier were over a hundred feet tall stood in mute testament to the power of Hurricane Michael. Their shallow roots, normally buried by several feet of decaying vegetation, baked in the afternoon sun. The detritus had been blasted into the trees that edged the clearing. "It's like a bomb went off," she said, slowing her pace and falling behind the Honduran soldiers.

Amanda slowed as well, and eventually the two ladies simply stopped and stared.

"Mrs. Scott," Lieutenant Garcia called, breaking their trance. "I must insist that you stay with us."

Amanda was surprised to see that they had tarried long enough for the squad to disperse into defensive positions along both sides of the choked road that lead to Tela. They held their weapons waist-high and scanned the jungle nervously. "Maybe we better go." She tugged at Bernice's blouse, suddenly aware of their situation and its potential. They hurried up to the officer, who gave a command, and the group reassembled with the women in the center. "The sound is almost deafening," Amanda said and they continued down the narrow lane and a half road that by Central American standards was a main arterial.

"Lieutenant, how did all these bugs survive?" Bernice asked after walking through a cloud of small black midges.

"I do not know," he answered, barely acknowledging the question as he scanned the jungle ahead.

"He's making me regret my decision to come along," Bernice whispered to Amanda. They both hesitated when Garcia suddenly jogged to the head of the column.

"Me too," Amanda answered just before the lieutenant halted the squad with a raised fist. A pregnant moment passed. Garcia grunted an unintelligible command and all ten men crouched and rotated towards the forest, guns raised. Amanda and Bernice found themselves inside a circle of very nervous and heavily armed men. Instinctively, they dropped to the ground.

"Stay low," Garcia said unnecessarily to the two women after he found his way back to them, his eyes and weapon constantly moving. Amanda stared at the jet-black rifle that swung in an arc a foot above her head. She marveled at its utilitarian design but was terrified by its capability. She knew nothing about weapons, military or otherwise, and imagined that a simple errant touch would suddenly make them go off, with obligatory lethal consequences.

A full minute passed and then Amanda heard a small pop. Just a single innocent crack, but it sent ripples of apprehension through the lieutenant. "Was that what I think it was?" She whispered to Bernice, who was inches from her face.

Before she could respond, a whole series of pops like a string of firecrackers followed. "MAC 10," Garcia whispered. "That's not us." He squatted and retrieved a small radio from beneath his flak jacket. "Maya seis, Maya seis." No one responded. He tried three more times without success and then changed the radio's frequency. Three more times and no answer. He let loose a short string of Spanish that both ladies knew was not suitable for mixed company. He duck-walked over to a soldier, pulled a larger radio from his field pack, and then sat back to back with the man.

"Damn it," Bernice whispered. "Smugglers. Tela is a part of the drug corridor; boats pull up in the middle of the night, take on fuel, and then are usually gone the next morning. No harm, no foul. Except five days ago a couple of boats that should have been watching The Weather Channel a little more closely pull in and then find that they can't leave. So they stash their boats and cargo in a warehouse by the river. They must be trying to protect it." Bernice turned to Amanda and found that her dirt-covered face had a questioning look.

"General Regara told me before we left; it's why he sent these guys with us," Bernice clarified

"I don't understand. The general knew there were drug smugglers here and didn't do anything?" Amanda tried to keep her voice low, but the lieutenant heard enough from fifteen feet away that he glanced over while talking on the radio.

"How long do you think the general would last if he started pissing off the drug cartels? It's their way, and it's been their way ever since we started turning a blind eye to foreign governments involved with the drug trade, so long as they hated the communists as much as we did. This is hardly the place for a political debate." Her voice was low, but it still communicated a rebuke for Amanda's naiveté. "Sorry," she said after a moment. "I didn't mean to get so carried away. Sometimes I can be a real bitch, and right now I'm a real nervous bitch."

Garcia crawled back to the center of the circle. "We've been ordered back to the landing field …"

"Contact, ahead," a voice hissed.

"Contact, left," a second one added, followed closely by a third on the opposite side of their circle.

"Down," Garcia said, and all ten men flattened themselves. "They probably heard the helicopters," he said to himself and the women.

Maybe they'll just pass by us, Amanda thought, but then took stock of the situation. Tela had one road in and one road out, and they were currently on it. Even if by some miracle they missed her group of thirteen, the presumed drug gang was on its way to investigate the helicopter landings and they would surely find her Red Cross team, which only had a handful of soldiers to protect them.

Two full minutes passed with almost no one breathing, and then even Amanda could hear them. At first it was just the snapping of a tree branch, then hushed voices followed by the smell of cigarettes, and then finally six men rounded the corner. They were dressed in fatigues and carried rifles that looked decades older than Lieutenant Garcia's. They had their heads down and shuffled more like zombies than Honduran soldiers.

"¡Alto!" Garcia yelled and was suddenly on his feet, along with his ten soldiers. The six men did indeed stop; they stared at their clean and rested colleagues with looks that ranged from confusion to relief. "Who is your commanding officer?" Garcia demanded, first in Spanish and then in English. The six men looked at each other, wondering who was going to answer.

"He is dead," a man in the back finally answered in Spanish. His uniform was ripped in several places, but Amanda still could read the name Listera over his left breast pocket. He was the least haggard of the group, but it still looked as if he were about to fall over. Three of his comrades dropped their weapons and sat in the dirt. "So are twelve more of us and just about everyone else in the city. There are bodies everywhere." His voice trailed off and he too dropped his rifle and slipped into the dirt.

Garcia turned crimson and screamed, "On your feet soldiers!" Three of them, including the spokesman, slowly climbed to their feet. "You need to give me a better report than that!" Amanda didn't need her high school Spanish to understand. "Form up!" he yelled in English and his ten soldiers immediately formed two columns. Garcia walked down the center of his men and then over the fallen branches that separated the two groups. He slowly walked among the exhausted soldiers, inspecting them closely until he reached the spokesman. "What happened here, corporal?"

He looked confused. "There was a hurricane."

"What happened to you, to these men, to the city?" He waved both arms, his impatience obvious.

"It started last night, a few hours after the rain began to slow." He stood straighter but struggled for words. "Before the storm hit we had divided up the civilians into three groups, and then Colonel Mencia split our platoon into three groups to protect them. The six of us were in the storm shelters by the airport with about a hundred civilians." He suddenly looked confused. "I think it was a hundred, maybe it was a thousand."

"It doesn't matter, Corporal. Where are they now?"

"We let them go, and then they all died. At least most of them, I think." He began to lean and then sway. Garcia grabbed the man just before he fell.

"Sit down, Corporal. Can anyone else tell me what's going on here?" The remaining men, following the corporal's example, sat in the dirt. They stared at Garcia, and like before, no one answered.

"I think a lot of them got shot," the corporal finally answered.

"Who shot them?"

"Colonel Mencia. But he didn't kill them all; the Columbians killed a lot, and then we killed the Columbians." He smiled proudly and Amanda noticed that his teeth were red.

"All right, Corporal." Garcia softened his tone. "Listen closely; why did Colonel Mencia shoot the civilians?"

"He didn't just shoot civilians. He shot Reyes, Quinteras, Alonsa …"

"He shot the mayor and the police captain," another soldier added.

"That's right; he started with them." Listera nodded his head and stared back at Garcia.

"You didn't answer my question, Corporal. Why did your colonel start shooting people?"

"He got sick; everybody was getting sick. See." Listera rolled up his sleeve to reveal a line of blood-filled blisters up his arm. Two other soldiers followed suit and pulled up their sleeves, and another opened his shirt. All of them had the same lesions.

Garcia backed out of the knot of soldiers. "Mrs. Scott," he yelled.

"Right behind you, Lieutenant," Bernice said. "I heard what he said. Does any of it make sense to you?"

"No," he answered quickly. "What are those things on their skin?"

CHAPTER 9

"She just walked in from the jungle and passed out," Mary Ecklers told Dr. Greenburg as the pair hurried behind Oso, the large Honduran private. He carried a small bleeding woman, whose moaning had ominously ceased.

"Senor, take her over to the tent." Greenburg pointed to the large pavilion that had been erected just minutes before. In time it would serve as triage and, if needed, an open air hospital ward.

"His name is Oso," Mary teased. The large man grunted at her; she had been calling him Oso since they had landed, and his fellow soldiers were starting to pick it up.

"My name is Miguel," he said, reaching the tent and lowering the stricken woman onto the only clear spot, which happened to be a stack of bottled water cases.

"Help me clear this, Oso." Greenburg had started to pull boxes off of a large wooden crate.

"Miguel," he said, brushing aside the physician and opening the side door of the crate. "I am guessing that you want the exam table." He slid the folded table from the crate and in a single move expanded the legs.

"I never knew they opened like that. Thanks, Oso." Greenburg stood back and examined the crate's side door.

The big man shook his head and gave Mary a long look as he lifted the unconscious woman onto the exam table.

"Sorry, but it suits you," she said, tearing open bags of saline and IV supplies.

"She's been shot," Greenburg said in surprise. "We're going to need more help." He applied pressure to a small wound in her upper right chest. "Get me a set of vital signs and a couple of IVs as soon as you can." He reached around the small woman and his hand came back bloody. "Shit, the bullet went all the way through. She's got an exit wound that's as big as my fist. We could use some help in here." He yelled, "Hey Oso, or whatever your name is, see if you can find us a pair of gloves."

Dr. Jorgenson and four other people rushed into the tent. "What's going on?" he asked his colleague.

"Gunshot wound to the chest; as if these people didn't have enough problems now someone is shooting them. Can you get me a blood pressure?"

"I can't get a blood pressure," Mary said, stabbing the woman's arm with a large-bore needle.

"She's still bleeding so she must have one. Get me some instruments—maybe I can clamp this damn bleeder off."

Twenty minutes later, and after fifteen minutes of CPR, David Jorgenson tapped his partner's back. "She's gone, Eli; you need to stop."

Greenburg reluctantly stopped chest compressions. He was dripping in sweat and had blood up to both elbows. "Not even two hours and we're already pulling the sheet over one of them," he said bitterly as Miguel helped him off the table. "I'll bet she's not even thirty." He brushed the dark, bloodstained hair from her face and then paused. "Hey David, what do you make of these?" He pointed to a crop of small clear blisters that had appeared over her otherwise smooth face. "She didn't have these when we started."

"Allergic reaction?" Jorgenson bent close.

"To what? All she got was saline and epinephrine. We didn't even have gloves for a latex allergy." He lifted both his bloody hands as proof.

"Doctors, she's got them on her arms as well, and she definitely didn't have them when I started the IV." Mary raised one flaccid arm, which was now covered in a cobblestone rash.

"Okay, I'm starting to get a little concerned here." Jorgenson pointed to the skin of the young woman's neck, which moments earlier had been completely normal.

"What the hell?" Greenburg said, watching her skin blister before his eyes. Instinctively, he checked for a pulse. "This is impossible," he said and then backed away from the table. "I need some alcohol and Betadine to scrub this crap off of me." He held up his arms and one of the nurses led him outside. She began pouring alcohol over his bloody arms. "Can someone find me some hydrogen peroxide?"

"How do you want to handle this?" Jorgenson asked Greenburg after his arms had been scrubbed raw. The body of the small woman lay unattended in the now off-limits tent.

"No way we can get this body out of here, huh?" Greenburg was sixty-eight and the senior physician by more than three decades. A retired internist, he had volunteered only to break the monotony of retirement. Jorgenson was a general surgeon who had just finished eight years in the employ of the US Army and was donating a month of his time to the Red Cross before starting a private practice position in Boston.

"Not until the morning," Jorgenson said as everyone looked up into the darkening sky.

"The lab is the one thing we have up and running, and I'd sure like to know what that shit is. How about I gown up and take some tissue?" Greenburg was asking for advice, but ultimately the decision was his.

"So long as we maintain isolation. I'd do skin scrapings only and reduce the risk of contamination. We might want to freeze some while we're at it, and bring it back home."

"Good idea."

***

Ten minutes later, the lights around the compound began to come on, and the drone of the jungle was partially replaced by the hum of small generators. Lieutenant Garcia led the way into the clearing and four of his ten soldiers followed, with Bernice and Amanda bringing up the rear.

"Are we just going to let those men spend the night in the jungle?" Amanda whispered to Bernice. They had had the first serious disagreement with the Hondurans over the fate of the six men, all of whom were clearly sick. Garcia had disarmed each man, then detailed six of his men to watch over them until his superiors could decide what to do with them.

"We could at least bring them to the clearing and give them food and water," Bernice had pleaded.

"They are soldiers and have been trained to do without," Garcia answered tersely. "My orders are clear: they are to remain where we found them." His tone closed the door on any further discussion.

"They are sick and dying men," Bernice said, stomping after the lieutenant. She fumed all the way back to the camp.

"I'm glad you're back," Greenburg said, greeting Bernice outside of the large tent. The corpse and exam table had been removed. He filled her in on the last hour's activities, and when he was done she shared her adventure. "So it's not an isolated case; we've got some sort of outbreak going on."

"Looks that way. I'll contact our people in El Progresso. Garcia has already talked to his superiors, who are busy pulling their puds trying to decide what to do with the six in the jungle. Can I see the slides so I can at least sound like I know what I'm talking about?"

"Absolutely. Any woman who talks about pulling puds can have anything she wants. Follow me; the lab is set up over here."

The pair walked to a smaller tent that sheltered the three small generators and an even smaller medical lab. Bernice noticed an odd collection of empty crates and boxes just past the arc of lights. "The body," he said simply, and she nodded.

"After you." He lifted the tent flap to find David Jorgenson bent over one of their two microscopes. "Did you figure it out yet?" Greenburg said loudly, causing his younger colleague to jump and knock over a bottle of water.

"Damn it, Greenburg, you better sleep with one eye open tonight."

"Relax, it's only water. What do you see?" He peered over the smaller man's shoulder, as if seeing the slide would answer his questions.

"Nothing; you have a look." Jorgenson backed up and let the internist take over.

"Dermatology was never my strong suit." Greenburg pulled up a small stool, and Jorgenson and Bernice shared a look and broke out into broad smiles wondering if the stool would bear Greenburg's weight. "I can feel you smiling," he said as he adjusted the focus. "Hmm. Extensive dermal damage. Even the subdermal blood vessels are necrotic. That would explain the fluid."

"How about in English, Doctor?" Bernice asked.

"Something has affected the cells of the skin, not just the epidermis, the outer layer, but the living skin beneath, and its blood vessels. When the dermis is injured it loses some of its grip on the overlying epidermis, which can peel away, allowing fluid to accumulate in the space. Voila! A blister. The problem is that, whatever the process, it should have stopped with her death, but this one didn't." He pulled back from the scope and began to stroke his chin.

"Skin cells continue to grow and divide after death," Bernice said.

"Only for a very short time," Greenburg said. "So obviously whatever caused this had already been in the dermal tissue before blood flow stopped. Which means either a toxic or infectious etiology. In fact, I'll go further—it means either heavy metal intoxication or a viral infection."

Without warning, Jorgenson suddenly scrambled backward into a generator. Bernice nearly tripped getting out of his way in the close quarters and Greenburg spun in his chair. "What the hell are you doing?"

"Bernice, back away from Eli," Jorgenson said. She hesitated. "Bernice, now, back away." She looked at him and then back at Greenburg, completely confused until she saw the small red and clear blisters on the backs of his hands.

"Oh shit!" he said, more angry than concerned. "Well, I guess we can cross heavy metal intoxication off our list," he said, examining the backs of his hands. "You two need to get out of here. Go clear some space for me in the big tent, preferably by a window and the fire."

Bernice and Dr. Jorgenson slipped out the back of the tent and literally ran into an uncharacteristically disheveled Lieutenant Garcia. Amanda was only steps behind the officer. "I am so glad I found you," Garcia addressed the doctor. "We have a situation with some of the soldiers from town. Six of them were found wandering in various states of delirium outside of Tela. Their arms were covered in lesions. I left some of my men with them and they have radioed back that one of the six men has died, and the other five are close to death. I need you or Dr. Greenburg to go and see if it is safe to bring the men back here." Bernice and David hesitated and then looked at each other.

"What's wrong?" Amanda asked.

"While you were gone we had a woman come into camp. She had been shot, and we couldn't save her. She had lesions—small blood-filled blisters ..." Jorgenson began to answer.

"Yes, that's what these men have," Garcia interrupted.

"Dr. Greenburg has developed the same lesions," Jorgenson finished.

"Oh my God," Amanda whispered, and Garcia made the sign of the cross.

"We can't let those men into this camp until we have a better idea what's going on. I'm sorry, Lieutenant." Jorgenson tried to walk passed Garcia, but the larger man stepped in front of him.

"But they will die. Can't you just come and see them. It's not far." Garcia was pleading.

"I don't understand this sudden change in heart," Bernice said suspiciously. "Thirty minutes ago you were happy to leave them out there all night."

"They are soldiers, just like me. They have families just like me." He began to cry and then dropped to his knees.

Amanda took a step away from the sobbing officer. "He's been like this for about fifteen minutes. It happened so fast; one minute he was talking to the general on the radio, and the next minute he was crying and smashing the radio," she said quietly to Bernice. "Ours is still okay."

"Where's his rifle?" Bernice asked.

"I'm not sure. I think he handed it to someone when we went to radio the general."

"Good. Everyone who came in contact with the men in the woods, or with the dead woman, needs to be disarmed and isolated," Bernice whispered.

"I understand the isolation, but what does this have to do with weapons?" Jorgenson asked.

"The soldiers in the forest told us that after their colonel became sick he started killing people," Amanda answered.

"Great. Apparently whatever it is that's killing these people isn't doing it fast enough." The doctor shook his head. "We'll have to take it to secondary contacts as well, which I'm guessing pretty much includes everyone."

"Well, at least I'll have some company." All three turned to find Dr. Greenburg standing just outside the lab tent. "Can I come out now? I promise not to shoot anyone."

"What are we going to do?" Amanda asked the obvious question over the lieutenant's renewed sobs.

"First thing is to segregate everyone who is clearly infected, which includes the doctor and the lieutenant. Then we need to check everyone for signs of infection, and keep checking, let's say every hour. Then we need to get on the horn and get us some help." Bernice had once again become the grand organizer.

Greenburg still seemed unfazed. "We need to keep people away from each other. I'm afraid that our little meeting here has probably infected you two ladies. David, I'm guessing that you were infected earlier when we tried to save Patient Zero. I would spread the word that no one gets closer than ten feet to anyone else in case the agent is spread by airborne droplets."

"That's going to make it difficult checking for signs of infection, but I see your point." Bernice said. "I've got a bullhorn and I'll spread the news. One last thing—he has six men in the forest guarding the ones already infected from the village. Do we bring them in? They had been ordered to keep away from the sick men."

"Yes," three voices said at once. "I doubt that the risk here is any less or greater than out there. Do you think he's in any shape to give that order?" Jorgenson asked the other three. Garcia had rolled onto the ground and curled into a ball, but at least he had become quiet.

"No," Greenburg said flatly. "Is this what we have to look forward to?" He faced Jorgenson.

"Why is it affecting him like this? None of the men from the village were this bad." Amanda stared at the man who earlier in the day had been strong, articulate, and vigorous. "This is terrifying."

"You're telling me, sister," Greenburg said under his breath. "I'm guessing that whatever this is has a variable presentation. Let's hope that he's at one end of the spectrum and we're at the other." The small group nodded as the lieutenant began to moan again.

It took an hour to get everything organized and for the rest of Garcia's platoon to make it back into camp. Two more of the stricken six died before the remainder were left to die alone in the dark jungle. David Jorgenson and Mary Ecklers had both developed the tell-tale blisters, and along with Oso had joined Dr. Greenburg and Lieutenant Garcia in the large supply tent. Within minutes Greenburg had organized a poker game. Out of sheer luck it had been placed downwind of the rest of the camp, but that didn't stop Bernice from ordering everyone to wear surgical masks and cover as much skin as possible, even in the stifling heat and humidity.

***

"The lieutenant grabbed that man, remember?" Amanda asked Bernice, who sat the requisite ten feet away while waiting for the Honduran liaison to radio her back. The sun had gone down several hours earlier, and the air was filled with flying insects.

"I remember," Bernice said. "It's been a long day, and it's going to be a long night," she mused. "It's been several years since I've spent the night in the jungle. I remember the stars being brighter, but also the bugs being smaller."

"You want to know a secret?" Amanda asked.

"This is going to be about sex, isn't it?"

"No!" Amanda answered.

"Good, because if you were about to tell me that you had a thing for Dr. Greenburg I'd have to get off this chair, come over there, and punch out your lights. That man is mine!" Bernice tried to keep a straight face but failed, and the two women started to laugh. She stood and began to shake her considerable bulk. "Cause I like my men big and jiggly." She flopped back into her chair, barely finishing her pantomime through the laughter. "Oh God, I needed that," Bernice said after the laughter had begun to die away.

"No, despite my secret attraction to Dr. Greenburg, I was about to say that this is the first time I have ever been out of the country."

"I can't even remember how many countries I've been to. I've been all over the world. But I always like coming home the best. Maybe it's familiarity or convenience, but even with all its warts and worms I'll take the good-ole US of A."

"Did we just make a beer commercial?" They both started laughing again, and as it faded they fell into a comfortable silence.

Amanda had become so relaxed that when the radio squawked she nearly fell from her chair.

The first part of the message was delivered in rapid Spanish. "Slow down; I can't understand you," Bernice sent back. "This is the Red Cross camp in Tela, Honduras. I'm waiting for Dr. Leon Martinez."

"Yes, this is Dr. Martinez," a masculine voice responded in heavily accented English. "Is this Mrs. Scott?"

"It is. We have a situation here." Bernice gave a concise summary of the condition of Tela, the camp, and the mysterious illness. "Everything we know about Tela comes from the soldiers in the jungle. None of us have actually been in the city, but we did get close enough to hear gunfire."

"The military has had other reports of violence in the area. It is your belief that it is the rash that is causative?"

"I'm not certain I am being clear." Bernice turned to Amanda and rolled her eyes. "It is my belief that whatever is causing this rash is also responsible for personality changes that can lead to violent behavior."

"I understand now." A short pause followed. "How can we help you with this?"

Bernice's eyes widened and she mouthed his last sentence with complete disbelief and frustration. "We need help. At a minimum the sick need immediate evacuation and someone needs to investigate what's actually happening in Tela."

"Uh, yes. We do have a problem with evacuation. There is simply no place that will accept such patients."

"I don't understand. You realize that we are an understaffed aid station short on supplies, with both of our physicians in quarantine. We are not capable of supplying medical care to anyone. Not even to ourselves."

"All our hospitals and clinics are overwhelmed. There is no room for anyone," he said in a distinctly bureaucratic voice.

"In the entire country?"

"Yes, in the entire country. We do not have the infrastructure that you Americans are used to." His voice was now full of disdain.

"Forgive me, but I don't understand your attitude. We are here to help you …"

"Then why are you making yourself a bother?"

At first neither Amanda nor Bernice understood the question. "Do you want to talk to this asshole?" Bernice walked away from the radio and kicked a box, swearing at the top of her voice.

"Dr. Leon, this is Amanda Flynn, Mrs. Scott's assistant. I understand that your country's resources are strained, so is it possible to contact our government? We had heard that the US Navy was sending a hospital ship. I'm certain that they can render some assistance."

"My government has declined the offer."

"I'm not sure I understand. We were told that *Mercy* was being sent here."

"Whether it was or was not, it is not now coming."

"So we are alone here." Bernice had been listening and motioned for Amanda to hand her the microphone.

"I need to speak to the Red Cross's international representative or to a representative of the United States."

"Yes, I'm certain you do, and you have our permission to do so."

"But we don't have any long range communications. It was all left in El Progresso; you're probably standing on it right now." Bernice was beyond her boiling point.

"I assure you I am not. Perhaps in a few days we will be able to deliver your remaining equipment, and your government can assist you directly. If that is all, I must sign off as I am very busy."

"Wait, can we speak to General Regara?"

"Once again I am sorry, but he is not here. Perhaps you should try in the morning. Good night." If it had been a phone, Martinez's sign-off would have been punctuated by a loud "click."

"Fuck," Bernice screamed and threw the microphone at the radio console.

"Bernice, please don't break the radio; it's our only lifeline." Amanda broke the isolation rules by retrieving the dangling cord.

"Life is cheap down here, and the lives of a few Americans and peasants mean nothing next to bruised egos. You were warned about this," a voice said from the dark, and Eli Greenburg slowly walked into the light. He maintained his distance from the two women, but even from twenty feet away the change in his physical appearance was shocking. What little skin not covered in tense, blood-filled blisters had taken on a sallow yellow hue. His blood-shot eyes were sunken, and he was gasping for air. Both Amanda and Bernice jumped to their feet and after less than a moment's hesitation started for him. "Stop!" He demanded. "You can't help me, and I refuse to die knowing that I killed you as well. Just stay where you are and listen." He staggered over to the chair that Amanda had been using and painfully lowered himself into it. Both ladies waited as his breathing slowed. "The civil government in Honduras is pissed off with the US government over the coup in 2010. You can't rely on them, and in fact you have to avoid them at every turn. Use the military; they're much more reasonable and pragmatic. Wait for the morning; try and get a hold of that general who sent us to this hell-hole, and get out. If you can't get a hold of him then take anyone who is not sick, go to Tela, find a boat, and get to the Barrier Islands or up the coast."

"We're fine; it's getting you and the others out," Bernice said.

"You're not fine, Bernice. I've known you for years, and if you were fine you could have schmoozed that jerk into driving here himself. Maybe it's just the stress, maybe it's not." His dying eyes were fixed on Bernice. "Oso and the lieutenant are dead. Garcia had a knife, biggest God damn thing I ever saw. Did you know that they were Special Operations Group? Mary was stabbed in the arm and David in the neck. He's not going to make it." He tried to laugh, but all he produced was a bloody cough. "Hell, I doubt any of us are going to make it."

"We didn't hear a thing," Amanda said, her eyes wide with shock.

"I was right there and barely heard it. The whole thing was over in less than a minute. Our Special Forces trained these guys, and they are really very good. I had a long talk with that Oso fella. Nice guy. His real name was Miguel. He had a family." Greenburg sat in thought for a while. "Everyone around me is dying and all I can think about is how much I hurt. I think I'll go back to bed." It took him thirty seconds to reach his feet. "Bernice, I need you to hear me. Get out of here as quickly as you can. If the general can't rescue you, then you rescue yourself. At some point somebody is going to quarantine this whole area, and if you're here when they do, you will die here. It has been an honor knowing and working with you." He lurched to his left as his balance momentarily failed. "Good thing I'm not driving." He tried to laugh again. "Amanda, I'm sorry your first trip had to be this one. Good luck." He staggered back into the darkness.

"I never liked that man," Bernice lied, with tears in her eyes.

***

Amanda sat on a fallen tree branch, avoiding her old chair, and watched as Bernice trailed behind the doddering Greenburg. Her mind was reeling and everything had an unnatural feel. It wasn't possible that they would be left out here to die alone and forgotten; people who cared about them knew where they were. There were expectations of contact, daily reports had to be filed, requests for more supplies were part of the routine, and without them red flags would go up all over. They had a massive, well-oiled machine behind them, and it was only logical to assume that in time that machine would rescue them.

But how much time? she asked herself. She glanced up as Bernice returned to her chair. Bernice gave every outward appearance of being normal, but Greenburg's insinuation that she was not quite herself echoed in Amanda's mind. To be trapped here without Bernice was unthinkable.

"Any thoughts?" Bernice asked.

"I don't see that we have any choice. I agree with what he said; if we stay here I'm afraid we're going to die. I was just wondering if we should pack up now and head out."

"It's too dark and dangerous. If we don't get shot we'd probably end up breaking a leg on a tree stump. What time is it?"

Amanda held her watch up to the light. "Eleven-ten."

"Okay, I'm going to try and get some sleep for a couple of hours. I know that I should be checking myself every hour, but if we can't get out of here, what's the point?" Bernice rose, gave Amanda a weak wave, and disappeared into the darkness behind the radio tent.

Tiny alarm bells were going off in Amanda's mind. Bernice had always been mercurial, but never irresponsible. She put it out of her mind and decided to get some sleep as well. She moved her sleeping bag into a patch of darkness and slipped inside after quickly checking her skin.

CHAPTER 10

Amanda listened to the sounds of the living jungle and wished that she had moved her sleeping bag closer to the small cluster of tents and people. Unlike the rest of the team, she had rarely slept outdoors and never alone, and she certainly felt alone now. Darkness and strange, eerie sounds enveloped her, and they intensified Amanda's free-floating anxiety.

"Go to sleep, MONA," Amanda whispered to the night. When she was a little girl and certain that some unnamed evil lived in her closet or under her bed, her mother had warned her about MONA—Middle Of the Night Angst—a small, sneaky gremlin that worked its way into your sleepy mind and poisoned your thoughts and dreams with whispers of dread and doom. It had taken years for Amanda to fully appreciate the meaning of angst and MONA's ability to paralyze with unfounded fears, but on this particular night MONA's whispers didn't seem so very far from the truth. Three times Amanda's fitful sleep had been disturbed by heated exchanges in both Spanish and English. The team had been here little more than twelve hours and already two people were dead, at least three more were dying, and any cohesion between or within the two groups was falling apart. It was hard to be optimistic, and MONA was taking full advantage of their situation.

The sun broke over the horizon with such intensity that it ripped Amanda out of the only restful sleep of the night. She had been dreaming about her husband, Michael, and awoke with the familiar empty feeling when she found they were not in their bed with his arms around her. The emptiness was replaced by fear when she remembered where she was. She quickly checked her skin and was relieved to find nothing new. Her face was covered in dew, and she really needed a bathroom. It wasn't completely light yet so she quickly kicked out of her sleeping bag and ran behind the nearest thicket of jungle. No one had ever accused her of being prissy, but she never could get used to peeing outside.

Walking back to her sleeping bag, she realized that she hadn't seen her backpack since they left El Progresso. Her teeth felt furry and she was covered in dirt; she desperately wanted a toothbrush and some soap to wipe away the layer of grime on her face and neck. She angled towards the large pile of supplies that had yet to be sorted and spotted her pack about halfway up. Stephen, one of the volunteers, was standing just to the right of the pile, and it appeared to Amanda that he was appraising a task in front of him.

"Good morning," she said from a safe distance. Stephen was one of the oldest members of the team, but remarkably fit for a man in his seventies.

"Well, hello young lady. I'm not so sure it is a good morning but it's always nice to see a pretty face." He was a cross between a kindly grandfather and a disapproving college professor, and in their brief time together Amanda had found it hard to really understand the man. "I was supposed to make some sense of this mess, but I don't see much point in that now."

It came to her in a flash that she hadn't thought about the three people still left in their form of isolation. "Have you heard anything about how Mary and the doctors are doing?"

He gave her a strange look that confirmed what she had suspected. "I'll be out of here in a moment," he said, not bothering to go through the formality of answering her question.

Twenty minutes later Amanda felt better physically. She dropped her pack next to her sleeping bag and set out to find Bernice. She searched the upper portion of the small camp but couldn't find a soul. Reluctantly, she walked to the large pavilion and found several people staring at a prone figure just outside the large tent. "What's going on?"

"It's one of the soldiers; he just collapsed," answered one of the other nurses.

"Oh my goodness!" Amanda couldn't remember the woman's name and circled around the small group to get a better look. "Where is Bernice?" she asked, realizing that the young Honduran was dead, his upturned face covered in the now all-too-familiar lesions.

"She's in there," the nurse answered, pointing into the dark tent.

Amanda's heart sank. "Oh my God," she whispered and turned to face the woman, whose name continued to escape her. "Wait a minute. What are we doing? We can't have any contact, physical or respiratory." Amanda backed away from the others.

"What's the point?" the only male of the small group answered.

"We're not here even one day and all of our training and discipline goes out the window?" Amanda scolded, but they seemed completely uninterested in her thoughts.

"It was a very bad day," the nameless nurse said. "I'm going to see if I can find something to eat." The others followed, leaving Amanda alone with the corpse. Reluctantly, she turned away, knowing that something should be done with and for the body, but having no idea what.

"Bernice," she called, walking around the south end of the tent.

"I'm over here, Amanda." A grey head bobbed among the boxes. "Are you all right, dear?" She sounded like her old self.

"I'm fine. Are you all right?"

"Depends on what you mean by all right." She grunted. "Lift that up," she said to an unseen assistant. "I don't think I'll be making that call to the general, Amanda. That task falls to you." Her head popped up again and a taller, darker head could be seen just in front of her.

"What are you doing?" Amanda's question was half a plea.

"What I have to," Bernice said, out of breath. "Stop here for now," she said to her companion. She stood up to her full five feet two inches and Amanda could see the upper half of her face; small red blisters covered in sweat reached as far as the bridge of her nose. "What a difference a day makes." She made eye contact with Amanda. "First thing, keep everyone away from here. Things got pretty messy last night. Second, get a hold of that general and have him get you and the rest of our people out of here. If that doesn't work, you get them out yourself. Third ..." she stopped suddenly as the beating of an approaching helicopter echoed through the clearing. "Praise Jesus," Bernice yelled.

"Thank God," Amanda added.

"Don't stand here, child, go. Get our people home."

Amanda ran back the way she had come and found eight people waving their arms at the approaching helicopters. Two of them started to hug and Amanda had to stifle a warning to maintain their distance. She craned her neck and found the helicopters just above the tree line, heading straight for their little camp.

"Six. seven, eight, of them," Stephen, the grandfatherly professor yelled, and then waved as they made a close pass overhead.

"Look, there's more," someone screamed. Amanda turned back towards the west to find another six helicopters approaching. The first group split into two, with four of the crafts banking left and the other four banking right. In less than a minute they had encircled the clearing. The helicopters' rotors were perilously close as they took up hovering positions, and Amanda said a silent prayer that there wouldn't be an accident just as they were about to be rescued. Ladders and ropes dropped from both sides of each helicopter and moments later soldiers began to rappel to the ground. The surviving Red Cross and Honduran platoon began to cheer as each soldier touched down.

"Why aren't they just landing?" someone yelled. The noise was deafening and Amanda couldn't tell who had asked the question, but it struck her as funny that they would risk the soldiers by having them rappel out of the craft as opposed to waiting until it landed.

"Maybe it's an exercise," Stephen screamed back.

It took less than five minutes for the helicopters to empty, and one by one they banked out of the field. The second group of helicopters screamed overhead and Amanda expected them to perform the same maneuver, but they continued on towards the city. She looked back to the soldiers, but it took a moment for her eyes to adjust after the bright sky; she found that they had formed a ring around the perimeter of the clearing. *What in the world are they doing?* she asked herself.

"Attention!" A soldier with a bullhorn had taken a step into the field. "This area is a quarantine. Please stay where you are, do no moves and do no approach the military personnel." The voice was very heavily accented and the English so poor that if the message had not been repeated Amanda didn't think she would have understood its meaning. Stephen walked beyond the perimeter of lights screaming that he was an American and demanded to see a representative of his government. He was answered with a hail of bullets aimed ten feet in front of him. The meaning of that message was crystal clear.

Amanda ran to the radio tent as the perimeter soldiers watched her intently. The bullhorn sounded again: "Please stay where you are," but she ignored the warning. To be nearly completely without hope and then have what appeared to be salvation dangled in front of her—only to have it snatched away—enraged her.

"Shoot me then," she screamed. She threw back the tent flap and triggered the mic. "This is the Red Cross camp in Tela; someone better tell me what the hell is going on."

More helicopters flew overhead and they began to drop large pallets, which the soldiers began to rapidly unpack. The rotor noise completely obscured any response from the radio, which only further enraged her. She started yelling into the near white noise of the helicopters and after two minutes of screaming a pounding in her head forced her into a chair and into a sullen silence. She was angry enough to want to reach through the radio, grab the officious Dr. Martinez by the throat, and tear the silly little smirk right off his face. She was certain that the petty bureaucrat was laughing at all of them. General Regara was probably with him, waiting for Amanda to radio back and plead for mercy. "Fuck you!" she screamed at the radio, and it dawned on her that this was the first time she had ever said that expression out loud. It felt good; it was empowering and liberating. She screamed it louder, and it got better each time she said it; only the exertion made her head hurt more.

The helicopter noise began to fade and she could finally hear the radio. "... Minister of Health. We will lift the quarantine once we have an idea ..." Amanda didn't allow him to finish.

"I don't know who you think you are, but if you think you can hold us against our will then FUCK YOU!" She punctuated her point by banging the microphone onto the radio. A chip flew off and hit her in the face. "There! Do you assholes like that?" She lifted her arm to smash the vile piece of equipment again but an arm caught her on the down swing.

"Easy, pretty lady. We're going to need this at some point." Amanda hadn't heard Stephen come in, and for a moment her anger flared and she nearly hit the old man in the face. He grabbed her other arm and they both saw a small patch of the cobblestone rash.

She pulled away from him and drew her arms close, suddenly regaining herself. "Oh my God, Stephen."

"It's okay." He pulled back his collar. "I've got my own." He spun Amanda's shoulders towards the opening in the tent flap and retrieved the microphone. "You stay there for a minute and let me try and straighten this out." Amanda nodded. "This is Stephen Hoyt; to whom am I speaking?"

"This is Dr. Leon Martinez of the Honduran Ministry of Health." Amanda took a start at the radio as soon as she heard the name, but Stephen held up his hand, stopping her.

"Excellent. As I understand, you have quarantined this entire area."

"That is correct."

"I understand your predicament. Now I hope that you understand that under Honduran law and by international agreement, once you have declared a quarantine zone that includes foreign nationals, you are obliged to supply medical care, as well as—and this is critical—inform our government that we have been included."

A long silence followed. Stephen turned to Amanda, waiting for Martinez's response. "In my earlier life I was an international relations lawyer. I helped draft the UN agreement." He winked. Amanda smiled and had visions of Martinez frantically combing through a large legal book. A strong desire to tell him to fuck off welled up inside her, but Stephen's presence was enough to suppress it.

"Mr. Hoyt?" Martinez finally responded.

"Actually, it is Dr. Hoyt, Dr. Martinez." Amanda nearly kissed Stephen for kicking this spic's ass. That was another term she had never used in a coherent thought before. It felt okay, but not nearly as good as any phrase that included the word "fuck."

"Did you know the word 'fuck' comes from an old English term? For Use of Carnal Knowledge. F-U-C-K. Fuck." She sounded drunk and wondered when the last time was she had really been intoxicated.

"Amanda, honey, please sit down and let me finish with this man." Stephen slid a chair under her and she obligingly sat.

"Spic. Not a man; a spic." She felt sick and dizzy and was glad Stephen had found her a seat.

"We are having communication problems of our own but will contact your embassy as soon as we can." Martinez's bureaucratic smugness seeped through his words.

"So long as that is within twenty-four hours, you'll be fine. And the medical care?"

"We are doing the best that we can. Hopefully, the situation will stabilize within a few days. May I ask where Mrs. Scott is? It was my understanding that she was in charge."

"She is ill," Stephen said, without offering details.

"How sad. We will try and keep you informed as much as we can. In the meantime, please comply fully with the rules and the military. I am afraid that they have been given a great deal of latitude in dealing with this most serious situation."

Stephen dropped the microphone. "Prick," he said under his breath.

"You kicked his ass," Amanda said, smiling awkwardly.

"Unfortunately, all I did was win a meaningless argument. He still has all the authority. Why don't you come with me and let's go talk with Bernice."

CHAPTER 11

Amanda awoke in a cot that smelled more of mildew than canvas with an IV in her arm. She traced the silastic tubing taped to the back of her hand to a small plastic bag that hung above her head. Her unfocused eyes could just make out the word Midazolam. She was sick and didn't need the infusion of the sedative to confirm it. Every part of her was covered in ugly red blisters, her bones ached, and any movement prompted vertigo bad enough to make her retch. The sun was just clearing the horizon and her fractured mind tried to understand what had happened to the day. She recalled flying in on the helicopter, setting up camp, Bernice's blistered face and then … The memory of her psychotic behavior fell into place. Wild, bizarre, disconnected thoughts and images had raced through her mind for hours, days, maybe even weeks. Despite both having died years earlier, she remembered watching as her father and brother walked through the tent and out into the sunshine without even acknowledging her. *This is not real; it can't be happening,* she told herself, but they seemed just as real as the Honduran soldier who had stopped to chat with them. Paroxysms of rage had alternated with bouts of paralyzing terror, and if she hadn't been restrained there was no doubt that she would have hurt herself or someone else. She closed her eyes and felt the sedative pulling at her. She didn't want to sleep; sleep would only bring back the nightmares. Her thinking became mushy and she struggled weakly to remain lucid, but the medicine in her IV won and she drifted away.

***

She opened her eyes and watched as shadows moved all around her. She thought that she was lucid, but couldn't be entirely certain that this wasn't just another well-formed hallucination. A hand touched hers and it was enough to snap the world back into focus.

"How are you doin', honey?" Bernice's face came into view, but it looked different, bumpy and misshapen.

"Bernice, is that you?" Amanda asked through cracked and bleeding lips.

"For now it is," Beatrice responded, and Amanda understood her cryptic answer perfectly. "You're going to be like this for a while, and then maybe it will pass."

"Maybe it won't," Amanda said. A burst of sharp reports distracted them and Bernice leapt on Amanda, their combined weight collapsing the cot. A half-dozen people around them dove to the floor just as splinters of wood and metal showered down. One of the supports for the large tent gave a loud crack and canvas dropped over everyone.

"Don't move, Amanda," Bernice struggled to say, her face smashed into Amanda's chest.

"How can I with my hands strapped to this damn thing and you on top of me?" She tried to kick her legs but found them tied as well. The canvas smelled of mildew and Bernice smelled of vomit and suddenly Amanda was flooded with claustrophobia. She squirmed and tried to kick the older woman off of her, then started screaming as more gunfire erupted all around them.

Bernice tried to snake an arm up to Amanda's mouth but couldn't reach; someone next to the pair managed to find Amanda's mouth and clamp a hand over it. She tried to bite the hand but it gripped tighter. A face appeared before hers; it was distorted in rage, and despite the muted light it appeared just as badly misshapen as Bernice's. "Shut your God damn mouth or I'll kill you." Spittle covered her face and she relaxed, fear now overwhelming her.

Nothing moved for several minutes and the gunfire had ceased. The hand across her mouth relaxed and eventually slid away, allowing her to breathe again. Her head was clearing and she recognized the sound of people and running feet. In a moment the canvas was lifted and the sun streamed back in. Bernice climbed off of her and then fell awkwardly back to the broken cot. "Damn, I got up too fast." She had managed to miss

Amanda's restrained legs and looked around trying to figure a way back to her feet that did not involve using Amanda as a springboard. She rolled towards the end of the broken cot and her feet landed in a pool of blood.

Amanda had already found the source. Kelly Byers, the youngest nurse after Amanda, was lying face down in an expanding circle of blood. Her blouse, once green, was now a dark shade of red. "Oh my God," was all Amanda could say, so she said it over and over again. Bernice found a sheet and covered the poor girl. "Wait, Bernice. She may not be dead!" Amanda's mind was suddenly clear.

"Trust me; she's dead," Bernice said to the sheet.

More people arrived and the "Oh my God" refrains continued. Amanda was suddenly struck with a completely random thought: *With all the praying going on around here, where is God, and why did things just keep getting worse?*

The silhouette of a tall man stood next to Bernice as two others wrapped Kelly's body in more sheets. They had turned her over and Amanda had to look away; the pretty young face of Kelly Byers was gone on one side. She squeezed her eyes closed and tried not to listen as the body was lifted from the wreckage. After several long minutes Amanda opened her eyes to the early morning sun of a beautiful new day.

"There are fourteen of us left," the tall silhouette said to Bernice. The voice was distantly familiar, and it took a moment for Amanda to place it. "Hey sweetie. Are you still with us?" Stephen took a step forward and propped some of the fallen tent with a broken pole.

"I think so. How are you, Stephen?"

"I'm okay. A little older, a little uglier. How do you like the new voice?" His voice was deeper and had a rough, raspy edge.

"You sound like an old cowboy." She smiled and tried to reach for his hand.

"Great. I always wanted to sound like Roger Staubach," Stephen said, but Amanda didn't understand the reference, and by the expression on her face, neither did Bernice. "Troy Aikman? No? You live in Dallas and don't know Roger Staubach or Troy Aikman? If anyone asks me about the decline of Western society I will have to tell them that it started right here." He shook his head.

"There are only fourteen of us left?" Amanda asked, looking for an explanation.

"You've been out of it for three days."

"Three days?" She was shocked and disappointed, and quickly examined her hands, but the cobblestone rash hadn't faded.

"Everybody has it now; we've dropped all the isolation rules. Whatever else this is, it is extraordinarily contagious." Bernice said, her face looking more swollen than blistered. "Are you thinking clearly?"

"I think so, but you can't trust anything I say."

"Well said," Bernice answered and then bent painfully to undo Amanda's Velcro ankle straps. "I'm going to let you go, but you will have to stay with me." Amanda nodded and Stephen released her hands. He helped her to stand, and she nearly fainted when pain assailed every joint in her body.

"Walk around and it will get better." Stephen helped her with the first few steps and then Amanda felt stable enough to let go of his arm. They walked around the tent for ten minutes until she fully regained her balance.

"Where did that come from?" Amanda squinted in the bright sun. A new chain-link fence had been erected in the tall grass just outside the tree line.

"They finished it yesterday," Bernice said behind them. "Don't go near it." She pointed at a dark shape next to the east end of the fence. "One of our soldiers. They shot him from the woods yesterday morning."

"They put up cameras this morning," Stephen said to Bernice and pointed out four towers that supported small rotating cameras.

"Well, they have enough resources for fences, bullets, and cameras, but none for medical care." Bernice moved slowly as the trio walked the length of the camp's main tent.

"We started with thirty-one people. What happened to the other seventeen?" Amanda asked as Bernice stopped in front of the same plastic chairs they had used the night they had arrived.

"We lost four the first night; the two doctors, the lieutenant, and Oso. Mary lasted most of the next day." Bernice's voice broke. "I knew her for almost twenty years, and to watch her die that way …" Her voice trailed off and she slowly, painfully lowered herself into the chair. "Dr. Greenburg had the right idea; get it over quick." She wiped her face with her dirty sleeve. "The soldiers got into it the day before yesterday, and when they were done we had seven more bodies. It looked like the orders to avoid contact with those soldiers from town weren't followed as precisely they were intended. Yesterday we lost two to the virus, and one to those bastards in the woods." They were closer to the body now and Amanda recognized him as one of the two soldiers who had helped with her pack. "And this morning, poor Kelly."

"You're one short," Amanda said.

"Our shooter this morning," Stephen said sadly. "I had no choice. I tried to just wound him but I'm a pretty poor shot."

"Seventeen," Bernice added. "What a God damn mess."

"Is someone working to get us out of here?" Amanda asked.

"They say they are, but I see no outward signs of it. We have yet to speak to anyone from home," Stephen answered.

"So when are they going to let us go?"

"When all of us are dead or our people trip to the fact that we have been incommunicado for four days and come looking for us," Bernice answered, and then turned back to Stephen. "So have we finally accounted for all the weapons?" A pair of soldiers with bloodstained uniforms emerged from one of the three tents the platoon had erected, and slowly walked past them.

"No, and they aren't talking to us. If we had managed to get them all under lock and key maybe this never would have happened."

Amanda watched as the pair stalked Stephen with their eyes. He had just killed one of them. It didn't matter that the soldier was in the midst of a homicidal rage that took the life of a young woman; what mattered was that the dead soldier had comrades who remained armed, resentful, and mentally unstable.

"So we have two armed camps, us and them, surrounded by a whole lot more of 'thems.' That, my dear, is the situation," Bernice concluded as the soldiers disappeared behind the radio tent.

"Both of you look like you're on the mend."

"I think we are starting to understand this infection a little better. If you survive the first day or two the illness seems to stabilize. What happens next is anyone's guess. We've only lost three to the virus, at least directly." Bernice began to look around. "What is that awful smell?"

Amanda had begun to smell it as well. It was a thick, acrid odor, almost as if someone were burning plastic. A light breeze blew in from the sea, carrying more of the smell. "Look!" Amanda pointed to the east. "Over the trees." A plume of thick black smoke was starting to rise into the sky. "There must be a fire in Tela," she surmised.

Bernice and Stephen stood and watched as the plume of black smoke rose into the morning sky.

"It can't be," Amanda said incredulously. "You don't think …"

"They're burning the bodies," Bernice said in disbelieving awe. "Those Nazi bastards are burning the bodies. It's insane."

"How do you know those are bodies?" Stephen asked, unconvinced.

"Because there's only one thing that smells like this." Bernice turned and grabbed Stephen's arm. "Help me to the radio. I've got to get a hold of General Regara, and not that asshole Martinez."

***

Five minutes later, sitting in the medical lab they found the radio and their small group's armory. "A couple of us moved everything in here when the guys across the hall started to become a little goofy," Stephen said nodding to the rifles. "These are the only weapons we could find. Let's hope no one has to use them again."

"El Progresso, this is Bernice Scott," she dispensed with all radio etiquette. "I need General Regara now!" she demanded.

Surprisingly, it took him only about two minutes to respond. "I have been expecting your call," he said.

"So the smoke we are seeing … Are you burning the bodies in Tela?"

"Regrettably, we have no choice. The infection that has involved your people and my platoon was much worse in the city. We could find no survivors and most of the bodies showed undeniable signs of infection. We do not have the means to dispose of almost one thousand contaminated bodies properly."

"But do you understand that if this contagion is viral—and our doctors were certain that it is—burning the bodies may spread the virus if it is not heat sensitive?"

"We were also concerned about that, which is why we are using thermite. It will consume any organic material."

Bernice paused her attack. She understood the general's position. Cleaning up a thousand infected bodies would strain the resources of the United States in the best of times and was clearly beyond the means of Honduras during the worst of times. Destroying the bodies with Thermite also made sense. Like living things, a virus was made of proteins, but heat-resistant viruses had developed unique shells of proteins that could stand up to ordinary fire, protecting the delicate genetic material inside the shell. Thermite, composed of iron, aluminum, and magnesium, burned at such a high temperature that it would reliably denature any known proteins, splitting them into broken strands of small molecules.

"Are you still there, Mrs. Scott?"

"I'm here, General, although I wish I were any place but here. I agree with your logic; I don't like it, but I agree with it." Bernice sat back and shrugged her shoulders. "A couple other points, General, while I have you. We have a body of one of your soldiers out by the fence and no one is willing to retrieve it, because they think they're going to be shot."

"Please send some of his comrades to bring him back to your camp. His death has caused much sorrow here."

For a moment Bernice was going to tell the general that there were sixteen more bodies in the camp and they too were causing a great deal of sorrow. "Sorry, General, I think I just bit my tongue. What about the supplies that we were promised? We are running low on gas for the generators, water, saline, and food."

"They are being delivered this afternoon. Please closely observe the transfer procedures we discussed earlier."

"We will. Now for the hard one. When are we going to be able to speak to a representative of the United States government?"

"As I told you this morning, this is a matter for the Ministry of State. I have relayed your concerns and they insist they are trying to work out the ..."

***

Amanda was listening closely, but something in her peripheral vision drew her attention. The bright tropical sunlight dimmed for an instant and then returned to its usual level of brilliance. Like some cheap special effect in a low-budget thriller, time seemed to slow and then stop, her perceptions reduced to still-frames. Stephen stepping into the tent and reaching for the microphone just as two soldiers slipped from the shadows with weapons raised. The next frame saw Stephen lurching forward, sparks flying from the radio and Bernice falling off her chair into the microscopes. The final frame, the briefest, was simply the Hondurans advancing shoulder to shoulder, a muzzle flash from each weapon frozen in time. The loud clicks from their empty clips moved time forward. For an instant the Hondurans vainly attempted to fire their empty weapons, their faces masks of insanity and their eyes filled with rage as they screamed like feral animals.

A blackness filled Amanda's mind, and when it lifted she stood over two mutilated corpses, a smoking rifle in her hand. The body on the left twitched and instinctively she fired. It would never move again. Time seemed to slip off its rails again as two more soldiers came running around the old radio tent. She watched their knees pump through their khaki uniforms and the shock wave from each footfall pass up their legs. It took nearly an eternity for their facial expressions to turn from confusion to anger when they saw Amanda standing over their fallen friends, and then to alarm as they processed the fact that the weapon in her hand was aimed at their chests. It took the rest of their lifetimes to try and bring their weapons to bear and for Amanda's bullets to tear through them.

The echoes faded and Amanda stood alone. She began to register the weight of the weapon and stared at it in complete confusion. She was terrified of guns; how did she manage to have one in her hands? She tried to decipher what had just happened, but her memory had large gaps. She was in there—her head turned to the destroyed medical tent—and then she was here. She swiveled her head between the two corpses at her feet and the dying men ten feet away. Without thinking, and still not certain how she had found herself in this situation, she walked over to the bleeding men and kicked away their weapons.

"Are they dead?" Bernice had crawled out of the medical tent.

Amanda reflexively swung the rifle in her direction but then lowered it. Her mind took a second to process the question and to formulate a suitable answer. "Yes."

"Good. I only wish they could have died slower. They killed Stephen, and clipped me in the knee. Bastards." She twisted into a semi-sitting position and dragged her bleeding leg from the fallen tent. "Blew up the only radio as well." She shook her head. "I knew that they would come after Stephen. They were all sick and acting really strange, even worse than you. We should have disarmed or killed them after what happened earlier."

Amanda stared at Bernice blankly. The older woman was speaking, but Amanda was capable of registering only a few of the words. She slung the rifle over her shoulder, its red-hot muzzle burning her arm briefly.

The pain seemed to take a long time to reach her brain, and she languidly rubbed the red mark. She reached for the two fallen weapons and dragged them over to Bernice. "What just happened here?" she asked after helping Bernice up to a crate.

"You're in shock, dear." Bernice lovingly brushed the hair out of Amanda's eyes.

"I don't think so. I know I shot them, at least those two," she pointed at the far pair. "But all I remember is seeing those two"—she pointed at the pair very near their feet—"firing into the tent and you and Stephen falling. The next thing I know, I'm out here with this in my hand, standing over them, and they're dead."

"Are you okay?"

"Yeah, I'm fine; just a little confused about the last few minutes."

"You're okay with this? You don't feel bad about what you had to do?"

Amanda looked at Bernice as if she had just asked the most inane question ever. "Fuck no," she said without emotion.

"Interesting choice of words," Bernice said with concern.

"It's my new favorite word. Here," she handed Bernice a rifle. "I'm going to get some help."

Amanda did the math as she walked through the camp looking like Rambo but feeling more like Rain Man. Their Red Cross team was now down to three nurses, two volunteers, Bernice, and herself. Half the team was dead and they had been here less than four days. The Hondurans were down to two, from their original seventeen. She peered into the few tents that remained standing, looking for any help, but everyone seemed to have scattered with the gunfire. She tried not to think about Bernice's question but it kept bobbing to the surface. She had asked with such sincerity that Amanda felt perhaps she was missing something. Yes, she had killed those men—four of them to be exact—but they were going to kill her, and Bernice. They had already killed Stephen, although in fairness she didn't know that at the time. Was she supposed to feel bad that they were dead? She walked towards the pavilion pondering the question. Yes, she admitted, she was sorry they were dead. It was a tragedy that they got sick and became murderous psychopaths, and their families would probably mourn them deeply. But should she feel sorry for having to put down murderous psychopaths bent on killing her? No, she concluded. She understood Bernice's question and all its meanings and rejected the notion that she should feel guilt for doing something that any rational person would feel was right.

"Hello?" She called into the large tent. She heard rustling, and then a face appeared over the unpacked crates and boxes. It was the nurse with no name, and Amanda still couldn't recall it. "I'm sorry, but for the life of me I can't remember your name."

The plump, round-faced brunette gave Amanda the same look that she had just given Bernice after being asked an inane question. "What are you doing out there? Didn't you just hear that?"

"Everything is taken care of. I need some help with Bernice; she's been shot."

A dark cloud of suspicion covered her cherubic face. "You need to go; we have weapons." There was more rustling behind the boxes and Amanda brought her weapon to bear.

"You need to calm down. I am no threat to you and I didn't shoot Bernice, the soldiers did. They killed Stephen. I'm guessing it was in retaliation for him killing one of theirs."

"Where are they now? The soldiers, I mean," she asked with a little less suspicion, and not a trace of concern for their fallen colleague.

Apparently death is becoming all too common around here, Amanda thought. "They've been taken care of. Now, please, I would like to get Bernice over here so we can get her stabilized."

There was more clattering of boxes and the plump unnamed brunette disappeared for a moment; then she, along with another nurse whose name Amanda couldn't retrieve, appeared around the south end of the tent. The pair strolled up to Amanda and then put their hands on their hips. "Okay, we're here." Their sullen attitude reminded Amanda of spoiled teenage girls.

"I'm sorry for the inconvenience, but you do realize that even with all that's happened we still have a job to do?" Amanda stood face to face with the plump brunette, who simply rolled her eyes. "Oh, fuck it. Follow me," Amanda ordered and turned back into the bright sun. It was like being in grade school all over again, with Amanda as the teacher's pet. She had felt the poisonous attitude from the moment she had been introduced to the first unnamed nurse back in Dallas, and despite the fact that people were dying all around them, this middle-aged, insecure bitch continued to have a giant chip on her shoulder.

"Is that gun loaded?" Bitch Number Two asked.

"It wouldn't be much good if it wasn't," she said without turning or missing a step. She smiled at her answer; it wasn't hers of course—she just remembered it at the opportune time. It made her sound like a genuine bad-ass, a concept she was warming to.

"Do you know how to use it?" For a moment Amanda wanted to give her the benefit of the doubt, but the subtle undercurrent of disdain prompted a different approach.

She stopped and turned. The weapon swung casually outward. "Would you like me to show you?" Their eyes widened and their pupils dilated. "It's not very smart to try and anger someone with a gun. However, if you have a genuine doubt"—she turned, walked a few paces, and pointed to a pair of corpses—"you can always ask these two, or perhaps the pair over there." For the first time in her life, Amanda enjoyed intimidating someone.

It took the two women, Charlotte and Cami, ten minutes to carry Bernice back to the tent. Amanda walked behind them, happy to be the guard.

"Okay," Bernice said to Amanda after being plugged into a saline IV with a morphine chaser. "What did you say to them?"

Amanda smirked. "I was just having a little fun. They have been rude from the first moment I met them, especially Charlotte."

"You scared the hell out of them." Bernice gave her a drunken smile. "We've got two more on the verge with the flu. I mean whatever this is. I am high as a kite." She took Amanda's hand. "The ranks are getting pretty thin around here. We can't afford petty games and swabbles."

"Squabbles," Amanda corrected.

"That's what I said." She pulled Amanda down to her face. "I need something from you." Her eyes had cleared momentarily. "I do not want to die like Mary Ecklers. If I start to go down that road I want you to give me some dignity."

Amanda's smile instantly disappeared. "You can't ask me to do that."

"Well I'm askin'. Not only that, I'm makin' you a promise that I'll do the same for you. This morphine is some fiiine stuff, full of dignity." She smiled and winked, then her face became stern and serious. "I want you to promise me that right now." Her voice was sharp and clear.

"Okay, if you go down that road …"

"Make sure I'm going down that road now child," she sang as if she were in a Baptist revival.

"I will make sure that if you're going down that road, I promise to give you some dignity." Amanda had known Bernice Scott less than three weeks but felt closer to her than she had ever felt with her own mother. Morality aside, if Bernice was suffering she would end it. Maybe in the end, if it came to that, morality was the issue.

"Now turn the light off and let this old woman go to sleep."

Amanda walked from the tent out into the field and stared at the muted sunlight. Her adrenaline high was beginning to fade and her body ached more than she could ever remember, but her mind was as clear as she could ever remember. The smoke from Tela cast a grey haze from horizon to horizon. She had expected some kind of ash or particulates from all the burning, but her outstretched hand caught nothing. She could see the Hondurans outside the fence, and they could see her. Someone was scanning her closely with binoculars, and she was fairly certain that it had nothing to do with the quarantine. She restrained herself from giving him the finger and simply began walking through the tall grass just outside the tent.

Hours of walking had helped to ease the pain in her joints and gave her legs a warm glow of soreness. She kept checking on Bernice, who snored loudly in the arms of intravenous morphine. There were two other Americans, one a nurse and one a volunteer, in their makeshift hospital, and both were barely clinging to life. Their rash had progressed to involve the entirety of their bodies and over the last few hours had begun to ooze plasma and blood. Neither was truly conscious, although it was impossible to be certain. Their breathing was ragged and at times intermittent. She paced the length of the tent and stopped just in front of their cots. Nothing could be done for them except make sure that they didn't die alone. Charlotte and Cami were sitting in the shadows and she heard them talking quietly; she took a step into the shade and their conversation abruptly stopped. Their furtive glances and sudden rapid and secretive exchange told Amanda that her presence, no matter how remote, was not wanted. In a way, she understood; the dying nurse had been their friend and her death was a private affair, not to be shared with strangers.

Amanda walked once more around the tent and finally felt ready, both emotionally and physically, to deal with Stephen's body. She retrieved her weapon and made her way to the medical tent. She skirted the bodies of the last two men she had shot—as well as the first two just in front of the fallen medical tent—without a thought. The tent had collapsed and she began to struggle with the unruly canvas when a second set of hands began to help.

"I'm glad to see you back," Larry Hanford said, holding the flap of the fallen tent high enough for Amanda to walk under. "God damn it!" he said suddenly after recognizing the body of Stephen, the only other male volunteer, slumped in front of the shattered radio. "So this was the result of all that gunfire," he said softly. Amanda had managed to find a portion of the center pole and propped enough of the canvas to allow Larry to enter. "Fuck!" he said as he ducked in and looked at Stephen. His glasses were askew and his eyes open. Larry closed them and straightened his glasses. "I shared a tent with this guy for three months when we were in Haiti. Worked his ass off there. An old guy digging through rubble, carrying boxes, carrying babies. Thought he was going to have a heart attack, but he didn't." Larry looked around the tent for something that would cover the large bloody wound in Stephen's chest. He tore off a square piece of opaque plastic from a fume hood and tried to arrange it across Stephen's chest. "He cheated in cards, but what do you expect from a lawyer? Damn thing isn't big enough, but it will have to do." He looked at Amanda with a confused and pained expression. "We're here to help these people. This shit should never happen." He pointed at Stephen's body and balanced anger with grief. "Fuck!" he screamed again and then brushed by Amanda as he ducked out of the tent.

"Yep, that about sums it up," she said, following him outside. "I need you to help me move him. We can't leave him here."

"I know; just give me a moment." He had walked a few paces towards the fence and hung his head. "I had a heart attack a few years ago. I smoked too much, drank too much; I made millions off of people's retirement funds. Money real people had earned through a lifetime of labor, and I would skim off the top ten percent, all for punching a few buttons. I was what was wrong with the face of capitalism. It was people like me who precipitated the banking crisis, the foreclosure crisis; if there was a crisis, just look behind the curtains and you'd find me or someone just like me. But I got out of that." He turned back towards Amanda and straightened. "And now I am going to die in this shitty little field. I can accept that; in a lot of ways it's appropriate and just." He pointed back at the tent. "But that's not just. That's not something I can accept. He could have done anything with his life, but he chose to work for the UN to write charters on human rights. Instructions for assholes like me on how to live our lives. And he dies like that. Fuck!" He screamed and stamped his foot. Amanda could see that the perimeter guard was now on his feet, rifle in hand.

"Larry …"

"I know; we have to get him out of there." He walked back into the tent, but not before kicking one of the dead Hondurans. "Where do we put him?"

"The old radio tent," Amanda said, gathering Stephen's feet.

It took a good five minutes to maneuver Stephen's long frame out of one tent into another. "How many more do you …" Two nearby shots, fired almost simultaneously, made them both scramble to the ground. Amanda had shed her rifle just before Larry had arrived, and she could see it lying next to one of the dead soldiers. A wailing woman's voice carried across the field and Amanda thought it was Cami, or perhaps the older Charlotte. Aside from her screaming, nothing moved or made a sound.

"Jesus, that woman needs to shut up," Larry said, and it dawned on Amanda that it was Larry's hand that had nearly smothered her earlier that morning.

"I'm going to try and reach that gun." Amanda pointed at the weapon fifteen yards away.

"Are you insane? There are still two soldiers left in this camp. Special Operations Group! Do you know what that means? They'll shoot you before you get five feet. Even if you did reach it, there are two of them."

Amanda looked back at Larry and nearly smiled. "They'll shoot us both in five minutes if someone doesn't do something," she said, turning her gaze back outside. She was waiting, almost hoping, for time to once again slip off its rails, but it kept ticking along at the standard pace. She waited a heartbeat and then sprinted for the gun, expecting either a bullet or some significant time compression, neither of which occurred. She snatched up the gun and rolled into the medical tent for cover; nothing followed, and as far as she could tell nothing was moving in the entire camp. Cami was screaming now, and she was certain that Larry was fuming over it, but there were no signs of the Hondurans or any other threat.

After a minute Larry risked a look out of the old radio tent, and Amanda waved back at him. She looked to her left and could see an edge of one of the three tents the soldiers had been using. She knew that they had converted one into a morgue and were unlikely to snipe from there, but didn't know which of the three. Minutes passed and the only thing that happened was that Cami's screaming died away. Amanda was bent into an awkward position, and her calves began to cramp. She tried to rub the cramps away, but the muscles knotted even tighter, forcing her to stand. Larry was frantically signaling her, but she ignored him. If the Hondurans were going to shoot her it would probably hurt less than her calves. But no one shot her. She limped back towards Larry, keeping an eye on the Hondurans's tents, but nothing moved.

"Let's try and make it back to the big tent," she whispered to him, crouching low.

He hesitated, then nodded. He went first. Bending low slowed their progress, but they reached the entrance of the large tent alive and intact. Amanda followed him into the relative darkness of the shelter, and they both found piles of boxes and crates to hide behind. "Cami, Charlotte, are you okay?" She risked the question knowing that it might restart the screaming. And it did. It was definitely Cami because Amanda could hear Charlotte trying to calm her.

"I can't take any more of this!" she screamed loud enough to hurt Amanda's ears from several feet away.

"God damn, it's like being in an airplane with a screaming child in the seat behind you," Larry said through clenched teeth.

Amanda realized that if they had just kept going around the south side of the tent, literally only a dozen or so more feet, they could have put the majority of the large tent and its unopened cargo between the Hondurans and themselves. And as a bonus they could reach Cami, in which case Amanda could unleash Larry's death grip on the screaming woman. "Larry ..." Amanda's whisper was easily concealed within Cami's screams. "Follow me around the corner." This time he saw the logic and nodded vigorously. Amanda hoped he was warming up his hand.

They sprinted out and around the tent, and again no shots followed. They spotted Charlotte on her knees in front of a red-faced Cami, who was alternating between wails and inarticulate screams. Larry veered towards the two nurses, and Amanda worked her way towards Bernice, who was awake on the ground and trying to throw things at her hysterical nurse.

"Bernice," Amanda said, breathless.

A decade of concern fell from the older woman's swollen face. "I thought it was Stephen all over again."

"Not this time. Don't know where they came from or who shot them," Amanda said, her breath returning.

"Well, if she doesn't shut up I'm gonna have you shoot her." Amanda joined her on the ground, but her smile was cut short. A new crop of blisters had appeared all along Bernice's collar line, and her pupils were widely dilated.

"Bernice, are you okay?"

"No, I'm not okay. I've been shot, and if that fool doesn't shut up it's going to happen again." Abruptly Cami was quiet. "Well, praise Jesus," Bernice said. "Where the hell have you been?" She looked at Amanda with those frighteningly large pupils. Her IV with the morphine drip was still running, and Amanda was questioning whether morphine dilated or constricted pupils. She was fairly certain that it constricted pupils, which made Bernice's condition all the more concerning.

"I moved Stephen's body into the radio tent. Larry helped." She studied Bernice closely, almost coming nose to nose with her, yet she didn't respond. "Bernice, can you see outside?"

"No, it's nighttime. Why are you asking such stupid questions?" That subtle shift in personality had reappeared. Amanda checked over her shoulder; the light was muted by the smoke, but there was no way any one with sight would mistake it for night. In a matter of hours Bernice had become blind.

"I'm going to check on Cami. You stay here and I'll come back to get you when it's safe."

"Well, do it quickly," Bernice said sharply. "An old woman shouldn't be crawlin' along the floor. Probably snakes out, and there are definitely spiders. I saw ..."

Amanda crawled away, leaving Bernice deep in her own conversation.

"She's calm now; Charlotte gave her something," Larry said as Amanda approached the trio.

Charlotte looked back at Amanda. "Morphine. It's the one thing that we aren't going to run out of." There had been a subtle shift in the power structure. Larry deferred to Amanda, and now so did Charlotte. "Bea died; so did Charlie," she said in a purely unemotional matter of fact tone. Just for an instant Amanda wanted to slap her.

"What are we going to do about them?" Larry motioned towards the Honduran tents. "We can't keep hiding over here. Our water supply and the food are on that side. Not to mention the generators are going to need more fuel in a few hours."

"Do we need the generator on? What are we using it for?" Amanda asked.

"The bodies. Yesterday we put them all under a tarp and hooked up a cooling unit." Larry seemed uncomfortable with their solution, but Amanda thought that it was rather clever. "There's no more room under the tarp. I thought maybe we could use the radio tent. Problem is that I don't think it will accommodate…everybody," he said awkwardly.

"Doesn't much matter if we can't reach them," cheerful Charlotte said.

"We're all going to die out here," Cami added pitifully as she briefly came out of her morphine stupor.

Amanda had had enough of Cami and took a step away. Larry followed and Charlotte redosed her friend. "I think Bernice is sick again. She can't see and her rash has returned. I am not going to cower behind some boxes and watch her die. I'm going to sneak over there and see what they're up to."

"Do you have a death wish?" he asked.

"No," Amanda said quickly—much too quickly to have fully considered the question. She had to admit that her behavior over the last eight hours was at odds with her personality. She was terrified of guns, yet now she didn't feel comfortable without one slung across her shoulder. She was distinctly nonviolent, yet she had killed four men today and couldn't muster a trace of guilt. She had threatened and intimidated Charlotte and Cami when they were rude and dismissive, yet in her entire life she had never threatened or intimidated anyone for any reason, and what was truly surprising was how much she enjoyed it. More to the point, all her life she had been somewhat passive, letting things happen to her, yet now she insisted upon directing events, even if that direction entailed risk. Did that equate to a death wish?

"I can't leave Bernice like that." They both looked down the tent and found an obviously disoriented Bernice crawling out, her bloody leg leaving a trail.

"I'll help her get back into bed. Don't get yourself killed and leave me alone with the sunshine sisters."

Amanda hefted the rifle and walked back into the waning sunlight. She stayed close to the edge of the tent just in case the Hondurans decided to use her for target practice.

"See, a desire for self-preservation," she whispered to herself as she reached the south end of the tent. This was her last real cover, and the next steps would give them a clear shot at her. The platoon's third tent, the one she judged most likely to be occupied, was less than twenty yards in front of her, but it would mean running directly at men who meant to kill her. The only other option was to leap-frog to the radio tent, then the medical tent, and finally the first of the platoon's tents—the one least likely to be occupied—where she would have to work her way down to the other two. Impulsively, she sprinted for the third tent.

Add that to the list, she thought as she raced across the open ground. She slid the last few feet into tall grass that effectively covered her, and waited for a response. *I've never been impulsive*, she thought, silently catching her breath. Decisions usually paralyzed her.

The absurdity of the situation hit her like a bullet. She was lying in the grass waiting for soldiers to come bursting out of their tent to shoot her dead, and all she could think about was how strangely she was acting. So many people had died around her in the last three days that death had become a matter of course, and she was stressing about how her behavior had changed? *No more introspection until I get the hell out of here*, she swore to herself.

Five minutes passed and she hadn't heard a sound from any of the three tents. It was unnaturally silent. Not a creak, a snore, a cough, nothing. She crawled closer to the grey tent. It had a small flap and a mesh window. She held up a hand to the tent but it cast no shadow. She stood as quietly as her stiff joints allowed and then quickly looked into the window. She didn't take it all in but caught enough to know that she had nothing to worry about from this tent. Two bodies were sprawled against the wall facing her, a halo of blood above each upturned head. She looked again, this time longer, and confirmed the original glance. The only things living in this tent were the flies that flew in and around the faces of the dead soldiers.

She crept to the second and then the third tent. The entire platoon was gone. Seventeen men dead in four days, and that didn't even include the soldiers from Tela. She turned to the left and found her contribution. The four corpses were only a few hours old, but already she could imagine that she could smell them. She slung the rifle over her shoulder and followed the mechanical noise to the smoking generator. An empty fifteen-gallon gas can lay on its side. She looked for more but only came up with three other empty containers.

"More good news," she said ruefully and started back to the tent and the other four survivors.

Larry's head appeared briefly over the crates as Amanda approached. Tentatively, he stood. "I take it that everything is secured?"

"As secure as they are going to get," she said with a smile. "They shot themselves. That's what we heard. They were pretty bad off, the infection I mean." Amanda didn't have to elaborate. "How is Bernice?" The sky was finally beginning to darken and bring this biblically bad day to an end.

"Angry," he said and then started to push the obstructing crates and boxes aside. "I'm tired of this being in the way." He managed to shift enough of them to create a corridor. "There, isn't that better?"

"Much," Amanda said, walking through to the medical side of the tent.

"I think that's the most useful thing I've done since we got here." He reached for her arm as she passed. "Amanda, I just wanted to apologize for what I said earlier. I don't think you have a death-wish. You're just trying to do what's right for everyone."

"Thanks, Larry." She found his light grip on her arm somewhat uncomfortable and shifted out of it.

"Bernice wants to see you." Larry's eyes widened. "I mean she wants to talk to you."

"Okay," she said, turning away. *One more thing for the list that I'm not thinking about,* she told herself. She had always been a person who enjoyed physical contact. A touch of the hand, a brush of the cheek, and especially hugs. She had always loved getting and giving hugs, but the thought of a hug was just as disagreeable as she had found Larry's grip on her arm. *But I'm not thinking about this,* she warned herself.

She skirted some boxes on her way to Bernice's cot, but a sullen Charlotte cut across her path. "I heard what you told Larry. So what do you want to do about the bodies?"

Amanda looked over Charlotte's shoulder and saw Cami asleep on a cot. Next to her were two bodies wrapped in blood-soaked sheets.

"There's no more room under the tarp. Besides, the generator is going to run out of gas any minute."

The weight of the rifle caused Amanda to shift it on her shoulder, and she restrained a very distant but enticing desire to use it. "If you and Larry could carry them to the radio tent?" She was proud of herself for phrasing it more as a question than an order.

"Fine," Charlotte said, and stomped off like a petulant child.

Amanda turned the other way and found Bernice. "I heard you were back," she said soberly. "I didn't hear any gunfire, so I assume you didn't get shot." She had an almost accusatory tone.

"No, I did not get shot. I take it by your tone that you know what's wrong."

"Give me your hand." Bernice was clearly angry now and Amanda knew what would come next.

"No," she said pulling her hands and face out of range of the older woman's flailing arms. "Stop it, Bernice," Amanda commanded with enough force to get Bernice to stop trying to slap her. "I'm trying to see if you need anything."

"What I need is to see!" Bernice yelled. "They keep telling me that I can't see, and I keep tellin' em I can." She started crying, and as an exception to Amanda's new rule of "no-touch" she took Bernice's hand. "I know what's happening and so do you. You're a smart girl."

"I have an idea." She took the penlight that either Larry or Charlotte had left and flashed it into Bernice's eyes. Her abnormally large pupils constricted briskly, and then slowly dilated again. "Did you see that?"

"I don't know; maybe I saw a flash."

The occipital lobes—the back portions of the brain—are the vision centers, and when they are injured in isolation the patient becomes blind but the person still maintains that they can see. The pupils, which are controlled by centers in the brainstem, dilate, but constrict normally when exposed to light. "Cortical blindness," Amanda said.

"I don't want to die like this, Amanda."

"I don't know that you're dying and neither do you." She tried to sound definitive and forceful but her true beliefs betrayed her.

"If you lie to me again I will slap you." Bernice's words were stern, without even a trace of her trademark playfulness. "I may not be able to see but I can still feel, and I feel these things burning through me." She pulled down her collar, and the collection of blisters Amanda had seen earlier had spread across her chest and breasts. Tears started to flow down Bernice's face. "You made me a promise a little while ago and I'm holding you to it."

Amanda reached up to the IV and turned it up a notch. "Not yet, Bernice. Things could still change."

"The only change that's happenin' here is for the worse." She wiped her eyes, and Amanda was glad that Bernice couldn't see the blood that she had just smeared across her face. "Ah, there it is ….Mr. Morpheuss," she began to slur.

"It's just to get you back to sleep. I promised you that you had to be on that road. I'll stay with you tonight."

Bernice opened her eyes and looked for Amanda. "I'm holdin' you to it," she said, and then she closed her eyes. In less than a minute she had begun to snore quietly.

Amanda went looking for her sleeping bag and backpack and found them not far from her first set of dead soldiers. She walked back to the tent as the light was rapidly failing. Larry waved to her from the tall grass just beyond the camp's lights. He looked a little close to the fence, but there was no reaction from the soldiers in the jungle. She stretched out at the foot of Bernice's cot, not bothering to look for Charlotte. Cami was snoring almost as loud as Bernice.

Amanda stared at the stars. This hadn't been the worst day of her life, but probably the second. She rubbed the scratchy rash on the back of her left hand and a strip of skin peeled off, leaving behind red raw healthy skin. She quickly ran her hand over the rest of her accessible body parts and found that most of her lesions were in various stages of healing. It dawned on her that she hadn't eaten in three days, but she didn't feel hungry. She closed her eyes and her mind floated away to a happier time.

CHAPTER 12

The bang was just a backfire, her sleepy mind told her. Stay in bed; it's so warm and comfortable. No need to wake up. Only, it wasn't comfortable, and the screaming that followed was Charlotte. She wasn't at home with her husband; she was wrapped in a filthy sleeping bag, lying in the dirt of Honduras. She opened her eyes and the thin light of dawn greeted her. She rolled over and saw through blurry eyes a figure running through the field and a second one on his knees in front of the fence. She kicked out of the sleeping bag and ran after Charlotte before she reached what could only be the body of Larry. Several soldiers began yelling and waving their arms, and another shot rang out through the morning air. Charlotte dropped to the ground and Amanda froze. Larry had been shot, his hands clinging to the chain-link fence as a large red stain expanded across the back of his shirt, but Charlotte was physically uninjured.

Amanda raised her hands and walked through the knee-high grass to the nurse. "Come on, Charlotte; there's nothing that can be done now," Amanda said, grabbing the woman's arm and dragging her to her feet. She was crying loudly, and Amanda nearly slapped the woman. "Control yourself, otherwise we could be next." She looked over her shoulder and saw that Larry had slipped into the grass, one hand still caught in the fence. The soldiers split their time between Larry and the retreating pair of women.

"He found me and asked me to look at something," Charlotte cried as Amanda led her to a chair. "His back was covered by those damn blisters and he was bleeding. He asked for a shot of morphine and I gave him eight milligrams. I thought it would make him sleep, but he started running at the fence." Her face was red, wet, and turned up towards Amanda, pleading like a child.

"There's nothing more we can do for him. You have to be strong for Cami."

"Cami's sick. She's going to die just like the rest of us." She started to cry and scream at the same time, and Amanda was almost convinced that the time was right to slap the woman. Instead she grabbed her by the arms and started to gently shake her, but the disagreeable sense was so strong that she was forced to pull her hands back and let the woman cry. It took a minute before Charlotte could speak again. "I was up with Cami. After I gave her the morphine last night she never really woke up. So, early this morning I tried to wake her up." The crying started anew and her thoughts came out in fragments. "But. She had them … everywhere. Even her eyes. Oh God, even her eyes." Amanda stood and felt more than a little empathy. "And now Larry." Her head dropped into her lap, and her tears started to turn to blood. She screamed again, and jumped to her feet, her face covered in blood. "What's happening?"

Amanda's first thought was that Charlotte had indeed been shot. In just a few seconds she had soaked the front of her blouse. Amanda did the only thing she could think of and grabbed a folded towel and smashed it into Charlotte's face. She squeezed the woman's nose and eyes and led her to the only clean cot. "Charlotte! Charlotte! I need you to hold this," Amanda said, bringing the woman's right hand to the towel. "Now squeeze as tight as you can. It's just a nose bleed," she lied. Charlotte lifted her head, exposing her neck and a fresh set of blood-filled blisters. In the few minutes that it took to get her down and the bleeding under control, Amanda watched them spread like a living organism down her neck into her chest. "Oh my God, it hurts," Charlotte moaned through her blood-clotted nose and mouth.

"Let me get you something. Just lie right here; we don't want the bleeding to start all over again." It took her only a few minutes to find and administer the morphine. Charlotte was finally calm enough for Amanda to take away the blood-soaked towel, and even after all she had been through, Amanda was not prepared to see what lay beneath. Large strips of skin had come away with the towel; all of the skin on Charlotte's nose and lower forehead had sloughed down to a bloody pulp. Her ragged eyelids refused to close completely, and the conjunctiva of each eye protruded with tense red blisters. Amanda looked away in horror and quickly stood. The only saving grace was that by this point Charlotte was only barely conscious from the morphine.

She glanced over at Bernice, who had rolled towards all the commotion, and then to the cot two over from Bernice and saw the face of Cami. Like Charlotte, her face was in tatters, her unseeing eyes staring at the roof of the tent. Amanda waited a moment and then reluctantly walked the ten feet and covered her body. She couldn't bring herself to close the eyes on the mutilated face.

"Where are you, dear?" Bernice's voice was soft and raspy.

"I'm right here," Amanda answered, stepping quickly away from Cami's body.

"My mind's pretty clear now, Amanda. I heard what happened to Larry and I can guess what's happening to Charlotte. Are you all right?"

"Physically." She knew what was coming.

"I'm well down that road now," Bernice said simply. "I know this is hard for you, and I'd do it myself if I could."

"What is happening here?" Amanda was angry—angrier than she had ever been. Angry with Larry for leaving them, angry at Stephen for getting shot, angry at Charlotte for being a screaming bitch, and angry at Bernice for what she was asking her to do.

"I'll ask the Lord for ya', and then I'll get a message back to you." Bernice smiled and her lip cracked and started to bleed. "Oh my, I'm gonna ruin my dress," she said, wiping the blood with a blistered hand.

"I can't do this; I'll be alone," Amanda cried pitifully.

"You're gonna be alone no matter what you do. What was your husband's name?"

Amanda didn't follow the sudden change in topic. "Michael."

"Michael. 'Who is like God.' Could there be a better name? I'll bet he was tall and handsome. He have long blond hair like you?"

"Bernice, my hair is short …" Amanda said through tears. "No, Michael was a Marine and got used to short hair." She dropped her head and everything started to slow to an almost peaceful pace.

"That ain't right. I'll change that for you. Now tell me, what was your son's name?" Reluctantly, Amanda reached for the IV and opened it wide.

"Josh," she said. "He was two and liked to do somersaults."

"Josh. Short for Joshua?"

Amanda nodded, then said, "Yes."

"Good strong name. 'Jehovah is Salvation.' Should be Jesus is salvation, but I'll bet your Michael has that allll straight now." Her voice was slowing. "You remember what I told you when we was come down here? You need to find out what's important to you and cling to it. Me and Jesus are going to take care of your Michael and Joshua until you get up to see us, but you still got some work down here. You understand me?"

"Yes." Amanda's heart was breaking.

"Now give me a kiss." Amanda bent down and gave Bernice a kiss on her cold forehead. "That was nice. Now give me one more, right here." She tapped her right cheek, and Amanda gave her a second kiss. "That was even better. Now, one more, right here." She tapped her left cheek. And again she gave Bernice a kiss. "Wonderful. The first was for me. The second one I'll give over to Michael and the last goes to Josh. I might even give him a hug or two." She smiled weakly and her grip became weak. "I'll just hug Josh." Her hand dropped from Amanda's. "There you two are," she barely whispered. "You're every bit as pretty as your momma. Come and give me a hug; I got something for you." Her voice faded away and she became still.

***

It was hours before Amanda could return to the tent. For a time she debated following Larry's lead by rushing the fence and ending it all in a sudden hail of bullets, but giving up, letting those bastards win, was adding insult to injury, and she wasn't going to give them the satisfaction. They wanted her to rush the fence so they could shoot another American.

"Fuck you," she screamed at a group of soldiers, who watched with undisguised leers as she stomped through the grass. Shooting her wasn't the only thing they wanted. "Disgusting, fucking pigs," she screamed at them on her next lap. They were responsible for all the death and misery that surrounded her.

No, she corrected herself. They're mindless animals. It's their masters, the ones who drove them. They're the ones responsible. That spic Dr. Martinez and his pal General Regara. Amanda's mind reeled with possibilities. They were the ones who created this infection. Maybe they even faked the hurricane to lure us down here. It was suddenly all so clear. That's why the bastards made them take helicopters in, so the team would be deprived of long range communications. That's why they hadn't heard from home.

That's why the hospital ship had been turned away. It was all an elaborate ruse to conduct a human biologic experiment.

"Bastards," she screamed at the soldiers as she rounded the corner of the tent. They were being secretive now, not looking at her directly, fading away into the jungle where they could use their binoculars and cameras. Maybe she was their reward, the bone Martinez and Regara would throw to their dogs for watching the Americans die. And when they were done with her they would shoot her. Or, maybe they would shoot her first and then molest her corpse. "Fucking degenerate bastards," she said to herself and then slumped in the grass, physical and mental fatigue overwhelming her.

After a moment her mind began to clear. As much as she hated Dr. Martinez and his officious disinterest in their plight, he wasn't responsible for it, and the soldiers who surrounded her weren't waiting for a chance to rape her. They wanted to go home as much as she did.

She closed her eyes and willed herself to be anywhere but here, but when she opened them she was still sitting in the tall grass with bugs crawling all over her. She studied them and tried to figure out why she had always harbored a fear of bugs. They were fascinatingly complex and diverse.

"When I get home, maybe I'll become an entomologist," she said to a large caterpillar-like bug that walked up her arm. She played with it for a while, and then finally turned her mind back to the task at hand. "Sorry little guy, there's something I have to do," and she placed the insect back in the dirt. She stood and looked at the covered body of Bernice Scott, and then with a start remembered Charlotte. Amanda had completely forgotten the petulant, rude woman and was a little ambivalent about the possibility that she had died alone.

She slowly walked back to the tent, avoiding the wrapped body of Bernice. Charlotte was still asleep, but her breathing was ragged. She looked for another syringe of morphine, but had to walk by Bernice to retrieve it. After a long while Charlotte began to stir and Amanda reluctantly fetched a handful of loaded syringes. When she returned, Charlotte's eyes were open. Surprisingly, she didn't look much worse, although it would have been hard to do.

"I saw you out there."

"I needed to be alone for awhile," Amanda answered with a touch of frustration and anger.

"Is she gone?" Charlotte asked, and Amanda didn't know if she meant Cami or Bernice.

"Yes." Amanda didn't want to answer any questions. She was an emotional wreck. It seemed that everyone around her, including her present circumstance, died. Her father when she was a child, her mother when she was a young teenager, and her only brother just a few years later. Michael and later Josh had helped her bury them in her mind; it took another year to get Michael and Josh buried, and now it was happening all over again, except now they were all out of their graves and running around in her mind.

"Was it peaceful?"

"Yes." She was about to ask Charlotte if she wanted another shot, but then decided to just give her one.

"Wait." She could see well enough to divine Amanda's intent. "You were sick before," Charlotte accused, her implication obvious.

"I got better," she answered, without giving the question much thought. She reached for the port on the IV and out of habit swiped it with an alcohol pad.

"Hold on; I want to know something." Amanda paused, needle in hand, and stared down into Charlotte's ruined face, its expression lost in the blood and tattered flesh. "What makes you so goddamn special? Why do you get to live while everyone else dies?" It was meant to be mean and hateful, and she would never know how accurate her aim had been.

Amanda got up, syringes in hand, and walked away.

CHAPTER 13

"As far as we can tell they arrived on the ninth, with a full platoon of Honduran SOG." Captain Shore stood at attention, waiting for his commanding officer to give him permission to stand at ease.

"That was nine days ago and we're just hearing about this now?" Rear Admiral Howard Hemming was commander of the US Navy's 4th Fleet and had been ordered to redeploy six capital ships immediately. The Chief of Naval Operations himself had informed Hemming that he was to personally attend to it. "Relax, Captain, and sit down. We have some work to do."

Captain Shore sat only because he had been instructed to; he maintained an at-attention posture, waiting for his commander to stop pacing behind his desk. "They contacted the State Department five days ago and told them that everything was being handled."

"And no one followed up!" The admiral slammed his open hand against the wall and the room shook. Hemming was a large man, and the urban legend that circulated their Jacksonville home port was that when the admiral was a mere lieutenant, and flying jets off of the very carriers he now commanded, on two separate occasions the steam catapult that launched planes off the deck failed immediately after Hemming's plane took off. "What a bunch of know-nothing jack-asses."

Shore had been braced for a more colorful tirade. "The information that we have is that there is now only one survivor." Normally he would have used the word "intelligence," but decided on "information" to avoid the inevitable reaction. Despite outward appearances, Captain Shore knew the admiral to be a cerebral man, highly intelligent, well-educated and read, with more than thirty years of experience to bolster his academic credits. He balanced that with a deep passion, and occasionally a blind spot, for anything American or Navy.

"So thirteen of our people died and those sons of bitches just stood around and watched. How much firepower do you think it would take to finish what that hurricane started?" He stared seriously at the captain and then smiled. "All right, that's enough of my bitching; let's try to solve this problem. What do we know about this General Regara?"

"Old Honduran family with lots of connections."

"To the old government or the new one? Wait, let me guess, both?"

Shore nodded. "Relatively honest. He does have his hand in at least one Columbian cartel's pocket."

"Hell, no one's innocent down there. Why did they wait so long?"

"I get the feeling from State that the local officials really thought they had a handle on things. The bureaucrats dragged their feet some, probably because they're still angry over our lack of support for their coup. I get the sense that they would have acted faster had they known what they were up against."

"So what are they up against? It looks to me that they lost a whole city." The admiral's desk was covered in satellite photographs. "And then they started burning bodies?" He shook his head in disgust.

"All we get from them is that they have quarantined the area and stopped the spread of some illness. They suggest that it's some version of Ebola."

"I read that. Is it credible? Because it sounds to me like they just hung the nastiest label they could think of on this giant mess to justify some very questionable behavior."

"We have to assume that it is correct."

"Okay. Redirect the battle group. Tell them I want them on station before noon tomorrow. They'll have to move, but shouldn't have to blow out any boilers getting there."

"They will permit only one helicopter to land." Shore braced for the admiral's reaction.

"How do they expect us to make that work?" he asked without embellishments.

"We can only take the survivor. The bodies have to stay."

A thirty-second string of very creative profanity followed. The admiral hit his intercom button. "There's a Honduran general named Regara. Find him. I want him on the phone, now." He smashed the button and sat loudly into his chair.

"Would you like me to stay, sir?"

"Yes. Your presence tempers my behavior."

The intercom buzzed a few minutes later. "On line three, sir."

"Damn, that was fast," Hemming said, picking up the phone. "General, good of you to take my call. Bruce Calloway sends his regards." In friendlier times, Bruce Calloway and the US Special Forces had trained the Honduran Special Operations Group, one of the units Regara commanded. The conversational gambit was false; Hemming had never met Calloway; he was simply trying to set a tone. "I've got you on speakerphone with my XO Captain Shore."

"Good morning, Admiral. I'm afraid I will have to dispense with the pleasantries, as you can imagine I have my hands quite full."

"All right." Hemming took a breath and cracked his knuckles.

Shore smiled. Low-grade animosity suited Hemming much better than artificial civility.

"We have been informed that only one sea-based helicopter will be permitted to land and that the bodies of the thirteen deceased will not be repatriated. Is this true?"

"Yes. It is not optimal, nor is it my idea. I have simply been ordered to see it done, as I assume you have as well."

"We have the capacity to take them all home, General. It would relieve your country of the burden."

"I agree with you, Admiral, but others do not. Our two governments have agreed to this and it falls to us to work out the logistics."

The situation became clear to Shore: Regara objected, but didn't have the authority to change things.

"We will be available tomorrow at thirteen hundred local time. I will send three helicopters in hopes that between now and then our representatives will come to their senses."

"I agree, but as it stands, I am permitted to only allow one into Honduran airspace. If there is nothing else, I must say good-bye."

"Good-bye, General." Hemming replaced the phone and turned to his adjunct. "A man of few words. Get a Chinook out to Teddy and tell them to send along a couple of Seahawks as well. Go get our people back."

"Once we get her, what do we do with her?"

"The survivor is a woman? I don't know why I assumed it was a man. I guess my wife is right; I am a misogynist." He reached for a single sheet of paper. "A representative of the Combined Services Medical Group will then assume control. The representative, a Colonel William Bennett, will deploy with the rescue team." He finished reading. "That comes from The Chief himself. Ever hear of the Combined Services Medical Group?" Shore shook his head. "Neither have I."

CHAPTER 14

There were very few places she could go. Four days ago she had gently moved Bernice's body into the old radio tent. She had left Charlotte and Cami where they were, partly out of sheer vindictiveness but more because of practical reasons. The generator had failed and the tarp-covered bodies exposed to the tropical sun did what was expected of them, and there really wasn't room in the radio tent for two more. The old medical tent, being surrounded by four decaying bodies, was off limits, as were the Honduran tents. This meant that the two women were still in their deathbeds, which left Amanda with only the eastern portion of the large tent—where the water and food had been stored—and all the grass between the tents and the fences to await death or rescue.

She had walked through the grass enough to beat down a path, a feral energy driving her day after day. The Hondurans had fatigued from boredom and were stretched out in the eaves of the jungles. If there had been any gaps in the fence, she was sure that she could slip into the jungle unseen. Of course, that begged the question: what would she do next? The answer was fairly obvious—die from a bullet or exposure.

On one of her uncounted laps around the big-tent, as Amanda had come to know it, she noticed that the twelve sheets of paper that chronicled the events of the last week were getting wet from the light drizzle that had just started. She had taken a full day after Bernice's death to mourn the loss and adjust to her new situation, but before the second day had fully dawned she finished her account. She had accepted the fact that in all probability she would join Bernice sooner than either wanted, and in her mind the only thing that could make this obscene situation worse was the inevitable lies and half-truths that others would use to cover it up. She knew that in all probability her effort at setting the record straight was little more than a futile gesture, but it was all that was left to her. She gathered the papers and once again looked for a safe place to store them. It was more than reasonable to assume that once Amanda was gone, either alive or dead, the entire camp and everything in it would be burned, just as the Hondurans had burned the bodies in Tela. All the medical supplies and personal effects would be consumed in a purifying blaze, including her precious twelve sheets of legal paper. After once again scouring the entire tent for a safe, fireproof, and discoverable hiding spot, she dropped her work on to an empty exam table and slumped into the only decent chair open to her. If she was made to disappear, her work would not survive her for very long. Dr. Martinez, or someone just like him, would fashion the truth in any way that suited them, and the only thing she could do to prevent it was to survive. The drizzle had changed into a steady rain that drummed on the roof of the big-tent, and she spun her chair outward and watched as the soldiers started to run for cover. Their discomfort gave her an iota of delight.

The only problem with isolation is being alone with oneself. Introspection had become Amanda's only form of recreation, and she focused on the trace of joy that came with the Hondurans scrambling. Intellectually, she knew that these individuals were not responsible for her situation, and that they had been almost as miserable as she. Under normal circumstances, she imagined that she would probably feel sorry for them, but these were anything but normal circumstances, and she was not the same timid girl who had fretted over an open helicopter hatch less than two weeks earlier. This had been a transformative experience, and for the first time in her life the misfortunes of others prompted an emotion other than sympathy. She had already spent many of the lonely hours pondering her new emotional makeup, and had decided that on a whole she liked the new Amanda. She was more resolute, no longer afraid of making decisions. All her life she had been afraid. Afraid of guns, of violence, of taking a chance, of taking charge of her own destiny. The new Amanda would do everything it took to survive, even if it meant using guns or violence, and then follow the path that she wanted. She had grown up living her life only to meet the expectations of others. When she thought of herself, it was always through the eyes of others. When faced with a choice, she would filter the options through what she thought others would want. In fact, she found it difficult remembering a single time she ever been completely selfish. She had always been a "good girl." A door mat.

Of course, not every attribute of the new Amanda was as positive. She had developed a vindictiveness that was both disturbing and more than a little comfortable. Leaving Charlotte to die alone and in pain was at best morally questionable, but even days later it warmed her heart. So did the possibility of violence. In her many empty hours Amanda thought about taking out a guard or two—not in hopes of escape, more just to see what it was like. She had shot the four soldiers earlier, but that had happened so fast, and had been purely reflexive. Her sole motivation was self-defense. She idly wondered what it would be like to shoot someone just because she could. Would she feel remorse? Elation? Or would her emotions remain as silent as they had when she was forced to defend herself?

***

It took less than fifteen minutes for the shower to pass and for the bright tropical sun to return. After another fifteen minutes—as the boredom was beginning to overwhelm her—she resumed her walking.

"How you doing there, Charlotte?" she asked, passing the corpse. Charlotte didn't answer, so she kept on walking. Two hours and a few dozen circuits later she noticed that her captors had started to pack up and that many had already disappeared back into the jungle. No weapons were visible, and most of their packs and chairs had disappeared; even the ever-present cigarette smell had faded. She moved along the path a little faster and then detoured to the east end of the big-tent. It was mostly hidden from the Hondurans' view and was where she had collected and stored all the weapons she could find. She knew that in time a decision would have to be made; they wouldn't watch her indefinitely, and by far the easiest solution to the "Amanda problem" was a conveniently placed bullet. Already there were thirty bodies scattered about the camp, and most of them had their own bullets. Who would even conceive that she had died under anything other than "natural" circumstances? She crawled into a small recess that she had constructed under a number of large crates and pulled her weapons and spare ammunition close. She had no misconception that she could successfully take them all on, but she would be damned if she was going to make it easy for them.

She waited, but nothing happened. Part of the problem with being hidden so well was the fact that she had a very limited view. From her rabbit-hole she had only about a forty-five degree viewing angle that extended to the edge of the radio tent and the fence beyond. The jungle buzzed and the early afternoon air heated up under the tropical sun, and still nothing. She wished she still had her watch, but it had broken when a crate fell onto her arm as she was creating this very hiding place. She slowly started counting to a hundred, deciding that if nothing happened before then she would take a peek.

After the first hundred she started over. By forty-three she stopped. She heard the sounds of tires crunching over branches and gravel. She twisted to try and see what was happening, but beyond twenty yards her view was blocked. She whispered a curse. If she wanted to know what they were up to she would have to move, which was probably exactly what they wanted. A door slammed and she heard distant voices and then a loud, piercing amplified squeal.

"Hello in the camp," said a voice that Amanda recognized immediately. "This is General Hector Regara." He rolled his R's almost as well as the waiter in Chicago. "Will you please show yourselves so that we can talk?" Amanda didn't respond, and a minute passed. "We mean you no harm. I am here to inform you that a United States helicopter is on its way to take you home. For that to occur safely we must remove portions of the fence. It is imperative that you remain in our sight and within the confines of your camp until your countrymen arrive. Will you please show yourself?"

It's a very clever trick, Amanda thought. Off in the distance she could hear the signature thumping, but the sounds of helicopters overhead had become commonplace the last few days. "Although," she said out loud, "they could just toss in a few grenades and be done with it. Why go to all this trouble?" She countered. *And why would he be here?*

"Mrs. Flynn," Regara's voice boomed, and Amanda was startled at the sound of her name. "We need you to respond, now." His last word echoed across the large field. "The helicopter you hear is from an American aircraft carrier waiting to bring you home, and it has limited fuel capacity. I can not permit it to land until I know that you will cooperate."

Amanda crawled out, but as a consolation to her more-cautious side she brought along a weapon. She walked out of the big-tent and down its side, still not completely convinced they had her best interest in mind.

Just beyond the fence on the eastern side of the large field stood Regara, resplendent in his dark uniform and medals and ribbons. Several very stern soldiers in jungle fatigues flanked him, and each held a weapon identical to her own.

"I assure you that your rifle is not needed." He smiled. She wasn't buying his relaxed, everything-is-all-right tone. His soldiers, who looked like they were ready to pounce, told a more accurate story. "All right, if it makes you feel more comfortable. All I ask is that you stay right where you are. Can you do this?"

She looked around and found a second group of soldiers almost directly behind her, but they were armed only with bolt cutters. "You've already killed two of us, and one was your own soldier," she accused Regara.

He took several steps forward and now was only inches from the fence. His security detail was about to follow but a quick hand motion froze them in place. Amanda could see that she had touched a nerve; Regara's face had lost all its graciousness. "His name was Fernando Oklana. He was born three miles from here, and I had to tell his mother in an evacuation center that her only son is dead." He pointed at the dark form that had once been Sergeant Oklana; his words fired at Amanda as if she had been responsible for his death.

His anger only fueled hers. "There are twenty-nine other bodies in here, and you and your Dr. Martinez watched them die one by one!" She screamed and pointed her weapon at one of the cameras mounted high on a metal pole.

"My responsibility is to protect my country; I do not care if you ever understand that. I only care to know if you will comply with the instructions, or do we shoot you now and be done with it?"

It was an intriguing offer. She was certain that she could raise her weapon and fire at least several good shots before they took her down, and at a minimum make Regara and Honduras pay a small amount of what was owed to Amanda and the rest of her team.

"I take your silence as a willingness to be reasonable," Regara said before Amanda had completely made up her mind. She lowered her rifle, which had somehow found its way into a firing position, and then after several long moments, with nothing better to do, she sat in the tall grass. Regara turned and nodded to a figure in the shadows and a moment later she could hear the sharp snap of metal breaking, followed by a tinny sound as the fence recoiled. It took at least ten minutes to clear the west end of the large field, and then the drumming of rotors filled the air. Amanda stood and watched the largest helicopter she had ever seen clear the trees just outside of Tela. It came in deceptively fast and, after flying over the camp once, banked around, flared its nose slightly, and settled gently into the grass. Amanda could have cried when she saw the roundel of stars and stripes. A dozen armed men in white suits poured out of the front hatch of the behemoth and she started to run towards them.

"Mrs. Flynn," a blessedly unaccented American voice said over the helicopter's speakers. "Stay where you are. We will come to you. Repeat. Stay where you are!" Amanda dropped the now heavy rifle and stopped just before the end of the big-tent. Men approached her and guided her back into the tent, where they quickly stripped every bit of clothing from her, doused her in a slick yellow liquid that dried almost on contact, redressed her in surgical scrubs, and then repackaged her in the same white suit they wore. They moved so quickly and efficiently that she had no time to object. What little modesty she had left was swept away by the relief that she was finally going home. Once done, they firmly guided her to the large twin-rotor aircraft. As they hurried her along she looked back and saw Regara arguing with an American in a white suit, and then they ducked her head and she was strapped to a stretcher.

"Sorry about the rush ma'am, and about this …" The airman plucked at his own isolation suit. "We'll get you out of it as soon as possible." He smiled through the visor and for a moment she wondered how bad she looked. The airman was at least ten years older than her, yet he called her ma'am. "I need to get some information from you …"

Amanda gave him a brief timeline of events, but he kept coming back to the lesions. How big were they? How fast did they appear? Where were the majority? Finally, she interrupted him.

"The infection was bad, but it's effect on people's thinking and behavior, that's what we need to focus on. The virus itself was responsible for only seven of our casualties." He nodded patiently, waiting for her to finish so he could get back to what was truly important.

Once he had finished his checklist of questions, Amanda felt a little frustrated that she hadn't quite got her point across but reasoned that there would be other and more comprehensive opportunities. The airman rose quickly and disappeared. She expected the frenetic activity to continue and an immediate departure, but once she had been strapped in and interviewed things slowed to a crawl.

After more than fifteen minutes the airman reappeared and Amanda reached for his arm. "Why aren't we going?"

"Sorry, ma'am, but there are some things that need to get straightened out before we leave," he said over the idling rotors, and there was that word again.

"Where are we going?" she asked before he retreated from view.

"That's one of the things that need to be figured out," he said cryptically.

"Are you going to be closing that door?" She pointed to the large hatch.

He looked confused. "Not until we leave, ma'am."

She stared at the ceiling, strapped into a stretcher she didn't need, and waited for another hour, hoping that nothing had happened that would leave her stranded again. Even the crew was getting antsy; they kept looking out the hatch, then walking down the small ramp, and then later she watched as two of them lazily walked around the large helicopter. The "Ma'am-man" periodically checked on her, and once turned on a fan over her bunk. It was a silly but thoughtful gesture; her suit denied her any real benefit. Finally, the rear hatch opened and a half-dozen white-suited men started loading and securing box after box into metal compartments. Each box was wrapped in biohazard stickers.

The rear hatch closed and suddenly the capacious interior was crowded with soldiers, their weapons, and isolation suits. A rush of emotion hit Amanda and she began to cry. "This isn't me anymore," she whispered and reflexively tried to wipe her wet eyes, but her gloved hand only banged off her visor. The helicopter began to shake and then lift. She had left Honduras, and along with it Bernice and twenty-nine others. She had no guilt, survivor's or any other kind, just sadness—a deep enduring sadness. She closed her eyes and for the first time in days wondered what she would do once she got home.

CHAPTER 15

But she didn't go home. Almost a day later, more white-suited people led her down a grey corridor, through multiple sets of double doors—each of which forced them to wait for the locks to electronically disengage—and finally into what looked like a very unfriendly and utilitarian hospital room equipped with three ceiling-mounted cameras.

"Once you hear the door close, you may remove the isolation suit, Mrs. Flynn." The man's voice was all business, and he turned to leave.

"Hey, wait a minute. I was told that once we arrived to wherever this place is someone would explain what was going on!" Her patience was long gone. They flew her to an aircraft carrier, and before she could enjoy the experience she had been bundled onto a small plane and flown from Air Force base to Air Force base until she landed here an hour ago. She assumed this was the ultimate destination, as she had been constantly warned not to try and take the now very sweaty and smelly isolation suit off. In addition, this was the first bed she had been offered.

"The doctor is already here and will explain the procedures." He had barely turned and acknowledged her, and his tone was one of bored disinterest. The proverbial clock watcher.

"Asshole," she said, waiting for the door to close and lock. She had a ceiling and three blank walls to stare at; the fourth wall was almost entirely taken up by a mirror. She had watched enough TV to know that her mirror was certainly one-way glass. She looked for a light switch but found none. There was no thermostat either. The only other feature beyond the Government Issue bed and the stainless steel sink and commode thoughtfully hidden behind a virtually see-through drape, was a recessed air duct that stretched along the bottom of all four walls. A white air dam on the ceiling completed the picture. She was in a reverse airflow room; not even air could escape.

She pulled the drape and worked her way out of the suit, her scrubs soaked through with sweat. She tried to clean herself as well as possible and then pulled back the curtain and fell into bed.

"Can you at least turn off the lights?" she yelled, and an instant later the overheads dimmed.

She slept the sleep of the exhausted. She tossed and turned and woke several times wondering where she was. There was no clock on the wall, and her broken watch was last seen in the dirt of Honduras. Her mind cycled between Bernice and Lisa. They would have been instant friends and she would have loved to have seen that. She rolled over and brushed a tear from her eye. Grief hung in her chest like a ten-pound weight, but it stayed there; it didn't pull her down into the abyss as it had so often in the past. It seemed as if she had spent most of her life in that abyss of grief, pain, and helplessness. It wasn't yet time to think about silver linings or anything good coming from the horrific last two weeks, so she rolled over. As her mind floated freely she recalled her last interaction with Charlotte, and she finally felt a trace of guilt. *Or is it that I just think I should feel bad?* That actually felt closer to the truth. A part of her was manufacturing emotions that seemed to be lacking.

"Good, I could use a lot less guilt," she whispered as she resumed the habit of talking to herself. It dawned on her that she hadn't had a real conversation, besides the ones she had with herself, in several days. Her body didn't care; it was trying to decide whether to stay awake or to retreat back into the oblivion of dreams. This was the first bed she had been in for nearly two weeks, and it was so comfortable. Her body relaxed into the cotton sheets, having decided that it was time for her mind to turn out the lights, and she closed her eyes and gently drifted away.

***

"Mrs. Flynn," a voice said in her dream. The voice repeated itself, only louder.

"Mrs. Flynn is my mother-in-law's name," she said, trying to get the voice to go away.

"Amanda," the voice said sharply, and her eyes snapped open.

The lights were still muted and she was still in her hospital cell, as she had begun to think of it.

"I'm Dr. Keyes; I'm one of the assistant directors of this facility." He sat in a plastic chair that had magically appeared with him. "Excuse the suits; I'm sure you realize that for a time they are necessary."

"Well, good morning, Dr. Keyes, if it is morning. Would you mind telling me what facility we are in?" Her frustration with everyone's compartmentalization of information came roaring back.

"We are in the Tellis Medical facility, which is in Oklahoma."

"Tellis, and not Tela. Hmm, too close for my comfort." She noticed a new set of scrubs at the foot of her bed and a small overnight kit sitting on the shelf above the sink. "I don't mean to be rude, but could you excuse me while I … take care of some things?"

"Of course. There is a call light on the arm rail." He pointed at the bed rail. "Please press that when you are ready."

He left, and Amanda tried to clean herself up. Ten minutes later, the call of nature answered and feeling a little more presentable, she faced Dr. Keyes.

"Let's start at the beginning …" For the next two hours he took a detailed medical and family history and then went step by step through the activity of the last two weeks. He was more than thorough, he was exhausting, and remarkably good at prompting things that Amanda had forgotten or in a few instances suppressed. She tried to be honest, even with the more difficult events, but still kept a few things to herself. For his part, he remained purely clinical and nonjudgmental. Only once did he ask her about her emotional state, and simply nodded his head when Amanda recounted the details of Charlotte's death.

"Wow." He took no notes, and Amanda was certain the entire session was being recorded. "Quite an ordeal." He stared at her, almost as if he were expecting a response to his summation of one of the worst times of her life. "Are you up for a physical exam?" he asked suddenly, the time limit for her response having expired.

"Okay," she answered reluctantly. She knew it was coming, but that didn't make it any easier. Her reaction to physical contact or even proximity had persisted throughout her journey to Tellis, and it was unlikely to have left her overnight.

He examined her fully, but she had to stop him several times as her aversion to his presence nearly overwhelmed her. He checked every square inch of her without commenting except when he agreed to step back and give her a moment to refocus.

"As far as I can tell, you appear to be completely healthy," he said after a very difficult thirty minutes. "We will need some samples from you to confirm that."

"And then I can go?" It was a natural question, and she had expected a simple yes. It was only prudent to have her fully evaluated before releasing her back to the population, and she was willing to comply, but her willingness had a limit and she desperately wanted to be back home and see Lisa and Greg.

"I don't see why not, but cultures can take quite a long time."

"How long?" Her radar detected the first signs of evasiveness.

"Well, tuberculosis cultures often don't turn positive for six weeks."

"Six weeks!" she screamed. "You want me to stay here that long?"

"Calm down, Amanda. You are a nurse, and I would like you to think like one. What option do we have here? Something unknown just killed thirty of thirty-one people in your little camp in a matter of days. Imagine what would happen if this somehow found its way into the general population. You have to be patient until we know for certain that it's safe."

Of course, she knew he was right, and if the roles were reversed she would quite willingly counsel patience as well. Only, it was so hard to accept it when she was on the receiving end. "I want to contact my family," she demanded.

"Logistically that will be difficult. I believe that they have been informed of your transfer here."

"My aunt lives in Oklahoma City; surely accommodations can be made."

"Not until we start getting some results back. It would be irresponsible before then." He stood and prepared to leave. "We will try and make this as comfortable for you as possible, but I will tell you right now that our main concern is the health and welfare of the citizens of this country. Your needs are a secondary concern."

***

"You lied to her," Nathan Martin said to Byron Keyes as he emerged from the airlock.

"You have some nerve, Martin. I was ordered to, and I have a strong suspicion you were behind it." Keyes was an internist and a lieutenant in the newly formed Combined Services Medical Group. "I have a pretty good idea why you wormed your way into this case, and I will remind you of two facts. First, she is not your guinea pig, and second, a lot of people know that she is here, especially me."

"That is the most insubordinate thing …"

"You're not in the military or the chain of command, so go to hell with your insubordinate crap. As of six minutes ago she became your patient, Doctor. Remember that a long time ago you swore an oath to do no harm, and I will be around to ensure it."

A smug grin crossed Martin's face. "No, you won't. You've been reassigned. Nome, Alaska, I hope. I would suggest that you go find Colonel Bennett."

"What was all that about?" Stanley Cripps asked Martin after Keyes had stomped up the stairs.

"We have a history, a long history," Martin answered. "I'm not sure he's comfortable with his lot in life."

"It sounded like there was a lot more than jealousy, Nathan. I know Keyes, and he can be insufferable at times but his judgment has always been excellent."

"What are you saying, Stanley?" Martin had turned to the Professor Emeritus of the University of Chicago, who had literally written the book on special pathogens even before they were called special pathogens.

"I'm saying that I see the potential for great good and great evil in that young woman. Something inside that pretty lady beat off this very nasty bug, and if we can determine her resistance we will go a long way in furthering our fight against these outbreaks."

"I agree; that is exactly why I came here," Martin said, his motivations out there for the whole world to see.

"What I am worried about is in that focused search for the revelation, Amanda Flynn will be forgotten. I understand the pressures that you are under; you have some pretty big shoes to fill, if I do say so myself." Martin had recently been appointed to become the second director of the the Centers for Disease Control and Preventions Special Pathogens Department after Stanley Cripps retired to Chicago. "It is only human nature to try and make a big splash the first time you jump into the pool. I believe that this is the root of Dr. Keyes' concern."

"That is beyond insulting, Stanley," Martin said. He knew that Dr. Cripps had never been his advocate, and rumors abounded that he was not even on Stanley's personal list of replacements.

"Ambition has a price, Nathan, and sometimes that price is transparency."

"So you have concerns that I can't do this job; is that what you're implying?"

"Absolutely not. You are an excellent virologist, first rate. I wish I had half your brain. The problem is that I wouldn't want the other half." Stanley found his coat, slipped into it, and then turned to the smaller man. "You are politically astute, Nathan, and those who appointed you are also politically astute. Perhaps to run a department nowadays that's more important than … other attributes." The unspoken word "ethics" hung in the air. "Good night, Nathan. I will be here through the week to review the tissue samples from the other victims and to periodically check on her."

Martin watched the old man climb the stairs to the ground floor. In the span of five minutes two colleagues—one he could ignore, but one who held great influence—had questioned his morality. He couldn't understand how both men could be so blind. There was only one morality here. Within Amanda Flynn's blood, white cells, or DNA was an answer that could immediately save thousands, and if down the road things went really wrong, perhaps the entire human species. How could her life be balanced against that? Where was the morality in not searching for that answer with all their resources?

Martin was alone in the observation booth; all the recording and monitoring was done in a room above, and he secretly watched his patient pace the length of the small room. She was a beautiful woman, there was no denying that, and she moved with a natural grace. *Maybe not so much grace, but arrogance?* he wondered as he studied her in the dark. Had society elevated her to a life of privilege simply because she had won the genetic lottery, allowing her to live by a different set of rules? She finally tired of her pacing and sat at the edge of the bed, her legs crossed demurely. *What makes you so special, Amanda; why did you survive above all the others?* It was as much a metaphysical question as a medical one. The noisy approach of a pair of medical technicians snapped Martin back to the real world.

"Evening, Doctor," the first man down said. "We were going to draw her blood now. Did you have plans to see her?"

"No. I don't need to see her. Dr. Keyes did an adequate job examining her earlier. Are you just collecting blood samples now?"

"We'll get the rest in the morning. They can only process blood work at this hour."

He almost ordered them to collect everything now, and if the samples weren't useable they could be collected again, but simply nodded his head. No sense pissing everyone off on the first day.

CHAPTER 16

At least they had given her a television. The first couple days all she could pick up were the local channels out of Enid, but ten days ago someone ran a wire to a cluster of plugs and outlets on the wall and she suddenly had basic cable. She searched the 24-hour news channels for any information, but it appeared as if either no one knew or cared about the lost Red Cross team. It was strange, because the news cycle was fairly sparse and the loss of so many Americans in a foreign country should have invited hours of the typical empty speculations and over-analysis of official statements, at least until the next big thing happened.

They had asked her the same questions either directly or with subtle twists, over and over again. Her family history as far back as she could remember was scrutinized in frustrating detail. Her medical history, although scant, was dissected to the point of absurdity. Every cold, flu, and sniffle she could remember drew tremendous interest. They asked her to review a six-page list of medications and check the ones that she had ever taken, circle the ones she had taken within the last six months, and underline those that she had taken the past thirty days. The following day they gave her back the same six-page list and asked her to review it for any allergies. They spent several days interviewing her about what exactly happened in Honduras. Each aspect was examined from every conceivable angle, from the moment that she landed in El Progresso until she landed on the USS Theodore Roosevelt. She was given a pen and drawing paper and asked to sketch the lesions and their locations on as many of the victims as she could remember. After several days of the intensive, almost non-stop debriefing, everything began to run together and she started to contradict herself, which led to only more and deeper questioning. She began to sense their frustration and perceived a subtle shift in their attitude. She was no longer the victim, no longer the sole survivor of a horrific experience.

On her fourteenth day they suddenly shifted their focus, and a nurse spent three hours with her recounting the events of the previous three months in detail. She had come armed with a computer tablet that contained most of the answers, and every time Amanda deviated from their timeline she was asked to explain. When the woman corrected her for at least the tenth time, Amanda simply took the tablet from the woman's hand and scanned through it.

"You have reconstructed my entire life." She turned the screen of the notebook to the stunned woman. "You know more about me than I can remember; why are you asking me this? I'm not hiding anything." The poor woman stared back at Amanda with wide eyes, seemingly afraid to reach for the notebook or even move. "I'm not going to hurt you, whatever your name is." When the woman had first arrived she hadn't even bothered to introduce herself; she simply sat in one of the two plastic chairs that had been added to the room's decor and informed Amanda that she had some questions. Amanda's anger, fueled by isolation and loneliness, flared for a moment with this latest demonstration of the institutional mind-set of depersonalization, but instead of acting on it she cooperated for as long as she could.

"Here, take it." Amanda extended the small notebook. The frightened woman didn't move. "Okay, I'll leave it here if you change your mind." She placed it on the chair next to her.

"Now it's my turn to ask some questions," Amanda said after her interviewer recovered and retrieved her notebook. "I have been here two weeks now and have yet to hear back from my family. I was told that they were informed of my whereabouts." She waited for a response.

"I don't know anything about that." Her voice had found some of its former authority.

"Well, I am telling you and whoever is watching this that I will not cooperate further until I hear from them." No one responded, although she was convinced that she had been heard. "Well, I guess we have nothing more to discuss," she said to her nameless guest. The woman quickly stood and walked as fast as her self-respect allowed and entered the airlock. Amanda watched through the glass as the woman stripped out of her suit, but only after storing the small computer tablet in a sealed container. They were taking her isolation seriously. She idly tried the door and once again found it locked. Obviously, someone had been watching to release the electronic lock and then re-engage it.

***

"Okay, now what do we do?" Paul Oxford asked his partner, Gage Moore. On loan from the Army Medical Corp, the pair were distinct from the Combined Services Medical Group that staffed the rest of the facility. They were both battle-tested medics with twenty years experience between them, and the best they could rate was monitor duty. It had taken them only hours to learn that they were in with some very fast company; even the laboratory technicians had more training and experience than either of them.

"You know what we have to do," Gage, the senior NCO, answered, reaching for the phone.

"Hold on just a second." Oxford grabbed the phone. "Why don't we keep this in-house? Colonel Bennett is here. I'd rather deal with him than that asshole Martin."

"That asshole just showed up," said a voice behind the two medics. They turned to find Martin, in his clean white lab coat, and their temporary commanding officer, Colonel William Bennett. "What's the problem?" Martin ignored the insult.

"She refuses to cooperate until she hears from her family," Gage answered, while Oxford literally and figuratively kept his head low.

Bennett turned to Martin. "This is your call; you set this in motion." It was a small violation in protocol for Bennett to be so forward in front of enlisted men, and if Martin had truly carried rank he would have excused the two medics.

"We continue as we have."

"Just so I am clear, we continue to lie to her." The last thing Bennett wanted was for this house of cards to fall on his head. The addition of Martin at the last minute had changed everything, and the executive order that put him in charge was enough for the colonel to consider retirement.

"Would you rather tell her the truth?"

Martin had meant the question to be rhetorical, but Bennett saw it as an opportunity. "Yes," he said clearly, in front of two witnesses who would be unimpeachable.

"We would be knee-deep in lawyers and would lose this opportunity forever. I am following the letter of the law, and it is my decision, my responsibility."

"None of her cultures have turned positive," Bennett said, satisfied that Martin was now clearly and solely on the hook.

"It's only been two weeks, and we have only blood and fluid cultures."

"So you still plan on moving on to an invasive investigation?"

"I don't see that we have a choice," Martin said as he bent to exam the image on the monitor.

"Once again, just to be clear, you wish to perform invasive procedures on this patient to determine whether she is safe to be released, or to identify the source of her resistance, which exceeds your mandate?"

Martin's face reddened. "I am very tired of the military second-guessing every decision I make. It is not up to you or your superior officers to interpret my mandate," Martin said sharply. He laid his briefcase on the table, opened it, and gave Bennett a series of photographs. "That, Colonel, is an unidentified virus that in four days killed over a thousand people. It could have been tens of thousands if the Hondurans hadn't evacuated. Exactly one individual survived that outbreak." He pointed at the monitor. "We don't know what this thing is …" he began to tick off each point with his fingers, "where it came from, or how it got there. And most importantly, how to treat it if this thing suddenly pops up in Detroit." He snatched back the grainy pictures of a six-sided wheel. "In case you haven't been paying attention, we are the only ones trying to answer those questions."

"Then level with her. Tell her what you just told me. Let her family know that she is alive instead of lost in Honduras."

"I never told them that she was lost in Honduras," Martin said with a false sense of innocence. "Besides, we can't take the risk of losing her."

"No US military personnel will assist you in violating this woman's civil rights." Normally Bennett was in command of the Tellis Medical Facility, and while he still retained command of the troops working there, he had been ordered to place all his resources at the disposal of Dr. Nathan Martin and the Centers for Disease Control. "Not even the President of the United States can order them to ignore their duty."

"It's an interesting legal point, but completely moot. I am not going to ask anyone to ignore their duty or violate this woman's civil rights." Martin pulled from his jacket pocket a single sheet of paper and handed it to Bennett. "Tomorrow a small group of technicians and physicians will arrive and perform these tests. They should be here less than a week, so we won't inconvenience you too badly." Martin turned back to the monitors as Bennett read the directive.

"What you are doing is immoral and unethical by all reasonable standards," Bennett said. Appealing to Martin's morality was an exercise in futility, but it was all Bennett had left. Martin had the legal authority to "examine and treat" Amanda Flynn; he was not bound by reasonable standards, moral or ethical. A decision had been made far above Bennett's head that this woman posed an exigent risk, and Martin had been given the responsibility to quantify it, presumably by whatever means he felt prudent.

"I think it's time I met Amanda," Martin said, leaving the room without further comment.

CHAPTER 17

The isolation suit prevented Amanda from fully assessing the man who had just entered her cell. He was shorter than most of the soldiers who had attended her; dressed in the first business suit she had seen in months, he appeared to be someone of importance. "So someone is finally taking me seriously, and all it took was for me to hold my breath and turn blue."

"That we could deal with, Amanda. I am Dr. Martin, one of the physicians looking after you."

"Good. So let's start with why you are keeping me in this cell?"

"I promise to get you into a less restrictive environment once we know it's okay. So far everything looks encouraging." He smiled and crossed his legs. "We have discussed your situation with some of the experts in the field of infectious disease and we are all in agreement that for now this is the best place for you."

"Have you discussed this with my family?"

"I believe that they have been kept abreast of your condition." He said confidently. "We need your full cooperation, Amanda. I don't need to tell you how bad this could have been had this contagion showed up in Miami, as opposed to Tela, Honduras. And I'm sure that you understand that we need to know everything that happened down there, as well as everything there is to know about you, so that we can determine how you survived."

"I understand that. I also understand that you haven't answered my question." Amanda stared into Martin's eyes and realized that she didn't like what was beneath them. He was more of a politician than a physician.

"Part of the difficulty we have with outside communication centers around our location." He paused. "This is a military base that, shall we say, has no real address. Bringing unauthorized individuals here would violate about a half-dozen laws that would probably land a lot of people in jail."

"All right, what about a phone call or the internet?"

"My hands are tied. Once here, no one has communication in or out of this base. It is the only way we can maintain the security that is required for these types of situations." He gave her a pained smile. "Believe me, I want to leave here every bit as much as you."

She waited a long minute staring at his shoes and then looked up at him. For a moment he held her stare, but then quickly stood to cover the effect she was having on him. "All right," she finally said, "for now." Martin's suit made an irritating crinkle sound as he took a half step towards the airlock. "No more for today. I will take your silly tests, and answer your inane questions again tomorrow, but not today."

"That sounds fair. With the way that we've been pounding away at you, I can see that you need a break." He smiled again and then tried to open the airlock, but for a second it remained closed. She heard a very soft click and he was gone a moment later.

He was lying about something. She didn't know how she knew, only that she was certain that he was hiding something. She hadn't sensed any real dishonesty from any of the other twenty or thirty people who had visited her cell in the last two weeks—only disinterest. She heard the other end of the airlock cycle and after a few seconds knew that he was watching her. She imagined him standing just in front of the one-way glass studying her, his white lab jacket draped over a sink in the corner, and another man, a tall man just in front of it staring at her as well, a disapproving look on his face. She walked to the mirror, picked a spot, and then tapped her finger where she imagined his nose to be. *I see you,* she thought.

***

"You lie well," Bennett greeted Martin at the airlock. "Just the right mixture of truth, deflection, and small lies, and poof! The truth disappears. For a moment I actually believed that you had an interest in her welfare."

"I'm not a monster, Bennett. I don't want to hurt that woman." He watched as she turned to face the mirror. She had an odd and intriguing expression, as if she knew a secret. She walked directly in front of him and then tapped the glass less than an inch from his nose. He took a step back and a smile slowly crossed her face. His mind was split between Amanda's strange behavior and the irritating Colonel Bennett.

"But you don't want to treat her like a real person either," Bennett countered.

"I don't want to have this discussion. I appreciate that you have limited your focus to this one individual, and as a physician that is your responsibility. My responsibility extends well beyond her welfare." Martin walked up the metal stairwell, trying to come up with another way of holding Amanda that didn't involve the military.

***

"Unless you can give me a reason that this patient needs to remain in a restricted reverse laminar flow room, I can't authorize the expense," General Dixon said over the phone. "I have reviewed her four- and six-week culture results and they remain negative. Aside from the humanitarian aspects of keeping an individual in the same room for 46 days, you have spent eleven million dollars, a third of it directly related to isolation."

Martin wanted to bang his head against the wall. It seemed that at every turn he had a military officer questioning his approach, and now they were pulling the plug on his financing, his one true Achilles' heel. His executive order gave him control of the patient, but the funding flowed through a military spigot. He could fight this, but in the end he knew that he would lose. "I understand your position, General. I think it is reasonable to move her to a ward. I do not think that it would be prudent to move her offsite, as we are still waiting for more results."

"Hmph," the general responded. Martin knew that the general had played his best card, but also that he was stuck with this situation until Martin gave permission to release her. "Of course, once she has been transferred to a less restrictive environment we will look to your people to take over."

It had been a month since Martin had last visited Tellis, and after his small group of technicians and physicians had finished their various biopsies of Amanda Flynn, Martin had become completely reliant upon military personnel to direct her care. "I don't understand, General?"

"Read the charter, Doctor. We are responsible for acute care alone, not custodial care. Tellis will remain at your disposal, but with only minimal personnel. The labs, housekeeping, kitchens, those sorts of things. The medical personnel will need to be supplied independently."

Martin pounded his desk, making his secretary jump at her desk. "Cut that out," she screamed at Martin.

The general had tricked him. Interest in this virus, now called EDH 1, had fallen exponentially with the passage of time and with no further outbreaks. Tela, Honduras, and Amanda Flynn were becoming old news in the circles that made decisions. For six weeks they had given him everything that he had asked for, and there was precious little to show for it. He could guarantee that no one would authorize another eleven million dollars chasing down an outbreak that was starting to look to the uninitiated as a one-trick-pony, and it was the uninitiated that were paying the bills.

Although, he thought, *my own people would make things considerably easier.* The funding of the CDC was always tight, but they did have discretionary and emergency funds. A couple-million-dollar expenditure on a potentially infectious patient could be justified with a little work. And as a bonus, Amanda was falling off of the radar; fewer people were inquiring about her. "Of course, General. I believe we can have everything in place in a couple of days."

"Another option is to simply release her."

Martin was always shocked by the short-sighted nature of the military mind. "Just a little longer, General." His voice was almost smiling.

"That's the response I was told to expect. Bye, Doctor." Abruptly, the line went dead.

CHAPTER 18

At first Amanda was shocked as the door opened and Colonel William Bennett walked in without the now-ubiquitous white isolation suit. He was a good-looking man in his early fifties, his attractiveness enhanced by the fact that Amanda hadn't seen a human face not wrapped in plastic in seven weeks.

"You are being moved to one of our wards, and as you are the only patient in the entire facility, my guess is that you will get first choice in beds." He smiled and Amanda found him even more attractive.

"How long have I been here?" she asked as he sat in one of the now well-worn plastic chairs.

"About seven weeks."

"Seven weeks," she repeated. "I thought it was longer." She dropped her eyes so Bennett wouldn't see her face.

***

The last month of near-complete isolation, locked in the same ten-by-twelve room, had taken a heavy toll on Amanda's mental stability. The first two weeks she had been at Tellis had been relatively busy, filled with daily physical exams and lengthy medical interviews, which were tedious, but innocuous. Then came the biopsies, which were uncomfortable, and occasionally worse. They had inserted needles into a variety of body parts for seven straight days using only minimal amounts of anesthetics, but the discomfort was a small price to pay for the chance to be free of her cell and to interact with someone besides herself.

It had been a month since they completed their procedures, and Amanda hadn't been out of her room since. For the first few days she appreciated the solitude, but the last few weeks had taught her just how effective isolation could be as a technique of torture. Deprived of external stimulation, the brain's defenses weaken and it begins to create its own reality. She had started to hallucinate about the world beyond these three solid walls and the mirror that watched her incessantly. She created complex and well-formed visions of the control room behind the glass and of the stairs that led to a larger control room, manned twenty-four hours a day with monitors for each of the cameras that tracked her. Sometimes she imagined that she was sitting in one of the black leather chairs, watching herself sleep, read, or watch television. But the visual hallucinations, although increasing in both frequency and complexity, were still relatively rare compared to the voices in her mind. These were with her every waking moment and hounded her even as she slept. Random thoughts, usually only peripherally related to her, seemed to be broadcast straight into her mind. Before, during, and after nursing school she had cared for mentally ill patients, and now she began to relate to them. Hallucinations and the broadcasting of thoughts were symptoms universally seen in patients with major psychiatric disorders like schizophrenia. She was in the appropriate age group for it and had a family history of major depression, which made her more vulnerable to mental illness. Certainly she had had enough life-altering events to act as a trigger for almost any form of psychiatric illness.

A week earlier, her resistance had weakened enough that she almost asked to see a psychiatrist. Late in the afternoon, a technician had appeared with a needle and a handful of specimen tubes; after drawing her blood he paused and asked her if she needed anything. Without thinking, and a little too forcefully, she answered, "No." He took a step away from her and backed his way into the airlock. She watched him leave with half her mind chastising the other half for being weak.

Later, after counting the ceiling tiles and confirming that none were missing, she made peace with herself. The visions and voices were a problem, but they were benign and non-threatening; in fact, they rarely addressed her. So long as they remained as background noise, and nothing more, she resolved to keep them to herself.

***

"Don't worry about your things." Colonel Bennett looked around the small room and it was obvious that she didn't really have any things. "Well," he said, slightly uncomfortable. "Just follow me." He led her out of the airlock and into the small control room behind the glass. Amanda stood and stared, her mouth open. "Glad you're out of there?" he asked, misinterpreting her hesitation.

She scanned the very familiar room. She had passed through it several times before, but with each trip she had worn the isolation suit and had usually been on a stretcher with its rails up. She had never really seen this room, except in her hallucinations, which had been exactly correct down to the small crack in the porcelain sink in the corner. "Yes," she said, hiding confusion mixed with excitement and wonder. "Those stairs lead to another control room, only that one has monitors." She asked and told him.

He nodded and his smile returned. "Good guess. We won't need the monitors, or the cameras." He reached for a panel that contained several switches and began to flick them off. "Or these microphones."

She followed him up the stairs and found an exact replica of the room from her mental images. Her imagination had even supplied the correct smells: a mix of leather, coffee, and just a whiff of cigarettes. The three monitors were now dark, but she was certain that if they were on she would have seen her cell. She did a full circle in the dark room while Bennett patiently held a door for her. Her startlingly prescient hallucinations had never gone beyond this point. "Oh, I'm sorry. Thank you," she said, passing under the arm that held the door open.

"No problem. I can only imagine how good it must feel to be out of that room."

"The cell," she said softly. "Can I ask you a question?" They were half-way down a long, dark, and deserted hallway. "I would like you to be completely honest."

"Uh oh, I never like being COMPLETELY honest."

"Did you or someone else put something in the air or my food, or even the water? Maybe to sedate me?"

"No. Absolutely and completely, no." He stopped inside a doorway that led to a large, darkened hall. Voices from the opposite side echoed loudly. "We are not in charge of your care and are only peripherally involved with the investigation of the virus that killed your friends. This entire situation is being directed by the Centers for Disease Control in Atlanta. I and others have had disagreements over the approach and course of this investigation, but if anyone had gone as far as poisoning you, or drugging you without your knowledge and agreement, I would have known and been able to intercede."

The sudden change in his demeanor told Amanda that those disagreements had been substantial. "You're taking quite a risk telling me this." She said it as a statement, not a question. "In fact I would guess that you have been ordered not to tell me this."

"Tell you what?" He feigned ignorance and resumed his walk down the dark corridor and into the bright light beyond.

"What do you do here?" she asked after several more turns.

"Anything we want," he said as a joke. "Actually, we provide medical support to all branches of the military. We generally take their more unusual cases."

"Which makes me unusual," Amanda teased, with just a trace of a flirtatious tone.

"As strange as they come," he smiled down at her. "When we aren't playing Doctor House, we provide laboratory support."

The voices in her head were remote, except for one that quietly projected a sense of intrigue and uncertainty. She followed him through another dark hallway, then into and out of a brightly lit kitchen. He descended a set of stairs and into a short corridor lined with doors on each side. "Take your pick," he said. "They're all the same, though."

She opened a door and said, "This one will be just fine." There was a bed, a chest of drawers, a door that she surmised led to a shared bathroom, and a television hanging from the ceiling. "Cozy," she said. "Where are the cameras?"

"No cameras; you now have complete privacy. Which reminds me." He reached in front of her and closed the door. "Can I show you one more thing?"

He led her up the hall to a large recreation room, where ten soldiers were lounging, reading, or watching what looked like a NASCAR race on television.

"Officer on the deck," someone yelled, and everyone stood and immediately came to attention.

"As you were. Mr. Lambert is from the Navy, and believes that we are aboard a ship at sea. Please excuse his delusions." The ten young men turned to face Amanda, and she could feel the hormone level soar through the roof. "From this moment on, no one may use the south hallway. It is reserved exclusively for our guest. This is an order, gentlemen. Any infractions will lead to immediate reassignment. Am I clear?"

"Yes, Colonel," they said in unison after most of them had returned to an attention posture.

Amanda looked at their young faces and realized with a start that she recognized at least four of the ten by name, and another three looked very familiar. She must have met them a month ago during her many trips back and forth from the CAT scanners and procedure rooms. She was surprised by how intensely familiar they were. "Mr. Lambert just became a father—about six weeks ago?" she asked the muscular red-haired young man to her left.

"Yes ma'am," he said with surprise.

In her mind she saw a pretty, young red-haired woman who had yet to fully lose her baby fat, and then a small bundle of baby wrapped in a blue blanket with hair the color of new carrots. "A boy, right?"

"Yes again, ma'am." He looked even more surprised.

"Mr. Lambert, I am only a few years older than you and if you keep calling me 'ma'am' I will be forced to reveal how you get little Carl to go back to sleep." A vision of Cameron Lambert singing "I'm a Little Teapot" while acting out the lyrics with his newborn son in his arms burst before Amanda's eyes. She felt light-headed, and while the chorus of male voices assailed Cameron Lambert she grabbed the door jam to steady herself. "Colonel, thank you for showing me the way, and everything else that you did on my behalf." The words were flying out of her mouth, and only after she heard them did she understand them. An image of Bennett arguing with a man who could only be Nathan Martin, the man who had lied to her weeks earlier, now filled her mind. "I need to lie down," she said, turning away quickly enough that Bennett reached for her arm. A small burning sensation ran from his touch up to her shoulder, and she reflexively recoiled.

"Whoa, sorry, Mrs. Flynn. I didn't mean to grab you so roughly." He hadn't grabbed her roughly, and he knew it, and now she knew it. A strange and familiar sensation seemed to pour through her body.

She began to shake as images and voices flooded into her mind faster than she could make sense of them. She stepped away from the officer, who watched her back down the hall, his arm partially raised. "I'm all right, Colonel; just a little dizzy. All this activity after a month of isolation," she explained unconvincingly.

She picked a door and slipped inside, maintaining eye contact with Bennett, holding him in place. She locked the door and quickly checked her arms for the lesions, and then stripped off her clothes and searched the rest of her body. Finding nothing, she began to dress. The déjà vu feeling that had overwhelmed her in the recreation room was beginning to pass, leaving clarity in its absence. She had experienced it before. She had been lying in a dirty cot in Honduras, watching her father and brother walk past her, as an eerie sensation overwhelmed her. She wasn't free of the infection; she hadn't miraculously beaten it. It was still with her, hiding in her brain.

"In some people it has a bimodal course, resurfacing after a short interval." They were her words as she described the infection to one of Martin's minions over a month ago. Soon—minutes, hours, maybe a day—the blisters would return, the madness would intensify, and she would die. She was a danger to everyone around her. It was possible she had already infected the colonel, and through him everyone else in the recreation room. She opened the dorm room door and found the hall empty. Voices, laughter, and life poured out of the rec room, but she turned the other way and stole her way back to the hated cell. She opened the outer airlock and a faint rush of air brushed back her hair. She paused, went back to the control room at the top of the stairs, and found a phone exactly where she knew it would be. A shiver of déjà vu struck again. The phone had a dial tone, and on an impulse she dialed Lisa and Greg Flynn's number, but an automated voice immediately warned that outgoing calls were not allowed. She tried zero and after a second a male voice answered.

"Operator."

"This is Amanda Flynn," she said in a rush.

"Yes, Mrs. Flynn?"

"I need to speak to Colonel Bennett; he's in the hematology lab." Once again the words were out of her mouth without conscious thought or awareness of their origin.

The phone began to ring and then a voice answered. "Hematology." It was the same disinterested tone that she had experienced since arrival, and its normality almost made her cry.

"I'm looking for Colonel Bennett," she said quickly.

"Just missed him, by about two seconds. Oh, how about that? Here he comes again. Sir. Sir, it's for you, I believe that it's Mrs. Flynn." She heard the phone exchange hands.

"Colonel, I need to see you in Control Room Seven." Once again she had no idea where her thoughts originated. The words were being squeezed out of her brain without her permission or control.

"Control Room Seven?" He sounded confused. "I'm not sure where that is, Mrs. Flynn."

"I don't know either." An edge of panic filled her voice. "The room above my cell, with all the monitors."

"Okay, now I'm with you."

"Come alone," she added before hanging up and cutting off his question.

Two minutes later, she heard his soft footfalls, and then he appeared at the doorway. Amanda had slid one of the black leather chairs against the console, as far from the door as possible. "Don't come any closer. I need to be back in isolation."

"Why would you say that?"

"Because it's coming back; the infection." He stared at her, waiting for clarification. "I know I don't have any of the blisters, but I have everything else." She held her bare arms out for his examination.

"Nor do you have the virus in your blood or any of your tissues, Amanda."

"You're wrong; it's in my head, in my brain. I'm seeing things and I hear voices in my head. I'm saying random, crazy things. This is how it starts; you start seeing things, then you lose control of what you're saying, and then you lose control over everything. I've been through this before. I watched my dead brother and father walk right in front of me when I was in Honduras, and when we were up here earlier I watched you and that other doctor, the one who lied to me—Martin —arguing in this room. Almost exactly where you're standing now."

"And that's what has you worried?" He sat in one of the two remaining chairs.

"I saw Cameron Lambert dancing with his baby singing 'I'm a Little Teapot.' I didn't even know his name was Cameron."

"That surprises me. He was one of your escorts when Doctor Martin was having you tested. He reported that you were very friendly."

Amanda tried to remember, but everyone looked the same in an isolation suit. "I never saw him dance or sing."

"I'm not saying that you did, and I don't think that you actually saw Dr. Martin and me arguing in this room or any room. You were isolated from human contact for over a month in a tiny room with limited intellectual freedom, and that came directly after watching thirty people die and being trapped with their bodies, alone, in a jungle, surrounded by armed men. And let's not forget what happened to you last year." He sounded very reasonable, but Amanda remained completely unconvinced. "Okay, how about this: I divulge a secret that Dr. Martin and I were not on the same page, and then you meet face to face a man you had been friendly with a month earlier who is bursting with pride over his newborn son, and your brain goes to work. Your mind simply added color to the picture that others gave you; you didn't create it." Amanda's features began to soften. "I doubt this is the virus, or any serious mental affliction, but if it makes you feel safer to be downstairs, then stay downstairs."

"I saw this very room in a hallucination," she confessed. "And the one downstairs; I saw them exactly as they are. I even saw these chairs." Her voice rose and she didn't know if she was angry or terrified of the implications.

"Amanda, you walked through this room when you arrived. I was right behind you, and then we walked down those stairs, through the observation room, and into the isolation room."

She suddenly felt very foolish. He had answers for everything, and they made far more sense than hers. She dropped her head into her hands but didn't cry. She was so humiliated; the only saving grace was that he was the only one who knew, and that he viewed her breakdown as an anticipated event. "I am so embarrassed."

"Don't be. In fact, I applaud your strength. After all you've been through, if your biggest problem is a little cerebral confabulation you are one special lady." He nodded his head. "I think we'll keep this conversation between us. If Dr. Martin finds out, he'll want to do a brain biopsy next."

"If it's okay with you, I'll stay here tonight."

"It's going to take some time for your mind to adjust, and learn to feel safe again. I see it a lot in my world."

"Post traumatic stress syndrome."

"I think that's a reasonable diagnosis. The only difficulty in your case is trying to figure out which one of your traumas triggered it."

"Thanks," she said, and a part of her wanted to give him a hug, but another part strongly resisted.

"I do need to tell you that I won't be around as much. Dr. Martin and his crew are taking over the day-to-day operations. I'll still be here and I'll check on you from time to time."

Her heart dropped. She trusted the colonel, and despite the fact that she had only met the man once, she didn't trust Martin. "He's the one keeping me here."

"He's the one that has been directing your care," he said evenly, but Amanda sensed a deep well of darker emotions. "I really don't think there's much more to do with you anyway. I'm guessing that you'll be going home soon." He stood, preparing to leave. "I hope when all this is over I have the opportunity to see you under different circumstances, Amanda." He smiled and Amanda blushed.

"I think I would like that, Colonel." He was more than twice her age, but that didn't seem to matter. She simply felt comfortable around him, and for now that was good enough.

CHAPTER 19

Amanda stared at the ceiling, and as the hours slowly passed the hope and trust she had placed in Colonel Bennett's assessment began to fade. She had seen him several times in the past seven weeks, and had talked with him several more; his simple, unassuming demeanor radiated a quiet confidence that in ordinary circumstances she would find very comforting and reassuring. She rolled onto her side as MONA whispered in her ear that these were not ordinary circumstances. Bennett's reasoning and logic were impeccable in the warm daylight hours, but in the cold dark of the night—when the impossible not only became possible but likely—reasoning and logic, no matter how impeccable, were no comfort.

Alone in the cell, the voices were blessedly distant, but a single repetitive hallucination irritated her like no other. Each time she closed her eyes, her mind seemed to float through the walls of her cell and glide unseen through the dark corridors of Tellis. Like a kite without a string, she drifted at the whim of an unseen breeze, aimlessly floating. At first the disembodiment was a curious and enjoyable distraction and reminded her of the rare occasions when she drank to the point of intoxication. She wasn't much of a drinker but had in her earlier years enjoyed just enough excess to realize that it was not the life for her. She hated the loss of control and the unreliability of mind and body, and that was the major difference with this experience. If she opened her eyes she immediately snapped back. No vertigo, no nausea, just a quick trip out of her cell—the perfect hallucinogenic experience. Only now she was tired, closer to exhausted, and the tedious trips that never went beyond the darkened rooms of the Tellis Medical Facility were preventing her from getting any sleep. Their novelty had worn off, and the unbidden ghostly trips were fast becoming irritating. Unlike the previous hallucinations, which were always intimately associated with an individual or a specific location, these were completely devoid of meaning or purpose. They retained the strangely hyper-real sense that the previous visions had, just not their significance.

She returned to staring at the ceiling, wondering if this bland hallucination represented a change for the better or a further unbraiding of her mind. Her eyes began to close and once again she felt the lightening of her mind as it prepared for another meaningless jaunt through the halls. She abruptly sat up, and in a bid to stay awake forced herself to analyze the situation. Something was affecting her mind; that much was clear. Colonel Bennett assured her that it was nothing more serious than PTSD, and the educated, rational portions of her mind agreed. After all that she had experienced, some transient mental instability was to be expected. Only her id ruled the rest of her brain, and it was awake and restless. It whispered in MONA's voice that no matter how illogical or impossible, she was still infected, and the situation was deteriorating, not improving.

She tried to reject the idea. *It has been almost two months,* she thought.

A virus can stay dormant for years. Varicella will present with chicken pox, and then decades later return as zoster, and the shingles, MONA countered.

Both of those primarily involve the skin, she countered right back.

Herpes Simplex starts as a cold sore, but in some people returns as a virulent medial temporal lobe encephalitis that most die from, and those who survive are usually impaired.

She had remembered this very fact weeks ago but quickly put it out of her mind; apparently MONA had found it. This new virus, EDH 1, as it had been christened, had more than a passing similarity to Herpes Simplex I. Both presented with a rash. A cold sore was nothing more than a rash in the lining of the mouth, and, in an unfortunate few, the virus attacked the inner portions of the brain—centers that were intimately involved with the creation of memories, and when disturbed were capable of producing vivid and recurrent hallucinations. *No one survives Herpes Encephalitis without treatment.* It was a weak response but the only one she could think of.

At this point we are the only one to survive.

Bennett says they can't find the virus in my blood or tissue. She clung to this one thought like a shipwreck victim clings to a log.

That doesn't mean it's not there, or hiding in the nerves or in the brain.

It was the logical counter to her one best hope. MONA had developed abilities beyond her usual Middle-Of-Night-Angst. Tired of the argument, she closed her mind to MONA and surrendered to the fatigue. Her eyes closed and her mind drifted away, at first through the corridors of Tellis, and later into the oblivion of sleep.

***

She awoke with a start; it took a few seconds for her to recognize her familiar cell. She could hear voices through the open airlock and felt several more in her sleepy mind. During the short night, she had traded the hallucinations for the voices. She slipped out of bed and attended to her personal needs. Like every other morning, she found a new set of surgical scrubs and toiletries in the cubby next to the airlock. She ducked behind the curtain and began to dress. Modesty may be the first victim of hospitalization, but her mind was dark this morning and she didn't have the slightest desire to indulge the lonely fantasies of the men around her. She finally pulled back the curtain as Nathan Martin ducked his head under the airlock's seal.

"Good morning," he said, and immediately she doubted whether it was "good" or "morning." He was of average height and slight build and was not, by any standards, an attractive man. He wasn't repulsive; just, like his height, he was average. His dark hair was thinning on the top and streaked with grey. Amanda guessed him to be in his late fifties. "I hoped you slept well." He was amiable, but her mood darkened even further. He pulled one of the two plastic chairs from a corner and sat without a word. Amanda edged closer to the bed and decided to remaining standing. "We met several weeks ago, I am …"

"Nathan Martin. I know who you are. You are the person who is keeping me here."

"It's really not that simple. We just don't know if it's safe to release you back into the population." He crossed his legs and she noticed how well he dressed.

"But it's safe for you to breathe the same air I breathe and to sit five feet from me."

"Fair enough." He nodded casually, as if his contradiction was of no real concern. "With your permission I would like to run you through some of the tests that we performed earlier. Just the interviews at first. Perhaps we can jog something loose that will shed some light on what happened down there." He smiled and it invoked a strong desire in Amanda to knock out a few of his perfectly straight white teeth. That way he couldn't lie through as many.

"And if I decide not to give you my permission?" Her eyes narrowed, reducing extraneous visual input as she focused on her visitor. He was lying, and it wasn't just what he was saying; his demeanor, affect, and body language were all false. She couldn't identify his tell, but her subconscious mind had picked up on it and was preparing for a confrontation.

"I think that with your complete participation we will be able to get you home sooner." Once again his words were warm, his smile friendly, and his face completely relaxed.

I don't believe that you have any intention of letting me go home, but I do believe that you are an accomplished liar. She wondered if there was any benefit to giving voice to her thought. As the moment stretched, his smile slowly faded but didn't quite disappear. He watched her, waiting for a sign or an answer, and she knew that she had been correct. No matter how much she participated, he was going to do everything in his power to keep her.

It's his eyes, she thought. *The steady gaze of an accomplished liar.* He was going to make her disappear. No one outside this facility knew that she was still alive, and even the people who had taken care of her these past seven weeks were being replaced.

"So can I count on your cooperation?"

"I don't seem to have much choice," she answered as defiantly as her situation allowed, vowing to change it.

CHAPTER 20

"Damnation! I can't manufacture a positive result, no matter how angry you become," Newton Moore drawled to his temporary boss, Dr. Martin. Moore was one of eight laboratory and medical technicians who had been given a day's notice and uprooted from Atlanta to this hole in the ground miles from civilization. He was voicing the growing frustration that was shared by his seven comrades. "Can you please take a step back?" Martin was literally standing over him, the virologist's tie draped over Moore's shoulder. He and his colleagues had all agreed to deploy into the field in the event of an outbreak, but one woman, no matter how "hot," was not an outbreak by anyone's definition.

"I am trying to see if you're doing this correctly," Martin answered testily.

Moore abruptly stood. He was nearly a foot taller and a hundred pounds heavier than his boss and in a rare moment used it to intimidate Martin. "I will gladly watch you do it." He forced Martin against the wall as he yielded the stool. Moore knew that Martin knew nothing about the new enzyme-linked assay that could reveal even the slightest traces of the EDH 1 virus. Moore had been a principal investigator into the technique and was arguably a world authority, which was exactly why he had been dragged from his lab and brought to Tellis. "I haven't seen the sun in almost two weeks, and I'm getting pretty damn tired of you and the rest of your staff dogging my every step."

Martin was forced to look up at the angry man with his wild hair. Moore was a super-star in the field of immunoassay, and virtually untouchable. Even before leaving graduate school he realized his undeniable value and banked on it as he purposely tweaked the establishment with his hair and clothes.

"All right, just call me when this sample has been run." Martin backed his way to the doorway, giving Moore some space.

"It's going to be negative," Moore said as Martin slipped out of the door. "Just like all the others," he finished to himself. He returned to his seat and finished pipetting the last of the 96 wells in the microtiter plate. Martin's team, with the full support of the CDC, had moved remarkably fast in isolating the virus and then fabricating an antibody to a portion of the virus's protein wall, which was what made Moore's test possible. An antibody solution had been bound to a chemical that changed color whenever it came in contact with the protein unique to the virus. Moore sat waiting for any of the samples to change to the bright yellow color that signified the presence of EDH 1. After fifteen minutes, each of the 96 small wells remained clear. "Negative," he said, getting up from his seat. Four hours of work for the same result. He took the assay plate and tossed it into the large red medical waste bin. At least ten other plates had landed there in the last two weeks. He turned off his light and walked back to his room.

"Are you off?" A voice caused Moore to pull up short.

"Hey," he answered as Scott Price approached from behind. Price and Moore had worked together in the same microbiology lab in Atlanta for twelve years. Moore tolerated the usually grim man partly because they worked closely, partly because every spring they played on the same softball team, and partly because no one else would suffer Price and his near constant black-cloud. "I'm done; at least until they find another part of that luscious body to poke."

Price held up a small tray filled with needles and blood tubes. "They want some more blood. Want to help?"

"No, but I'll be happy to hold her hand, or anything else she'll let me hold."

"Hmpf," Price responded with his trademark grunt.

"So you're going to tell me that she's not the finest thing you've ever poked?" The double entendre only made Price grunt a second time, and Moore shook his head. "I'm calling Buuull Shiiiit on that one!"

"I said she's fine," Price said. They descended the stairs to the main isolation room, or the Cell, as everyone had begun to call it.

"I said she's fine," Moore mimicked Price with the voice of a prepubescent boy.

"Are you ever going to gown up?" Price said after putting down the phlebotomy tray. He pushed Moore aside and reached for an isolation suit.

"What the hell are you doing that for? She's not infectious." Moore pulled at the suit's sleeve as Price tried to slip an arm in.

"Stop it, asshole.," Price yelled and Moore let go. "I don't care what anyone says; I'm not touching her or any of her blood. Are you going to help?"

"No. I think I'll just stay out here and watch." He faced the glass and Amanda was staring directly at him. "Sometimes I think she can see through that."

"The airlock is open, genius. She can hear you."

"Can she hear this?" Moore flipped off Price with both middle fingers. He watched his colleague stoop and walk into the small room, and then returned his gaze to the lovely lady. She watched as Price negotiated the open airlock and then she very deliberately turned and faced Moore. He stared at her and she seemed to stare right back at him; after a long moment he waved but she didn't respond.

***

Amanda couldn't hear the obscene gesture, but Price's response was clear enough. She had heard their voices over the chorus of inarticulate voices in her mind. Occasionally one would take the lead and add its own aria in some unintelligible language, but like now they usually blended into a cacophony of strange white noise. She was convinced that they weren't drugging her and that the mental instability was purely organic, earned through stress and isolation. She clung to the hope that if she was ever released, her mind would naturally right itself, and if she was never released what did it matter if her sanity had slipped a little.

She saw Price bang the top of his isolation suit against the airlock that opened to her room, and her mood instantly darkened as he emerged with a scowl on his face.

"I need to draw some more blood," Price introduced himself.

"Why not? It's been almost eight hours." Amanda sat crossed-legged on her bed and pushed away a novel as Price approached. She presented a bruised arm, and with gloved hands he tapped her skin looking for an unused vein. "You don't usually do this," she said with an even tone. An aura of dissatisfaction surrounded him, and Amanda found herself in the middle of it.

"No. We don't have a regular phlebotomist, so we all have to take turns," he said tersely, and Amanda didn't have to ask him how he felt about that arrangement.

"At least it gets you out of the lab." Amanda tried to jar some positive emotion from Price.

"My lab is in Atlanta," he said sullenly as he wrapped a rubber tourniquet around her bicep. "Squeeze your fist," he commanded, and Amanda complied. "Don't move." He jabbed a large needle into her forearm and predictably he missed the vein. He cursed quietly as one of Amanda's mental voices suddenly took it up a notch. She focused on the strange, incomprehensible words as Price tried and missed again. He cursed a little stronger this time, and her mental soloist ratcheted up another notch. He tried a different vein as a large bruise began to form on her arm, and for a third time he blew the vein.

"Fuck!" he said out loud, and even though it had become her new favorite word, Amanda was taken aback. His sullen demeanor had deteriorated into outright anger, and he callously ripped off the tourniquet and reached for her other arm. "Let me have that one," he commanded when she hesitated.

"No! Not until you calm down." The heat of his emotions was like a sunlamp on her face, and the voice in her mind had reached a piercing level. It took a supreme effort to maintain her focus on Price as pain burst through her head.

He grabbed her other arm and quickly rewrapped the tourniquet. For the fourth time he stabbed her and, like in the previous attempts, missed. He started ranting as he lined up for a fifth attempt, and Amanda grabbed his arm. The pain from his rough attempts, combined with the shrieking in her mind, nearly made her vomit.

"No more! Get somebody else to do this!" She could hear his companion in the control room, or at least thought she could. Reality began to blur as the screaming in her mind began to resolve itself into a long tirade of obscenities. A distant and detached part of her mind was almost happy with the sudden clarity. Words, no matter how foul, were preferable to the inarticulate shrieking. But the resolution gave her no respite from the pain, which was beginning to threaten her level of consciousness. A hand reached her face in the fog of the half-reality and pushed her into a pillow. A sharp jab in her arm was followed by another scream in her ears and in her mind. Price and the voice vied to see who could cause Amanda the most pain.

"God damn BITCH!" he screamed as he twisted her arm. He forced her face further into the pillow and she began to gasp for air as he finally cannulated a vein. He kept his arm across her back as the blood began to flow into the specimen tubes.

I hope she passes out and dies from anoxia, said the voice in her mind. It followed with more invectives that Amanda knew were meant for someone else. Suddenly her mind began to fade and her body began to lighten. She felt an arm in her back, only she felt the arm more than her back. The synergy made her dizzy and she fought to stay conscious. Images of the sandy-haired Price and a small woman arguing in a car flashed through her mind.

All I want to do is go home, and this bitch is keeping me here! He punctuated his thought by pushing her deeper into the pillow, and the sensation of pushing and being pushed overwhelmed her. She was suffocating, and her dying brain began to hallucinate wildly as she watched Price and the small woman renew their argument in a restaurant.

It's his wife, Amanda thought, and as her consciousness began to fade a flood of alien emotions and memories raced through her. Price and Moore walking down the hall. Price arguing over the phone. Price losing his temper. Price driving. Price sleeping. Price. Price. Price. And finally Amanda made the connection. The voice in her head was Price's. His thoughts, senses, and life had merged with hers.

Abruptly he released her. Her head popped off the pillow and she gasped for air. Her scrub top had been pulled up and for a moment his eyes lingered. A large man with wild hair stood over Price, and he too stared. She angrily pulled her top down. "No wonder your wife left you," she spat at Price. The words were out of her mouth before she was even consciously aware she was speaking. His memory of the small, dark-haired woman running from their apartment raced through her mind. *You're nothing more than a coward!* echoing in his mind, and Amanda wasn't sure if she had yelled them or if it had been Price's abused wife.

He was on her in an instant. Amanda felt his blows as well as his anger as they reestablished the strange connection that had broken when he let her up. He was screaming in her ears and her mind, and she rejoiced in his impotent rage. Moore pulled the much smaller man off his feet and literally threw him across the room, where he struck the one-way glass. His face shield cracked and he ripped off the hood that covered his head. "You're a fucking bitch and you should have died with all the others." His face was red and his spittle flew halfway to Moore, who had interposed himself.

"Get out, Price. Now, or so help me they be carrying your ass out of here."

Price's voice still played in Amanda's mind and she could hear him weighing his options. Finally he stooped to retrieve the four vials of blood and, after a moment's hesitation, threw them against the wall. Glass and blood splattered over Moore. For a moment nothing happened, then both Moore and Price began to move at the same instant—Moore towards Price, who raced to the airlock.

"Asshole," Moore screamed as Price slipped out ahead of the larger man.

"You're friends with that fuck?" Amanda asked as Moore turned to appraise the damage.

"Friends is too strong a word. We work together, but that ended about five seconds ago." He picked a shard of glass from a tangle in his hair. Amanda tossed him a towel and he wiped the blood from of his face.

"He beats his wife, or should I say ex-wife."

"Worst-kept secret in Atlanta," he answered, and she liked the way he pronounced Atlanta. He leaned over and examined her face. "You're going to need stitches," he said.

She ignored what he said and searched her mind for a voice that fit this not-so-gentle giant. It was soft compared to Price's screams. *He's going to need more than stitches. Damn, how could he do this to that face?* She blushed.

"Turn your head," he said, and for the second time she felt her body lighten as his hand lightly touched her chin. She felt his powerful physical attraction, but also a strong sense of propriety. She leaned away from him and the connection became more remote. "Sorry,"—he misinterpreted her response—"I'm not going to hurt you." He was still close enough that she could hear him complete the sentence in his mind: *I'm going to hurt Price.*

"It's okay; it doesn't even hurt," Amanda said, subtly retreating from the large man.

"It's gonna; he hit you pretty good. Sorry I wasn't faster." He stood to his full height. "I'll get someone down here to fix you up."

She tried to ignore his inner monologue. "Thank you for what you did."

"Should never have happened. And it will not happen again." An odd look crossed his face. "Did you just say something?"

"No," she answered, and realized that their connection was possibly reciprocal.

"Okay." He still looked confused. "Are you going to be all right down here alone? I've got to get some help and find the future-former Mr. Price."

"I'll be fine." She smiled, and even with the developing bruise and the cut under her right eye, she felt Moore's heart skip a beat.

He walked to the airlock and turned back. The confused look returned. "You didn't say any ..." She shook her head. "I think I need my hearing checked."

She slid off her bed and looked in the mirror. She had seen her face reflected in Moore's mind and the mirror's reflection confirmed it. She touched her bloody cheek and began to laugh. Moore paused in the airlock.

"Are you okay?" he asked, ducking his head back into the cell.

His clear but confused thoughts floated across the room to her. "I am very okay." Her acceptance of the assault only confused him even further. He paused a moment longer and then returned to the airlock.

Amanda looked back at the mirror. She was already developing a first-class shiner, but it was a small price to pay for clarity. Her mental aberrations weren't aberrations at all; in fact they weren't even hers. She hadn't actually seen Cameron Lambert dancing with his newborn baby; she had somehow tuned into the young man's powerful memory of the event. It was the same with Colonel Bennett arguing with Dr. Martin, and with Price abusing his wife. She had become a receiver for the memories, thoughts, and emotions of those around her.

"Damnation," Amanda drawled.

CHAPTER 21

"I appreciate that a single incident should not prompt precipitous actions, but neither can we ignore it," Marcus Sobel said to Nathan Martin.

Sobel's clipped and precise elocution was more than an affectation; it was a defining characteristic. Sobel's appointment as Director of the Centers for Disease Control and Prevention coincided with the untimely retirement of Stanley Cripps. Sobel had been Martin's chairman at NYU, and the pair had managed to maintain a professional relationship for twenty years. The appointment of a protégée was fairly common practice, so Martin's nomination to Director of Special Pathogens was met with little resistance. Sobel was the epitome of insider politics. He was groomed from an early age for high places, his family's wealth afforded him an Ivy League education, and his father's connections ensured a position of respect and power. He possessed an uncanny ability to surround himself with people of great ability, insulating him from the mundane duties of his position and ensuring that they were done exceptionally well. He saw in Martin the tenacity of a bulldog and the look of one as well. He was comfortable that Martin would always get the job done and never pose a threat to him politically.

"It has been dealt with, Marcus." Martin had had a long discussion with Scott Price, before the younger man was fired.

"Which leaves the larger issue of the young lady. I have given you great latitude, and a good deal of our budget, both of which are in very short supply at the moment. I believe that without any further developments, once this last set of cultures and antigen studies has been completed, we will be in a position to release Mrs. Flynn. Don't you agree?"

Martin had to bite his tongue as a comment about Sobel's inability to interpret a clinical situation nearly made it out of his mouth. "Of course, that is one way of proceeding." He paused for Sobel to respond, but his boss just waited for Martin to convince him or hang himself. "When I was a resident. you gave a lecture about how humanity's future will be affected by the emergence of more resistant and pathogenic microbes. Do you remember?"

"Vaguely." Sobel's tone made it sound like his mind had already shifted to the next order of business.

"You posited that unless the rate of scientific advancement kept pace with population growth we would ultimately reach a tipping point. That the interaction between the human biomass and the microbial biomass would inevitably lead to 'pandemics of biblical proportions.' That was the very term you used."

Sobel took a long moment. "Unfortunately, I am still of the same opinion. However, you have yet to prove that this patient represents anything more than a potential PR nightmare."

"Marcus, you have to let me do the job you hired me for. This woman is everything that you talked about, only in reverse. Instead of humanity selecting out more virulent pathogens, the pathogen has selected out a more resistant human. This is a singular opportunity—for everyone." Martin's implications were blatant but effective. He knew that Sobel had aspirations well beyond the CDC.

"All right, Nathan," Sobel finally said. "I will give you a little more time to complete your work. A little more time, and then one way or another this situation must be resolved."

"I appreciate that."

"Thank you for your work on this, Nathan. Hopefully, we will all learn something from it. Now, on to other matters …"

They talked for another fifteen minutes before the director dismissed Martin. He walked back to his office wondering what Sobel meant when he said that he hoped "we will all learn something from this." His tone had made it sound like both a rebuke and a compliment. That was the trouble with Sobel: you never really knew where you stood.

Five minutes later Martin threw a muted greeting to his secretary and immediately retreated to his office and computer. The EDH 1 virus in all its glory popped up as soon as Martin moved his mouse. It was the best electron microscope image they had and he was thinking of making it into a screen saver. His division had amassed a tremendous amount of information in record time. In less than three months they had isolated, cultured, dissected, and created a simple screening test for infection. Unfortunately, none of it came from their single test subject. She remained stubbornly resistant to revealing her idiosyncratic resistance. All the progress they had realized had come from blood and tissue samples collected from the bodies on site—bodies that ultimately and foolishly had been destroyed. After twelve weeks, Amanda had contributed nothing to their cause.

Martin idly studied the image on his screen; he had caught himself doing a lot of that lately. EDH 1 was completely unique, which itself was unique. Every other known virus shared characteristics with at least one other virus, which was one of the primary means of identifying and categorizing them. Only EDH 1 was unlike everything that had come before; it was literally in a category of its own. Its size, shape, clinical characteristics—everything made it completely alien and horribly dangerous if it were ever to reappear.

He closed the file as a mixture of personal and professional dissatisfaction welled up. Special pathogens were special because of their ability to infect, and in most cases kill, quickly and in large numbers. They were mostly viruses, and the CDC's ability to treat the outbreaks was fairly limited. His department's job was mostly about containment of the outbreak, isolation of the pathogen, and laboratory studies that were aimed at that giant breakthrough that would ultimately arm them with the clinical tools to stop an outbreak rather than just contain it. One day, in some lab, this nut would finally crack, and the medical world would radically change. He tried to bury his innermost secret under a pile of medical imperatives, but knew that the desire for his lab to be the one, the only one to finally discover that silver bullet, was what drove him.

EDH 1 and Amanda were the key; he knew it, and the opportunity was slipping through his hands. He already had the preliminary results of the final pathology and antigen studies, and like all the rest they were negative. He could hold the results for maybe a week, but eventually Sobel would receive them and pull the plug. All he needed was one positive result—just one, and that would justify the extreme measures necessary to finally unlock Amanda's resistance.

He toyed with the idea of falsifying one of the reports, but that would do him no good. The CDC staff members in Tellis were reporting their results directly to Sobel, and as they worked in labs outside of Martin's control they had no real loyalty to him, and he had no real sway over them—certainly not enough to have them falsify a report. An even darker thought occurred to him. They had synthesized a relatively pure form of the virus. It was possible that if Amanda was re-exposed to EDH 1 her immune system would rapidly deploy that holy grail of defenses.

He felt that he should turn off his office light and sit in the dark if he was going to consider such radical, unethical, and illegal behavior. He put it out of his mind, but it bounced right back with greater force. If she indeed was the key to curing outbreaks of hemorrhagic fevers, or even simply future outbreaks of EDH 1, was it immoral to challenge her resistance a second time? If six months down the road an outbreak of Marburg or Ebola killed a thousand Ugandans, would he be morally responsible because he didn't avail himself of every resource? Or worse yet, if years from now EDH 1 reappears and threatens tens of thousands, possibly millions, could he or anyone else say that putting her at risk was unjustified?

Those are questions for an ethics committee, not a physician, he told himself, and then sat quietly, afraid to follow his train of thought. He returned to his computer and checked on the progress of the tissue cultures and found that they had created more than two hundred test doses of EDH 1 for study purposes. *It is possible,* he mused, and wondered if he could get Sobel to sign off on it.

CHAPTER 22

It took a full day for the bruises to completely develop into a pair of first class black eyes. A medic had closed the small laceration beneath her left eye with a bead of super-glue, and nearly three days later Amanda could barely see it.

She stretched and gave herself a momentary break from another of Dr. Martin's endless forms. What a difference a few days made. She wasn't schizophrenic or psychotically depressed; she wasn't even suffering from post-traumatic stress; she was something more, something different. Tele-path. Psychic. Seer. She wasn't even certain what she was, aside from happy.

Her new talent gave her life a focus. Something to concentrate on between Martin's questionnaires and examinations. She had moved out of her "cell" and began to freely interact with the staff while secretly using her new toy. She was still little more than a passive receiver of thoughts and emotional energy but was beginning to learn how to fine-tune them. She had found that true clarity required either isolation or at least close physical proximity—contact if possible—but that was still something she tried to avoid.

She also tried to avoid examining the ethics of her new talent. She knew that what she was doing represented the ultimate invasion of person-al privacy, but, she rationalized, she was only having some innocent fun with it. She would never use anything she learned for her own benefit. Be-sides, this was something that she hadn't asked for and was completely out of her control. The voices came to her; they were invading her sanctuary.

***

"Knock, knock," Colonel Bennett said, walking into the empty recreation room.

"Well hello," Amanda said warmly. Her receptive greeting generated a spark of excitement in Bennett, and Amanda felt it just as keenly as the colonel.

"I haven't seen you in a while and wanted to check in." He pointed to her face. "I heard what happened. I also understand that you didn't want to press charges."

He was too far away for a good connection, but his emotional energy was clear. A cool shade of blue seemed to warm her face. The synesthesia was becoming a familiar part of her life. "I was never asked whether I wanted to press charges or not."

His warm blue darkened, and she felt small, circulating red splotches in his emotional color wheel. "I see," was all he said, and a single name, *Martin,* floated in the ether between them. "I should have expected as much, but it always surprises me when I am lied to so directly." He pulled up a chair opposite her and let the moment of unpleasantness pass. "What are you doing?"

"Contributing to the deforestation of the planet." She waved at a thick set of forms. "I'm fairly certain that I've answered these same questions three other times. Are they running out of forms and tests?"

"Yes," he said, giving her an unexpectedly direct answer.

His tone suggested that this was more than a casual visit, and she felt his mind shift from social mode to professional mode. "I'm concerned about your safety," he said without preamble, and his mind added that he was powerless to do anything about it. "The virus that you were exposed to appears to be a new form of hemorrhagic fever. Similar to Ebola or Marburg."

"I've heard that." She had actually overheard it weeks ago from some less-than-discreet staff members. She had visited Newton Moore a day earlier and had learned even more.

"Martin is determined to figure out how you survived. He's convinced that you are the key that will unlock a giant medical mystery." A rising tide of powerful emotions obscured Bennett's thoughts, and the harder she listened, the more difficult it was to hear. "He is also convinced that you are not being entirely forthcoming." His carefully chosen words told her more than his hidden mind.

"And you're not entirely convinced that he's wrong," she surmised.

He hesitated, and his gaze dropped to the paperwork on the table. A long, quiet moment passed and then Bennett looked up. "No, Amanda, I don't think he's wrong," he said with conviction.

Her heart dropped as she stared into his brown eyes. Despite their age difference, his interest in her went beyond medical responsibilities, and he was willing to risk that for the truth. His sincerity shone brightly and she was embarrassed by her secrecy and duplicity. "So I will ask you not as a physician or as an officer in the United States Army, but as a concerned party. Are you telling us everything?"

She had always been proud of the fact that she was a hopelessly transparent liar, but at this moment, as her faltering eyes betrayed her, she regretted her transparency. He waited patiently as she chose her words carefully. "Nothing I can tell you will help answer your questions." She wanted to tell him everything, but a sudden wave of distrust stopped her.

"So there is something to tell." Amanda immediately sensed his frustration with the word games.

"Doctor Bennett, I have told you everything I know about what happened in Honduras and before. I have no idea how I survived, but I do know that the answer is not going to be found among these stupid questions." She flipped the small sheaf of papers and felt his heart slip a little when she addressed him so formally.

"So tell me what happened after Honduras, Amanda."

Her mood darkened. "I tried to tell you before and you wouldn't listen."

He stared at her impassively, and then a look of recognition crossed his face. "You told me that you were still infected and had been seeing things. Are you saying that you still believe that?"

"It's not a question of belief, and if you approach it with that attitude, there's no point in discussing it." Amanda folded her arms and looked away. His doubt and patronizing tone grated on her. Their connection was strong, and a loudspeaker in Amanda's mind broadcasted his thoughts. Bennett's disbelief colored her emotions and suddenly she was furious with the man. "Fine! You want proof?" she said angrily, and she grabbed Bennett's wrist. Intent on uncovering and then divulging a closely held secret, Amanda instead found herself falling through space. Bennett's thoughts, memories, and desires swam around her, and she felt the line that separated their individualities begin to blur and then dissolve. Their lives began to intermix and Amanda couldn't tell if the images that flowed through her were from her life or Bennett's. Each was powerless to hide anything from the other as for the moment they shared a single identity.

Abruptly, she slammed back to Earth and into her own mind, suddenly feeling more alone and isolated than ever before. Her sluggish mind had a hard time reorienting. She was confused about where she was and how she had come to find herself in such an odd room with an unconscious man sitting next to her. Her thick brain slowly pieced her disjointed memories together and familiarity began to return.

Bennett groaned and lifted his head. "Oh my God." He swayed in his chair as he tried to right himself. "I suddenly have the worst headache of my life." He looked at Amanda, confusion still painted across his face. "Hi there. I was hoping to see you today."

Amanda sensed his sudden and complete disorientation but didn't dare probe deeper. "I'm right here," she said tentatively, not completely certain where "right here" was.

With wide eyes and a perplexed look on his face, Bennett looked around the room. "Yes you are," he answered, and began rubbing both his temples. "I forgot what I was supposed to tell you." He waited a moment, then his smile faded. "I'm afraid I have some bad news for you. Dr. Martin wants to put you back in isolation."

***

"You sure you're all right, Colonel?" His aide had been the fourth person to ask him that question in the last three hours.

"I'm fine, Corporal; just a headache." He guessed that he must look like hell. "Has Mrs. Flynn been moved back to isolation?" The last thing he wanted right now was to discuss his state of health.

"Yes, sir." The corporal had taken the hint. "Begging your pardon sir, but I don't understand this sudden turnaround."

It had been a terrible mistake to turn this facility over to a civilian agency and then expect his men to blindly follow orders. Tellis Medical Facility was not just a secret military hospital—a fact that had been lost on most outside the military chain of command. It was staffed by the Combined Services Medical Group, a small and highly cohesive group of exceptionally well-trained medical professionals who had been assembled to respond to and treat a full range of medical emergencies. Every individual under his command had been hand-selected. Just to be considered, an applicant had to have scored in the top one percent on entrance aptitude tests, and had to have demonstrated their ability to work and think independently. It was easier to get into the Special Forces than the Combined Services Medical Group.

"It will become clear soon enough," he said as he walked into his office and closed the door on Corporal Tator's follow-up questions. In a normal unit such questions would not be tolerated; Corporal Tator would be told directly and severely that it was not important for him to understand, just to follow orders. But in this unit it was necessary in most situations to understand the reasoning behind the orders to accomplish them.

Bennett spun his smooth leather chair around and slid into it. It was his one luxury forty-seven feet below the surface of Oklahoma, and at this moment he was beyond grateful for it. He had been walking around in a fog for the last few hours, an unexplained headache pounding away at his temples. Something had happened earlier and for the life of him he couldn't recall what. The day had been somehow reset. He remembered waking up that morning; he remembered his workout with some of the Group; he remembered starting the day with a phone call from Martin, and then not much beyond that. It was late afternoon, but his mind told him that it still should be mid-morning. He ran through the medical differential diagnosis that would explain both a memory gap and the atypical headache, and if he were anyone else he would recommend a CT scan of the brain, looking for a hemorrhage. He had access to a CT scanner, as well as every other form of medical hardware, but he was not anyone else. He was the commanding officer of this post, and while some of the rules of military command were allowed to be relatively lax, the rule concerning the infallibility of the commanding officer had always been adhered to closely.

The phone on his desk ran loudly and he answered it before the third annoying ring. "Yes," he said, uncharacteristically terse.

"You wanted to be informed when Dr. Martin had arrived. He was just cleared through the main gate."

"Did he bring anything with him? Any medical supplies?"

"I don't have that answer, sir, but I will shortly."

"Thank you, Corporal." He hung the phone up quietly. Martin's sudden phone call, and now appearance, coupled with his instructions to re-isolate Amanda Flynn, was nothing short of ominous. If he hadn't had access to her lab results, his first thought would have been that Martin's team had found something with their reexaminations, but he knew that all the tests had come back negative. Martin was a driven SOB with a fairly flexible moral line, and he was certain that the man from Atlanta was about to step over it.

Bennett's thoughts of Amanda suddenly triggered a memory of a short conversation that seemed to have been set out of time. He was talking about some paperwork with Amanda, who despite her bruised face was absolutely radiant. He puzzled over the unattached memory, concluding that he must have seen her during his lost morning. He teased at the fragment, hoping that it would reveal its context, but it remained little more than an image. He let it go and surrendered to his headache by searching his desk for some ibuprofen. He took a full dose, four tablets, and washed them down with the stale remnants of that morning's coffee.

It would take Martin at least ten more minutes to reach the facility, which gave Bennett ten minutes to make a decision. From the moment Amanda had arrived at Tellis, her official status had always been somewhat undefined. She wasn't a soldier, and all the civil rights that defined her as a US citizen had been suspended. Bennett didn't know if due process had been served, or whether it had been postponed because of exigent circumstances; all he knew was that Nathan Martin had in his possession documents from the US Attorney General that in effect made Amanda the property of the CDC, and that he had been ordered by his commanding officer to turn his facility over to the man from Atlanta, and to keep her presence at Tellis a secret. After watching Martin in action for three months, Bennett was convinced that Amanda's presence on US soil, even her survival, had also become a secret known by only a few dozen people.

In the twenty-eight years he had been in the United States military, he had never come close to disobeying an order. Even as a medical resident at Walter Reed, he had been creative enough to technically follow orders that were ill-conceived and potentially dangerous without harming the patients under his care. If he picked up the phone and dialed one of the two numbers that were listed in Amanda's chart, no amount of creativity would protect him. His best defense would be to simply state the truth:

Martin had illegally ordered him to hold a US citizen, against her will, while he performed medical experiments upon her person. A flash of her naked "person" burst before his eyes in startling detail. The power of the image forced him to reflexively push away from his desk, and he waited for his office to reform around him.

That was strange, he said to himself. His heart was racing, and everything about him was brighter and louder as the adrenaline surge reached his brain. He was attracted to her, both physically and emotionally. He had lost the love of his life eleven years earlier, and it had taken him nearly that long to accept the possibility that perhaps he could be happy with someone else. But there were proprieties; he wasn't a teenage boy lusting after a picture in a magazine. Amanda was more than just a pretty face, and the connection that he had hoped for extended far deeper than a superficial physical tryst.

His breathing and pulse slowed, and with an effort he mentally shelved the experience, noting that this particular shelf was getting crowded with unexplained experiences. He turned back to the matter at hand. He weighed the options while waiting for his corporal to confirm what he had already suspected. His phone rang again.

"Yes," he said, more like his usual self.

"Dr. Martin carried a biohazard box with him and refused to have it searched. He did present the appropriate clearances for the material and was allowed to pass."

"Thank you, Corporal." Bennett paused. "What do you suppose is in the box, Corporal Tator?"

"I doubt it's cookies, sir." Now Tator paused. "Would you like me to have him detained?"

"Yes. Inform security that Dr. Martin may be bringing potentially dangerous material into a secure facility, and ask them to detain the good doctor and whatever he is carrying."

"Yes, sir," Tator said enthusiastically. The animosity directed at Martin personally and some of his officious and overbearing staff had filled Tellis like a poisonous gas since they had arrived.

Bennett smiled. Martin's hubris had presented him with a way out of his dilemma. He picked up the phone and hit a single button. "This is Colonel Bennett for General Dixon." He waited for the general's office staff to make the requisite transfers, but instead of the usual two or three exchanges, General Dixon answered himself.

"Bill, I was expecting your call. I'm guessing Dr. Martin has arrived."

"Yes sir, he has, and in his possession is a biomedical container that he refuses to have searched."

"Unfortunately, that is his prerogative. I got a call earlier from the Secretary of Health and Human Services. She reminded me that Dr. Martin is to have unfettered access to Mrs. Flynn. Have you been fettering Dr. Martin when he has tried to access Mrs. Flynn?"

"No sir." Dixon's tone was light and unconcerned and Bennett was worried that he was about to get brushed off. "Sir, I have a concern for her safety."

A short pause and a more typical Walter Dixon answered. "Explain," he ordered.

"I also received a call this morning, from Dr. Martin. He told me that for safety reasons Mrs. Flynn was to be placed back in isolation. The problem is that all of her cultures and tests have been negative." Bennett was talking fast, trying to hook Dixon before the general's notoriously short attention span cut the conversation short. "At this point in time there is no good medical reason to keep Mrs. Flynn, much less isolate her."

"Go on," Dixon nibbled at the hook.

"They have run eighty-nine tests on her, and at last estimate have spent twenty-three million dollars with nothing to show for it."

"The woman is alive, isn't she?" Dixon wasn't going to swallow the hook blindly.

"That is true, sir, but no one can take credit for that. She never exhibited any signs of EDH 1 infection or any other illness. Just as we talked a month ago, there isn't a single reason she couldn't be released back into the public. Dr. Martin's focus from the beginning has not been treatment but an investigation into her resistance to the virus, something that could be just as easily accomplished on an outpatient basis."

"Bill, you know I'm not a physician, so I have to rely upon you folks to do what's right. I can't possibly referee a medical dispute."

"This isn't a medical dispute, sir; this is about ethics and morality."

"I'm sure Dr. Martin would have a different point of view, and he is one of the CDC directors, with the Secretary of Health and Human

Services behind him." Bennett was losing the argument to Martin, who wasn't even on the phone.

"I'm concerned that he intends to inject Mrs. Flynn with a reconstituted virus to gauge her response."

A very long pause followed. "Okay, Bill," he finally said. "You are asking me to climb out on a limb with you, and if I do and you are wrong that will be the end of the both of us and the Combined Services Medical Group." The CSMG was Dixon's pet project, and Bennett was the man he had chosen to create it. "Is your concern strong enough to bear all that weight?"

Bennett sorted through the evidence in his mind. Already the reports of a synthesized EDH 1 were making the medical rounds. In addition, the CDC workers in Tellis had been told that their stay was to be extended and that they were to prepare for a third round of biopsies and testing, which only made sense if the situation had changed. Only nothing had changed, at least not yet. Now Martin was literally on the doorstep with a biohazard container. "It is a very strong circumstantial case, General."

"I need something concrete, Bill."

"Let my lab techs examine what's in his case. If I'm wrong, I will gladly escort him to Amanda and then resign. If I'm right and he infects her, we would be accomplices to her murder."

"That doesn't sound like unfettered access." His tone wasn't as negative as his statement.

"We are all professionals, working to achieve the same thing. What's wrong with a little transparency?"

"That sounds very reasonable, but I've had the displeasure of talking with Dr. Martin, and I don't think reasonability is one of his strong suits. He seems to have a bee in his bonnet about all things military." Dixon paused again. "I want you to escort Dr. Martin to the patient. Allow him to do anything he wants except administer medications to her. I will bump this up the chain one more time. Just so you know, my butt is starting to get a little sore from this entire situation."

It was a middle-ground decision, but one he could live with. He had hoped to escalate the situation that would in the end expose Martin, but Dixon needed to avoid an open conflict between the military and the CDC, which for now had the backing of a Cabinet member. "I appreciate that, sir. There is one more thing: we still have not been given permission to inform the patient's family of her condition."

"This whole situation is starting to stink like a three-day-dead dog." Dixon was a Texas native and dropped in a colloquialism at every opportunity. "I'm starting to share your concern. With one hand he makes this woman disappear, and with the other he convinces his boss to allow him to do anything he wants to her. It's god damn Nazi Germany all over again. You watch that SOB and make sure that he doesn't harm her, and you contact her family, personally. I'm going to put an end to this experiment in intergovernmental cooperation. Good luck, Colonel."

As soon as Bennett had replaced the receiver, it began to ring. "Yes?"

"He's here sir. Security has him in a conference room upstairs, and they tell me that he's quite upset."

"Good. Keep him there. I have one more phone call to make."

***

"Professor?" An overly painted coed ducked her head into Emily Larson's office. "You weren't answering your phone ..."

"For a reason," she said loudly. Emily knew she was hard to work with, and in the rare moment of introspection she vowed to try and change, but this was not one of those moments. She had one inviolate rule: she was not, under any circumstance, ever, to be bothered while she was writing. Years ago she had gone to a graphic designer and had them create a three-foot sign with a large red light attached warning the entire populace to stay out if the light was on. And at this moment the light was most definitely on.

The coed retreated behind the door but didn't close it. "I'm sorry, but there is a telephone call that I think you need to take." Her voice was below the level that only dogs could hear, but not by much.

"Is it the President?" she screamed, without pausing her furious typing.

"No, it's ..."

"Is it Brad Pitt with a marriage proposal?" Her decibels had decreased, but she still threatened to shatter glass.

"No, it's a ..."

"Is it Jesus Christ, Mary, or Joseph?" She stopped typing, and the frustration was evident on her upturned face. "Come out from behind the door; you've already interrupted me," she demanded, and the small girl reappeared. "Do I know you?"

"No ma'am; I'm a work-study student."

"Who is on the phone?" The damage done and her thought lost, she lowered her voice and softened her tone.

"It's an Army officer. He said it was in reference to your niece."

Emily stared blankly. "Amanda?" The name pierced her heart. She had spent a month in Honduras trying to find someone who had any information about the fate of the Red Cross team, but had learned nothing more beyond the official story that all had been lost to a mysterious illness that had also killed more than a thousand Hondurans. Her stony heart had nearly broken when they told her that all the bodies had been destroyed at the site, which was still closed and cordoned off by the military. The US government had very little influence with the Hondurans, and all they could offer were condolences. Rumors of survivors abounded, and the internet was alive with sightings and the secret locations of the survivors. For a time, she and the Flynns—Amanda's in-laws—chased down every lead, but each one came to a dead end. After nearly three months, all her hope had been exhausted and she secretly mourned the loss of her beautiful niece.

"It's line three." The coed quickly closed the door.

"This is Emily Larson," she said.

"Doctor Larson, my name is William Bennett. I am a colonel in the United States Army, and a medical doctor."

"Good for you. What does this have to do with Amanda?" Her suspicion meter was in the red.

"Has anyone informed you of her whereabouts and condition?"

"You sick bastard. I am going to have our campus police track this number and have you arrested." She covered the phone. "Hey kid, whatever your name is, get in here!" she screamed at the door, which opened a moment later as her personal secretary walked in. "Caroline, where have you been? Track this number; it's some asshole asking about Amanda." Caroline hurried off.

"Actually, it's some asshole who is trying to update you about Amanda, but feel free to track the number. If you want I can give it to you." Bennett said after Emily returned to the phone.

"Nice try."

"All right, how about this: do you have internet access?"

"Just keep talking; we'll find you."

"I'm trying to tell you how to find me, if you'll just take a moment and listen. Open your browser and type in this address." Bennett rattled off a series of numbers and letters, and asked Emily to repeat them.

"Combined Services Medical Group," she read from the website. "Never heard of it." She navigated through the site. "And indeed there is a Colonel William Bennett, but that doesn't make him you."

"No, it doesn't, but do you see the 'Contact Us' button? Punch it. See the number? That's the one your police are tracking. Do you want me to wait, do you want to listen, or do you want to call me back?"

"This is very elaborate."

"Put me on hold and call the number. I will have my staff put you right through."

A sliver of hope sliced through her painfully. She had raised Amanda after the death of her mother, when the poor girl was just fourteen. The loss of her niece, Emily's last relative, had been completely devastating, at least by Emily Larson standards. Every moment, thought, and action since had been colored by it, and Emily doubted that would ever change. She quietly put the call on hold and dialed the number.

"Combined Services Medical Group," a male voice answered.

"Well, you are organized, I'll give you that. I would like to speak to the man in charge."

"Certainly, Doctor Larson; he's expecting your call."

"Did I pass?" It was the same voice that called itself Colonel Bennett.

Emily's face immediately flushed and her heart started beating wildly. Hope almost exploded out of her chest, and for a moment Emily had trouble catching her breath. "Where is she?" Her voice cracked with uncharacteristic emotion.

"She is back in the United States and by all accounts is doing well …" Bennett tried to continue, but Emily was flooding the phone with loud sobbing interspersed with inarticulate words and the occasional "Thank God." She went on for more than a minute.

"So, she is alive?"

"She is alive. I saw her earlier today." His confirmation prompted another emotional outburst, but it lasted only about half as long as the first. "I know that this has to be quite a shock to you."

Suddenly, Professor Emily Larson returned. "Where has she been? Why weren't we informed? How did …"

It was Bennett's turn to interrupt. "She has been in strict quarantine in a US military facility. The Centers for Disease Control and Prevention has been directing her care."

"That still doesn't explain why none of us were informed of her whereabouts. For Christ's sake, you let us believe that she was dead. Do you have any idea what we have been through? It's unconscionable!"

"I agree, but it was not my decision. Technically I am violating an executive order by contacting you."

Emily's anger slipped into neutral as she digested what Bennett had just said. "The CDC, huh. Bureaucrats masquerading as doctors."

"Not all of them," Bennett said. "At the moment," he said with emphasis, "she is under the care of Doctor Nathan Martin, Director of the Special Pathogens Department. It is my suspicion that not many people outside of that department are aware that she has been held for nearly three months. Perhaps if more people were aware, her current situation would improve."

"And I gather that you are not in a position to do that."

"Doctor Larson, I am simply making a call that should have been made a long time ago, and informing you of your niece's unique situation."

"Did anyone else survive?"

"No," he said definitively. Emily's mind pushed aside the elation, relief, and joy and began to sort through the logistics.

"Well, I can sure as hell make people aware. I think I'll start with the senior senator from Georgia; Saxby Chambliss just happens to be a friend of mine." She shifted mental gears again. "When can I see her?"

"Only after she is released."

"Son of a bitch!" Emily cursed. "All right, when can I talk with her?"

"I believe that I can help you with that. It may take an hour or so to arrange."

"Good. I will call you back at this number in one hour, and I swear before God that if you are not who you say you are and this is some elaborate hoax I will hunt you down like a dog."

"I would expect nothing less, Doctor Larson. Call me back in one hour."

Emily slowly hung the phone up. She tried to temper her joy with the possibility that Bennett either wasn't Bennett and/or couldn't produce what he promised, but her heart and thoughts raced wildly. She stared at the phone and focused on the speed button labeled "Flynn." She debated whether to call Lisa and Greg. They had stayed in Honduras weeks after she returned home, hoping to find someone who knew firsthand what had happened, and finally left with nothing more than official apologies. Lisa had taken the loss of Amanda hard. Coming almost a year after losing her son and grandson, she had aged ten years in the past three months. She would greet the news with uncontrolled emotion and Emily was afraid for Lisa if things didn't turn out well. She decided to wait, and turned her mind to what it was best at: getting things done.

It took her less than five minutes to track down the senator and get him on the phone. "Senator, I need your help," she said.

***

In at least one way, Amanda was glad to be back in the cell. Her head throbbed, and the isolation afforded her sore brain the opportunity to rest, away from the unguarded minds that surrounded her. It had been hours since she had been escorted from the dorm room that had served as her home for nearly a week, and after settling back in, everything had come to a halt. She was alone; the observation room beyond the glass was as empty as the monitoring room above. She stared at the cameras that had recorded her every move for almost three months, but they too seemed to have been forgotten. For the first time in weeks her mind was free of other voices, except one.

William Bennett still floated through her consciousness. Their encounter had formed a mental connection that tugged at her, inviting her to continue the exploration of his mind. And perhaps a little more.

After their initial encounter, Amanda allowed herself to glide across their bridge three more times. Her first trip was little more than a quick glance. Frightened by their original encounter, as soon as she felt the pull of his mind towards hers she quickly retreated back into herself. But even as she fled the attraction tore at her, threatening to once again merge their two consciousnesses. After a moment of confusion, she was fully back to herself, but Bennett's presence was all around her. She could feel his frustration and concern, and a warm flush filled her as she realized that she was the focus. His coherent thoughts began to fade, but his emotions lingered.

Their second encounter was initiated by Bennett. Amanda felt his mind reach for hers; it was as if his lingering mental presence coalesced into a metaphoric tap on her shoulder and her mind reflexively turned towards it. In an instant Amanda was swept up into the strange blending of their identities, but this time she was able to maintain a small degree of mental cohesion. She flowed through him with a distinct awareness of her own individuality, and then he suddenly severed their link, leaving her breathless and mildly disoriented.

She recovered much faster that time and marveled at the power of their connection. She had just experienced what it was like to be William Bennett in high definition, and began to wonder if the intensity was unique to them or if it was the natural state. Bennett was attracted to her, and in her own way Amanda was attracted to Bennett. Did that influence the power of their connection? Or more basic still, was the desire to merge, to lose oneself in another, unique to them as a couple, or the natural reaction any mind had when the confining barriers were removed? That was a more interesting question. If all the barriers were removed, and everyone could do what she could do, what would become of humanity?

Her mood immediately darkened with the thought that others might learn to duplicate her secret. It was hers, and hers alone, and she did not want to share. She enjoyed her secret intrusions.

Bennett's mind tapped her on the shoulder again, and she felt his presence stream through her body and soul. It beckoned to her and initially she resisted its pull, but he was insistent. Her mind kept slipping towards his and then righting itself. Their tug of war continued until Amanda reached a flash point. A swell of emotional energy surged through her, and the idea of hurting Bennett was suddenly very appealing. Amanda let go and shot into his mind. Immediately a whirlwind threatened her identity, but anger insulated her. She sliced through Bennett's thin layer of conscious thought and dove to his core. She had never been this deep before, and like a thief in the night she explored the inner workings of another human being.

She had no expectations but was quickly disillusioned. On the surface, William Bennett was calm, cool, and collected, but beneath it he was a raging tempest of sublimated memories, thoughts, and ideas. Amanda began to feel betrayed as Bennett's deepest instincts and repulsive desires flowed over her and made her face burn. Everything about him was a lie. The foundation his life had been built upon was nothing more than a sewer, and his handsome smiling face, his simple morality, his chivalrous behavior, were all affectations, parts of a facade that hid the filth beneath.

Afraid that Bennett's perversions would somehow contaminate her, Amanda pulled back into herself but didn't completely leave his mind. She knew that she could do more than just sift through the life and times of William Bennett. She was a physical presence, and like a computer virus in a mainframe she could wreak havoc. She had the ability to control him or to hurt him. One of her own deepest and darkest desires began to pulse with life, and she realized that she wanted to control Bennett. She wanted to hurt him. She tried to resist the seductive step away from sanity and to dispassionately examine her motivations, but her reasoning powers had been corrupted. She wanted to hurt Bennett because she could, because it would be fun, because she wanted to. Her desire grew into a need that demanded release. Pressure to hurt the man began to build in Amanda's mind but she couldn't release it. She couldn't pull the trigger that would give her blessed relief. A single thought restrained her.

Despite what's beneath, William Bennett is a good man.

Most of her mind wouldn't recognize, much less acknowledge, that inconvenient fact. The compulsion to control, punish, and inflict pain strained against that single truth, but it was unbreakable. The moment passed and a slightly disappointed Amanda retreated back into herself.

An hour later she sat in her bed, her mind in neutral and thoughts of William Bennett turned down low. The realization that she had the capacity to commit unwarranted acts of extreme violence was causing surprisingly little emotional dissonance. She had in the end controlled the seductive desires. She refused to explore the logical extension of her rationalization and instead waited for Nathan Martin. Bennett had been ordered to protect her, but she didn't think it would be necessary.

CHAPTER 23

"I'm glad you're here, Colonel—oh sorry," Leo Arguerra said as Bennett walked into the monitoring room. His comment was cut short as Dr. Martin followed.

"Leo, right?" Bennett asked the CDC employee.

"Yes, sir," he addressed the colonel and nervously nodded at Martin, his boss. "I think the monitors are broken," he said, and moved to one side, letting the two new arrivals have a clear view of the three monitors that recorded Amanda's activities.

"They seem to be working just fine," Martin said gruffly. A different perspective of Amanda Flynn filled each screen.

"Just wait," the second tech said, without turning away from the monitors. The four men watched for almost a minute before Amanda turned and faced one of the cameras directly. After a moment, the middle screen turned blue and a message appeared: "No Input." Ten seconds later, Amanda reappeared, her back against the wall and her legs stretched the length of her bed. She smiled and turned to the second camera and the monitor to the right flashed, went blue, and then an image reappeared seconds later.

"This is starting to get real creepy," the second monitor tech said.

"It's been doing this since we turned them back on," Arguerra said.

"Turn them off," Martin said dismissively, and started towards the stairwell and the isolation room.

"It's okay; turn them off. Give us ten minutes, gentlemen, then resume your duties." They stared at Bennett for an instant and then left quickly, neither wanting to be privy to the inevitable confrontation.

The metal stairway clattered as first Martin and then a moment later Bennett descended to the observation room. Martin walked to the window and stared at Amanda, who seemed to be staring right back. "Colonel, do you know who Mary Mallon was?"

"Typhoid Mary? Your justification for what you've done and are about to do is Typhoid Mary?" Bennett turned and faced the smaller man, who continued to study Amanda.

"I'm not justifying anything. I am simply having a conversation while we wait for the secretary to order the general to let me do my job."

"Your job does not include purposely infecting an American citizen with a known lethal pathogen."

"Mary Mallon infected 53 people with Typhus. Three of those people died. The State of New York felt that she posed such a danger to the health and welfare of the people that they deprived her of her liberty for the rest of her life. Now, instead of Typhus, imagine if she carried EDH 1, a pathogen thousands of times more infectious and lethal. This one individual could potentially kill millions, possibly more."

"Mary Mallon refused to be tested, and when she died was found to have active bacteria in her gallbladder. Amanda Flynn has done nothing but cooperate. You have put her through 89 different studies, and each one has been negative. Eighty-nine," he repeated slowly. "There is not a physician or a court in this land that would believe that she poses a risk, and you know it. This is all a pretext to justify re-exposing her."

"I think I see the problem here. You have made the assumption that I am going to re-expose her to the EDH 1 virus," Martin said, as if he genuinely believed that their disagreement was based solely on a misunderstanding. "I would never think of exposing her to such a risk. What I have here is a nascent vaccine. We have removed all genetic and infectious material and have only the viral coat proteins. Her immune system will respond to them as it would if this were the real virus, giving us the opportunity to define her resistance."

"Is that how you sold this?" Bennett was incredulous. "That what you're doing poses no threat?" Martin had finally turned towards Bennett, who fought to restrain himself. He wanted to rip the case from Martin's hand and inject him with his nascent vaccine.

"The threat is negligible and justified," Martin said smugly, and now Bennett wanted to simply punch him in the face.

"Listen, you can lie to whomever you want, but don't lie to me. You have no idea what's in your nascent vaccine, and we both know that preserving the viral proteins while eliminating any infective material is an impossibility. If any genetic material was missed the viral particles will auto-assemble and you will be injecting her with live virus."

"I have more faith in our ability to separate proteins from nucleic acids."

"That is bullshit and we both know it. Did you run this by Stanley Cripps?"

"My predecessor is no longer involved in this case."

"So you got rid of anyone who would know better. Did you test this in culture or any animal testing?"

"I do not answer to you, Colonel, but in the spirit of cooperation I will tell you that we have done both, and this vaccine has proven to be safe."

Bennett knew that Martin was probably not lying completely. It was likely that some form of testing had been done, but it was equally likely that those tests had not had enough time to prove that the vaccine was unequivocally safe. He would have more respect for Martin if he openly admitted that he wasn't certain that the vaccine was safe, but that it was a calculated risk. Amanda's immune system had already faced the mature and deadly form of the virus and had somehow contained or destroyed it. In all likelihood it would respond vigorously when re-exposed to the virus or even to its proteins. In theory, Amanda's cells would destroy EDH 1 just as effectively as they would a common flu virus.

But there were a thousand "what-ifs" that normally gave pause to an ethical researcher. What if injecting the virus, instead of contracting the infection through touch or respiration, allowed the infection to spread faster than her immune system could mount a response? What if she had never been infected in the first place and had simply been a statistical anomaly? What if she had only limited immunity, like some develop with the chicken-pox virus? Re-exposure would then be lethal. What if Martin's reconstituted virus had mutated and her previous immunity offered no defense? What if they were incapable of determining her resistance? What if her resistance was idiosyncratic, unique to her and not applicable to others? He could stand here and rattle off a dozen other possibilities that had already been given the official brush-off. His only hope, short of physically barring Martin access to Amanda—a thought that prompted a smile—was that General Dixon could talk some sense into Martin's boss's boss. As if on cue, his phone began to vibrate.

"Sorry Bill; it's a no-go. The Secretary, the head of the CDC, everybody agrees with Martin. The Chairman of the Joint Chiefs has ordered that you stand down."

"General, begging your pardon, but you, the Chairman, even the Secretary, have no idea what he intends to do, or why he's doing it."

"Bill, this is not my first rodeo. Martin is replacing a legend, and he wants to pull an Aaron Rodgers. He wants to one-up Professor Cripps, and he sees Mrs. Flynn as his ticket. I think everyone knows that, but his point that she could help a lot of people is rather compelling." Bennett silently cursed. "They've taken it out of my hands, Bill. They wanted you replaced, but I think they'll accept you taking a vacation, at least until all of this is over."

It dawned on Bennett that maybe the Director of the CDC and the Secretary of Health and Human Services weren't so naïve. Martin had played his role well; he maneuvered anyone who could offer any resistance off into the wings and then promised his masters that he could deliver the medical breakthrough of the century, with all the attendant acclaim. All they had to do was to run interference for him as he performed a harmless medical procedure on a woman who by all accounts should have already died. The unspoken bonus was that if there was an adverse outcome there was no one left to say that it wasn't from her initial exposure. It was all so nice and tidy, with Bennett as the single loose string. "So you want me to hand over the keys to the place and go to the beach." He had taken several steps away from Martin and kept his voice low.

"Basically," Dixon answered ruefully.

"General, we didn't build this program just to turn it over to some amoral asshole out to make a name for himself." Bennett's voice was beginning to rise and he no longer cared if Martin heard him.

"I understand that, Bill, and I am in your corner. The problem is that I don't have enough stars on my shoulder. I am asking you as a friend and ordering you as your commanding officer to walk away. Let this one go."

"So you are ordering me to allow a government employee to administer a potentially lethal injection to a US citizen without her knowledge or consent."

"This isn't my order, Colonel." The discussion took a decidedly formal turn. "It is the order of our Commander in Chief."

"It is an illegal order, General, and you know it."

"Every soldier must make that determination for themselves, and I would recommend that you make it quickly." Dixon's tone had a subtle undercurrent of conspiracy.

Bennett was about to respond when the sound of boots on the metal stairway made him turn his head. He watched as his chief of security approached, the weight of the world balanced on his shoulders.

"I am sorry, sir, but you will have to come with me."

"I'm sorry, Bill. I didn't think they would move so quickly," General Dixon spoke into Bennett's ear.

"Captain Lewis, why have you brought a firearm into my facility?" Bennett addressed the base's chief of security as if he were a raw recruit.

"I have been ordered to escort you to your office, sir."

Martin turned to face Bennett. "For what it's worth, I do admire your ideals. It's sad that there is no real world application for them."

Bennett took a breath and turned towards Amanda. Once again she seemed to be staring right back at him, almost through him. "Thank you, General," he said, and closed his phone abruptly. A strange sense of calm descended as Amanda's crystal-blue eyes seemed to fill his mind. "Captain, a moment please," he said, briefly turning to the security chief and then back to Martin. He had a hundred things he wanted to say, but rejected them all. From two feet away Bennett's right fist shot into Martin's upturned chin. The smaller man's head snapped back with enough force to propel him backwards into the corner sink. The porcelain struck him mid-back, arcing his spine until the back of his head struck the wall with a resounding thud. On the way to the floor, his head caught the edge of the sink, whiplashing his chin into his chest.

"That's going to leave a mark," the captain said with a deadpan expression.

"I expect you to report exactly what you saw, Captain."

"I saw Dr. Martin slip on the polished floor, striking his head on the sink, sir." He smiled at his colleague. "I must say, sir, you really laid him out."

"Never do anything halfway."

"You son of a bitch," Martin spat his bloody words at Bennett as he tried to scramble to his feet.

"I warn you, Martin, this floor is very slippery. You could slip again. Now, you just sit there and wait while I go find you some medical attention. It shouldn't be more than an hour." He turned to Captain Lewis. "Do you have a detail upstairs?"

"Yes, sir."

"Bring someone down here and have them watch the doctor. I believe that he may have sustained a head injury and shouldn't be allowed to walk."

CHAPTER 24

Amanda had witnessed the entire encounter from Bennett's perspective. She had wanted him to hit Martin from the instant she felt his mind draw near, and was fairly certain that she had nudged Bennett in that direction. She rubbed her right hand and the lingering sting that she shared with Bennett. She couldn't remember ever striking someone in anger, and the experience left something to be desired. For one thing it hurt, and even Bennett, his mind receding into the distance and into the white noise of a hundred other minds, was wondering if he had cracked a metacarpal on Martin's chin. For another, it did nothing to relieve the pressure that was once again building inside her—the same pressure that had nearly compelled her to hurt Bennett. Martin saw her as an expendable asset, a thing to be used for his advantage. His very presence stoked a firestorm of emotions that needed to be vented, and she wanted to lash out. She indulged herself as wonderfully violent images played through her mind.

Make it happen, a voice, the very essence of seduction, whispered from the darkness. It wasn't the first time the alien voice had offered advice. Amanda had heard its whispers for weeks now. *Lose yourself.* As much as she wanted to deny it, the darkness and its voice were and had always been a part of her. It wasn't alien; it was homegrown. More than twenty years of societal pressures and learning how to be a "good girl" had silenced it, but now it had recovered its voice and strength. But it was still innocent, still a small child. It had encouraged her to hurt Bennett only because it didn't know better. She had to teach it, direct it, and when appropriate, use it.

"Not yet," Amanda whispered to herself.

After Bennett had left, Amanda's view of the observation room became poor. The strong emotions that fueled and emanated from the darkness in her mind obscured its vision. She tried to find Martin in the chorus that sang in her head, but her energized mind lacked the focus. It kept defaulting to Bennett, whose voice was remote but recognizable. She closed her eyes and willed herself to focus, but her mental stream kept diverting down the well-worn groove to William Bennett. After countless futile efforts she finally relented, and his familiar mind seemed to flow around her. Hoping that her mental spelunking would slow her racing thoughts, she decided to camp out in his mind, but the memory of Emily Larson suddenly flooded her thoughts. In details too real for life, she saw her aunt's university photograph on Bennett's desktop computer and heard her strained voice in his ear. He had talked with her and she was coming. The possibility that this nightmare could be over so suddenly added to her emotional energy, and she very nearly missed Nathan Martin opening the outer airlock.

Her mind whipped back to the present and her mental focus became sharp as a knife. With almost no effort, she sliced into Martin's mind with all the force she could generate. It was a purely instinctive reaction to what her darkness had perceived as a mortal threat. It took her conscious mind half a second to realize that she had overshot the mark. The last thing she heard was Martin's scream as his body hit the floor. She awoke moments later, her head throbbing worse than earlier. For the second time in a day she learned that the mental connection was reciprocal. Too much force and it would rebound back into her.

Amanda felt and heard Martin groan as he regained a painful level of consciousness. His head, back, and chin all hurt, and now Amanda's head, back, and chin throbbed as well. This physical reciprocity was one aspect that she could do without. He climbed to his feet and slowly began to don the very familiar white isolation suit. He was clumsy at first but then managed to relearn to use his limbs and digits. He kicked the biohazard box with a gowned shoe and cursed as his foot now began to ache.

"Open the airlock," his muffled voice said, and Amanda heard the metallic click. Before he could open the airtight door it clicked a second time. He tripped into the locked door.

"Very funny; now open the airlock." The door clicked again, and then just as quickly the locks re-engaged.

"I am starting to become annoyed." Martin's voice was loud enough to penetrate the sealed chamber.

Click. Click.

"Who the hell is up there?" Martin was punching the intercom button.

"The locks keep re-engaging, Dr. Martin."

"Check to make sure that the airflow is reversed; the door can't be opened otherwise." Amanda heard the cutting and cynical comments that Martin left unsaid. His thoughts opened up before her and she saw a series of relays and pumps. She focused on the largest pump and imagined it suddenly grounding to a halt in a flurry of sparks and smoke. "God damn it, you just shut down all the air!"

She had just shorted out a pump she had never seen, and had done it with a simple thought! The realization that her thoughts could translate into physical effects overshadowed everything. Her mind reeled with possibilities. She focused on the plastic chair at the foot of her bed and imagined it sliding across the floor, and an instant later it slammed into the wall. Amanda squealed in joy and began to laugh. She turned on the television, then all the lights in her room, then turned them all off. Not a soul was watching her. They were all focused on Martin and his plight.

"I could kill him!" she thought. A vision of Nathan Martin being thrown around the small access chamber, his body rebounding like a basketball off the walls, the floor and the roof. "No one would know!"

"Dr. Martin, we don't have access to the air pumps. They're regulated automatically by the computer. You might want to think about getting out of there, because the recirculation pump is about to kick on and evacuate that chamber."

"What?" Martin screamed.

"The computer is reading that the inner door has been opened and that there is a containment breech. It will send all the air in there through the filters and replace it with fresh air; only, the fresh air pump is the one that just failed. Is your suit intact?"

Amanda felt Martin search the polypropylene suit and find a two-inch cut just above his shoe. A small line of blood ran down the fabric. "No, I have a tear in it just above my ankle. I accidentally kicked the box I was carrying." A pump cycled on and a loud whistling filled Martin's ears and Amanda's mind.

"Dr. Martin, get out of the suit and release the inner lock manually. You have only a few seconds before that chamber is evacuated of air. Once that happens the doors will not open."

Martin frantically pulled at the hood and zipper but his fingers weren't working fast enough. He started screaming to turn off the pump, but his voice was lost in the loud whistling as air was sucked out of the small access chamber and into the ceiling vents.

He was going to die in that tiny little chamber, and Amanda was going to happily watch the whole thing. It was the ultimate in poetic justice. On his way to kill her he dies in an industrial accident of his own making. Of course, it wasn't entirely of his making, but no one could prove that.

Martin banged on the door loud enough for it to resonate through her cell, and Amanda's mind. "Fuck," she whispered to herself and turned away, but his pleading consciousness pulled at her.

Just let it happen, her dark voice whispered.

I can't just let him die, she answered.

Why not?

Because it's wrong. She rolled off the bed and pulled at the airlock door. The magnetic clamps immediately released, and a gust of air knocked her into the struggling Martin. The whistling took on a lower pitch as the pump no longer strained to suck out every last molecule of breathable air. He had torn off the hood of the suit and his blood-red face was inches from hers. "Next time, I let you die," she said, pushing away his arm as he tried to use her for support.

***

"Why did you let him in there, Corporal?" Captain Lewis's eyes drilled the young soldier to the wall. "You were ordered to watch him."

"He said that he had authority. When I refused him access he made several calls and General Macintyre ordered me to allow him to proceed." The corporal stood at attention before his captain and the colonel, who towered over both of them.

"What happened in there, soldier?" Colonel Bennett asked.

"The doctor was trapped inside the access chamber when one of the recirculation pumps failed. He was suffocating and I couldn't get to him. The locks were engaged and then the doors wouldn't open with the vacuum. She opened the far hatch."

Both of the officers stared at the young man and then at Amanda, who had returned to her bed. Her arms were folded across her chest as she waited for someone to remember her. "So the patient, that small woman in there, opened up the door when you couldn't?"

"Yes, sir." His embarrassment was overshadowed by his confusion.

"You're dismissed, Corporal," Lewis said and then turned to the colonel. "Same story as Martin's monitoring technicians. An accident."

"Only, it doesn't feel like an accident, and if the monitors hadn't been running it would be hard to convince anyone that it was," Bennett said to his security chief.

Nathan Martin sat on a stool, his head propped against the glass as one EMT administered oxygen while another took his blood pressure. He had a blank look on his face that was accentuated by wide, empty eyes. "He looks like he's had a concussion," Lewis said to Bennett.

Martin turned his head slowly. "I fell on the slippery floor." He stared up at the two officers. "I think I hit my head."

"Better get him a CT scan," Bennett said, and a moment later his cell phone rang. "Colonel Bennett," he answered after taking an imperceptible centering breath.

"Bennett, where's Dr. Martin? I've been calling his phone for twenty minutes."

"He is sitting right next to me, General Macintyre. He's had something of an accident." He passed the phone to a stunned-looking Martin, who for a moment appeared as if he couldn't remember how the device worked.

"Hello?" Martin's blank face began to register confusion. "No, I didn't call you. I don't even know who you are." Martin listened for several seconds. "No one hit me, and I didn't call you. What do you want?" His baseline personality began to resurface. "Here, he wants to talk to you." He passed the phone back to Bennett.

"Yes, General."

"That man is absolutely certifiable." He huffed and then cleared his throat. "I understand that the two of you disagree on the management of your patient."

Bennett registered the change in Amanda's ownership. "Actually, sir, we have not disagreed an iota about her treatment, as she has required none. We do, however, strongly disagree about the ethics of human experimentation." Macintyre was a four-star general and the commander of the US Army, next in line for the chairmanship of the Joint Chiefs of Staff, but Bennett couldn't resist the opportunity to make his point.

"What's the status of the patient?"

"She is alive and well. Dr. Martin managed to nearly asphyxiate himself trying to re-infect her. Ironically, she was the one who saved his life."

Macintyre huffed again. "Colonel, I understand that this has been difficult for you. A commanding officer who is also a physician will invariably be placed in situations of conflicting loyalties." Bennett waited for an apology he knew would never come. "I would like you to collect Dr. Martin and his staff and have them escorted off of the base. Dr. Martin's access has been revoked."

The general allowed him a moment and Bennett took it. "What's happened, General?"

A longer moment followed, and Bennett began to worry that his single question was one too many. "I suppose you deserve an explanation. After all, I did fire you for doing your duty." He huffed for a third time. "Conflicting loyalties, Colonel. Our Commander in Chief had a sudden change in heart after he had a chat with a ranking member of the Senate. I doubt very many people would vote for a man who authorized the incarceration of a woman whose only crime was surviving."

"I would agree, sir."

"When you feel that this young lady is safe to be released, you release her. The records of her treatment are to be sealed and classified as Top Secret. Am I understood, Colonel?"

"Perfectly, sir."

"One more thing."

"Yes, sir?"

"Did you strike Dr. Martin?"

"I'm afraid that information is classified, General."

Macintyre laughed. "Well done, Colonel."

CHAPTER 25

It was a hug that threatened to go on forever, and each time Amanda tried to pull away her aunt only squeezed tighter. "I thought I lost you" was interspersed with "Don't you ever do that to me again."

"I don't think you have to worry about that." Amanda finally pulled away.

"I am so angry! You've been here the whole time? An hour away from home?" Colonel Bennett had allowed Emily onto the base for a quiet reunion.

"Most of it," Amanda answered. For the first time in almost four months, Amanda was dressed like a real person, and Emily plucked some lint from her sleeve.

"When we get out of here, I'll take you for some new clothes," Emily said, her face red and wet.

"You're going to go shopping, for clothes?" Amanda teased.

"Just this once," and she gave Amanda another hug. A tiny electrical buzz played across Amanda's skin; at first it had been slightly uncomfortable but now it was almost inviting. Emily abruptly pushed away and dried her tears with a handful of tissues. "Let's get the hell out of here," she said, very much like the Emily Larson that had raised Amanda. Emotions made her uncomfortable, and a public display of emotion was almost a singular event. "Where are your things?"

"They're all gone." A distant vision of a large fire in the middle of a Honduran field suddenly interrupted Amanda's stream of thought.

"Bastards probably burned everything," Emily swore. "Someone needs to be held accountable for this fiasco." A righteously indignant Emily Larson was a happy Emily Larson.

"I need to thank someone before we go."

"Okay," she said slowly, turning Amanda transparent with her patented x-ray gaze. "Thank the colonel for me as well." She smiled and winked as Amanda turned towards the door of the rec room. "See if you can find us something to eat. Crying makes me hungry."

***

"Come in, Amanda," Colonel Bennett said a moment after she knocked on his office door.

The energy of his thoughts bumped a quantum level as she walked into his office. "So that's what you look like in real clothes. I must say I approve." She did a little curtsy for him and flashed her thousand-watt smile. She didn't need her ability to sense the expectation in the room, and the darkness in her mind began to stir. William Bennett was a good-looking man, no matter his age. In fact, the slight grey at his temples and the crow's feet only enhanced his chiseled features. His broad shoulders and chest stretched his perfectly pressed uniform, and on more than one occasion she had admired the view as she watched him walk away.

"I just wanted to thank you for everything that you did for me." Her mouth was becoming a little dry and her heart was racing. The darkness began to swirl a little faster, stripping her of restraint. Flashes of their entwined, naked, and sweaty bodies pulsed through her.

"Of course." He rose from his desk and offered her a seat with a hand gesture. He rounded his desk just as she reached the office chair, and for an instant they were only inches apart. Amanda's breath caught as his aura brushed through hers. "I'm glad you came by. I was hoping to discuss something with you," he said as he sat on the corner of his desk.

"Yes," Amanda answered, barely understanding his words. She was consumed by desire and offered very little resistance. Reason, propriety, logistics—everything faded into the background as an animal lust raced through her being. A primal need, more powerful than anything she had ever felt with her husband, drove her to the edge of her seat. Without her even being aware of it, her hand had found his knee. She wasn't interested in making love. She wanted sex in its most base form. Pounding, thrusting, scratching, hair-pulling sex.

"Are you all right, Amanda?" Bennett asked, completely oblivious to her condition. "You seem distracted." He looked at her hand on his knee.

"I'm fine," she struggled to say, but kept her hand in place. Only a lifetime of conditioning stopped her from attacking him. She had always been the passive partner in previous sexual experiences, but being the aggressor seemed so much more natural and exciting. She watched herself tear off his shirt, handcuffing his arms behind his back as she raped him on his desk. She closed her eyes briefly and shifted in her chair.

"When you arrived here ..." His hand covered hers, pinning it in place. The contact with his skin burned for a moment, which only stoked the fire that blazed within her. "You were a very different person. Taking into account all that had happened to you, it wasn't surprising to find that you seemed somewhat lost ..."

A beautifully detailed hallucination filled Amanda's mind and obscured everything Bennett said. She was naked and bent over his desk, their clothes thrown into a corner. Bennett was behind her and deep inside, grunting as he pounded away. She was screaming words she had never even whispered, encouraging him to take her to new heights. She felt her bare breasts grating against the top of his desk and only wanted more.

"... vulnerable and fragile," he continued as Amanda's mind drove her towards orgasm. "But something about you has changed. I would like you to level with me and tell me honestly what happen yesterday with Dr. Martin." He paused, as Amanda's eyes had closed and her face creased in pain. The hand on his thigh began to squeeze and then it released. "Amanda, what's wrong?" He quickly moved to her side and felt her glistening neck for her pulse. Her body shivered several times and then she opened her eyes.

At first she was lost, and surprised to find Colonel Bennett at her side, and then the memory flooded back. The desire had faded but not dissipated, and she felt it rise again as his hand swept a lock of sweaty hair from her cheek. She flushed, and a muted whisper of shame echoed in her mind, but it was quickly replaced by loud cries of delight. She had just had an orgasm inches from the man she had fantasized about. A deep, soul-shattering orgasm that left her feeling wonderfully nasty and dirty. "I'm okay," she said, taking his hand and staring deep into his eyes. Her mind started to slide into his and she felt his pull. He kissed her, gently at first, and then with more urgency.

"This is so wrong," he whispered, and her arms snaked around his neck. He lifted her out of the chair and they renewed the kiss. Her legs wrapped around his midsection as he turned and gently lowered her to his desk. "Unprofessional," he managed to say just before he tore open her blouse and began to smother her heaving breasts. His shirt was off, thrown into a corner; in an instant the rest of their clothes were gone, along with his remaining restraint. She clung to him, nails in his back, as he entered her with an urgency that no force could deny. She screamed in his ear as he buried himself body and soul into this woman half his age. Then she was on top of him, leaning low to give him her breasts, as she drove her pelvis into his. He found himself standing, his hands on her hips, her body bent over his desk. He was grunting like an animal and she was screaming in ecstasy. They dissolved into each other and into the moment with only fragmentary thoughts of mutual pleasure.

***

"It's been an hour and a half," Emily accused Amanda.

"Sorry, we had something that needed to be worked out." Amanda had done the best she could at repairing herself. She didn't care if the rest of the world knew what had just happened, she just didn't want Emily to know.

Emily appraised her niece with a long stare, and Amanda's heart dropped when Emily's mind drew the correct conclusion. "I'm sure you did," was all she said.

CHAPTER 26

"Lisa, I can go to the grocery store on my own." Amanda had been back in Colorado Springs for two weeks, and Greg, Lisa, and Emily had taken turns making sure that she stayed within their collective sight. It was Emily's final night in Colorado, and before she flew back home the Flynns insisted on a memorable send-off.

"I know you can, but I need to pick up a few things as well," Lisa said. She and Greg were as much of an open book as Emily had proven to be, and Amanda easily sensed the white lie. "Besides, it will be good for us to have some alone time."

Spending two weeks in close quarters with her three surviving family members had been difficult on many levels. The Flynns didn't have a big house; it had three bedrooms and two baths, one of which Amanda shared with Aunt Emily, who demanded a degree of cleanliness that would put most operating rooms to shame. The proximity also made it difficult for Greg, a lifelong Democrat, and Emily, a staunch conservative, to maintain a respectable distance while the news was on, or after the newspaper was delivered. Amanda could deal with the cramped quarters, her aunt cleaning up after her, and the occasional loud "discussions" between Emily and Greg; what she couldn't deal with was the three of them constantly in her mind. At Tellis there were places that offered a degree of isolation and mental rest, something not available in a twenty-five-hundred-square-foot house occupied by three other adults. Slowly, she had been learning how to turn down their mental volume, but sometimes despite her best efforts the volume knob got stuck on eleven.

It wasn't entirely bad. The proximity allowed her to amass a good deal more information about the inner workings of the human mind, and Amanda came away surprised that sanity was so prevalent. The maelstrom of sublimated thoughts and dark desires that Amanda had witnessed in William Bennett seemed to be the norm. An individual was defined by how well they insulated themselves from these universal base instincts, and not by their simple presence. Everyone, including Lisa, the most virtuous person Amanda had ever known, carried them.

Fifteen minutes later Lisa was behind the wheel of her Ford Explorer, with Amanda strapped in the passenger seat and braced for the inevitable onslaught. "Have you been thinking about what we talked about earlier?"

No, but you have, Amanda's darkside answered. Two weeks in a loving environment had allowed it to mature a degree. No longer a child with impulse control issues, it had grown into a rather temperamental adolescent that required attention periodically, otherwise it would manifest itself in some creative ways. "I don't need to talk to anyone, Lisa."

Apparently Lisa didn't like Amanda's answer, as she abruptly pulled the Explorer into the parking lot of an antique store. "I don't think these guys sell butter, Lisa."

Lisa shoved the transmission into park and took a deep breath before turning to Amanda. "Something happened to you down there; everyone but you can see that."

Not true, her mind answered. I see it quite well.

"Even Emily, a charter member of the 'pack-up-all-your-troubles-in-your-own-kit-bag' club, thinks you need some help."

"I don't think that's how it goes, Lisa." Amanda smiled, but Lisa wasn't going to be put off with a little charm and levity.

"What's the harm in talking with someone?"

"It makes me uncomfortable," Amanda said. *And angry, and you wouldn't like me when I'm angry*, her mental adolescent added.

"I understand that, but a lot of things make people uncomfortable, and they still do them because they are necessary."

"I think you've been around Aunt Emily a little too much." Amanda's voice had taken on an overly playful tone, courtesy of her dark friend.

"I don't think this is funny." Lisa had become serious as a tax audit.

"Boy, now you really sound like her," Amanda said, laughing as her mental controls slipped into the darkness.

"This is the very thing we're all worried about. You aren't yourself. You're not even somebody I recognize." The pain in Lisa's voice brought Amanda back into the light.

"I think you're overstating the issue," she said, knowing that if Lisa knew just how close she had come to the truth they would be on their way to a hospital, or a mental institution. Amanda had become somebody that even she had a hard time recognizing. Her id was roaming freely in the guise of an adolescent voice that whispered—but more often yelled—from the dark recesses of her mind, and like a permissive parent Amanda rarely challenged it. She had tested the limits of her old personality and found them unnecessarily restricting, choosing instead to be loud, forceful, and often profane. For the first time in her life she was indulging her own desires and needs and questioning anything that threatened to contain them.

"It terrifies me to think of you on your own," Lisa continued.

"You know I can't stay with you forever, Lisa." This was their other point of contention. Greg and Lisa insisted that Amanda take more time before getting on with her life. Even Emily had offered her home for more recuperation.

"Two weeks is hardly enough time to regain your perspective after everything that's happened." Lisa was reciting her carefully chosen and practiced words cautiously. Amanda couldn't shield herself from Lisa's mental anguish, which was far more persuading than her argument. For now, her bond with Lisa, Greg, and Emily remained strong despite the steady unbraiding of societal bonds, but given time and continued proximity she knew that they too would begin to unravel.

"Two weeks is not a lot of time," Amanda agreed and then paused as she scooted her adolescent companion into a dark recess. With full control over her thoughts and emotions, she took a moment to revisit her greatest dilemma: whether to confide in Lisa or to continue the façade of near-normalcy. From the moment she had met Lisa, almost six years earlier, she knew that she could share anything with her, but this strange and wonderful truth would permanently change that. Their relationship had always been more akin to mother and daughter as opposed to in-laws, resulting in an inherent but subtle inequality. It was a comfortable relationship that even her petulant adolescent didn't want to see altered. "Please don't take offense, Lisa, but staying longer will ultimately make things harder for me."

It was a rare moment as manipulation and truth merged. "No one wants that," Lisa said with a downturned chin. "We just want you to be safe, and happy." She turned towards Amanda and locked eyes. "I want to see joy back in your eyes, not this wild, reckless light that frankly terrifies me."

Amanda tried to hold Lisa's gaze but immediately felt the now-familiar sense of falling as her consciousness tried to merge with Lisa's. The last few weeks had brought a degree of control, but not enough to withstand the powerful emotions that Lisa was experiencing. They would quickly engulf her, and she wouldn't be able to control her struggling mind, putting Lisa in real danger. "Are you afraid for me or others?" she finally asked.

"Both," Lisa answered with a tear rolling down her cheek. "I get the sense that something fundamental in you has changed, that you …" Lisa trailed off.

"Go on," Amanda said, a little too forcefully. Her dark friend was listening.

Lisa shot a quick and disapproving look at her daughter-in-law. "That you don't value life anymore. Yours or others," she said with a mixture of pain, anger, and fear.

Amanda watched as Lisa fiddled with her jacket's zipper. "I haven't told this to anyone, but when I was down in Honduras I killed four men." Amanda continued, despite hearing Lisa's gasp and feeling her emotional start. "Honduran soldiers—they were part of the platoon that was sent to protect us. They were going to kill me, just like they had killed the man next to me. They started shooting and the next thing I know I've got a smoking rifle in my hand and I'm standing over four bodies. Over the past month I've thought about that moment a lot. I think it was then that I realized that I had been nothing more than a spectator in my own life." Amanda noticed that Lisa had stopped playing with her zipper and that her hands were now clenched. Amanda reached over and covered Lisa's fists; her skin tingled and the contact sharpened her empathetic awareness. "I do value life, Lisa, especially my own, maybe now more than ever. I think that for the first time in a long time I'm finally trying to live it, instead of it just allowing it to happen. I might bounce against the walls now and then, but in time I'll find my way."

"What are you going to do?" Lisa asked, steering the conversation into less turbulent waters.

"I'm not going back to Dallas, or the Red Cross." She let go of Lisa's hands and absently rubbed her own.

"Good; they were of no help," Lisa said bitterly.

"I was thinking about maybe going back to school."

"You've given up on nursing?"

"I don't think so. I just want to do something more." Amanda sensed Lisa's relief and noted the return of her characteristic smile. "Feeling better?"

"Better? A little." She looked over at Amanda, the turmoil in her mind beginning to settle. "I think more importantly I understand."

Amanda smiled back and a part of her felt horrible. The half-truth she had told was much closer to a lie, something she had never done to Lisa, and it had come all too easily. And just as worrisome, she did it convincingly. Her dark adolescent friend was pleased.

***

"No matter how you look at it, we screwed up," Assistant District Attorney Randi Garner told a sullen Greg Flynn.

"So everything is out?" Normally an even-tempered man and slow to anger, his voice was raised enough that the ADA took a step back.

"Anything from the storage locker and everything that flowed from it was obtained illegally and is 'fruit of the poison tree.'" Garner was almost as tall as Greg, and even though she had been a prosecuting attorney for less than ten years she had the highest conviction rate in the state. She knew her business and was one of only a handful of people Greg trusted completely. "I can argue the point, but we'll lose, and it's likely that the judge will attach jeopardy."

"Which means that no matter what we find in the future, he can't be prosecuted again." He was as close to cursing as he had ever been. Garner nodded. "I'm sorry, Randi; I really made a mess of this."

"You got played by some experienced operators."

"So what happens now?"

"What happens now is that John Eden goes home with our sincerest apologies, and you get back to work. Find another way into that storage locker, or flip his wife. I don't see any other way to salvage this."

"Four months work, and we're back to square one." He ruefully shook his head.

"Just remember: beware of Greeks bearing gifts." She patted his shoulder and walked off.

Greg stood in the center of the courthouse annex with clenched fists, seething. It was early evening, well past the work day, and the few stragglers that were left in the large hall streamed towards the exits. He turned towards the door and found a couple of security guards openly eyeing Garner as she headed past them. She was an attractive woman and routinely turned heads. It was an innocent and natural thing, but today it was an offense, and he was filled with a rage better directed at himself, his detectives, and Mr. and Mrs. John Eden. He stomped towards the guards, and their smiles retreated the instant they caught sight of him. He reached their desk and suddenly didn't know what to say.

"Inappropriate," was all he could come up with.

"Yes, sir," they answered in unison.

Thirty seconds later he was on the courthouse steps breathing the clean mountain air, something that John Eden would be doing in a matter of hours. He let the wave of anger flow through him without catching a ride. He had to begin the process of leaving work at work. He slowly walked to his car while shoving all the filth, violence, and human waste that filled his days into a giant mental closet. He didn't want any of that in his house or near his family. The closet was getting pretty full after twenty-three years of being a detective for the Colorado Springs Police Department. It also wasn't airtight and had begun to emit a foul-smelling miasma that had begun to subtly color Greg's thoughts and behavior, and this latest episode would certainly add to the stench.

He reached his car and started it. It was a short ride home, and he had to paint a smile on his face. Amanda's aunt Emily was flying back to Oklahoma in the morning and the women in his life had decided that they were going to have a party to send her off in style. On any other day he would be looking forward to a houseful of people and a night of good humor, but at the moment he could only see himself acting the part.

Nine minutes later he made a right-hand turn into a cul-de-sac and watched Joseph Thomas, his lead detective, take a grocery bag from Lisa. She caught sight of him and waved and suddenly all his cares were gone. Even after thirty years of marriage, she still made him breathe a little faster and made his heart beat a little stronger. Together they had conceived and raised a son; together they watched as he went off to war and then returned broken in body but not in spirit; together they stood by him as he married the woman who he loved, and then they in turn gave them a perfect grandson; together, with broken hearts that still beat as one, they buried their son and grandson in a single grave and adopted Amanda for their own. Together Greg and Lisa could overcome anything, do anything, and tonight they were going to have a party.

"Well, hello," he said in a lecherous tone. "I'm looking for the lady of the house." He batted his eyebrows as he gave her cheek a kiss.

"Hello yourself, stranger. But I'm afraid there are no ladies in this house." She batted her eyebrows back at him.

"Excuse me; I can hear you," Amanda said from the other side of Lisa's Explorer.

"Okay, we'll behave." He grabbed a few of the grocery bags from the SUV and turned to find Joe Thomas with an expectant look on his face. "Later," he mouthed.

"Hi, boss," Andy Neiman said, coming down the steps of their house. Andy was the youngest and newest detective in the fourteen-man squad, and Joe Thomas's partner. "Mrs. Flynn, let me take those." Lisa was the den mother for the unit.

"Andy, if you call me Mrs. Flynn one more time, or anything other than Lisa, I will take my husband's gun and beat you with it."

"Yes, Lisa," he said, beating his retreat into the house.

The schlepping continued until the Explorer was empty. The women were back in the house and Greg found himself alone with his two detectives.

"So what happened?" Joe asked anxiously.

"Nothing happened. What is going to happen is that John Eden goes home." Greg's dark mood returned, and he slammed the Explorer's trunk closed.

"They're not even going to arraign him?" Andy asked.

"No. Garner thinks that if we push this we'll lose him forever." Greg watched as their heads dropped. Thomas kicked a stone into the street.

"I'm sorry Greg; this is all my fault," Joe said.

"Yes it is," Greg answered. Joe was a veteran officer, fifteen years as a detective, and he had made a rookie mistake.

"She made it sound like it was their storage locker. She had a key." He offered weakly.

"It was your job to check, and not to be taken in by some penny-ante hustler and his bimbo wife." Greg fired back. Andy looked up as his new boss displayed a side rarely seen.

"I will make this right, Greg," Joe said resolutely.

"I know you will, but not tonight. We will not discuss this until tomorrow. Tonight we have fun, drink beer, tell jokes, and act normally. Our screw-up will not affect this evening. Got it?"

Both officers nodded their heads.

"Tomorrow we start again, and the two of you will find a way to put Eden and his lying wife away for a very long time." Once again they nodded their agreement.

"Now, let's go have some fun," Greg ordered.

CHAPTER 27

The thoughts racing through Greg's mind were clearer than his terse words. Amanda was dressing in the bedroom that she had shared with her aunt. Emily loved the fresh air and routinely left the window open, allowing the cool air to circulate. Except this evening the cool air carried Greg's private conversation. It was an odd situation, but Amanda was more uncomfortable with her unintentional eavesdropping than she was with her mental forays that violated every norm of civility. She heard them conclude their conversation and waited for Greg to follow Joe and Andy back into the house, but he lingered by Lisa's SUV. His emotions seemed to carry his thoughts further and they teased her.

Amanda saw a tall, attractive blonde woman's face, and attached to it were feelings of regret and anger. Amanda had rarely seen Greg angry, and the image intrigued her. She listened a little closer and his thoughts streamed to her as if they were looking for a receptive audience. The woman, a prosecuting attorney, had told Greg that any chance of convicting someone named John Eden had been lost. An image of a smiling middle-aged man flashed through her mind like an internet hyperlink. Eden was a forty-one year old financial advisor specializing in complex art and real estate investments; at least, that's what he told his marks. In reality he was a con man. At one point in his life he had been legitimate; he had a degree in psychology from Cornell and worked for Merrill Lynch for eight years. After learning the system, and how to beat it, he drifted over to and finally embraced the dark side. He preyed upon middle-income retirees. He was cunning, never going for the whole nest egg, just a nibble. He would take just enough to sting his marks but not enough to make them cry foul too loudly. His was a volume business. Everything was going well until he met Ethel Idle. She was in her eighties, a little older than Eden's typical targets, but she seemed so eager to hand over her money that he thought it would be a crime not to take it. For twenty-nine thousand dollars, she purchased a one percent share of a theme park that was undergoing construction in North Denver. Eden had sold the same one percent to three other people, and what each had purchased was twelve square feet of landfill that was already mortgaged to a bank. When the principal investors suddenly pulled out, "the deal" fell apart and the bank moved in, leaving Edith Idle with a heartfelt apology and a tax deduction for a failed investment. Eden had recommended that Mrs. Idle get legal representation before investing, and he even offered to personally drive her up to Denver so she could review the project in person. As he had expected, she declined on both accounts, so the fault was her own. Only, her son didn't see it that way. Larry Idle began an escalating campaign of phone calls, e-mails, and letters that gave him no satisfaction, so he finally sued Eden Investments. Exactly seven days later, a cleaning crew heard a loud bang from Larry Idle's office and they found him dying from a bullet wound to the chest. A dark-haired man was seen running from the building.

***

Amanda slipped the light-blue sundress over her shoulders and it dropped perfectly to just below her knees. Lisa had taken it upon herself to supplement Amanda's wardrobe. "Good job, Lisa," Amanda said to the mirror. She turned to slip into her new pair of summer shoes when she heard Greg slam the mail box closed. An image of a man slumped over a desk forced its way into her mind, and her unruly adolescent began to prowl through its deep recesses. Suddenly she was reminded of her childhood dog, a yellow mongrel that would creep through their small house, sniffing every corner and dark place for a forgotten morsel or the occasional rodent. "Mittens," she said out loud, and realized that she hadn't thought of her for years. "It's as good name as any," she whispered.

"Amanda," Emily called out. Her aunt had fallen back into her old pattern of regulating even the most mundane aspects of Amanda's life, and she had obviously taken too much time getting ready.

"I'll be out in a minute," she called back. It took less than that to navigate to the kitchen, which was now filled beyond capacity. A couple of wolf whistles announced her arrival, and everyone applauded her new look. "I can't take all the credit," she glammed. "Lisa did buy the dress."

"Let's move this party outside please," Lisa cried out from deep in the depths of her kitchen, and the crowd slowly began to disperse into the backyard. Amanda followed and wound up trailing Joe Thomas out the door.

"Hi, Amanda," he said, his voice full of forced enthusiasm.

"Hi, Joe." She let a few other guests squeeze by her and then turned back to Joe. "I heard you guys out in the drive way," she said sheepishly.

He stiffened. "I am under orders not to discuss that. We are to have a good time," he said, miming a robot.

"Let me know how that works out for you. Are you in trouble?"

He tipped his head to the side in a gesture that said "sort of."

"Do you think you can get this guy?"

A flood of emotions poured out of Joe. "We have to. This guy and his wife are real pieces of work. They've been scamming people for years in three different states, and now he's moved on to murder. If he gets away with this, they'll disappear and set up shop somewhere else, and God knows what they'll do, but whatever it is I'll be responsible." He sipped his warm beer as Amanda drifted through his mind.

Joe had spent four months meticulously piecing together a case against Eden only to be tripped up at the finish line. He had interviewed Abby Eden two days earlier, just as the noose was tightening around her husband. His car had been spotted by a traffic camera two blocks away from Larry Idle's office minutes before the murder; he fit the general description of the man fleeing the scene; and his alibi—that he was in a mall, shopping for his wife's birthday—was shaky at best. He had retained a lawyer and refused any further questioning. His wife, however, graciously made herself available for Joe. She confessed to having concerns about her husband's stability, and when asked if she thought he was capable of murder she gave the detective a rather unconvincing answer of "no." Sensing that he was making progress, Joe pressed her for any possible information that might shed some light on her husband's dispute with Idle, at which point she informed him of the storage locker. He asked if she would let him see it and she said, "Sure, why not?" Five minutes into his exploration, Joe found a handgun that later proved to be the murder weapon. John Eden was arrested and charged with the murder of Larry Idle. Hours later,

Eden's lawyer presented Greg Flynn with documents proving that Eden Financial had rented the storage locker, that Eden Financial existed prior to the marriage of John and Abby, and that Abby had no ownership and therefore no right to access the storage locker. He concluded his presentation with the statement that Abby had in fact been trespassing on Eden Financial property, but they would not, at this time, be pursuing charges against her or the officers involved.

"I think maybe I'll mingle a little," Joe said as he spied a scowling Greg Flynn walking down the patio steps with a large platter of uncooked steaks.

Hours later, after all the guests had left and with Emily snoring away in bed, Amanda sidled up to a somewhat tipsy Greg as he ineffectively brushed the grill.

"Hi sweetheart. Did you have a good time?" He reached around her waist and pulled her close to his side. Amanda was surprised by how good it felt, like being home after a long absence.

"I did." She cuddled into him. "I heard you and the guys out in the driveway earlier."

"You did?" he said, surprise and a little concern flashing across his face.

"Yep. Aunt Emily leaves the bedroom window open and you were talking just outside it."

"Well, so much for my powers of detection. If the chief hears that I'll get canned for sure."

"Are you in hot water?"

"Hmm. I've swum in hotter waters." He scraped the wire brush on the grill's rack.

"Anything I can do to help?"

"You being here is all the help I need." He squeezed her tight and kissed the top of her head.

"Are you going to catch this guy?"

"In twenty-four … twenty-three years? I think maybe I've had a few too many of these," he said, taking a long draw from his beer. "But the point is," he slurred happily, "I have never seen a perfect crime. And this sure is not gonna be the first. Imagine: the guy drives a red Porsche 911 with personalized plates, MK MNY, to a murder. He should be arrested on the grounds of extreme stupidity."

"Maybe it was his first, or he didn't read the manual all that well."

"Well, it's going to be his last if I have anything to say about it."

"What do you need to get him?"

"Well, look who's suddenly become all curious." He shook her a little. "You know, idle mind, nothing to do."

Greg looked down at Amanda. "Idle," he said, and then went back to the grill. "Well, in your spare time if you stumble across a videotape confession let me know, or if you get his lying wife to grow a conscience." He teetered a bit and she had to steady him for an instant. "Let's keep this between us. Lisa hates this kind of stuff."

CHAPTER 28

It wasn't hard to find the address of John and Abby Eden. With a little magic—and the requisite internet skills—it was available to anyone. It was also listed in the phone book; that fact tempered some of Amanda's pride in her internet coup. The Edens' home overlooked the Broadmoor Resort, The Springs' only five-star hotel. Their house was perched on a ledge high above the foothills, and Amanda could only imagine their view. They lived in a guarded, gated community that for a week had been covered by the local and regional media. Murder was a big thing in Colorado Springs, and the press was squeezing everything out of this one. Under the pretense of finding a new home, Amanda drove her new Jeep Grand Cherokee through the neighborhood looking for any opportunity, but none presented itself. She even spent an afternoon touring the area with a realtor, who unfortunately could not broach the Edens' defenses any better than she could. It also wasn't the kind of neighborhood that would allow someone to simply park and wait, and it was completely impractical to keep circling the six-block perimeter until Eden or his wife ran down to the market.

After a week, John Eden came out of seclusion and returned to work. The media followed, and for another week anyone approaching or exiting the two-story Eden Financial Building found a microphone in their face. Once again, Amanda circled in her new SUV, searching for a way in until she was stopped by a patrol car and politely told to move on. After nearly two weeks, she was losing faith in her clandestine skills.

"Did you find anything?" Lisa asked Amanda at dinner.

She slowly turned to face Lisa, confused by the question. She had been quietly sifting through Greg's memory of the case and had come upon a possible opening. In the two weeks since Eden's release, Greg and his detectives had found nothing of real consequence, just more details of the couple's lives, one of which intrigued Amanda. Abby Eden had a standing monthly appointment with a therapist.

"Nothing yet. I was thinking that maybe I would rent awhile instead."

"I think that's a good idea," Greg said as he nosily slurped a long string of spaghetti into his mouth. Her husband used to do that very same thing, and her heart was suddenly stabbed with a deep sense of loss.

"What's wrong, dear?" Lisa said. Amanda was starting to worry that the Flynns were gaining too much access to her inner thoughts. Lisa was especially tuned into Amanda's emotional state. Her empathic connection was without a doubt a two-way street. Even when Amanda quietly, gently explored the mind of another, she left something of herself behind, and a faint but discernible trail back to her own mind. Lisa's subconscious was learning how to follow that bread-crumb trail back to Amanda.

"Michael used to do that," she said, nodding towards Greg, who had a noodle halfway down his chin. Silence hung in the air for a long second. "Please don't be uncomfortable. It was one of the things that I loved about him. Now I know where it came from." She smiled with a touch of pain back at Greg.

"Well, then, I shall do it proudly," he said, and he loudly slurped the rest of his noodle. Greg was a good deal like Colonel Bennett, a concept that suddenly made her uncomfortable. His thoughts were organized, disciplined, and ruled by a deep-seated, simple morality. Each time she ventured into his mind, or anyone's for that matter, she unintentionally took something back. More often than not, for a time after an encounter her thoughts and attitudes seemed to align with her subject, and then their influence would slowly fade away. It wasn't much different from adopting the accent of a long-time companion. With Greg, it was always his discipline and organization that followed her home.

"I was thinking about perhaps going to talk to someone about all that's happened," she said after the silence had stretched comfortably.

Greg and Lisa exchanged a glance. "I think that's a good idea, Amanda," Lisa said slowly. "Is there something that changed your mind?"

"Not really. I've had a lot of alone time and was thinking that maybe a different perspective wouldn't be such a bad thing. I found some information on a therapist called Christi Bates."

Greg's eyes widened and he coughed. "I'm sorry; did you say Christi Bates?"

"You know her?" Lisa asked with surprise.

"No, I don't know her. It's a work thing," he answered rather abruptly. "How's the new car working out?"

"Fine," Amanda answered.

"I can't remember when we last bought a new car," he said to his bowl of spaghetti.

***

"We have an opening on Tuesday the thirteenth at two o'clock. Will that work for you?" The receptionist at Christi Bates's office was overly solicitous after a little mental persuasion, courtesy of Amanda.

"Skye, how about two o'clock today," Amanda asked and instructed. "I don't mind waiting, so it's okay to double-book the appointment." She was starting to feel a little like Obi-Wan Kenobi of Star Wars and half expected the young girl to repeat her statement in a disembodied voice.

"Well, in that case I will." Skye bobbed her head and her pony-tail swished without any influence from Amanda. "Would you like to wait or come back in an hour?" Her smile was broad enough to cause permanent facial damage.

"Why don't I just sit and wait?"

"That would be wonderful. Can I get you anything?"

"No, nothing," Amanda said, and she eased away from the desk and out of Skye's mind. She chose a seat by the door and watched as Skye began to reorient herself. She shuffled papers randomly and then began to rifle through the desk drawers as if she were looking for something that had been lost. Skye was basically a helpful individual and didn't need that much direction to do what came naturally. Amanda had to only lightly steer her around the obstacles that she was paid to erect when faced with walk-in patients without a referral. Amanda was beginning to worry about the poor girl when the door opened and Abby Eden walked in.

"Hello, Mrs. Eden. You're right on time." Skye flashed her toothy smile again, making Amanda wonder if she had guided the poor girl at all.

"Hello, Skye, I'm just here for a quick visit." She crossed the office threshold quickly and then signed in. She turned and for a moment seemed startled to find someone else in the waiting room. For an instant her face registered annoyance, then she politely nodded at Amanda and chose a seat as far from her as possible. After a moment's hesitation she sat without taking off her long black cashmere walking coat; it was at least a size too large and much more coat than the weather called for. An oversized pair of dark sunglasses was pushed up into her streaked hair, and she pretended to busy herself inside the red and black purse that matched both her shoes and coat. Amanda watched Abby's reflection in the window behind Skye and was mildly surprised to see how different she looked in person. She had a face more comfortable with a grimace than a smile, and the signs of early middle-age were artfully concealed by makeup. If Amanda didn't know better, she probably would have guessed her to be in her early thirties as opposed to her true late thirties.

"Abby, are you ready?" Skye asked from behind her elevated reception desk. "You're here to see Christi, right?" The office, along with Skye, was split between three independent therapists.

"Yes," Abby said, her voice barely a whisper. She quickly got up and didn't wait for Skye to open the door.

Amanda was left alone with her thoughts and those she had quietly gleaned from the suspicious Abby Eden. She was definitely hiding something—something so big that she expended the majority of her mental energy trying to contain it. Amanda needed more time and to be closer in order to break through. Mittens, her unruly and bloodthirsty inner child, whispered that there was an easier way: she could slice through the woman's brain like a knife through butter. Split her mind open like a rotten melon. Carve her up like a Thanksgiving turkey.

Enough! Amanda screamed at her own alter ego. Her heart was beating faster and she felt the surge of adrenaline and the rush of excitement. It was an option; she could take care of Abby Eden right here, right now. She could dispense justice without benefit of lawyers, judges, or juries. Mittens was on her feet now, and the light Amanda tried to live within became muted. There was no question of whether she could do it, or of getting away with it.

What's holding you back? Mittens asked.

The fact that she may not have done anything wrong, Amanda answered herself, without much conviction. It wasn't just Mittens who wanted to let go. At a very basic level, Amanda wanted to let go. An animal instinct to rip and tear, to cause pain, and to kill pulsed through her. She wanted to be completely unleashed, and to exhaust herself in the pursuit of violence and brutality. If it happened to coincide with justice, all the better. Her hands began to shake, and the Tiffany crystal lamp on Skye's desk exploded, literally scaring the hell out of Amanda.

Skye came running back to her desk at the sound of the shattering glass. The metal base was smoking and she stood frozen in indecision. She looked up to Amanda, who had jumped to her feet. "What ... happened?"

"I don't know, but you need to unplug it before it starts to burn." Amanda's warning only made Skye back farther away. Amanda crossed the room, broken glass underfoot, and pulled the cord from the wall.

"Thanks," Skye said, taking a second before she approached her desk. "What happened?"

"I don't know; it just exploded." Amanda feigned surprise and confusion. Skye began to pick up pieces of multicolored glass from her desktop. Amanda knew that she had caused the explosion. She had no idea how, but was certain that she was responsible. She had shorted out the air pumps in Tellis and very nearly killed Nathan Martin, but she had directed that herself. This lack of control was a new and scary dimension. Even Mittens had retreated back into the shadows, and only a wisp of desire remained. "Here, let me help you," she said, suddenly feeling very guilty.

"No, I'll just call our maintenance man." Skye looked up at Amanda. "Uh, you're bleeding." She pointed to her own left cheek and backed away from the sight of blood. She pushed a box of Kleenex across the desk and managed to knock more glass shards to the ground. "Sorry," she said as they hit the tile floor at Amanda's feet.

"It's just a scratch," Amanda said, dabbing the bead of blood from her cheek. The door to the offices opened and Abby Eden pulled up short at the sight of glass and the smell of ozone and burned plastic.

"Careful, Mrs. Eden, there's glass everywhere," Skye yelled.

"I can see that," she answered, cautiously picking her way.

"Maybe I'll just come back another time," Amanda said to Skye, and backed her way to the door.

"Okay," the confused girl answered absently.

Amanda reached the door before Abby and held it for the older woman, who muttered "thanks" and then walked to the elevators. Amanda followed in her wake, trying to break through to the woman's closely defended secret. It took only a few seconds before the elevator arrived. Abby walked in first and Amanda followed. "Ground floor please," Abby ordered politely. Amanda hit the button and the car moved for a moment and then jerked to a violent stop.

"Oh for Christ's sake," Abby spat.

After several long expectant moments the phone rang and Amanda answered it. A voice said, "This is building maintenance; is everything all right?"

"I'm fine but the car has stopped."

"Is the door open?"

"No, the door is not open," she answered. *The power has just been cut off,* her mind added.

"Okay," the voice said with bored resignation. "I'll send somebody up."

"He said that help is on its way," Amanda relayed to Abby.

"Thank you," she said formally.

"Might as well relax," Amanda said, and she slid to the floor. Abby didn't react and remained standing, facing the sealed doors. Her resistance was still high, but the proximity afforded Amanda an insurmountable advantage. Abby screamed, grabbed her head, and buckled at the knees.

"God," she yelled as she staggered back to the faux wood paneling and dropped slowly to the floor.

"Interesting choice of terms, Abby," Amanda said, the older woman's pain suddenly rekindling the wonderfully sadistic desires in Amanda. "You heartless bitch. This was all a setup." It dawned on Amanda just how easily Abby had done it. She was about the same size as her husband; the right clothes gave her the approximate shape, and they shared the same hair color. "That's why it seemed so amateurish. Killing Idle was just a way of getting rid of your husband. And the innocent wife routine with the detectives, the sudden appearance of a key that opened a storage unit that just happens to have the murder weapon. Bravo." Amanda began to clap slowly.

"I have no idea what you're talking about," Abby said, her face fixed in stone.

"The hell you don't," Amanda said just before Abby screamed a second time. "I want to tell you something I have never told anybody." Amanda stood and took a step closer to the seated woman. "I can literally see into your mind. I know exactly what you did, how you did it, and when you did it. But that's only part of my secret." Amanda suddenly felt like a towering giant. "I can make anything I imagine happen. With a single thought I can stop an elevator. Or let it go." The elevator car suddenly dropped three floors, and then just as suddenly it came to a bone-jarring stop. Abby started to scream with terror. "Shhh, quiet down," Amanda said gently.

"You're fucking crazy; stay away from me," Abby screamed. "Help! Somebody get me out of here!" She climbed to her feet and began pounding on the metal doors.

"Calm down, Abby, please," Amanda pleaded. She could barely control Mittens, who, inflamed by Abby's screams, now demanded release. Power seemed to surge through her, and one of the fluorescent lights began to flair and smoke. "Sit down, NOW!" Amanda screamed. Abby flew across the car as if she had been shot out of a gun. She hit the back wall with enough force to rattle the light panels, causing dust to rain down on them. "Stop moving, and stop talking," Amanda said through clenched teeth. She retained control by only the barest margin.

Abby stared up at Amanda, eyes wide with fear. She had had the wind knocked out of her and was gasping for air, but dared not move.

"Let's let everything calm down," she told Abby and Mittens. "It is in your best interest not to lie to me or provoke me. Do you understand?" Abby nodded slowly. "You need to understand that no one is coming to rescue you until we resolve this issue. Are we clear?" Once again Abby nodded, but now tears began to roll down both her cheeks. "Okay …" Amanda began to nod her head as the adrenaline rush faded and Mittens stopped breathing down her neck. "We are going to discuss this calmly." She dropped to her knees and met Abby eye to eye.

"Who are you?" Abby risked a question.

"You mean what am I?" Amanda corrected. "Right now, I don't know." She stared into Abby's eyes and through them into her vacant soul. "Justice. Vengeance. A woman barely in control of herself. All three? But that's hardly the issue before us. How do we resolve this, Abby? I'm open to suggestions."

"I don't know what you want," she whimpered and started crying.

Amanda almost laughed. "I sure know what I want. I want you to meet my dog, Mittens. Only, I'm not quite certain I'm ready to take another life." Abby screamed again and butt-scooted her way into the corner.

"Don't do that, Abby. Control yourself, or I won't be able to control myself."

"You don't understand. He was going to kill me," Abby pleaded.

"I know you believe that, and maybe it's true, but why kill an innocent man? That's what this is all about. If you had to kill someone, why didn't you kill your husband? Simple, direct, and given the right circumstances, understandable."

"You don't know what it was like." She was blubbering now.

"Do I look like someone who can be fooled by your crying?" Amanda stabbed Abby's brain to punctuate the point. "Please, I must emphasize that to ensure your continued good health do not try and manipulate me." Abby stopped crying and her entire countenance changed in an instant to one of pure hatred. "Now that's an emotion I can deal with. The real answer to my question was that you didn't want to kill your husband. You wanted to make him suffer. It's that simple. All the elaborate plans were for one reason only: to make John Eden suffer for the rest of his life. The only problem was that his lawyer knew something you didn't, and you unwittingly committed the near-perfect crime."

"So now what do we do?" Abby's voice was raspy from the crying but had regained most of its haughtiness.

"You are going to call your husband and confess. And then you are going to call Detective Joseph Thomas and confess to him."

"And if I don't?"

"There's always Mittens. It works for me." Amanda smiled, and Mittens paced just inside the shadows of her mind.

"Then what?"

"Then we get off the elevator." Amanda's smile lasted for only a second and then her face abruptly hardened. "You still don't get it do you?" The anger was rising again and Amanda began to pace. "I can hear what you are thinking." The lights above her head began to flair brightly. "You will not tell your husband or Detective Thomas that some crazy bitch is forcing you to confess to something you didn't do. This crazy bitch is forcing you to confess to something you did do." In her mind's eye Amanda saw Abby's body being squeezed. She stared down at the woman as her face and body began to contort into unnatural positions; she held the painful pose for almost a full minute before Amanda released her. "Have I made my point?"

Abby started to cry in earnest. It took her another minute to silently shake her head. "I need my phone," she said with a broken voice.

Ten minutes and two phone calls later, Amanda released the elevator. Amanda could hear shouts from the rescue workers above as the car began to move, and seconds later the phone rang. She ignored them both and they rode quietly until the car slowed and came to a gentle stop. The doors opened and both women stared at the large gold lettering on the opposite wall that spelled "Level Three." Abby tried to scramble to her feet, but Amanda knocked her back on her butt with a slight mental nudge. "You stay here until Detective Thomas comes to collect you. Feel free to tell them what happened here. It might make a good defense. One more thing …" The doors tried to close on her and then started buzzing. "I will be watching." The doors finally closed and the elevator began to descend, only to once again jerk to a stop. Amanda walked to the stairs as Abby pounded on the sealed doors.

CHAPTER 29

"To broken elevators," Joe Thomas yelled drunkenly, raising his bottle of beer. Most of the bar joined him, including Greg Flynn.

"Slow down there, big guy; tomorrow is a school day." Greg pulled Joe back down to his chair just before he was about to give his fourth toast.

"I'm calling in sick." He wrapped his arms around Greg. "Don't tell the boss."

It was an unparalleled stroke of luck, or perhaps divine intervention. The murder of Larry Idle was fast becoming an albatross tied firmly around their collective necks, and suddenly Abby Eden confesses to everything.

Randi Garner slid into the seat next to Greg and tipped his mug with her glass. "Remember what I said about Greeks bearing gifts? Well, forget it." She took a sip. "Thanks for the call. I didn't think I'd be welcomed after what happened."

"Are you serious? You're the hero of the day. We were a search warrant away from convicting the wrong man." Greg had to shout over the din. "He's still an asshole, and I think the Feds will get him for fraud; he's just not a murderer." He tipped her glass in return. "Thanks for keeping us honest."

"Have you ever seen that before? She was in the clear and then suddenly confesses. It doesn't seem right."

Greg shook his head. When he first heard of her confession he immediately doubted it, but when he actually saw her, sitting in the interrogation room, eyes wide with panic, his doubts regarding her innocence vanished. She had killed Larry Idle, of that he was certain, but the doubts that they had the whole truth persisted. "No, it doesn't seem right. I think there's more to the story."

"She has a psych history."

"She didn't seem crazy; she seemed terrified. My only guess is the husband. She called him before she called Joe." It was the only conclusion that could be drawn from known events, but it still didn't sit well with Greg.

"I guess she thought she was safer in jail than at home with her husband. I hope this doesn't come back to bite us in the ass again."

"Do you have concerns?"

"None. There's not even going to be a trial. It's over, except for the sentencing." She looked back at Greg and they shared an uneasy feeling. "I should go. Congratulations." She stood and then weaved her way out of the bar, a half-dozen heads turning as she passed.

***

Even after three days, Amanda was still conflicted. It wasn't the outcome that bothered her; Abby Eden was going to pay for killing Larry Idle, and justice had been served. She had made an impromptu visit to Greg's office, and managed to exchange glimpses with Abby as she was being booked, just to ensure her continued cooperation. It was the fact that the entire affair seemed to throw in relief the issues she had been avoiding since arriving home.

For three weeks she had a diversion. Her days were filled with all things John and Abby Eden, and she had loved almost every minute of the hunt. But now all that was left was a void. What was she going to do with the rest of her life? She could hardly make a living stalking criminals. And despite what she had told Lisa, she couldn't see herself returning to school either. After all she had seen and done, the thought of sitting in a classroom taking notes and exams seemed almost ludicrous. She also didn't want to return to the world of nursing, in any of its varied forms. She needed something more active, dynamic, exciting—like stalking criminals.

"That's it, I'll be a superhero. I will keep the city safe from evil in all its guises. Jaywalkers beware," she told the geese that surrounded her. She had driven back into the mountains and found a small lake and a rickety picnic table. The early spring sun was growing a little thin and the temperature had started to fall, but the geese didn't seem to mind so long as Amanda periodically tossed more feed corn. She had been to this lake years earlier, shortly after Michael proposed and she accepted. They made love somewhere on the far side of the lake one long, lazy, wonderful afternoon. It had been one of the most special days of her life. But that life was over. It had died in pieces: the first with a knock on her door and a sheriff's deputy wearing a pained expression; a larger piece a week later when a single coffin was lowered into the frozen dirt; and the last piece as she watched thirty people die around her while a virus rewired her brain. The final vestiges of the old Amanda Flynn—an occasional memory or a transient sense of loss—were slowly and inexorably fading away, leaving a new and very different version behind. She remembered sitting under a sweltering tent in Honduras, trying to understand the nascent changes that were being wrought in her brain, an act driven by a mixture of her old and new personality. The innocence of trying to capture on paper what she had become made her laugh. This new version of Amanda didn't care what she had become or where she had come from; she had no past. All that mattered was this moment and how she could use it to shape the future to fit her needs.

Which led her to her most difficult problem. How was she going to live? What rules would guide her behavior? God's? Society's? Her own? In her old life she had never been given a choice. The rules had been written into her soul as she grew up, and like a good, obedient girl she had followed them, only to have her life lurch from one tragedy to another. So much for God and society repaying her fealty. Her new soul was nearly a blank slate; she had no instructions, no constraining morality. The only things stamped into it were Aunt Emily, Greg Flynn, and Lisa Flynn. Somehow those bonds had survived her transformation, and a part of her resented that fact. Without them she would be truly free to explore any form of behavior that occurred to her. She would be free to let Mittens off her leash; in fact she would be free to become Mittens. A life ruled by her passions and desires, free of guilt or consequences; no need for delayed gratification or impulse control. No need for rules of any kind. With what she had become, she was beyond rules.

Except Emily, Greg, and Lisa kept pulling her back to earth. "Damn them," she said to the geese, and then threw a handful of the corn as hard as she could at a nearby group. The kernels pelted the birds, and they scurried backed to the water, honking the whole way. The sadism made Mittens happy, and Amanda smiled. She had enjoyed hurting Abby Eden. No, she loved hurting Abby Eden, and had replayed the memory of the woman contorting in pain at least a dozen times. She had wanted to do more than just hurt her; she had wanted to squeeze the life out of her; she wanted to be inside the woman's mind as the pain and the certainty of her death drove her insane. And when it was over she would have torn the corpse to pieces, shredding any recognizable piece of Abby Eden, leaving only blood and tissue hanging from the walls and ceiling. The violent images and thoughts made Mittens growl and she began to pace through Amanda's mind; she had grown to love the feral feel of her energized id. Mittens made her strong, confident, and powerful—attributes that were almost completely lacking in her former life—and a desire to explore them fully was growing into an addiction. Abby Eden was a start, but Amanda knew that if she continued down this path, in time, more would be required. At some point, blood would be needed.

Amanda stared up into the mountains and contemplated the possibility of cold, calculated murder. Was she capable of it, or would her old tepid personality resurface at the critical moment as it had when Nathan Martin was suffocating inside an airlock? Did she have the courage to do what was necessary to feed Mittens and solidify her new life, or would she backslide into her old one?

"No," she declared to herself. "That life is over." She was a new being, free from anything that constrained her. Her only moral imperative was to do whatever she wanted, because no one could stop her. She lay back on the top of the picnic table and tried to remember what had stopped her from dismembering Abby Eden. She closed her eyes and reworked the memory.

***

Amanda awoke some time later to the sound of squabbling geese. Reflexively, she checked her watch and realized that she had to be going. Lisa would be worried if she came home late without calling. Once again, Amanda felt her soul pulled back to a life she no longer wanted. Moving out would help, and earlier today she had found a small furnished apartment on the west side of town. It came with all the creature comforts, few of which she would ever use. All she really needed was the freedom to explore what she had become.

She slid off the picnic table as the sun slipped beneath the tall trees covering this side of Pikes Peak, and for a minute she watched the shadows lengthen. The previous night she had watched her first episode of "Dexter," and a small part of her responded to the main character's need to "take out the garbage." Which involved a large knife, a great deal of plastic wrap, a fair amount of dismemberment, a few trash bags, and a midnight boat ride. Colorado Springs didn't have nearly the volume of human garbage that Miami apparently had to deal with, but perhaps it was a starting point. The geese crowded around her, the larger ones jockeying for the best positions. She poured the remaining kernels of corn into her hand and then tossed them into the air. As the birds tracked them Amanda aimed savage kicks at some of the more vocal birds. All but one managed to scurry out of range; the slowest of the lot was booted into the air. He landed on his side in a flurry of feathers and a loud squawk. She watched as he scrambled to right himself and then rejoin the fight for the few remaining kernels.

"I should have kicked you harder."

***

"Greg got home late." Lisa answered Amanda's expression that questioned her uncharacteristic early-evening inactivity. "He's taking us out to dinner as a punishment."

"Fancy or casual?" Amanda dropped her purse on a table by the kitchen door and hung up her coat. She noticed a goose feather stuck to the tip of her right shoe and quickly snatched it up.

"I think just casual; I'm not that mad at him. What do you have there?" Lisa asked.

Amanda swore to herself. She really needed to get out of this house and away from the Flynns, especially Lisa. She hadn't seen the feather, and couldn't possibly know that it was in her hand; she had unconsciously sensed Amanda's reaction to the offending and revealing object. "I seemed to have picked up a feather along the way." She opened her hand to reveal the partially crushed feather.

"Wash your hands after you get rid of it. Geese are such filthy birds," Lisa said with a shudder. "I'm going to check on Greg."

Amanda tossed the feather into the garbage and dutifully washed her hands in the sink. This whole home situation was rapidly becoming untenable. She hadn't been inside Lisa's mind for weeks, and in fact had actively closed her mind to Lisa's, yet their reciprocal connection remained strong. It was only a matter of time before Lisa's empathic sense solidified into certainty that this was not the same Amanda who had left for Central America months earlier. She dried her hands and decided to change out of her jeans and sweater, imagining that they had been impregnated with her thoughts and dark desires.

"We are leaving in exactly nine minutes," Greg said to Amanda as they passed in the hall. The return of his cheerful demeanor correlated exactly with the closure of the Larry Idle case. The heat was off Greg and his unit; in fact, somehow even their mistake had been turned to their advantage. Randi Garner, in her public statement following Abby's confession, had been asked about John Eden's arrest and sudden release. She answered simply that the system worked, and despite being lied to and misled, the police never developed tunnel-vision and ultimately uncovered the truth. An editorial in this morning's Denver Post lauded the Colorado Springs detectives for not throwing in the towel and whining about a nonsensical legal distinction that led to the release of a "killer," and encouraged the Denver police to adopt the professional attitude of Colorado's second city.

"I will be ready in three."

"Three Female-Minutes," he said from the kitchen.

A half hour later they were sitting across from each other at Luigi's Italian Restaurant, waiting for someone to take their drink orders. Lisa pulled a copy of the Denver Post from her purse and casually began to fan herself with it. "Sometimes it gets a little warm in Colorado's second city, don't you think so honey?"

Greg beamed, with a bread stick in his mouth. "It's like I always say: it's better to be lucky than good." The waiter arrived, took their order, and disappeared. "Did you ever go see the therapist, Amanda?"

Lisa stopped fanning herself and gaped at her husband. "Where did that come from?"

Amanda already knew. "Abby Eden confessed after seeing her therapist. It was the same one you mentioned, Amanda. Christi Bates." Greg turned to his wife, trying to be casual, but his light tone had a shiny edge of accusation.

"I haven't called yet, but if she's good enough to convince a murderer to confess, maybe I should call now," Amanda said. Instead of being uncomfortable with the tacit lie, her mind viewed it as a challenge. Greg liked to portray himself as just one of the boys, promoted more out of longevity than competence, but Amanda knew the real Greg Flynn. He was obsessed with details and had the tenacity of a bulldog. Decades ago he learned to trust instincts that time and experience had since honed to a razor's edge. He was in fact Colorado Springs' version of Lieutenant Columbo, and Amanda simply smiled back at him, waiting for him to ask "just one more thing."

"She said that someone else was in the elevator with her, but when the doors were opened she was alone." He leaned back as the waiter placed his iced tea in front of him. Once their order had been taken, Greg continued as if there had been no interruption. "She said that some Amazon woman rode down with her and tortured the truth out of her."

"Insanity defense," Lisa sang.

"There's not going to be a trial; she doesn't need a defense." He went back to the breadsticks. "I was hoping that by chance you had stopped by and maybe saw a tall black woman who had an affinity for torture."

Amanda cocked her head ever so slightly and looked confused. "Greg, I was with you when that woman was arrested. Remember? You took me to that hot-dog place. You left me there when you got the call."

Greg looked up from the wicker basket, confusion and then recognition creasing his face. "That's right. I forgot my keys and you brought them to me."

Amanda nodded, and Lisa stared at her husband. "Greg, maybe it's a good time to take some time off."

"No, I'm fine. This has been the strangest week. Let's forget about it." He smiled brightly.

CHAPTER 30

It took Amanda eight more days before she took her first life. She didn't count the four Honduran soldiers whom she had shot; that had been self-defense. This was murder in every sense of the word. Cold, calculated, pre-meditated murder, performed for her pleasure alone, and without hesitation. Angel Diaz was not a nice man by anyone's estimation, and some on the extreme right of the political spectrum would argue that Amanda had in fact done society a favor, but that had never figured into Amanda's thinking. She moved through society but remained distinct from it. For now, she required the infrastructure created by society—food, water, electricity, and a fringe element that served to meet her unique desires—but she had no wish to contribute to society, at least beyond what was required to maintain the pretense of normality.

***

Angel Diaz was the epitome of society's fringe element. A Mexican national, he had grown up in the barrios of Tijuana, literally a stone's throw from the promised land of the United States. Like his brothers before him, he gravitated into the drug trade primarily because of a lack of options and the easy money. It was fairly easy, mindless work: unload the truck, stack the product, carry it down the tunnel, and then hand it off to his American counterpart. Even the risk of incarceration was virtually non-existent, so long as he stayed on the Mexican side and kept his mouth shut. The only real inconvenience was that it was universally done in the dead of night. Everything hummed along in perfect harmony for years, until the Sinaloa Cartel tried to expand their operations westward. Angel barely knew that he was a tiny cog in the Tijuana Cartel; he and his brothers worked only when the mood suited them, and saw themselves more as independent contractors, happy to work for anyone so long as they got paid. When the shooting started, however, the Sinaloas failed to make the distinction. Two of Angel's three brothers were gunned down while unloading a pickup, and the third barely survived a shot in the head as the drug war weaved its way through the slums of Tijuana. Allegiance now became a matter of survival, and his choice was easy. Two years later, with the Sinaloa Cartel in full retreat, Angel Diaz had a tattoo of fourteen bullets encircling his right wrist and was a respected and feared lieutenant in the Tijuana Cartel, which now controlled all drug smuggling in Western Mexico and the Baja peninsula. The war had taught Angel and his overlords the undeniable lesson that stagnation invited confrontation, and confrontation was bad for business. Deciding to expand beyond their historic distribution, they sent the naïve and expendable Angel north to sniff out new opportunities. He eventually discovered Pueblo, Colorado, and that he was on a relatively long leash. It took him almost ten years to carve out a violent niche in an already saturated market, and to gain a degree of independence not available to his colleagues closer to home. Which is how Angel Diaz appeared on Greg Flynn's radar.

Colorado Springs is a relatively quiet city, not as flashy as its northern neighbor, Denver, or as dangerous as its southern neighbor, Pueblo. Relative to the region, unemployment is low, in part because of the extensive military infrastructure and tourism. Educational standards are reasonably high, and the prevailing political opinion is conservatism with a half step to the left. The citizens of The Springs paid their taxes, came to complete stops at stop signs, and more often than not said hello to strangers. So when the bodies of three prostitutes were found in a dumpster outside the bus station, people took note. Drugs, prostitution, and the inevitable violence associated with them could be found in Colorado Springs, but generally one had to go in search of them. The murders now brought it into the homes of every Springs resident who had a newspaper subscription or a television. For weeks a slow news cycle ensured that the three victims were not forgotten. Greg and his department devoted the majority of their resources to the case, but all they could come up with was a name never spoken aloud: Angel Diaz. His reputation preceded him, and an impenetrable wall of intimidation and threats shielded him. After weeks of banging their collective heads against it, the world began to turn again and necessity forced the triple homicide to slide from the front burner to the back burner, and then finally off the stove altogether. It was Greg's only unsolved multiple homicide, and he naturally turned back to the cold case once Larry Idle was off his plate.

His run of luck continued when a drunken bar fight a week after Abby Eden's surprise confession escalated into an exchange of gunfire. Both assailants missed their intended targets, and it was out of sheer luck that only two of the eighteen shots fired in the middle of a crowded bar found a mark. One of the now incarcerated pair insisted that he was willing to trade some information about the "dead hookers" for a one way ticket out of Colorado Springs. The criminal/legal quid pro quo was relatively common practice, and although Greg had never been completely comfortable with it, in this case he was more than willing to make an exception. Three hours into his day, he was asking Randi Garner to push the deal through.

***

Less than eight hours later, Amanda had a name, an address, and a new direction. Her mind buzzed with possibilities, and she had to shorten Mittens' leash as her alter ego wanted to charge over to Diaz's house and play with the drug-dealer and some of his vassals. Like with the Edens, she started out by simply driving by his house, acclimating to the smells of the neighborhood. Diaz lived in a sprawling compound that was itself surrounded by other sprawling compounds in the foothills between Colorado Springs and Pueblo. He counted among his neighbors a former governor of the state, an All-Pro offensive tackle for the Houston Texans, and an unusually successful psychiatrist named Eldridge Adegbite. She slowed her Jeep, and it coasted passed the psychiatrist's large wrought iron gates. Her GPS gave her the address and the county tax records gave her the name, and although her intended prey lived up the canyon, Adegbite's name gave her mind a tickle and a pause. Not surprisingly, she could see little from the street, just strategically placed scrub trees that gave the false impression of unrestrained nature. Google Maps gave her a satellite view of the area, and she was surprised by how close Diaz had placed his house to Adegbite's. Both properties were more than fifty acres, yet the two homes were a mere five hundred yards apart, separated by a small hill and a steep draw.

Curious, she said to herself as she accelerated up the street. Conforming to neighborhood norms, Casa Diaz was also not visible from the street, but instead of the rustic rock wall that encircled most of the other compounds, Diaz had a ten-foot stucco fortification complete with revolving cameras that tracked the progress of Amanda's jeep. She made a U-turn and cruised back down the canyon road, with Diaz's cameras following her. Her mind jerked again when she drove passed the Adegbites's gates.

Several minutes later, she was idling in a McDonald's parking lot sipping a Coke. A blue Prius pulled in next to her, and its interruption nearly stirred her to violence. Its three occupants gave her stern, reproachful looks as they made their way around her polluting SUV. Amanda flipped the nearest one her middle finger.

"Bitch," he screamed, and then he squared himself to the front of her Jeep. His two friends were halfway to the door when they turned.

Just for a moment, Amanda thought about slipping the Jeep into gear and giving herself a new hood ornament. She smiled brightly.

"Let's go, fuck-wad," one of his friends said. All three were stoned, but what made Amanda laugh was the realization that the eco-friendly car wasn't even theirs; it was Fuck-wad's father's.

"Fucking bitch!" He banged her hood with his open hand and turned back to his friends.

"Hey Fuck-wad!" Amanda was out of the car before he had taken two steps. "Did you just bang my car?"

"Yes, I did, skank." He turned back towards her and retraced his two steps. He was tall, lanky, and reeked of pot. His two friends didn't know whether to back him up, laugh at him, or drag him into the restaurant, so they simply stood by the door. "What the fuck are you going to do about it, BITCH?" He yelled in her face and the next minute he was airborne. He landed in the bushes just in front of a window covered by a poster of an impossibly large and juicy hamburger. After a moment's delay, his two friends ran to his aid, screaming the word "bitch" far too liberally for the situation.

She gave them a moment to extricate Fuck-wad and redirect their attention to her. "I really do object to your language, gentlemen," she said as the first tire in their Prius exploded with a loud boom that echoed across the parking lot. "I think you should perhaps apologize." The second tire exploded with a similar report. The small car listed to the driver's side.

"Whatever you're doing, just stop it, okay? We're sorry, he's sorry, everyone's sorry, okay?" The smallest and oldest of the three had taken a step towards her, palms up in supplication. Mittens was emitting a low and menacing growl in Amanda's head.

She held the young man's eyes and the moment began to defuse. "Maybe just one more?" She smiled mischievously, holding up one finger.

Their spokesman forcefully shook his head, his high now completely wasted.

"One question," she answered his pleading look. She was having a hard time reading them, both as a result of their intoxication and her energized emotional state. "Where did you get the pot?"

They exchanged a quick look, and finally Fuck-wad spoke in a much more respectable tone. "It's ours. We, ah, grow it ourselves."

Amanda stared into him and found that he was telling the truth. It was too much to hope that she would just happen to stumble on a trio of Diaz's dealers. "Pity," she said, and both of the Prius's passenger side tires exploded as one.

Their first instincts were to run to their stricken car or to attack Amanda as she walked back to her idling Jeep, but after a shared hesitation the trio just stood where she had left them. Amanda pulled out and gave them a smile with a little wave as she drove past.

***

"Why do you believe that you are a psychopath?" Eldridge Adegbite was the proverbial stately man. Tall, thin, well-dressed, and with a sharp, hyperarticulate manner of speaking. Amanda thought he should be sitting in a library chair, legs crossed as he puffed on a pipe, and a book in his lap as he introduced "Masterpiece Theater."

"Doctor, I know I am a psychopath." Amanda sat across the sixty-two-year-old man. It had only been slightly harder getting an appointment with Adegbite than it had been with Christi Bates, although she did have to wait a day. "I believe that it is something we share in common."

He smiled benignly at her. "I see; so you believe that I am a psychopath as well."

"Once again, Doctor, I know you are a psychopath." The previous fifteen minutes had completely reshaped Amanda's immediate future. All thoughts of the now rather banal Angel Diaz were forgotten. She desperately wanted to kill, slaughter, obliterate Eldridge. Even his name was an affectation, but a perfect one. Her mind was practically bursting with excitement over the untimely but exquisitely slow demise of the old fraud. Ahh, but what a fraud. At least in total numbers he wasn't the killer Diaz was, but what Adegbite lacked in volume he made up with style.

"I stand corrected." He nodded his head in condescending acceptance. "May I ask you how you know we are psychopaths?"

"Of course." Amanda leaned back in her own library chair and tried to unmask the psychiatrist-who-wasn't with her eyes. "We are both social predators. We take what we want and do as we please, without regard to social norms or expectations, and without the slightest sense of guilt or regret."

"I see that you've read Robert Ware." Adegbite nodded slowly and approvingly. "Then you know that there is no treatment for the condition. No therapy or medication can give you, us, the emotional complexity or empathy that is missing in our psychological makeup. We are irretrievably flawed." Amanda now nodded her approval. "Which of course raises the question of why you charmed your way into my office?"

Eldridge had been born Lucas Tyler in Davenport, Indiana. His father was a school principal and his mother a school librarian, at least until their untimely deaths when Lucas was nineteen. "I'm curious …" Amanda ignored his question. "What set you off, Lucas? Did you wake up one morning and suddenly decide to burn down the house as they slept? Or did the idea slowly evolve during all those years of stifling boredom?"

Amanda wasn't surprised at his lack of reaction. Externally, he still projected an unshakable sense of comfort and ease, and even his thoughts remained relatively calm. No panic, not a trace of fear or even concern, just a sense of intrigue, a thrill of excitement as his daily routine took an unusual turn. "My name was Lucas, but now it is Eldridge. And indeed my parents did tragically die in a fire, but I assure you I had nothing to do with it. In fact, I was away at school. Does that disappoint you?"

"Not in the least. In fact I am very impressed with your ability to lie convincingly."

"Apparently not well enough to convince you." His relaxed, comforting smile hadn't dimmed a degree. "But aren't we here to discuss your issues?"

Amanda felt the pull of his magnetic personality and very nearly ceded control by answering his question. "You've locked away a good deal of your life." She stared back at him, quietly sifting through his mind. "Shuttered doors and windows. I wonder what's behind them?" She could easily answer her own question, but that would prematurely end her visit. "Can we go back to your parents? I really am interested in your motivation. They were out of your life, yet you went back almost a year and a half later just to kill them."

"Mrs. Flynn, I believe that we have …"

"I know, I know. I have an unhealthy fixation with you and it would be unprofessional of you to allow me to continue. I can see the words in your mind before you do." Outwardly, he remained relaxed, but his thoughts were beginning to turn dark—a state Amanda could well relate to. "I'm not here to hurt you, or to turn you into the police; right now all I want is for Lucas Tyler to level with me, then Eldridge Adegbite can go on with his life." He wasn't the only one who could lie convincingly.

"Amanda …" he began, but she stopped him.

"Please, don't provoke a demonstration. Trust me when I tell you that I know what you did then, and later. I can see you blowing out the oven's pilot light and turning on the gas. I know that your father met you on the stairs and that you threw him over the railing. I can hear his body hit the floor with that sick, wet thud that still resonates in your mind all these years later. I know that you watched the house burn from Willis' Hill knowing that your mother would never be able to untie herself in time. I know what you did in the solitude of your car as the roof collapsed. I can see it because you still see it."

Adegbite's smile had disappeared and his mind was silent. A mental gag order in place while the secret parts of his mind worked on this latest development

"Well," he finally said, with only the subtlest change in his appearance. "You have my attention. What do you want?"

"Like I said, I just want to understand the why. Let's forget about what came later; it all flows naturally from that one decision." Amanda was sitting up in her seat, her face bright with excitement.

"Are you planning on killing someone, Amanda?"

"Perhaps." She smiled, and raised her eyebrows.

"Are you planning on killing me?" He asked, without the least bit of fear, or even concern.

"I'm not sure." She stared deep into his eyes and mind and began to sense his awareness of her intrusion.

"Interesting," he said as more doors closed in his mind. "I'm afraid the answer will disappoint you," he said after a moment. "If you read Robert Ware as closely as I believe you have, you already know the answer. I had, and still do have, a very low threshold for the monotony of life. Murder is exciting, but I am guessing you already knew that."

"They were your parents." Amanda probed him for any trace of human emotion.

"Meaningless at an emotional level; highly convenient at a practical level."

Amanda nodded blankly. Lucas Tyler, aka Eldridge Adegbite, had no soul. He had killed simply to alleviate the tedium of life. "A life without rules or restraints," she said, mostly to herself.

"Oh no, that's where you're wrong. There have to be rules, and one must exercise restraint. Otherwise one ends up on death row."

"Society and the rule of law are an unfortunate reality," she agreed. If she had a soul it was surely dying; her motivations were fundamentally no better or worse than his. "I would like to meet your neighbor, Senor Diaz."

He appraised her with eyes very much different from the ones he hid behind. "Ambitious." He smiled. "What makes you think I would help you?"

"You will either do it willingly or you will be … compelled."

"Compelled …" His smile broadened, his mind anticipating the challenge. "I could simply pick up a phone and call the police, or even Senor Diaz. Or perhaps I could simply compel you."

"If that's what you want." Her smile returned and Mittens was prowling through her mind. She really would enjoy draining Eldridge of life, but like him she was intrigued by another possibility.

"No. I would like to see if this confidence is deserved or simply delusional." He was fully unmasked now. "If you fail, he will kill you." He looked her up and down. "Although I doubt he will do it right away."

"I won't fail." She stood and straightened out her dress. Adegbite watched closely as her hands smoothed out the wrinkles.

"We have a zoning issue that he is anxious to resolve. I will ask him to drop by my house at eight tonight. Would you like me to call you after the arrangements have been made?"

"It won't be necessary," she said, staring into his shining face. He was excited about the prospect of watching at least one person die, and not by his own hand.

"One question before you leave. How did you know?"

She resisted the desire to show him only because she needed him clear-headed when he talked with Diaz. "It's a secret you don't ever want to learn." She turned and left.

<h1 style="text-align:center">CHAPTER 31</h1>

"I am happy to see that there is no family resemblance," Angel Diaz said just before he kissed Amanda's outstretched hand. The peck burned with enough force to focus her mind. From the moment she had driven through Adegbite's gates Mittens could smell death in the air, and she strained at her leash.

"Eldridge is a distant uncle," she said, giving him a vacant-headed smile and then turning to Adegbite, who nodded in agreement. "You travel with an entourage; are you famous?" Amanda adopted the stereotype that played in Diaz's head. He had darker, more obvious intentions as he took her by the arm, his forearm rubbing her outer breast.

"No, my dear, I am just cautious." Diaz guided her out into the torch lit patio. Two of the four impressively dressed men followed the couple. Eldridge brought up the rear.

"So that is your house, just beyond the trees." She pointed with her free hand and Diaz took the opportunity to lean in a little farther as he stood on his toes, pretending to follow her hand. He was younger than she had expected, and better looking. He had a dark complexion, a physique that spoke to hours of training, and coal-black eyes that reflected the light of the torches. He moved with a relaxed style that only partially hid the predator beneath. Amanda was enveloped by his aura of malice and contempt; left to his own devices he would have had "Uncle Eldridge" strapped to a chair with electrodes attached to a number of sensitive body parts and be damned with this false civility. She patted his arm in complete agreement.

"Yes, that is my home. Sadly, it does not have the view of your uncle's, but it does have some unique aspects." His flirtation had become a little too obvious and Amanda slipped her arm from his grasp. She enjoyed the playacting, and imagined herself as Marylyn Monroe. She pulled away from him, wanting the role to last a bit longer before they got down to business. "Oh! I apologize if I have offended you. My meaning was not clear."

"It's okay," she said, her tone implying that her mind was not fully closed to his advance. She casually approached one of Diaz's bodyguards. "Do they have to follow you everywhere?" she asked.

"Not everywhere," he said, following her to the edge of the patio.

She turned and found Diaz only inches from her. Eldridge Adegbite stood ten feet away, a glass of wine in his hand and a confused, disapproving look on his face. "Are your men good shots?" Amanda breathed.

"They all are expert marksmen." Diaz was completely in the moment, an image of a partially clad Amanda strapped to a bed filling his mind.

"Maybe we should put that to the test," she whispered to his lips. Just before they kissed, the guard facing Diaz pulled his weapon from inside his jacket and fired a shot across the patio and into the chest of his compatriot.

Diaz fell on top of Amanda, Adegbite fell to the stone, and the remaining two guards came running from the house long before the echoing report faded away. Amanda pushed the drug dealer off and climbed to her feet. Both guards watched her with guns drawn but pointed downward. She walked to Eldridge and offered a hand up, laughing. "I was beginning to think that we were in a really bad nineteen-fifties movie."

"What the hell just happened?" His eyes were wide and his pupils dilated.

She smiled and walked over to the body now sprawled across Adegbite's lawn. She looked down and then back up at Diaz. "You said they were expert marksmen. I wanted a head shot." Amanda began to feel Mittens take over.

Diaz had crawled on all fours and taken refuge behind a large stone planter. He didn't know where to look, and his head went from the guard behind him to Eldridge, to Amanda, and finally to his two frozen bodyguards, who were just as confused as their boss. He finally hissed at them in Spanish, and immediately they ran over to their dazed companion and disarmed him.

"I didn't think that would be so loud. My ears are ringing," she said to Adegbite, settling into in a patio chair. She crossed her legs and reached for Eldridge's hand. "Sit, we're just getting started."

Robotically, he pulled a chair opposite her and sat. "How did you do that?" he asked.

"You don't want to know, and you also don't want to know how close that guy came to hitting you." She realized that she was very nearly manic; thoughts and emotions flew through her head, blinding her to the thoughts and emotions of the men around her. "Okay, we all have to calm down," she said to Mittens.

"What are you talking about?" Adegbite asked. Diaz had risen and positioned himself behind his two loyal guards, leaving Amanda at his back.

"Just give me a moment." She closed her fists and shook them with nervous energy. "That was great," she finally said. "I've never done that before." She smiled brightly at the pretend psychiatrist, intoxicated by the emotional elixir pouring out of the men around her. "Okay,"—she clapped her hands—"back to business. You three take the body and go home. All the way home, and don't come back." They hesitated less than a second. "NOW!" Amanda screamed, and all three men buckled at the knees and grabbed their heads. Five minutes later their party was down to three. Diaz had tried to stop his bodyguards from abandoning him. Failing that, he tried to leave with them, only to end up on his knees holding his bursting head.

"I don't understand what's happening here, Amanda," Eldridge said after Angel's howling began to subside.

"He does, at least for as long as I want him to." She nodded to Diaz. "When you're feeling better, why don't you join us, Angel?"

It took him several minutes to gain his feet and stagger to the frosted glass table, and then into one of the two remaining chairs. "You're going to die, bruja," he sneered.

"Hold that thought," she answered and jumped to her feet. "I'll be back." She disappeared back into the house.

"What are you smiling at, old man? You're next. She's going to fuck you up worse than me."

"I think I liked you better when you were pretending to be civilized," Eldridge said.

"Do you want to die? Listen to me …"

"I'd really rather not listen to your pleading. Try to find some dignity."

"Fuck your dignity, man," he spat at Adegbite, and then his head slammed into the thick glass.

"OWW, a little too hard," Amanda said, padding her way back to the table. "Sorry Angel. I'm sort of new to this and sometimes I overshoot the mark. Does it hurt?" Amanda asked with a broad smile. "If you don't mind, I'd like to borrow these," she turned and asked Adegbite after placing a large bread knife and a pair of pruning shears in front of Angel. "Senor Diaz? I brought you presents," Amanda sang as Mittens fed on Diaz's impotent rage.

"Fucking bitch," he said, rubbing his forehead.

"You know, I'm getting really tired of being called a bitch. I want you to apologize." Amanda's playful attitude instantly became menacing.

"FUCK YOU, BITCH," Angel screamed and tried to spit again. Instead he picked up the pruning shears and clipped off the tip of his left pinkie finger. He howled in pain and managed to drop the tool and grab his injured hand in one motion.

"Hmph, I was hoping for more," she said and looked at Eldridge. "Several years ago, Angel cut off the fingers and toes of a warehouse worker in Tijuana. The poor man went to work one morning, found a hole in his storage shed, and a few of Angel's business associates. He lasted two whole days. How long do you think Angel will last?"

Adegbite moved his chair away from the bleeding Mexican and turned to Amanda. "I have personally never enjoyed the blood, or the brutality, but as you are my guest and Senor Diaz seems to be a willing participant, I believe that we should try to determine if he is equal to a warehouse worker in Tijuana." He had turned his back on the sobbing Angel, who now had his head down on the table, his left hand elevated and wrapped tightly in his right.

Two hours and eight snips of the shears later, Angel wasn't looking so good. "It's time," Eldridge said, looking at his watch. Initially, he had been a somewhat reluctant participant, but with each bloody scream he became more engaged and Amanda more disillusioned. "It's time, Amanda," he repeated.

"I heard you," she said rather testily. Her enthusiasm had run its course. Diaz's suffering wasn't giving Amanda what she needed. Forcing him to mutilate himself was about as challenging as shooting fish in a barrel. Even Mittens had retreated into a dark corner of her mind and fallen asleep.

"What's wrong?" a now-energized Eldridge Adegbite asked. His enthusiasm was beginning to irritate her.

"This isn't doing it for me."

"I don't understand—you can't stop now." A hint of desperation had escaped into his tightly controlled delivery.

"Why not?"

"Because you're not finished. Look!" He pointed at Diaz, who had rolled onto his side, blood oozing from his ruined left hand and right foot.

"It's getting cold and I didn't bring a jacket." Amanda looked up into the stars, her arms folded across her chest.

Eldridge shook his head. "This isn't doing it for you, and you're cold? How irresponsible can you be?"

"As irresponsible as I choose. I have no responsibility to you, to him, to anyone. I am a psychopath, remember?" Amanda stood and stepped over Diaz.

"There are rules that must be followed." He stood and partially blocked her way back into the house, punctuating his point with the large kitchen knife Amanda had borrowed earlier. "You killed one man and did that to another." He used the knife to point at his polished flagstones and the pool of blood that ended with Diaz. "People have seen you."

"First, I haven't done anything to anyone. Second, the only person to have seen me is you." Amanda had turned to face the taller man. He was in full predator mode, and his unguarded thoughts poured into Amanda's mind and Mittens caught the whiff of a strange scent. Self-preservation was his first and foremost imperative, and she was endangering it, and that caused him to emit a strange emotion. It wasn't fear; that had a distinct and delicious flavor. This was considerably more sour, but strangely appealing. It was an amalgam of rudimentary and stunted human emotions. "You smell interesting." She sniffed and took a step towards him. The sour emotion ramped up, and now Mittens began to take the mental reins from Amanda. The large, rabid dog breathed deeply and the lights in her mind began to blaze brightly.

Angel Diaz had disappeared from Amanda's consciousness; his agony had been reduced to a series of simple nerve impulses that were a far cry from what would sustain her. She needed fear, terror, and Angel was well past them. Eldridge Adegbite, however, was not. His mutant emotions tasted a little strange, but so did beets, and she had grown to love them.

***

His attempt to stab her met only air. Somehow he found himself facing the canyon, where an instant before he had been staring at Amanda. Diaz was at his feet and he nearly slipped in the blood as the Mexican reached for him. He kicked the prostrate man in the head and turned to find Amanda inches from him. He slashed at her face and found himself flat on the ground, the knife clattering from his grasp. He reached for the weapon, but Amanda stepped on his outstretched arm. He saw red as first one and then a second bone in his forearm snapped. A voice whispered in his ear that he was going to die, and he saw his mother tied to a burning bed.

"You're going to die," she screamed again over the roar of the flames. He kicked his legs and rolled to his feet, cradling his broken arm as the echoes of his dead mother flooded him with adrenaline. The thought of "not being," of the world continuing in his absence, prompted a state of near-panic.

"DIIIEEE," his father's voice yelled. He tried to shut it out, shut her out. Amanda was the source of his visions; she was manipulating his weakness. She had invaded his mind, his thoughts, his being, and in doing so had opened a door into her mind. From a far distance he could see her soul.

"Gone forever," his mother screamed. Knowing the source of his torment and being able to do something about it were two very different things.

"I know it's you, bitch," he screamed into the darkness. Somehow, all the torchlights had been extinguished, and his house lights had gone out as well.

"The lights aren't out, Lucas; you're blind," Amanda taunted him with the name his parents had given him. "Perhaps I should leave you like this, blind, dependent, and discovered." He stumbled after her and she fed off of his torment.

"I will find you, and …" A sharp pain in his back cut his declaration short. A second stab of pain dropped him to his knees and then into the sticky wet blood.

***

The world was starting to reform around him, only it was a world that made no sense. There was blood everywhere and his left hand failed to follow his commands. He was barefoot and a searing pain shot from his right foot to his confused brain every time he tried to move.

He was outside and it was cold. Freezing cold. He began to shiver and could swear that this was the coldest he had ever been, even after living almost a third of his life in the Colorado mountains. He rolled onto his side and nearly passed out from pain. His left hand was alive with fire, and when he brought it to his face he didn't recognize the bloody mess. He stared at the mutilated appendage and wondered what had happened to his fingers.

He heard voices and then something brushed his shoulder. A man's leg appeared, and as he reached for it with his good hand the leg savagely kicked him in the head. Stars burst through his confused mind, and instinctively he rolled away. Another wave of agony from his foot and hand seemed to focus his mind. He heard someone scream and recognized it as his neighbor, the shrink, and then the pieces started to fall into place. He was at Adegbite's house. The prick had invited him over to discuss the security fence Angel wanted to build, and then the mother-fucker shot one of his men.

A vision of Raul clutching his chest and falling into Adegbite's flower garden raced through Angel's head. "I'm gonna watch you die slowly, maricon," he tried to scream, but the words caught in his dry throat. He tried again as he heard a body scrambling near him, but the best he could produce was an unintelligible rasping sound. He rolled back on to his side and saw Adegbite above him, spinning his head around wildly while cradling his right arm.

"I know it's you, bitch," the old man screamed, and Angel looked for the bitch, but they were alone.

The pinche idiota is yelling at ghosts, Diaz thought as he began to drag himself towards Adegbite. "I'm going to cut your balls off and make you eat them," Angel whispered. "Then I'm going ..." he paused his diatribe as his right hand slid along the length of a large kitchen knife. The blade was covered in dried blood, and somehow he knew it had come from his mutilated hand. "Yo cago en la leche de tu puta madre."

Angel reached a leg of the patio table just as Adegbite stumbled into it. The old man twirled in place as if someone was behind him. Angel pulled himself to his knees, and just for an instant the world faded to grey. "Fuerza. Fuerza," he began reciting his work-out mantra, and he found himself standing with a knife in his one good hand, facing the broad, unprotected back of Eldridge Adegbite. The old man began to scream at the invisible bitch again, and Angel buried the knife, then pulled it out and stabbed Adegbite a second time.

"I got you, pendejo," Diaz whispered in the old man's ear. "You thought you could fuck with me," and Diaz stabbed Eldridge a third time. He fumbled with the knife handle but didn't have the strength to recover it, and they both fell to the floor. He tried to sit up but fell across the gasping psychiatrist. He rolled onto his back and saw an angel bathed in golden light standing over him.

"Madre Maria," he said and reached for her.

CHAPTER 32

"He's gone," Randi Garner said as an introduction.

"Who's gone?" Greg Flynn answered, balancing the phone on his shoulder as he brushed his teeth.

"Diaz. The Pueblo County DA signed off on the search warrant last night and they went in this morning, but the place was empty. No guards and no Diaz."

A whole lexicon of words he would never say out loud raced through his mind. He put down his toothbrush and wiped his face of tooth paste. "Somebody tipped him off," he concluded. A golden opportunity wasted.

"It's possible. I really don't believe that it took them three days to approve a simple search warrant."

"Did they recover anything useful?"

"Apparently a great deal. Computers, ledgers, bank records, just about everything was on site except the man himself. Pretty strange, don't you think?"

"I do. Even with a few minutes warning, he could have at least destroyed some of it." Greg was silent for a moment. "You think someone took him out?"

"I don't have a good feel for what goes on in Pueblo. For someone to take out Diaz and his entire security detail, they would need an awful lot of firepower." It was unlikely in the extreme that such an operation could be run in Colorado Springs without it becoming front page news.

"Anything on forensics?" Greg was grasping now; Angel Diaz was gone and would probably never be heard from again.

"Nothing. No bullets, blood, or bodies. Maybe they all just got homesick and went back to Mexico."

"Yeah, I'm sure he's sitting on a beach in Cancun at this very minute."

"Sorry, Greg. I will talk with you later." Garner hung up.

"Damn!" Greg yelled loud enough to pull Lisa out of a deep sleep.

"What's the matter?" she called from the bedroom, her voice full of early morning alarm.

"Sorry. Just something at work." He opened the bathroom door and saw his sleepy wife sitting up in bed, her short hair pointing in several different directions and her face puffy. She blinked her eyes at the intruding light. "Oops, sorry again," he said, and he closed the door. "I'll be out of here in a few."

"Please don't forget again to call Ted Alam," she said in a sleepy voice, and he could imagine hearing her head hit the pillow. Ted was a friend and occasional co-worker. He was normally stationed in the FBI field office in Denver, but for the last few months had been working out of Greg's office.

"You really want to push this," he said from behind the closed door.

"Yes, I really want to push this. He likes her and she seems to like him. I don't want Amanda to be alone." Her sleepy voice was gone, and her I-will-not-be-moved-from-this voice was in full force.

"Doomed to failure," he said to his reflection.

That had been the high point of Greg's day. His unit averaged a little over one homicide a month, along with the usual load of property and other forms of violent crime. This morning brought their third murder in four weeks. The first two had been cleared reasonably quickly; a man killed his girlfriend, and then—to even out the cosmic balance sheet—a wife stabbed her husband. Fairly easy, but the legalities demanded dozens of man-hours to be expended upon witnesses, forensics, and most importantly, paperwork. When this morning's call came in, Greg was just settling into his office desk and found nobody left to take the case aside from himself.

"You aren't going to like this one, chief," Courtney Pendleton, the dispatcher, said before handing him a yellow sheet of paper, a throwback to the original police blotter days. "It's at Memorial. A baby."

His head dropped as he scanned the form. "Okay," was all he could say. A devout Catholic, Greg was strongly against capital punishment, except in situations that involved children. "Five months." He shook his head after reading the victim's age.

Thirty minutes later he was sitting across from a drained and angry neurosurgeon. "Any way this could have been an accident?" He asked for a tragedy rather than a crime.

The doctor shook his head. "None. Baby had a left parietal and right frontal skull fracture, separated just about the width of an adult hand. Then there's the fractured femur in a child who can't … couldn't walk yet." He took a sip from his can of Coke.

"The mother reports that she picked the baby up from his father's house last night and that he was already asleep."

"Or in a coma," the surgeon scoffed.

"She says that she woke the baby up and fed him around seven …"

"Whoa! She said that she woke him up and fed him?"

"Yes." Greg rechecked his notes. "'He took a bottle around seven, and that's when I saw the bruise.' That's her statement."

"She's lying. Whatever caused those bruises caused the skull fractures and the subdural hematoma. No way this kid ever woke up and took a bottle."

"Subdural hematoma?" Greg questioned.

"Blood clot between the skull and the brain." He shook his head and stood up. "So Mom says Dad did this last night. What a piece of work." He drained his can and waited for Greg to stand. "Now I have to go tell those parents that one of them has killed their child."

Greg would wait at least an hour before interviewing the parents. He'd start with the father, who was alone in a family room, probably praying for everything to be all right, and moments away from learning that nothing was right. The mother was in a larger family room, surrounded by pastoral care, outsiders, and hospital nurses, all trying to help her through a process that she herself had probably initiated. "Which way to the operating rooms?" he asked a passing orderly.

It took less than half an hour to review the hospital records and view the baby's body. He had called a forensic team to take official photographs, more out of routine than need. The skull x-rays and CT scan told the story better than any photograph. He stared at the boy's tiny, perfect fingers and knew that they would haunt his sleep, but he couldn't turn away. Minutes passed and he continued to stare at those pale fingers and their delicate nails, avoiding the rest of him, which had been desecrated by violence. Tiny little Andrew Watts would never fit in Greg's mental closet, and he accepted that. This life, no matter how small, would not be forgotten.

"We need to take him, Detective," a voice said. A small black woman who he vaguely connected to the coroner's office tapped his shoulder. He turned away quickly after she unrolled an adult-size black body bag, and tried not to question whether the bags came in different sizes.

He took the stairs back to the ER, taking each step slowly. He paused at the last landing, needing even the briefest respite from the harsh realities of his job.

***

The murder of Andrew Watts was front page news, and the talking heads seemed to be on every television channel and radio station spewing facts and figures about the rise in domestic violence in a down economy. The entire country demanded an arrest, but the District Attorney, who had weighed in personally, waffled. Medical certainty had a habit of becoming somewhat murky under cross-examination, and without supporting testimony or forensics, the case against either parent was at best shaky.

"Day three of the 'Andrew Watch,'" Linda Stout said as she approached Greg, who was busy scraping the grill in his backyard. The Flynns were naturally gregarious individuals and it didn't take much of an excuse for them to throw a party, only now it had the festive atmosphere of a wake.

"Did you see the news this morning?" It was Sunday, and Colorado Springs had taken a hit in the hometown newspaper editorial pages and then again on the Sunday morning network news programs.

"Weren't we the toast of the town a few weeks back?" Linda was Greg's only female detective. Tall, with the physique of a long distance runner, she had the ability to always make Greg smile.

"The DA has got to get off the fence, Stick." Greg Flynn was the only person alive who could get away with calling her "Stick." "There's no forensics outside of the medical, and there are no witnesses."

"Did Diaz ever turn up?" Linda had been taking a course in Denver for the last week and was out of the loop.

"Nope. We are definitely going nowhere fast." He hung up the wire brush and turned to Linda, who handed him a bottle. "A beer. For me!"

"Lisa thought you could use one."

"Well, it's five o'clock somewhere," Greg said just before he noticed the approach of Linda's secret guest of honor. "Have you met Ted Alam?" Linda turned and offered her hand to a tall, dark-haired man in his mid-thirties. "Ted works for the FBI, and their agents have been ordered by the Director himself to wear suits to all backyard barbecues."

Ted grinned. "Sorry about that; I had to run up to Denver this morning. Hi Linda." He shook her hand, although introductions were hardly necessary as they had shared an office for the past month. He turned to Greg. "I've got something for you," he said in a slightly conspiratorial tone.

"Something besides a beer I hope," Greg said as he raised his bottle.

"Pueblo PD found Angel Diaz, or at least what's left of him," Ted said. Both Greg and Linda started. Ted shook his head and laughed. "You're not going to believe where…"

"Hi sweetheart …" Greg cut him off. Amanda skirted Ted and curled under Greg's outstretched arm. "You caught us. We were talking shop." He gave her a squeeze.

"I won't tell Lisa, this time. What's up? The baby?"

Ted looked at Greg and then quickly at Amanda. "It's okay, Ted. She's definitely heard worse," Greg assured him.

"He was at the neighbor's. They had a zoning issue over a fence, and from what Pueblo gathered, it got pretty nasty. Both dead, but here's the strange part: the old guy tortured Diaz. Cuts off his fingers and toes before Diaz manages to stab the guy. They both died four or five days ago."

Greg stood dumbfounded. "What?" he finally said as the shock wore off and the inconsistencies began to surface. "Angel Diaz, drug lord and murderer, gets tortured by a neighbor, over a fence? That's like Pablo Escobar getting killed by the pizza delivery boy over a tip."

"Believe it or not. In fact, the way we heard about it was because the old guy had assumed the identity of a psychiatrist who died back in the nineties. Truth is stranger than fiction."

"Cheese it guys; here comes the cops," Greg said in his best James Cagney as Lisa approached.

"NO WORK! You may talk about sports, the weather, the President, even religion, but no work." She stood behind the four of them. "Greg, you have hamburger patties to make, and Linda, you can help."

"Well, let's not let my wife's completely transparent motives delay us from pressing meat into patties, Linda." Greg released Amanda, took Linda's hand, and followed Lisa back into the house.

"Well, that was a little awkward," Ted said, and Amanda nodded her agreement.

"Yeah, Lisa is about as subtle as a bulldozer." Amanda sidestepped over to the picnic table and sat. "Greg tells me that you're going to Washington for a while." Even with her mental radar turned down to low, she could tell that her innocent statement had set off alarm bells in Ted's mind.

"Meetings, classes, work stuff." He recovered quickly but still seemed pre-occupied.

"You don't really want to be here, do you?" She smiled and pretended to be insightful.

"Does it show?"

"Somewhere else to be?" Her question unlocked a door in the back of his mind, and more anxiety came spilling out. Intrigued, she traced it back to its source and turned on a tiny penlight. Ted winced and shook his head.

"Ow. I just had a brain freeze." He rubbed his temples. "I'm sorry, Amanda, but I'm not very good company now; I think I should go." He was suddenly very uncomfortable in her presence; he stood and unconsciously looked around to see if he was being watched. "Will you please pass along my thanks and apologies to Greg and Lisa?" She remained seated, and he gave her a half wave and then disappeared around the side of the house.

"Oh Ted, what have you gotten yourself into," she whispered. When Lisa introduced them three weeks earlier, Amanda had sensed his checkered past and Greg confirmed it. Ted had been a rising star in the FBI ten years earlier, but disillusionment led to alcohol, eventually a less-than-discreet affair, and finally a very messy divorce. He managed to pull himself together in time to save what was left of his career, but only after he had been recognized as a security risk. Banished from Washington to the field office in Denver, he again found himself sinking into despair. Once the golden child living in the palace, now he was just an anonymous field agent living in a duplex. He managed to remain anonymous for several years, but eventually frustration took its toll and he found his way back down familiar streets. A drunken indiscretion led to another, and then more. After months of blackouts and sick-days, it took a bout of alcoholic hepatitis to bring him back around. Only this time it was without his integrity. The true cost of his indiscretions didn't become known until two weeks ago. It arrived in a large legal envelope that was delivered to his temporary desk in Colorado Springs, and inside were photographs of him with an unidentified Asian man. The following day a similar envelope contained copies of FBI files with a handwritten note: Southwest Corner, Washington Mall, April 12th, 2:00 PM, File: PLAX 7344963-8772. The same day, he received an email with the same message. An attached video showed him passing a thick file to the Asian man and laughing about how easy it was.

The party began to spill out into the backyard, and Amanda passed along Ted's apologies. Lisa was visibly disappointed, but the news that Angel Diaz had met a very timely and painful death seemed to have lifted everyone else. Greg had loudly assumed his role of master chef, and for the moment the murder of Andrew Watts was set aside.

CHAPTER 33

Amanda stared at the ceiling and listened to the house creak. Weeks earlier, she had come to realize that she needed less sleep. In fact, she wondered if in time she wouldn't need to sleep at all. She sat up in bed and the LED clock told her that it was 2:14 AM, or three minutes later than the last time she checked. She wondered what Suzie Watts was doing at this very moment. Was she sleeping comfortably, unencumbered by 2:00 AM feedings? Was she sedated, filled with remorse and guilt? Amanda had no proof beyond Greg's impressions that she had killed her son, but at 2:14 in the morning they would suffice.

Killing Suzie would be easy, even with the paparazzi dogging her every step. Grieving mother, consumed by guilt, takes her own life, complete with suicide note. The thought of watching Suzie Watts dying by her hand nearly pushed Amanda to the edge. She rolled out of bed and started pacing away the nervous energy.

"Calm yourself," she whispered to a growling Mittens. The relief she experienced with Adegbite and Diaz had faded quickly, and Mittens was becoming restless. Their deaths had been as much a learning experience as it was a release. For one thing, it taught her that torture for the sake of torture, and murder for the sake of murder, were incapable of satisfying her need. It was power and control over a human life that she craved, and violence was simply the most convenient tool to create the appropriate conditions. Mittens disagreed, but the empty feeling as she watched Diaz mutilate himself was undeniable. Within a matter of minutes he had surrendered to the inevitable, which made it completely unfulfilling.

Adegbite, on the other hand, refused to surrender or to cede control; he struggled to the end, a premature end.

Which was her second lesson. She had lost all situational awareness. Blinded by her desire to drain the old man, she had forgotten about the young man. Only after Adegbite was dropping to his knees did she remember that they were not alone. Devoid of her influence, Diaz's natural instincts asserted themselves, and he could have stabbed her just as easily as he had stabbed Adegbite.

"Stupid," she whispered to herself. She had lost every semblance of control, and it was only out of sheer luck that she survived. She wasn't much better than one of Diaz's addicts, nearly sacrificing everything for a fix. She wouldn't make the same mistake twice. Suzie Watts wasn't the cold-blooded killer Diaz had been. In fact, Amanda doubted that she was even a predator, but she would be treated like one. In all likelihood she had killed her son in a fit of rage, a true moment of insanity, but that wouldn't change Amanda's approach.

Why are you losing sleep over this woman? So she killed her son; what does that have to do with you? A voice that once may have been a conscience asked. *An admitted psychopath has no real human emotions, or interest in the artificial constructs of morality or justice. They are interested only in things that affect them. If you just need a release, why not go next door and kill the neighbors? It's far more convenient. In fact, you could make a night of it.*

She waited for her mind to process its own question. The house continued to creak, and she could just make out Greg down the hall snoring away his five beers. But no great insight that explained the apparent contradiction revealed itself. The truth was she didn't know what she was, or what she was becoming. Psychopath was just the latest coat she had tried on, but now it seemed too confining. She was forced to admit that her interest in Suzie Watts extended beyond simple convenience, and had to accept the fact that a part of her still clung to a fragment of morality.

Amanda slowed her pacing and finally sat on the edge of her bed. She could live with a small degree of morality, so long as it didn't interfere with Mittens. Her alter-ego made Amanda feel strong, resolute, and confident, and each time Amanda allowed Mittens to express herself they had both grown stronger.

A wave of fatigue rolled over Amanda and she lay back into the bed. She was tired of always examining her motivations. Life was so much easier without rules or reasons.

Like an animal. No thoughts of why, just of how, her conscience said in a voice that resembled her husband's.

It was an ugly, uncomfortable image, and Amanda tried to ignore it as she fell asleep.

***

Randi Garner stomped through the bullpen with an expression that scattered the early morning knot of detectives. "Is he in?" she asked without pausing. The officer outside Greg Flynn's office wasn't even on his feet before Randi was inside, the door closing with a loud rattle that shook the entire department.

"Well good morning to you," Greg said as the ADA dropped her purse and coat on his office sofa and dropped into the chair opposite his desk. "Are we grumpy this morning?"

She took a deep breath. "I have a message from Mr. Dunlop," she said, and Greg felt the temperature in the room fall considerably. Ray Dunlop was Randi's boss and the El Paso County District Attorney. "We have been informed by Internal Affairs that they have started an investigation into your unit and are requesting our assistance in appointing a special prosecutor."

Greg stared into Randi's eyes, looking for signs that this was a joke, but her gaze was unwavering. "Run that by me again?"

"Allegations have been raised about evidence tampering, intimidation, torture, and murder." Randi closed her eyes and dropped her head a fraction as she recited the list.

"You can't be serious," Greg answered, feeling as if he just fell down the rabbit hole. "Is this about the Watts case?" The bodies of Suzie Watts and her occasional live-in boyfriend had been found three days earlier in an east-side motel. She had requested police protection after her house was sprayed with gunfire. No one had been hurt in the incident, but the local media, who had been camped out on her doorstep, had quite a scare. An alert film crew had managed to tape the shooter's car, and the two men responsible were already in custody.

"Who picked the motel?" Randi asked pointedly.

"You know better than that." His tone was uncharacteristically severe. The city had contracts with a number of hotels for witnesses, juries, and occasionally suspects, which were used on a rotating basis.

"The Sky-Line was next up; why was she taken to the Mountain Aire?" She jumped on him as if he were a witness who had been caught lying.

"Because the Sky-Line said 'no.' Anybody with a television and half a brain would know who we were trying to protect." Greg was talking through clenched teeth. He could accept these questions from Ray Dunlop, or an internal affairs investigator, but not from Randi Garner. "We don't even know what happened. For God's sake, the autopsies aren't even back." He stared her down. "Do you seriously believe any of this?"

She hesitated only a moment. "I spent two hours this morning defending you and this unit, but there are things that I can't explain."

"Namely?" Her answer eased his sense of betrayal, but not entirely.

"You arrest John Eden, and then his wife says that a woman no one can find intimidates her into confessing."

Greg raised his voice. "No one intimidated that woman. She was alone in an elevator!"

"Like I told you before, there had to be more to the story. And now we have four dead bodies that are related to cases this office was investigating." She matched his decibel level. "And this suicide note sounds more like it came from a college professor than a guilt-ridden high-school drop-out."

Greg slumped in his chair. He couldn't fault her for voicing concerns that he shared. "I realize that, and I can only imagine how this looks from the outside, but no one, no one in this unit is involved with whatever has been going on these past couple of months." His eyes burned with sincerity and watched as Randi subtly eased back into her chair. "So is this an unofficial heads-up or a formal interview?"

"A heads-up. Dunlop doesn't want to deal with this any more than you do. So how do we make this go away?" She had calmed, although her complexion remained flushed.

He thought for a moment. This was uncharted territory; never before had anyone questioned his integrity or competence, and he didn't know who to turn to, or to trust. "You heard about this early this morning. I'm guessing the Chief of Police knew before you did and decided not to warn me. That means he wants this to go forward; so let it." He faced Randi. "Tell Ray that we have nothing to hide and will cooperate fully."

"You might want to think this through. Once it starts, you are guilty until proven innocent. Not to mention the fact that these investigations are a convenient way to settle old scores," she cautioned as they worked their way back to their normal comfortable relationship.

"Stonewalling will only make things worse. I'm not afraid of the truth, Randi, and I speak for the entire unit."

"Perception always trumps truth."

"If that's the case, then maybe it is time for me to leave." It was a thought he had a lot lately.

She stood and retrieved her purse and coat. "You have a responsibility to this unit and those who have come to rely upon you." She held his gaze long enough to communicate her meaning and then turned and left. He should have seen this coming, but hadn't. Despite his occupation, he was basically a trusting individual and expected the same courtesy from others, a naivety that had plagued him in the past.

There was little doubt in his mind that the sudden and far-too-convenient resolutions of these three cases were related, and even less doubt that the deaths of Suzie Watts and her boyfriend would officially be deemed homicides as soon as the autopsy results were available. He watched four of his detectives go about their business and toyed with the idea that perhaps one or more of them had taken matters into their own hands. It had happened elsewhere, on more occasions than anyone wanted to admit. It took less than five seconds for him to utterly reject the idea. He knew these people, he interacted with them almost every day, and not one of them had given him the slightest cause for concern.

Of course, that didn't mean that someone outside his unit, or even the department, hadn't decided to lend "justice" a hand. A very clever vigilante would go a long way in explaining the police's sudden unnatural good fortune.

He glanced at the clock and decided that it was early enough to check with pathology and see if they had come up with anything. He dialed the number from memory, hoping that it was the Chief Coroner who performed the autopsies, but that his secretary had the information.

"Hi Greg," Linda Miller said. "Don't you just love caller ID?"

"Hi Linda. Anything on the Watts case?" He had known Linda for at least a couple decades, and on this rare occasion he traded on that history to avoid small talk.

"For that you will have to speak to Him. Sorry." Everyone had the same opinion of Phillip Rucker, MD. Brilliant, but painfully awkward and well beyond any point of social ineptitude. Rucker lived inside of himself, and only rarely did he venture out.

"Detective Flynn, I have some information for you." No introduction, salutation, or even vocal inflection. Phillip Rucker could quite easily have been a computer program written by Linda. He smiled at the thought that Linda was secretly running the entire coroner's office. "Both bodies were without signs of struggle or injury. The toxicology report lists THC and alcohol, both in small amounts. Inspection of the external surfaces revealed no puncture wounds …"

Out of necessity, Greg cut him off. Rucker was incapable of filtering information and probably couldn't understand why mere mortals needed the condensed version of anything. "Do you have a cause of death, Doctor?"

"The female died of diffuse intracranial hypertension caused by extensive subarachnoid hemorrhage …"

"She had a bleed in the brain," Greg tried to clarify.

"That is not precisely correct …" Greg let Rucker drone on for two minutes, thoughts of Mr. Spock running through his mind.

"The male had a similar pattern of subarachnoid hemorrhage, but died of cardiopulmonary insufficiency initiated by a pulmonary embolus …"

"A blood clot in the lung," once again Greg clarified. "Both deaths were natural, then."

"At this point that is correct. However, it is subject to change should new information become available. " Rucker answered robotically.

"That doesn't fit with the evidence at the scene, Doctor. We have a suicide note."

"That is inconsistent with my findings," Robo-Rucker said. "Is it possible the note came from someone else?"

"Anything's possible, especially lately, but the note appears to be genuine, written by the female." Rucker's impersonal speech pattern was becoming infectious. Greg was silent for a moment. If the examining physician had been anyone other than Rucker, he would have asked that the exams be repeated, but Phillip Rucker did not make mistakes. Ever. "I am stumped, Doctor. We have a situation in which a mother confesses to killing her own son in a suicide note, and then both she and her boyfriend suddenly fall over dead from natural causes."

"That sounds unlikely." If Greg hadn't known Rucker better, he would have thought that the pathologist was making a joke.

"It sounds biblical." Greg shifted gears. "The two bodies from Pueblo, have they been examined?"

"Yes. The older man died from cardiopulmonary failure as a result of blood loss. He had multiple stab wounds that were the proximate cause of the blood loss. The younger man also died from cardiopulmonary insufficiency as a result of blood loss. He had eight digit amputations …"

"I see," Greg said forcefully. "So both were homicides," he concluded.

"No, Detective. The older man's death has been ruled a homicide but the younger man's death has been changed to suicide. He amputated his own digits. In addition, both men were found to have subarachnoid hemorrhages, but in neither of these two cases were they fatal."

"So all four of these individuals had bleeding around the brain?" Greg asked, for clarification.

"That is correct," Rucker answered succinctly.

"What would cause the bleeding around the brain?"

"Unknown. Subarachnoid hemorrhages are not uncommon in trauma situations. However, evidence of cranial trauma is conspicuously absent in all four victims."

"None of this makes sense," Greg commented to himself.

"Do you have any more questions, Detective?"

"No, Doctor, thank you." The phone went dead. Rucker's findings would give Greg and his unit a little breathing room. Suzie Watts and her boyfriend would disappear from any official inquiry. Diaz would also likely disappear, leaving only Adegbite, whose cause of death was clear. The Pueblo PD had hand and finger print matches to Diaz on the knife stuck in Adegbite's back. On the surface everything could be explained. Below the surface nothing made sense.

CHAPTER 34

Amanda fastened her seat belt and wrapped herself in a cloud of hostility to discourage the predictable and meaningless conversation from the man who sat next to her. She had no interest in hearing how much he hated to fly, or how much she looked like a girl he once knew (which was a lie), or any of the other dozen or so opening lines he was preparing. She nudged his attention towards the attractive flight attendant and restrained the impulse to punish him for invading her solitude. She curled into the leather seat and closed her eyes as the plane pushed back from the gate.

A week earlier, she had flown to Dallas to close out her employment with the Lieber Institute and collect her belongings, left in a hotel room a lifetime ago. By day, she dutifully attended the multiple exit interviews with the Red Cross and the Department of State, saying all the right things to allow them to close the book on this "unfortunate business," and played her dual role of both hero and victim perfectly. By night, she slipped into the more comfortable role of predator.

She opened her eyes as they lifted off and the long, flat expanse of north Texas rolled out to the hazy horizon. She was on a plane headed to Washington, and for the life of her she couldn't say why. Ted Alam was already there, and in less than a day he would pass top secret documents to a foreign agent, or die trying to protect them. So was it a sense of patriotism that drove her? She smiled at such a lofty and selfless sentiment. No, it wasn't patriotism. She wasn't going to protect Ted either. He had made his choices.

So why did you deceive everyone and get on this plane? her conscience asked in Michael's voice.

She tried to ignore the question but it dogged her. *Personal reasons,* she finally answered. It was the best she could come up with. Her mind was in so much turmoil that she simply couldn't trust any decision she made, and was running solely on instinct.

A voyage of self-discovery, Michael's voice mocked. *Or another opportunity to restart the cycle of disillusionment?*

Amanda was starting to burn with anger, and she wanted to lash out at something, at someone. But, like Ted Alam, she was the source of her own problems. Time had not brought her clarity, or even stability. With every life she took she became a little more desperate, a little more disillusioned, and a little more unstable. Violence and murder had become the focal point of her life, and for a time she had thought that it could sustain her, give her a sense of purpose, but all it seemed to do was hollow her out by increments. But still she defaulted to it; it was familiar, comfortable, and for the briefest moment made her feel whole again.

Cycle of disillusionment, she repeated to herself. Even the murder of Suzie Watts and her low-life boyfriend hadn't sustained her for more than a couple of days. By the time she had reached Dallas, Amanda was already in search of another opportunity. She was able to restrain Mittens for two full days, but then her alter-ego demanded another fix, and one without a trace of moral justification. Just pure self-indulgent, wanton violence. Two nights in a row Amanda tried to satisfy Mittens's desires. The first night she choose a street corner drug-dealer out of simple convenience, and the next night she found his supplier. She allowed Mittens to be as creative as she wanted and in the end took everything from each of her victims, only to awaken the following mornings to the now all too familiar gnawing emptiness.

Amanda had to finally admit that indulging Mittens had not made her stronger. Instead, each time she lost control and surrendered herself to her alter-ego she had dug the hole a little deeper and the gnawing emptiness filled it. Mittens was nothing more than an articulate manifestation of all the base instincts and drives that lived in the dark recesses of every mind and could never be completely satiated. Each death only increased her appetite. Everyone had their own Mittens. Unfortunately, Amanda's version had been amplified to a compelling level and came with the ability to indulge even the slightest whim without consequence.

The ultimate test of restraint. Are you up to it, Amanda? Michael asked.

His perspective flipped from first to second person with enough regularity that she began to wonder if the thoughts were even hers. Could this be her Michael communicating from a different reality? Was this another aspect of her evolution: communicating with the dead?

"Are you real?" She whispered, and waited for an answer. To have him back, even if it was just a voice in her mind, would change everything. But all she felt was silence.

Nothing more than voices of the past, Mittens answered after a long minute.

The bored flight attendant with the painted-on smile asked Amanda and her seat-mate if they wanted something to drink. Amanda declined, but he asked for a rum and Coke and took the opportunity to surreptitiously compare Amanda's cleavage with the flight attendant's. Amanda lost. She smiled, wondering how the horny traveler would feel if he knew what the smiling stewardess was planning to add to his drink.

***

Ted Alam had been walking the Washington mall for nearly an hour, trying to appear as inconspicuous as possible. He sidestepped the multitude of tourists who were snapping pictures of the cherry blossoms and of the distant Capitol, and kept moving. He was certain someone was watching him—either members of Lon Chang's organization or his own organization, the FBI, or both—and he refused to let them have an easy time of it. Two o'clock was late for lunch, but on a day like today, with mild temperatures and the sun warming DC for the first time in months, he had a reasonable excuse for his wanderings. Officially, he was in Washington to complete a class he had begun over a year earlier. He had worked through lunch to finish early, and then made a point of letting his proctors know that he was off to enjoy the day.

He tossed a handful of birdfeed to the very well-fed ducks that were returning in numbers to the pools. Lon Chang was late, which was typical but unnerving nonetheless. He strolled in front of a large group of elderly tourists and offered to take their picture. They thanked him, and the half dozen senior citizens slowly assembled and loudly yelled "Cheese" just before he snapped the picture. He retrieved his briefcase, which contained File: PLAX 7344963-8772, and continued his wandering. It wasn't a paper file but three CDs: the complete FBI security evaluation of the Port of Los

Angeles. His earlier indiscretions had been unimportant internal memoranda regarding budgetary allocations, and if Ted hadn't been so impaired at the time he probably would have realized that the information could have been legally obtained. This file was a whole different story. It was a blueprint for terrorism.

He walked by the southwest corner for the sixth time, but still no Chang. He was the epitome of a compromised agent, an absolute textbook example of what not to do, including keeping this latest development from his superiors. He knew what he was doing was a mistake, and he had debated long and hard about how to handle his predicament, finally deciding that handling this himself was the lesser of all evils open to him. The file required a key, a deciphering program that happened to be loaded on his laptop. He would open the CD file on his laptop, proving to Chang that it was the file in question, and then pass the worthless CDs over to the Chinese national. He would then stroll back to his life.

Of course, there was almost no chance any of that would happen. Chang would certainly know that the files were encrypted and would require a program to be opened, so he would either demand the key or Alam's laptop, or—worse still—would have his own laptop loaded with a copy of the deciphering program. In which case Ted would arrest the small man and both their worlds would unravel.

Of course, that was unlikely to happen as well. Chang played the part of a low-level agent, more fool than spy, but it was just a role. He would come prepared, almost certainly with a team of well-armed and well-trained operatives whose goal would be recovery of the CDs and, if necessary, and if possible, Chang himself. Ted was armed and prepared as well, but harbored no expectation he would survive a gun battle with an unknown number of hidden agents. He would draw his weapon if Chang resisted arrest, but then drop it once the small man played his last hand by calling in his team of operatives. Ted would let Chang and his men take the CDs and his case and allow them to leave. Once at a safe distance, he would detonate the charge that occupied half of the laptop's battery compartment. With a little luck, it would do more than just take off a hand.

Ted swung around the metal bench that he assumed would be the exchange point for the seventh time and started back up Jefferson Drive. After he passed Twelfth Street a distant clock chimed the quarter hour, and out of sheer frustration he glanced back at the empty bench. Nothing. He rounded the Smithsonian and a Frisbee skidded across his path. The lawns were filled with families and sunbathers, all enjoying life, and Ted felt more isolated than ever. He stepped over the disk and kept walking.

"Dude, a little help?" a longhaired twenty-something yelled. Ted glanced over; immersed in troubles of his own making, he didn't realize that he had violated Frisbee etiquette. "Toss it, man ..." The young man was dressed in a torn tie-dye shirt, cut-off jeans over pasty white spindly legs; a leather thong gathered his dirty black hair into a ponytail. He stood facing Ted with an expectant look, fifty years out of time. Ted flicked the disk back to the ersatz hippie, who caught it with one finger. "Seventh and Madison, just in front of the pool. Go now," he said quickly and then turned and jogged back to the center of the field, throwing the Frisbee to another pretend-hippie with practiced expertise.

For a moment, Ted wasn't certain he had heard what he thought he heard, and he remained rooted in place. The pair continued to toss the disk, yelling with each athletic catch, and after several more throws their game began to drift towards Madison Avenue and a small fountain inside a reflecting pool. Ted paralleled their progress and turned left on Seventh. Another group of tourists, all with headphones in place, stood facing the Capitol while their bored tour guide droned on in German. Ted skirted the group and found Mr. Chang propped against a tree, playing Angry Birds on a tablet.

***

"I am completely addicted to this game," he said as a surviving pig laughed at him. "But I can't seem to clear this level." His English was perfect, much better than Ted had remembered, and he shook the tablet in phony frustration. "You passed me three times and never even noticed." He finally turned from the game and faced Ted. "Or anyone else." His threat hung in the air.

"I just want to get through this as quickly as possible." Ted crouched down, slid the laptop out of his briefcase, loaded the first of the three CDs, and then handed the computer to Chang.

"Perfect. Is this everything?" Chang asked, immersed in the program.

"Here," Ted said tersely and handed the Asian two more CDs. Chang closed the program, swapped discs, and when that disc opened immediately, repeated the process with the third CD.

"Excellent," he said, closing the computer screen after pocketing the three discs. "Of course these files are encryp ..." Without warning, Ted jumped to his feet. Chang dropped the laptop into the grass and was on his feet only an instant after Ted.

***

A light brighter than the noonday sun suddenly filled Chang's mind. A moment later it resolved into the most exquisite creature he had ever seen. Her beauty was so overpowering that it made his head throb; he felt lighter than air and was certain that his feet had left the ground. He steadied himself against the smooth bark of the tree, and from her brilliance floated the most beautiful voice he could imagine. A mixture of music and soft caresses, it spoke in a language that no simple human mind could ever understand. Ted's rough and ugly voice interrupted its perfect harmony, and abruptly the spell snapped. A lovely young blonde woman wearing a yellow sundress approached them. Alam spoke again, and Chang's mind cleared enough to recognize the name "Amanda."

"What are you doing here?" Ted asked, and Chang wondered why Ted was so upset with the arrival of this exquisite creature.

"I can't let you do this, Ted," she said, and Chang struggled to understand what they were talking about. He felt drunk, and his mind slowly translated the English words to Korean. Alam was worse than a fool. He was an American fool. He saw an Asian face and immediately accepted that Chang was from China. It amazed and shamed him that such a narrow-minded, egotistical society was responsible for his proud country's survival. Still, they had brought with them the wonderful concepts of free markets and unrestrained capitalism.

"What's going on here, Ted?" Chang said, a little thickly, trying to shake off this woman's narcotic effect. He looked past Ted and found one of his four colleagues across the street, alert to the fact that things were not going to plan. Chang was running point for the five-man team that had worked the American agent for more than a year. A great deal of money and effort had been expended in maneuvering Ted to this very spot, and now this woman's unexpected appearance threatened their investment. "Who are you?" He took a step forward and had a clear view of Amanda.

"He's not who you think he is," she answered, ignoring Chang's question. "Ted, you don't have much time ..."

Chang reached for the gun beneath his jacket, but his mind exploded into an infinity of stars, and the wondrous voice filled the spaces between. He was on his knees, then on his back, and finally on his stomach as the beautiful angel transformed into a hideous and vengeful demon. An invisible hand forced his face into the dirt and he watched Ted scoop up the laptop and the precious discs. He could hear them talk, but their words held no meaning. He heard his name, his real name, and the astonishment made him struggle. He tried to move, but the invisible hand only pushed harder; he was breathing dirt now, and his body was being crushed by the unseen force. He began to panic, and images raced through his mind. His parents, their Seoul apartment, school, university, induction into the Army, and then an alien but crystal-clear memory of a small blonde baby. A tall, muscular American with an inviting and mischievous smile followed.

Josh and Michael, are you there? a woman's voice whispered in his mind, and repressed emotions of love, longing, and loss—having finally found an outlet—filled his soul. They were her emotions and it was her voice; the woman Alam had called Amanda. Images of her life mixed with his as the two talked above him. He was forced to listen but prevented from understanding until they came to a long pause and the woman turned her attention back to him.

I'm going to let you up, Bong-hwa, she boomed into his mind in a language that was neither English nor Korean. *Sit there and be good and I won't hurt you.* The pressure on his back eased off, and he gasped to re-expand his lungs. His head was released, and he rolled on to his back.

"What are you?" he panted. Amanda was a few steps closer, but Ted had retreated into the shade of a tree several steps up the sidewalk. Chang looked around for the rest of his team.

"I sent them away," she answered, and turned back to Ted. "They were going to take you, and the discs," she told the American.

"You can't be here," Alam said, fear filling his voice.

Chang tried to reconstruct the previous two minutes of his life, but they seemed to be lost. Something important was happening, but he didn't have the capacity to recognize it, only to sense it. It was difficult and somewhat painful to formulate coherent thoughts, and then a childhood nightmare flashed through his mind. He was running through the streets of Seoul, but they were covered in waist high snow and an unseen horror tracked him. The vision passed but the terror it reliably produced remained. Both time and reality seemed to have been warped, and his mind searched frantically for something solid to hold on to. He rolled into a sitting position, and his hand brushed against the cool metal of his fallen gun. It slipped into his hand with a familiarity that helped to clear some of the mental inertia.

There had been rumors about the American "psychic soldier" projects since before he had been born, but he had no idea they had made such progress. Not even a whisper of their success had reached his ears, or the ears of anyone else who lived in his world—a world that used information as currency. This made everything he, his boss, and their clients had worked for completely obsolete. The Port Authority plans were worthless when the Americans could tell when, where, and how the attack was coming. In fact, they must have seen him coming. Alam's willingness to deliver vital US secrets was a ploy to draw him and his men out into the open. It was likely the FBI was closing in on him at this very instant.

Panic stricken, Chang jumped to his feet. Ted sensed the movement, saw the weapon, and began to run towards Amanda. Chang's first shot struck Ted just beneath the left scapula as he tried to shield the woman. The second shot struck him in the knee and he fell fifteen feet short of her. Chang recentered his aim and fired his third shot in less than three seconds. Amanda's eyes were wide with surprise but narrowed with something else just as he felt the weapon recoil.

Time seemed to have stopped, and in the instant that lasted an eternity, Bong-hwa Son, AKA Lon Chang, had an almost perfect clarity. He saw the tourists reacting to the gunshots; their attempts to flee the carnage were frozen in his mind. He saw Alam down on his left side, blood already staining the concrete. He saw each of his four colleagues running in different directions, their minds confused and their intentions scrambled. But mostly he saw Amanda. She filled his sight and mind. He felt where the bullet had struck her, just below her right collar bone. Not a kill shot, but close; only, to their mutual surprise, she was for the most part unharmed. It felt no worse than being struck by a paintball; a paintball that in actuality had been a hollow-point 9mm bullet traveling at fifteen hundred feet per second.

"You really should not have done that," she said, and Chang didn't have enough time to wonder where the voice had come from. The gun seemed to ignite in his outstretched hand. He tried to drop it, but the molten metal and plastic dissolved into his hand and then poured up his arm. His jacket sleeve ignited in a flash, and instinctively he began to pat it with his left arm. The living, red-hot metal jumped to his other arm, and an instant later he was engulfed in flames. His only scream was cut short as the fire poured down his throat. He fell to the grass with his mind yelling that he was burning alive. The woman refused him the peace of unconsciousness, and she whispered that he would suffer for as long as he lived. Time had no meaning as months and years passed. He felt a pull on his right arm, and with perfect clarity he watched it fall to the grass; a similar pull and what was left of his left arm fell across the charred remains of the right.

Beg to die, her mind screamed, and he had no choice but to obey. He was well beyond human suffering and should by all reason already be dead.

Please, he pleaded across the mental bridge that separated them, and then all at once he was on his back, the sun shining brightly into his eyes. His hands, which should have been charred remnants, flew to his perfectly intact face and chest. An ache in his right shoulder and a spot just below his collar bone told him that he was still alive. He felt something slither up his left pant leg, and then his right. He tried to jump to his feet, but his legs no longer functioned. More cool, slithering somethings found their way into his jacket and then down across his waist. He tried to twist his body but nothing seemed to work.

Snakes! his mind screamed.

You didn't think this was over, did you?

The first bite was just below his knee, the serpent blunting its fangs against his shin bone, then into the fleshy portion of his thigh. The venom was like acid and his leg began to liquefy. His belt snapped as the mass of snakes found his midsection. The terror broke his mind. His mother's oldest threat was finally being realized. The next bite was to his left testicle, but instead of it dissolving, the serpent began to tear at the tissue. A second, then a third, then too many to count as the organ was ripped from his body. The agony was everything he had been promised so long ago by those who should have loved and protected him. He begged to die, but the only answer he received was a bite into his right testicle. Later, when the snakes had fulfilled every aspect of his mother's threat and he could no longer breathe, they started on his penis. His heart gave out just after they finished.

CHAPTER 35

Amanda knew that she had to move, but she was beyond exhausted. Instead of energizing her, Chang's long slow death had depleted her. She stood over his body, his head oddly misshapen. She kicked his foot for good measure and a small metal object rolled from beneath his shoe. She stared at it, its existence somehow compelling. She stooped to pick it up and nearly lost her balance when the world around her began to spin. She staggered over to Ted, but before reaching his body she turned away. He was dead beyond question. Death had its own unique flavor.

She hurried up the promenade and away from the two bodies. She slipped behind a copse of trees, ran across Madison Avenue, and disappeared into the afternoon crowds.

Two hours later she was in the middle seat of a Southwest Airlines flight to Chicago. It would be a long night of flying before getting back to Dallas, but she could use the rest. Her batteries were drained and she wasn't home yet. It didn't take a lot of energy to project the persona of Dalice Lewis, the name she had chosen to fly under, but circumstances now demanded perfection from her. An FBI agent, someone she had known, had been killed in broad daylight. The situation had spun out of control and she needed to distance herself from it without leaving a trail that led back to Colorado Springs.

***

"I'm sorry you had to come back early, Amanda." Greg embraced his daughter-in-law just in front of the baggage carousel.

"Don't be. I was finished anyway, and wanted to be home. How are you?"

"I'm okay," Greg said, with a mixture of unusual formality and typical male detachment. "I know you and Ted were friends," Amanda said, grabbing the first of her two suitcases.

"Friends is probably too strong a term. I don't want to talk about him," he said abruptly.

"All right. Where's Lisa?" Amanda had resolved to respect the mental privacy of her inner circle. As there were only three members, she didn't expect it to be a terrible imposition.

"At home. We aren't exactly communicating well at the moment." Greg opened the door for her as she wheeled her suitcase out into the cloudy afternoon. "Before you ask"—he cut off her question—"there's something we need to talk about." Greg suddenly showed a side of himself she had never seen. Professional, serious, and somewhat intimidating. She followed him to the car and they drove silently back towards town.

"Greg, you missed the turnoff." She finally broke the silence, which had lasted more than ten minutes.

"I don't want to talk at home," he said softly.

They drove several more miles and he took a familiar exit, followed by three familiar turns, before he pulled into a very familiar driveway. The house facing them was empty, and for Amanda it would always be empty. "Greg, I don't want to be here," she said, and for the first time in months she felt the familiar pain of loss.

"That may be the first completely truthful statement you've made since you came back," Greg said, with more sadness than bitterness. "You know that Lisa and I love you as much as we loved Michael and Josh," Greg said stiffly. "Nothing you do will ever change that."

"I know, Greg." The moment of truth had arrived. Greg would need to explain his suspicions and the proof that supported those suspicions. He would admit that Lisa was concerned but didn't completely agree with him, and then Amanda would have to make a decision. Continue living the lie, or confess everything. There really wasn't much middle ground.

"Something happened to you in Central America." He waved off what he had just said. "Something more; something you haven't told us." Amanda let him continue. "I can understand the new attitude, the way you talk, the things you say. God knows you've been through enough." He turned and looked at Amanda. "The day Abby Eden confessed, you came to the station to bring me back my keys." Amanda nodded. "I saw how she reacted to you. I didn't think much of it at the time, but then I remembered the therapist, Christi Bates, and Eden's story that a woman, tall and black, coerced her to confess." He opened his jacket and pulled out a single sheet of paper wrapped in a clear plastic evidence bag. Amanda followed the letter as Greg smoothed it out over the dashboard. "It's the suicide note of Suzie Watts. No fingerprints on it except hers. Only, she didn't write it. She put the words down on paper, but they weren't hers." Silence hung heavily between them. "The office manager of Dr. Eldridge Adegbite told us that the day before he was killed a woman, tall and black, talked her way into an unscheduled appointment. He was a psychiatrist who worked here in town, and he lived next to a drug dealer named Diaz. Diaz was a bad man, a very bad man, and I very much wanted to catch him, but just before we were going to bring him in, he kills the shrink, and then he cuts off eight of his own fingers and toes and bleeds to death." Still Amanda was silent. "Three cases I was intimately involved with, and three sudden resolutions, all of which have a rational explanation that stinks to high heaven." Greg turned away and wiped a tear from his eye, and silently held the floor for over a minute. "You know, I still can see Josh walking across that porch with his monster walk. And I see you bent over him, eyes full of love and life." More tears began to fall. "God forgive me, but sometimes I wish I would have a stroke, or something that would wipe my memory clean; maybe then I could sleep." He used his sleeve to wipe his eyes exactly like Michael used to do, and a pain so intense that Amanda gasped awoke inside her.

"Greg, I want to go," she said forcefully. "Now!" she demanded when he didn't move.

"Dalice is an unusual name, don't you think?" Greg said matter-of-factly, returning to his recitation. "I remember Michael mentioning it years ago; she was your roommate in college. Although I think her last name was Watkins. I don't know why I remember it; maybe it was that Joe Ely song: 'Have you ever seen Dallas from a DC-9 at night …' You should have chosen a different name." His voice was devoid of emotion, almost calm, while Amanda's emotions began to boil to the surface. Mittens was awake as well, but she was powerless against Greg. "Why Ted? I know he was on the edge, but he didn't deserve that."

She didn't have the energy to maintain the lie any more. Greg knew, and anything but a full admission would only cause him more pain. "I didn't kill Ted; the Korean did." It was out, and suddenly she needed to tell the entire story. "But I did kill the Korean." She reached into her pocket and extracted the small fragment of metal she had found at Chang's dead feet. "He shot me in the chest." Amanda felt the full complement of protective instincts rise in Greg's chest. "For what it's worth, I didn't want anyone to die. At least, I don't think I did." Now Greg let Amanda have the floor. "I'm responsible for your three cases."

"How?" he asked, turning in his seat to face her.

"Instead of killing me, the virus did something else. I can't explain how or why." Amanda turned to Greg. "A couple weeks after they flew me to Tellis, I started to hear things—in my head." She tapped her temple and for the next twenty minutes took Greg from Tela, Honduras to Washington, DC.

When she finally finished, they sat in silence for a full two minutes. "I don't understand, Amanda," Greg whispered weakly. "I don't understand how you could do this."

"Are you asking me how it was done, or why it was done?"

"For now, let's tread softly and explain how it was done."

Amanda fiddled with her fingers for a moment. "I can't tell you how it's done because I really don't know. At first it was just happening to me. All of a sudden there was a chorus of voices in my head, and I began to question my sanity. Later, I realized that I had become a sort of receiver for the thoughts and emotions of those around me. Just before I left Tellis and came home I learned to filter and amplify those signals, and then it was a reasonably short step to control them." She paused, but Greg's body language told her that he needed more. "I imagine that at some level we all are physically connected, but a barrier keeps us apart. A wall or something that fastens our consciousness to the physical world, and confines it to our individual bodies and senses. This is how all of us experience the world. But when that barrier is removed, our minds naturally reach for each other; it's like two magnets being drawn together. Instead of two magnetic fields, we get one larger field." She glanced at Greg. He was closer but not yet comfortable with her explanation. "I think part of the reason you suspected me is that each time I visited your mind"—her verbiage was awkward, but not nearly so much as the thought it expressed, and Greg winced—"I left footprints behind that led back to me. At some level you were aware of what was happening."

"So when the two magnetic fields merge, you direct them." He looked at Amanda for the first time in several minutes. He held her gaze and then looked away. "My world is fairly simple, Amanda. I believe in the Newtonian laws of physics. I believe that every person has been given the choice to allow God or Satan to direct their actions, and all are capable of great good or great evil. And I believe that absolute power corrupts absolutely. It may be that the barriers that separate us were erected to prevent the moral erosion that has been eating away at you."

Their discussion was going as badly as Amanda could have imagined; the last thing she wanted was to alienate Greg and add to his pain. The second to last thing she wanted was for Greg to lecture her. "I didn't ask for this, Greg," she started softly, but her volatile emotions began to roil. "For a moment, I want you to imagine every one of your darkest thoughts and desires, all the things every person buries deep in the recesses of their mind, suddenly dragged into the light and amplified to unbearable levels. Then, I want you to imagine that you have the power to indulge those desires, without consequence. Do that, and then talk to me about moral erosion." By the end, her voice had become angry and bitter. "All my life I have followed the rules of God and man, and things like this keep happening to me." A small part of her wanted to cry, but a larger part of her mind shouted down the weakness.

"I can't possibly know what you're going through, Amanda, but you can't use it as an excuse for murder," Greg said softly.

"It isn't murder if they deserve it; every one of them was guilty. They all had blood on their hands."

"And now so do you."

Amanda waved off his retort. "Justice was served. Simple, expedited, and completely infallible."

"Is it justice you were after, or an excuse?"

"You've had thoughts of doing the same thing I've done. The only things that have stopped you are the possibilities of making a mistake and of discovery. I can't be wrong, and the only reason you discovered me is that I led you."

Greg took a minute to study the backs of his hands. "Every cop at some point in their career secretly wishes to become a vigilante; I'm no exception. Whether it's right or wrong, we are motivated by something greater than ourselves. Justice is a natural law, a harmony that is hard-wired into all of us, and the motivation to take matters into our own hands is to re-establish that harmony, not vengeance, or retribution, or personal gain." He turned back towards Amanda. "Your motivations are completely different."

"So you don't condemn the act, only its motivation." She held his gaze.

"I don't know, Amanda. I'm a police detective; my entire professional life has been dedicated to the laws that protect society. You exist outside those laws; they weren't written for someone like you. You've made yourself judge, jury, and executioner, and despite your belief of infallibility—or maybe because of it—I can't shake the feeling that that there is something fundamentally wrong here. God forgive me, but I'm not sorry those people are dead, so maybe I can't condemn the results, but the process, our process, no matter how cumbersome and inexact, has a purpose. It prevents any one individual from having the power of life or death over another. I just don't know, Amanda." He shook his head and turned away. "Forget what's already been done. Right now I have to decide if you are a threat to society. What's going to happen if someone cuts you off in traffic? Are you going to blow out their tires and send them careening into a wall?"

Greg's perspective was a new and unwelcome slant, and as much as she wanted to deny it, his assessment was likely much closer to the truth. "So you think I could be a danger to others?"

"How much of a step is it from killing the guilty with complete impunity to killing the innocent? After twenty-three years of police work, the one thing I know for certain is that anything can be rationalized. And if you continue to change, are you going to reach a point where you won't even bother to rationalize your actions? A point where even Lisa and I won't be safe around you?"

It was the worst possible thing Greg could have said to her, if only because there was a grain of truth in his question. What little human emotions remained inside her were concentrated around the three people in her circle. The realization that at some point she could rationalize hurting them terrified her. She grabbed her purse and opened the car door. "I need to be alone, Greg. I'll be home before Lisa finishes dinner." She pulled away from the door.

"Lisa, it's a five mile walk. It's not safe." Greg's face was full of concern.

"Nothing on two or four legs can hurt me," she said with her back to him, and then realized that not all of Greg's concerns were for her safety.

CHAPTER 36

Amanda couldn't remember ever being so uncomfortable in the presence of Michael's parents. Even when she first met them, the awkwardness began to fade immediately, but now, after a silent and tense dinner, no one seemed to know what to do or to say.

"I will clean up," Lisa said, rising from her chair.

"I'll help," Greg said sullenly.

"I don't want it," she snapped at her husband. "Go watch TV or read something. I want to do this alone." Her last sentence was directed equally at Greg and Amanda.

Greg pushed back from the table and stomped his way into the living room. The couch creaked as he dropped into it in obvious frustration. Amanda caught Lisa glancing at her, and they both looked away quickly. "I want to do this alone, Amanda," she said in an injured voice.

Hours later, after unpacking her suitcase, Amanda was back to pacing her small bedroom, her mind warring with itself. She wanted to be free, to use the gifts that God or the Fates had given her, without any moral restraint. She felt like an eight-year-old screaming at her mother that "they were hers; why couldn't she use them like she wanted?" Why did Greg and Lisa have to interfere? After all she had been through, after all she had lost, it wasn't fair that she couldn't do what she wanted. She was being childish, and immature, and self-indulgent, and she really didn't care.

Of course you care. Michael, her conscience, had returned.

Why? Why do I have to care? Why do I have to keep accepting things graciously?

I doubt Suzie Watts or her boyfriend would agree that you've been gracious.

"Very funny," she whispered to her dead husband. She could imagine the broad smile on his face, so much like Greg's.

It's not really a question of control anymore, Amanda; it's a question of exercising that control. He didn't have to read her mind—extrinsically or intrinsically, he was a part of it. Greg had implanted the fear that she could one day lose control and plow a row of death and destruction where ever she went. It was a hideous vision, and her regression into the petulant pre-teen state was simply her mind's way of coping with that terrible possibility. Only, she had gained some perspective on Mittens's and her blood lust, and with it a degree of control. What had once been an imperative would in time become a simple tool that she could take out and use, or lock away.

Maybe we don't need to do it, but you can't deny that it is the most exciting thing we've ever done. Mittens had to have her say.

"Amanda? Are you all right?" Lisa asked after a soft knock.

Amanda opened the door. "I guess no one in this house is going to get much sleep tonight," she said, inviting her mother-in-law inside.

"I saw your light on." Lisa stood for an awkward moment and then decided to sit in the rocking chair she had once nursed her son in. "It's a good excuse to talk."

"I'm sorry I hurt the two of you," Amanda began.

"I know," Lisa answered. "Greg filled me in. I didn't want to believe it, but I guess he was right." She stared at Amanda. "I knew something was wrong, but I didn't say anything. No don't …" Lisa cut off Amanda's response. "Just give me a moment and let me get through this. I don't ever want to know any of the details, okay?" Amanda nodded. "We move forward from here. We don't forget what's happened, but we don't dwell on it either. Agreed?" Amanda nodded again. Lisa began to gently rock. "Can you control this?" she asked, and Amanda's first thought was that Lisa had been talking to her son.

"Yes," she answered—and admitted to herself.

"Do you want to control this?" Lisa followed up, and now Amanda was certain that she had been talking to her son.

"That's the real question." Amanda sat at the edge of her bed.

"I don't think I have to tell you what's at risk here." Lisa took Amanda's hand. "We can't follow you down this road."

Amanda squeezed her surrogate mother's hand, and instead of the usual uncomfortable tingling that came with human touch, she felt a reassuring warmth. "I know, and in moments like this it's not a road I want to go down." She released Lisa's hands. "But there are other moments when I realize that I have an opportunity to do or to be anything I want." Lisa visibly reacted as something about Amanda changed. "Before this happened I was a timid, scared little girl, always doing and saying things because they were expected of me, avoiding confrontation at almost any cost. I could count on one hand all the times I had raised my voice in anger. Imagine living with Greg and never raising your voice." Amanda couldn't help but sense Lisa's unease, and her natural reaction was to console her. "I can't live like I did before, and I know I can't live like I have been. I have to find a middle ground."

"When Michael was around ten," Lisa said after a protracted, uncomfortable silence, "we saw a film; I guess it was a documentary or something. In it was a brief clip of a tiny Japanese girl, probably four or five years old. She was half-naked and more than half-starved and was just sitting on a rock wall. I don't remember for sure but I think it might have been outside Hiroshima or Nagasaki, because all around her was absolute devastation. But she didn't have a scratch on her. She was all alone; everyone and everything she knew was gone in a blink of an eye, and she couldn't understand why. An American GI slowly approached her and tried to give her some food. When he was about ten feet away she started to shake with fear. The closer he got the more she shook. She stared at the GI as if he were Death himself, but never moved. Never made an attempt to run. Her eyes …" Lisa wiped a tear, then continued. "They were filled with fear and resignation. She wasn't even old enough to understand the concept of death, but instinctively she accepted it." More tears fell. Amanda reached for a box of tissues. "Thanks, dear," Lisa said and dabbed at her face again. "The image of that girl haunted Michael for years. He would have nightmares about her." Lisa stood after a quiet moment and walked to the dark window, her back to Amanda.

"I'm about to break the last promise I ever made to my son," Lisa said to the window, Amanda, and the ether. "Two months before he died Michael brought Josh over unexpectedly. School was out, so I was home alone. I can't remember where you were." She snuffled loudly. "I played with Josh for a time, and he just silently watched us; it was almost as if he was reassuring himself about something. I finally asked him what was wrong. He had a lot of Greg in him, so it took some time to drag it out of him, and then only after he made me promise never to tell you." Lisa turned and sat on the window sill with her head down, not willing to look up at Amanda. "He had the dream again, only Josh was the little girl and you were the GI, and you weren't trying to help." She closed her eyes. "Maybe it was just a dream; maybe he saw something. I don't know. I do know it terrified him, and now I can understand why. The woman he loved, the mother of his child, had turned into something unrecognizable."

Lisa looked up and Amanda looked down. Even before the Change, did her husband believe that she was capable of hurting their son, just as Suzie Watts had done? Could he look into her soul and see the evil that hid behind her accommodating nature? And if he looked into her now, what would he see? Would he recoil in terror? Would he take their son and escape, leaving her with the certainty that she had destroyed the one perfect thing in her life?

It was just a dream, his voice said from a deep recess of her mind. *Everyone has them, and they mean nothing*, he tried to soothe her.

This was as close as the Michael-in-her-mind had ever come to lying. The reality was that, given the right circumstances, this version of Amanda Flynn could be the terrifying GI in Michael's dream. Maybe she had taken a step away from the abyss, but it still pulled at her. It was no longer a demand; it had become a seduction.

"I'm sorry, Amanda," Lisa said from across the room. "I can only imagine how that must hurt."

"No, you can't imagine it, Lisa. You've never betrayed their memory." Tears fell into her lap as the shell around her soul cracked.

***

"No matter how you slice it, we don't know what killed this man. No drugs, no toxins, no radiation. That's my official and FINAL word on the matter." For three weeks a steady parade of increasingly senior agents of the FBI had been hounding Dr. Parisi for something that would explain the death of Bong-hwa Son. His presumed murder had become the feared proverbial international incident. A South Korean national, with remote ties to the National Intelligence Service, had killed an FBI agent in broad daylight, only to die under as yet undetermined circumstances. Fingers were being pointed in both directions as the investigation worked its way through Washington, Denver, and Colorado Springs. No one knew if Ted

Alam was a hero or a villain, but it was generally agreed that the Korean, who had liked to introduce himself as Mr. Chang, was not the innocent bystander his government claimed. "If you didn't have the video to the contrary, I would be forced to call this a natural death." Parisi anxiously shifted his weight in the uncomfortable chair, hoping the Assistant Director of the FBI would take the hint and let him get back to work.

Tim Kerr ignored the coroner's obvious annoyance. "How does this fit with the cases from Colorado?"

"Do you guys bother talking to each other? I've answered this question twice before. Son's intracerebral hemorrhages were much worse than any of those cases. The one that came closest was in a hypertensive elderly male. Hypertensive elder males often die from bleeds in the brain. There's no connection."

"Sorry to have kept you, Doctor. Thank you for coming in," Kerr said with the required perfunctory civility. He stood, shook the older man's hand, and then walked him to the door.

"Well, he was loads of help," Paul Lister said once the door had closed. "I don't care what he says, there has to be a connection. For months Alam worked in the Colorado Springs police department just as they experienced a handful of poorly explained deaths. Way too coincidental. " Lister shook his head.

Kerr nodded his head in agreement. Unfortunately, their mutual gut feelings had no evidentiary support. He walked back to his desk and noted that Lister was comfortable enough to sit in one of the sofa chairs without being invited. He silently appraised the agent. Lister was what Ted Alam had been destined to become before alcohol addiction had its say. He was the oldest graduate of the FBI training class a year before Alam and had gone from local law enforcement over to the dark side of federal law enforcement. His maturity and experience allowed him to quickly outpace his fellow students, and like Alam he was tapped for the Washington Bureau and rapid advancement. "Nothing more from the ATM video?"

"Same story as last week. Female between five-four and five-six. Light hair. Beyond that all we get are bigger and blurrier pixels."

"I thought that they had a program to clean up the image."

"The camera was too far away."

"Nothing to back up the airline manifests?" It was a routine part of every investigation to review and compare the incoming and outgoing flight manifests. Five minutes of computer work gave the agents the names of one hundred and fifty-six individuals who flew into the Washington area in the twenty-four hours prior to the shooting and then left within twelve hours following it. That was the easy part. The real work was tracking down those one hundred and fifty-six individuals. After three weeks only one name remained: Dalice Watkins, and no one seemed to belong to it.

"Dalice flew to Dallas," Kerr said idly. "You think this is our girl?"

"I'm betting she's the girl on the video, and I'll double down that she's the one who killed the Korean."

"How?"

"When we find her we'll know."

"Go to Colorado. Talk to the locals, but don't step on any toes."

***

"There may be inconsistencies in the investigations, but there are no inconsistencies in the pathology results," Phillip Rucker recited to Lister. The FBI agent had nothing to show for the week he spent in the Denver Field Office, so he drove the sixty miles to Colorado Springs. Another week's worth of work only managed to produce a very brief report detailing an investigation involving the same unit that Alam had been stationed with for weeks. The report was two pages long and closed within a day due to a lack of forensic support. It was unlikely in the extreme to lead anywhere, but Lister wanted a second take on the forensics. It was all he had left. Everything that connected Ted Alam with the Korean had vanished. No e-mails, phone calls, forensics, nothing. He promised himself that after he ran the traps in Colorado Springs one more time he would head home.

"All right, let's approach it from a different direction." Rucker's reputation of inhuman precision and oddity fell far short of the mark. Lister would have no trouble believing that Rucker was proof that aliens lived among us. His autopsy reports were flawless: no typos, misspelt words, smudges, or imperfections of any kind. "Can you review the autopsy report of the victim in Washington and look for any similarities?" Rucker nodded his head. Lister had been warned earlier about avoiding direct physical contact with the pathologist, so instead of passing the thick folder directly to Rucker he placed it on his unnaturally clean desk.

Rucker waited for Lister to sit back into his seat before reaching for the file and carefully opening it. While waiting for Rucker's impressions,

Lister assessed the man through the lens of an FBI profiler. Rucker never made eye contact; consistently used formal pronouns; even while sitting he remained rigid, his back never touching the chair. His office had no personal touches, no pictures on his desk or his walls, no vanity wall dedicated to diplomas and awards. Nothing to indicate that he even occupied this office, aside from the name stenciled to the door. He turned the pages mechanically and rapidly, too fast for any normal human to read, but Lister was certain Rucker read every word and missed not a single detail. If this man ever decided to become a serial killer, the FBI would have zero chance of ever proving it.

Less than five minutes later, Rucker turned the last page of the file and returned it to his desk. Lister took his cue and retrieved it. "Impressions?"

"Yes, I have impressions." Rucker said without expression.

"Can you share them?" Lister followed up.

"Yes, I can." Rucker answered.

"Can …please tell me your impressions," Lister corrected himself.

"Incomplete work, but that is not unusual. Drawing inferences from the data in this file, one can see similarities," Rucker said to a spot on the wall behind Lister.

"Can you elaborate?" It was a little fun talking to Rucker. He had asked the man if there were similarities and Rucker had answered.

"Yes," he said, without the slightest inflection. "Would you like me to list them?" he said after Lister waited for him to continue.

"If you don't mind."

Rucker gave the agent a brief strange look, as if his answer to a simple question made no sense. "There are seven areas in which these findings could overlap at least one of the four other cases." Rucker spoke rapidly for almost fifteen minutes. Less than halfway through, Lister stopped taking notes. "I do have to caution you that my conclusions are predicated on information collected by another, and that the information given to me is in my opinion incomplete."

Lister had to contain a smile; he was certain that he had found the author of every legal disclaimer ever written. "I'm sorry, Doctor, but you lost me about ten minutes ago. Can you, in simple English—English that I can understand—tell me if in your opinion either the same person or the same process was responsible for the events both here and in Washington?"

"Yes," he said precisely.

"Yes, you can tell me, or yes it was the same individual or the same process?"

"Yes, I can tell you in simple English that in my opinion either the same individual, and or the same process, was involved both here in Colorado Springs and in Washington, DC."

Lister was about to ask Rucker if he was sure, but that would have been a foolish question. "Just to be clear, I'm a little slow"—everyone was a little slow around Rucker, he thought—"these local cases have not been labeled as homicides. I don't think they are even being investigated. But now you are saying that an unknown individual or process is involved. Are you changing your mind?"

Rucker gave Lister that same strange look again that made the agent feel like a six-year-old who couldn't tie his own shoes. "You are not correct. I have labeled the deaths as 'apparently natural.'"

A distinction that only Phillip Rucker could appreciate. Lister stood and offered his hand but then snatched it back. "Thank you for your time, Doctor." For a brief moment they made eye contact, and Lister stared into the empty eyes of the pathologist. They reminded him more of his autistic nephew than a serial killer.

CHAPTER 37

"Well, this is an unexpected visit," Amanda said after Greg Flynn showed up at her new apartment.

"I wanted to see what the place looked like once it was all spruced up." He walked through the small living room to the floor-to-ceiling windows that opened onto a cloudy day. "I think I can see our house from here."

"Use the telescope," Amanda said from behind him. Greg slid over to the telescope.

"NO! Lisa's putting onions in the salad again." He pulled away with a smile that didn't have the wattage to disguise his true intent.

"What's wrong, Greg?" Amanda retreated to her couch; Greg followed. He studied her carefully. "Are you okay here, alone?"

"The isolation is good for me. Comforting. Sort of helps me with my perspective. How are you doing?"

"Worried, but that will never change."

"I need the space," she said, taking up an old argument. It had been several weeks since their tense confrontation, and neither Greg nor Lisa felt it was an appropriate time for Amanda to be alone. "I've made you a promise and I will live by it. No more letting Mittens off the leash."

Greg nodded. "I wish you had a better name, though."

"You're not here to discuss the name of my psychotic alter ego," she gently prodded.

"The FBI is in town. They have a task force looking into Ted's death, and now they're looking into the … other cases."

"Well, that doesn't sound good." Her tone was light and she sat crossed-legged on the couch.

"Honey, this is serious. They will put this together."

"To what end? They have no evidence that it was me."

"This is hard for me, Amanda. I'm breaking an oath I swore to uphold before you were even born, along with half a dozen laws, and to be honest your lack of remorse makes it all the more difficult," he chastised.

"The only remorse I have is that it has affected you. I'm not sorry those people are dead ..." She cut herself off before they strolled further into the minefield.

"If they find you they will arrest you, evidence or not. One of their own is dead."

"How are they going to find me?" It was more of a question than a boast. Greg hesitated and the answer hit Amanda with the force of a hammer. "They think you're involved."

"I am involved," Greg snapped. "Sorry, that didn't come out right. I was interviewed for an hour this morning about my role in the Suzie Watts case, and of course what I knew about Ted. It won't take long before they have your name."

Amanda got off the couch and began to slowly pace in front of Greg. She wasn't concerned about her safety—a part of her thrilled at the possibility of confrontation—but Greg and Lisa were another matter. "How ironic—the one time I was actually defending myself." She stopped in front of Greg. "I'll go to them and turn myself in. I can't have you protecting me."

"No. That is the one thing you can't do. If it was just the FBI I would say yes. Hell, I'd even drive you. But it won't be just the FBI; you'll be putting yourself back into the hands of those bastards who were experimenting on you, and if that happens ..."

"All right, then what do I do if they come a-callin'?"

"First thing is to not overreact. Don't make the situation worse." His meaning was clear. "And try not to let them know what you can do."

Amanda nodded. "Maybe I should just disappear."

Greg was quiet for a very long minute. "Lisa would have my head on a plate if I agreed with you, but it may come to that." His voice had dropped as if Lisa were in the other room. "At least for a while."

***

"She's the right size, shape, age, hair color, and her college roommate's first name was Dalice. On top of all of that, she was in Dallas at the time. How can you say it's only suspicious?" Paul Lister asked his boss over the phone.

"The only real evidence is the roommate's name—everything else is suspicious but still easily explained away. Give me something that puts her on a plane to Washington and then we've got something," Tim Kerr answered.

"But she knew Alam." Lister knew that everything he'd uncovered amounted to little more than a big pile of circumstantial evidence, but thirty years in law enforcement had given him the nose of a bloodhound, and he had caught a scent. "At least ask for a search warrant."

"Is the father-in-law involved?" Kerr ignored Lister's request.

"I don't know. My gut says no, but if she's involved he has to be."

"He is the chief of detectives in Colorado Springs. If we go after her, he gets caught up in it; even if he's not involved, it will ruin him. And if later we find that we were wrong, the possibility of us getting any local assistance on anything will be exactly zero for a very long time. And it won't be just Colorado Springs. You worked in Kansas City for ten years; how would you react if the FBI raked a fellow detective over the coals and then asked you for cooperation?"

"Okay, I'll keep digging. I guess I'm off to Dallas," Lister said with resignation. He wasn't surprised, just disappointed and tired of being on the road.

***

Amanda had always loved the solitude of running, now more than ever. It was one of the few times when she was alone in her mind. The world was remote and for the most part asleep as she wound her way through a canyon trail. Dawn was at least a half hour away, but the nocturnal world was already closing up shop. A solitary coyote watched her from the edge of the woods, the rest of his pack already beginning to bed down. Wild animals had strange, indecipherable mental signatures, and his floated to her on the morning air. She tasted traces of curiosity, fear, and possibility, but his thoughts—if he had any—were remote. Dogs had great mental signatures, but most humans didn't need telepathic abilities to read them. Their simple thoughts, needs, and desires were a welcome respite from the complexities of their masters.

The road began to slope upward after a long downhill and Amanda caught the residual trace of a pair of humans. They had been running in the opposite direction sometime last evening and had stopped at this point to rest. Isolation and time had helped Amanda refine her senses; invariably, humans left a lingering presence wherever they went. It clung to inanimate objects, and she could feel the two girls' scent covering the ground like fog. In time it would slowly dissipate, but for now it offered her an opportunity to reach out and touch them. A small part of her mind pulled at her, but she continued up the hill; she wanted to run now and wasn't interested in the mundane thoughts and lives of a couple of coeds. Even the ever-present desire for mischief was taking a break.

Life had become serious and complicated. Somewhere in the miasma, individuals with authority and power had turned their attention towards her. She was no longer moving through the world anonymously, and she imagined eyes on her wherever she went. Intellectually, she knew this wasn't possible; the FBI, no matter how many resources they had at their disposal, couldn't track her secretly. No one could. But they were investigating her, of that she was certain, and at some point they would know enough to try and collect her. Then everything would change.

Angry with herself, she ran harder. She had not been nearly as clever as she thought. The psychosis that drove her to kill blinded her to the subtle footprints that led back to Greg and, through him, to her. Instead of providing her with cover, her unique mode of execution was proving to be her undoing; it had become the unifying characteristic of all five bodies.

"Experience is a hard teacher; she gives the test first, and the lesson afterwards," she panted while cresting the hill.

***

"I remember her. Oh, boy, do I remember her." Lionel Black handed the photograph back to Paul Lister.

He couldn't have asked for a better witness than Lionel. Mr. Black was indeed black, as black as coal on a moonless night. He wasn't a big man; he was huge. Six feet eight inches tall, weighing in north of three hundred pounds. Lister couldn't picture him fitting inside the airport shuttle bus, much less driving it. A certified Baptist minister, Black ran a mission for the Dallas homeless in his off hours. He also wrote poetry.

"It's been weeks; how can you be so sure?" Lionel Black was literally Lister's last option. A few people in the hotel remembered Amanda, but nothing beyond vague recollections. The Red Cross personnel recalled her well and insisted that she had been in Dallas the entire ten days, but when pressed for details their certainty began to crumble.

"Have you seen her picture?" Black's laughter was as loud as a cannon going off. "But that was only part of it. She got on the bus at the Hilton. That's where I start my run, so the bus was pretty much empty. She didn't say much, maybe just hello. Sits down like an angel." His broad smile displayed brilliant white teeth. "Then these two gentlemen get on at the Hyatt and make a big fuss over her. Except she doesn't want to be bothered. They sit across from her and keep tryin' to talk to her. They were gettin' pretty loud and inappropriate and just before I said something they both start to cough and choke. They're grabbing their necks and knocking things over …" Black began reeling and waving his arms in a pantomime of suffocation. "Everybody jumps out of their way; only she stays. I pulled the bus over to help and I saw her watchin' 'em with this little tiny smile. She kinda leaned forward"—Lionel inclined his bulk towards Lister and dropped the volume on his deep baritone—"and just stared with those eyes. Made the hairs on the back of my neck stand up. Really, they were standing on end." Lionel returned to his former altitude and began to nod. "Won't be forgetting those eyes anytime soon."

"Where did you drop her?"

"The American counter. The seven-ten flight to Washington."

Lister was amazed. You remember that?"

Now Lionel was puzzled. "Odd," he said with a perplexed look. "Don't know why, but I do. Maybe she said it," he said unconvincingly.

"Thanks for your time. I'll let you get back to your lunch." They shook hands, and Lister weaved his way through the airport traffic back to his car. Lionel Black had put Amanda Flynn on a plane to Washington, DC. It took him three minutes to track down his boss by phone.

"She was on the seven-ten flight to Washington," he said as a greeting. "And there is no Amanda Flynn on the manifest." He quickly relayed the meeting with Lionel.

"So Amanda Flynn is Dalice Watkins," Kerr said cautiously. It was still possible that Amanda was traveling under an assumed name because of her family's tragic history with airlines, but she had flown from Colorado Springs as Amanda Flynn. It still didn't mean that Dalice Watkins was involved with Alam's or Chang's death, but she knew Ted and was a perfect fit for the woman on the video. "Pick her up."

"Arrest her, or invite her in for questioning?" Lister was excited.

"Arrest her. Let's go full bore and see if we can scare her into a confession."

"I want to use an HRT." Lister braced himself the moment he said it.

"A hostage rescue team? Don't you think that's a little over the top for one woman?"

"We have no idea how she killed Chang, or the others." He repeated Lionel Black's story of Amanda's encounter on the bus. "This whole situation is strange. I'm talking Mulder and Scully strange." The X-files reference had special meaning to Kerr; as a younger agent he had appeared in an episode. "Then there's the whole international aspect; she survives this epidemic down in Central America and then kills a former Korean intelligence officer for no clear reason. I would rather be accused of overreacting than underreacting."

"All right," Kerr agreed. "We certainly can't use the local SWAT team." It was likely Amanda had met at least some of the members of Colorado Springs small special tactical unit, and using them would create a true conflict of interest. "I'll make some phone calls. I think there might be a team in Denver already. Get back there and get this done as quickly and as quietly as possible."

"I'm already at the airport, and I've got on my quietest running shoes."

CHAPTER 38

"I'm sorry to bother you this late, Detective." Lister had shown up at Greg's door unannounced with four agents in tow.

Greg looked over Lister's shoulder. "I see you've brought company." Greg stepped out of the way. "Come on in." Lister entered alone. Greg closed the door after watching the other agents fan out across his front yard. "I'm guessing this is more than a social call," he said, drawing even with Lister in the entrance way.

"I'm afraid so." Lister had to look up at the taller detective. "I've got some questions for both you and your wife."

Greg's eyebrow rose. "My wife?" Lister nodded solemnly. "Lisa, we have company," Greg called. "Well, follow me to the kitchen; that's where I keep her chained up."

Introductions were made and the three sat around the kitchen table. "Do you know where Amanda is?" Lister asked Lisa, without the usual pleasantries.

Her face spoke volumes. "Why?" She fired back, using a tone Greg had heard countless times before, all from guilty suspects.

"We would like to question her regarding the murder of a man in Washington, but I'm guessing you already suspected that." He waited for an answer, but both of the Flynns remained silent. "She wasn't at her apartment."

"You're making a mistake, Special Agent," Lisa said with conviction. Greg started, and she turned to him. "I won't keep quiet. She's not responsible for this, and in my mind she's done nothing wrong." She started to tear up and angrily wiped her eyes. "The son of a bitch shot her," she yelled at Greg. "He got what he deserved," she said, turning back to Lister.

"That's not my call to make, Mrs. Flynn. All I want to do is bring her in safely."

"Good luck with that," Lisa said sarcastically.

"Lisa, you are making this worse," Greg said, raising his voice.

"How, by telling the truth? For three months they kept her from us, made us think that she was dead, while they experimented on her. Now they want to arrest her for defending herself. That's just too much." Lisa shook her head at Greg and then at Lister. "No. Too much has been taken from that woman already."

"I can arrest both of you for obstruction of justice." Lister's tone was more coercive than hostile.

"Back off, Lister. I've seen your evidence and it's paper-thin. Your medical examiner is not even sure there was a murder, so don't start threatening us." Greg's tone was completely hostile.

"We will find her; it's only a matter of time. The only question that remains is how she is brought into custody." Lister had waited a few moments for the atmosphere to calm.

Greg stole a glance at Lisa and she stared back. "Special Agent, I have been in your shoes more times than I care to remember, and I know how I would respond to what I'm about to say, so I'm hoping that you show better judgment." He paused and took a deep breath. "You are not going to take Amanda into custody. She won't allow it. If you threaten her, she could become unstable."

"So you're warning me that any attempt to arrest her will become violent …" A car pulling into the driveway interrupted Lister.

"What the hell?" Greg yelled when he recognized the Jeep's familiar shape. "Why am I cursed with such head-strong women?" he said, already running to the door. He opened it just in time to see one of Lister's agents being launched into the hedge grove. Lister himself tried to squeeze around Greg. "Whoa there," Greg said, grabbing the agent's right arm and collar. "Drop the weapon." Greg forced Lister's arm down, and the handgun fell to the floor.

"God damn it, Flynn," Lister said as Greg pushed him back into the house. Amanda slowly walked up the steps and into the entranceway.

"There were three more out there." Greg faced Amanda, his back shielding her from Lister.

She nodded. "When they wake up they'll be going back home," she said casually. She kissed his cheek and brushed passed him. Lisa immediately enveloped her in a hug. "Hi," she whispered into her mother-in-law's hair. "I'm okay; you don't have to suffocate me."

Lister stood to the side, clearly at a loss. "Amanda Flynn, I am placing you under arrest …" Amanda waved him off and walked into the kitchen. Lister followed, reciting her rights. "Do you understand your rights?" he asked as she sat in one of the chairs.

"Mr. Lister, will you please sit down?" Amanda answered.

"Where are my agents?" He remained standing, Greg looming over him.

"They're fine. They might have a headache, but they'll get over it. Now please, can we all sit and work this out?"

Lister moved tentatively towards his chair and then sat as Lisa took her seat. "There's nothing to work out. I have an arrest warrant."

"I know, and a Hostage Rescue Team at my apartment. The first problem that needs working out is that I need to get into my apartment before I leave. The second problem is you bothering Greg and Lisa. I can't allow that." She looked up at Greg. "And I can't allow you to put yourself at risk." She looked back to the FBI agent. "So, since we have a Hostage Rescue Team, I was thinking we need a hostage." Amanda smiled at Lister.

"You can't be serious," he scoffed. "Talk some sense into her, Flynn." He looked up at Greg.

"I know what I'm doing," Amanda mouthed to her father-in-law. "Let's be clear. They have nothing to do with this. This is just you and me." Her eyes blazed as they bore into Lister. "So, Special Agent Lister, why don't you have a seat while I get ready and then we'll go." Amanda stood, and Lister followed suit. "Come with me if you want."

"As a hostage?" Lister looked to Greg and then back at Amanda. "Let's say for the sake of argument that I am a hostage. What's to stop me from leaving?"

"Absolutely nothing. If you want, I can take one of your agents outside. In their current state they will be far more compliant." Amanda pointed to the window, her manner completely relaxed. "Can you please take a step back, Special Agent?"

Lister barred her way. She tried to go around him and once again he stepped in front of her. "I can't let you do this."

"Mr. Lister, this is childish and very irritating. Remember what Greg told you about me becoming unstable." She tried a third time to skirt the agent; again he blocked her way, this time reaching for her arm. In an instant he was slammed into the refrigerator door, his right arm pinned painfully behind him. "I have no issue with you, Paul. I understand that you are just doing your job, and I don't want to hurt you. I just want to be left alone." Almost a full minute passed as Lister struggled to breathe.

Lisa stifled a cry. "Let him go, Amanda!"

Lister slumped to the floor and Amanda bent to face him. "Now do you see?" She whispered, and he returned her intense stare.

"Yes," he said, panting.

Amanda stood and turned to find a mixture of fear, horror, and revulsion pouring out of the Flynns. "I'm sorry you had to see that."

"What did you do to him?" Lisa asked.

"I didn't hurt him, Lisa." The look on Lisa's face wounded Amanda's soul; never before did she look so much like Josh. "I showed him what happened, and what could happen." She turned to Greg, who had always looked like Michael. He took a step away from her. "I have to go," she said quickly, and she practically ran from the room.

Ten minutes later Lisa knocked on Amanda's bedroom door. "Come in, Mom," she said.

"I've always liked the sound of that," Lisa said. "I don't know how, but I saw what was in your mind, Amanda."

"The connection works both ways. My son would see me as a monster, and my husband would be terrified of me." Her voice and eyes were dry. "I have to go, Lisa, and not just because of this little FBI thing." She threw the scarf that she was trying to untie to the floor. "I can't see that again. The reality of what I've become reflected in your eyes is enough to destroy what little humanity I have left. I feel like a shipwreck victim clinging to a scrap of wood, wondering if I should just let go and accept my fate." She stood and Lisa wrapped herself around her. "Did I ever tell you that you and Greg are the only people I can touch?"

"No," Lisa said, pulling away. "Let's go. Greg's starting to get worried." Lisa turned to leave. Amanda felt her mother-in-law's torment and inner strength. Lisa was going to let Amanda go, even though it tore her heart out.

Amanda reached for Lisa's hand. "You are the mother of the only man I have ever loved." The two woman stared as a tear ran down Amanda's cheek. "And this isn't the end." Lisa turned away and hurried out of the room. Amanda let her go, and then looked around her room one last time. She had wounded Lisa and Greg and now any chance of repairing that injury was being taken away. She followed Lisa down the hall and into the kitchen, enveloped by a cloud of dark emotions.

Special Agent Lister had fully recovered, and the lingering connection told Amanda that he understood his role. He would clear a path for her and ensure that no one got hurt. "Are you ready?" he asked her.

"Yes," she said simply. "Why don't you go to the Jeep," she ordered.

Greg looked back to his adopted daughter as Lister left for the front door. "Are you controlling him?"

"No. He understands now. He knows what happened in Washington, and he knows how close to the edge they've pushed me." She hugged Greg. "No tears or lingering goodbyes, okay? Just know that you and Lisa are my only real connection to this world." She pulled away and didn't explain her statement.

He wrapped his arm around her and guided her towards the door. "We are always here for you," he said, tears running down his face. "Sorry," he said as one of his tears fell onto her cheek.

Lisa stood at the door, a plastic-wrapped teddy bear in her hand. Instinctively, Amanda recoiled.

"Take Fred with you." Lisa offered her the bear.

Amanda shook her head and backed away as if the bear were radioactive. "I can't." Her voice broke. "You don't understand what would happen if I touched that. It would kill me." Lisa pulled the bear back. "Keep it for me. Someday, maybe …"

***

The reality that she was leaving the only place where she had ever been happy was eating into her self-control. Mittens was no longer the dog of her youth; she had morphed into a beast from Hell, and she raged at the injustice, searching for someone to punish. She started screaming *kill them all!* and Amanda quietly began to join the chant as she drove up into the foothills.

"Are you saying something?" Lister asked cautiously.

"No," she said abruptly. She even resented the presence of the special agent. She didn't really need him to get to her apartment; she only needed him if no one was to die. "I am going to stop at this gas station and you are going to call the HRT commander and have him move his team back into their vehicle. They have ten minutes from when you make the call. After that anyone who gets in my way will be punished." She looked over at Lister and repressed a sudden desire to throw him from the moving car. "Are we clear?"

"We are clear. I don't want anyone hurt, Amanda. Is there anything else I can do to ensure that?"

His calming demeanor irritated her. "Just keep them away and all this will be over." She pulled into the station and slammed the transmission into "Park," straddling both gas pumps. A few seconds later, a woman in a Subaru hatchback pulled behind Amanda and beeped. Amanda closed her eyes and counted to ten. Mittens screamed louder, and a loud explosion eased some of her anxiety. *There, bitch. Now you need tires more than gas.* She looked over at Lister. "Make the call. We really do not have much time," she said through clenched teeth.

It took ten minutes of arguing, pleading, and threatening for the HRT team to be recalled. Amanda was pulling back into traffic before eight. The closer she came to her apartment, the closer the walls of the world pressed in on her. She felt the presence of the team sent to arrest her, and Mittens very nearly escaped from her leash. For a moment she seized several of their minds, and only just let go before Amanda broke her promise to the Flynns. Her emotions were blinding her as she raced up the narrow streets. Lister was saying something, but she shut him out. She was running on thoughts of death, murder, torture, pain, blood, screams—images flashed through her mind in a psychedelic, psychotic fury.

Amanda flew into her parking spot, barely conscious that Lister was still with her. "Stay here." He balked and she forced him back into the seat. "If you want to live, stay here!"

It took her only a few seconds to climb the three flights to her apartment. The air around her had thinned; a bow wave of compressed air pushed everything out of her way. She reached her door and found that it had been breached by the HRT. One of the hinges was sprung, and the door hung at an awkward angle. She touched the wood and found the minds of the two men who had violated her private space. They were close and tantalizingly vulnerable.

Kill them all! Mittens screamed. Amanda seized their minds and resisted the imperative to squeeze the life from them. She relented and felt their unconscious forms fall to the ground. Mittens was roaring so loud that Amanda had a hard time seeing. The lights of her apartment suddenly burst on and she looked around. Power pulsed through her, and at some level she knew it would need to be vented.

"Bastards!" she screamed as an introduction to a tirade of profanity. Her bedroom had been searched; everything she owned had been touched and examined by total strangers. Strangers who were forcing her to flee the only refuge she had known. Thoughts were racing through her head, and the three windows in her bedroom exploded outward, venting some of the rage. She quickly gathered her things into a suitcase and an overnight bag. She left her bedroom and went to the fireplace mantle to collect a small, sealed brown box. She touched the polished wood and felt a modicum of relief to find that no one had disturbed it. Inside were a watch, a wedding band, fragments of a wallet, and a pair of dog tags. It was the only thing she really needed from her apartment. Everything else could easily be replaced.

She reached for the box and felt something brush by her shoulder, and then again by her opposite ear. The two bullets deflected into the wood of the fireplace. Mittens's tirade had caused her to lose all situational awareness, and now men were shooting at her. She found the first sniper, the one who had fired the two shots, on a roof nearly a quarter mile away. Before she threw him off the three-story structure, she congratulated him on his marksmanship. She cushioned his fall just enough not to break the oath she had sworn, but not enough to save the bones in his left leg and arm. The second sniper didn't have a clean shot and remained poised on the roof opposite her apartment's wing. She chastised herself for allowing them to get so close, and forced Mittens to calm down so she could focus. She sighted down the barrel of the rifle and began to melt the metal and plastic. The sniper dropped his weapon as it began to burn in earnest.

She scanned the area and found only Lister and the two snipers. Even her neighbors had been evacuated, something that she should have detected. She had made the same mistake with Adegbite and Diaz and had very nearly been killed by it. The psychotic rage only blinded her; the energy had to be directed with cold, dispassionate deliberation. She broadened her scan and found the HRT and their captain, Albert Reese. He was the one responsible for giving the order to end her life. Did her promise cover that contingency? Was she allowed to defend herself?

She sat down on her sofa and wondered if she should call Lisa and Greg and ask for a ruling. Of course they would say that he was simply doing his job; he was no different from Greg when he was called upon to use deadly force. Mittens was considerably more old school: an eye for an eye. Reese was on the phone with someone and Amanda idly shorted out the receiver. While she was at it she shorted out the electrical circuits of their transport van, and then their klieg lights, and then everything else. She felt the team scurrying around in the dark, under attack by an enemy that was unseen.

"Yum …" Their confusion and sudden fear floated to her through the cool mountain air. She breathed deeply and felt a slight intoxicating rush. She stood, gathered her suitcase and overnight bag, and mentally said goodbye to her apartment. She passed the broken door and doubted that she would ever get her damage deposit back.

Lister was locked in the Jeep, only Amanda didn't remember doing it. He was yelling into his cellphone and then stopped when he saw Amanda approaching. She unlocked the doors with her remote and he jumped from the car. He stood next to the open door with an uncertain look on his face. She opened the trunk and dropped the suitcase in.

"What happened up there?" he asked tentatively.

"Your team didn't follow orders," she said, walking to his open door and closing it inches from him.

"They won't let you leave, Amanda. They've already set up road blocks, and helicopters are on their way. This is way out of my control."

"Not my control," she said as she walked to the driver's side door. "Go; you're free. I have no interest in you."

"What are you going to do?" He positioned himself at the front of the vehicle, which was odd as she had parked nose first.

"If you're trying to block me again, you'll have to go back there." She started the Jeep and backed up.

"Please Amanda …" He was waving his cellphone.

"Tell Greg that our agreement does not apply when people are trying to kill me." She drove past the FBI agent and into the dark street.

CHAPTER 39

She didn't get very far. The street lights had been turned off, and if her focus had been as fuzzy as when she first drove up the street, she would have missed the tire spikes that had been laid across the road. The thought that they had planned on damaging her brand new car pushed her even closer to the edge.

As soon as she climbed out of her car, two pairs of headlights clicked on, followed shortly by an amplified voice. "Stay where you are …" Amanda shorted out the speaker and sealed the four state troopers in their now-disabled vehicles, then rolled up the chained spikes. "Attention FBI, state police, Hostage Rescue People, and anyone else," she screamed into the darkness. "This was very irresponsible. Somebody could have been seriously hurt." She threw the spikes in the general direction of the im-mobilized cruisers and climbed back in her Jeep. She slowly drove by the dumbfounded troopers and then stopped. She found her cellphone and quickly took a series of pictures of the irate men. The look on their faces was priceless and she began to laugh hysterically.

Before she put the phone away, it began to chirp. "Hi Lisa, can I call you back? I'm busy taunting the state police."

"Amanda what are you doing. Special Agent Lister just called us …"

"I know, Lisa. They shot at me, twice. I'm fine, but they aren't. I didn't kill anyone, just immobilized them." Amanda's roller coaster ride of emotions suddenly dipped into a dark psychotic abyss. "I warned them, but they didn't listen." Mittens the beast was back, and Amanda quickly turned the Jeep around a corner before her vision of two burning state police cruisers became a reality.

"Just go, honey. Disappear. You don't have to fight this battle," Lisa pleaded, and the roaring in Amanda's head eased.

"Unfortunately, they're not giving me a choice, and honestly I don't know how much longer I can restrain myself." She let the Jeep coast to a stop. Two blocks up the road, shrouded in darkness, was the makeshift command center for the HRT and the newly arrived state police. There were at least thirty minds bent on stopping her, and for the first time she began to question the limits of her ability. At best she could control half of them, but the other half … "Lisa, I have to go now. I love you both." She hung up.

Kill them all! Mittens the Demon hissed. Killing them would be easy. Fire, explosions, compressed air blasts—it was all child's play to her, and when they were all dead she would drive through the carnage and maybe snap a few more pictures.

How many lives is your life worth? her conscience asked in Michael's voice. It was a tiny whisper against Mittens's roars, but it echoed through her mind.

I really don't need to hear you now, Amanda answered. *Prove to me that you are my husband, and not some residual memory of him, or a trace of the morality that has brought me only heartache.* She was tired of following rules, of making promises and keeping them, tired of restraining Mittens and all her wonderfully indulgent base instincts. Tired, tired, tired.

She turned off her car lights and got out of the Jeep. They could still see her, and would probably be using their microphones and bullhorns at this point if she hadn't shorted out all their electrical circuits. Two pairs of heavily armed and armored men began to steal along the lawns that faced the residential street. They used bulky night vision goggles to skirt anything that made noise, and Amanda was surprised that she had missed those devices. For a few seconds she watched them creep towards her, weapons up, safeties off. The street light above them suddenly blazed as bright as the sun, blinding everyone except Amanda; the sodium vapor bulb exploded from the sudden charge and once again they were plunged into darkness. The four men were down now, their goggles overloaded by the brilliant light, and Amanda fed off their pain. She walked slowly to the pair on the south side of the street and pinned them to the ground. The line between herself and Mittens had begun to blur.

"You were going to shoot me," she said to their prostrate forms, and then bent to pick up one of their weapons. "It's so light …" She stood and felt more than two dozen minds react to the fact that she was now armed. "Don't test me," she said loudly to the darkness.

"Let the men go, Amanda, and drop the weapon," a voice ordered from the dark.

"Captain Reese," Amanda answered, and then squatted next to the restrained pair of snipers. "You sent them to kill me; why can't I kill them, or you? I would just be responding in kind." She took off their goggles and stared into the faces of the men who would have shot her. "It would be so easy," she said to the terrified men. "Do you know how many times I've been in this situation? How many times I've had to decide whether to let someone go or whether to crush them?" She asked the nearer of the two as the stock of the weapon disintegrated in her grip. "Of course you don't," she smiled. "Do you want to see what it's like?" She reached for the second man and slid him across the grass as if he were no more than a ragdoll. "Do you want to feel the life slowly drain out of another human being? I warn you, it's addicting." He stared back at her in stark terror.

"There is no possibility of escape, Amanda. Lay the weapon on the ground and put your hands on your head," Reese ordered.

"Or what? You'll fire on me again?" Amanda quickly stood and redirected her thoughts to the captain. She tossed the weapon back down the street. "How did that turn out the last time?" She walked past the prone snipers towards the dark command center. Out of the gloom she could start to discern figures; dozens of men in black helmets, fatigues, and body armor were aiming a variety of weapons at her.

"Stay where you are and put your hands on your head. This is your last warning." Captain Reese's voice was becoming more forceful. He boldly stood in the middle of the street with a broken bullhorn in one hand and a handgun in the other.

"I am unarmed." Amanda raised her hands and continued walking towards him. The air began to lighten as a static pressure wave began to build around her. She felt the air molecules compress and watched as they began to emit a faint glow. When she released it, the wave would annihilate everything and everyone within a block's radius. She took another step and her foot barely made contact with the road. She stood virtually weightless, her decision balanced on the point of a pin when the most unlikely of things happened. A dog barked, and then barked again.

Amanda looked to her right and found a familiar, medium-sized Blue Heeler staring at her intently, her head cocked to one side, excitement written all over her face. "Sydney, what are you doing here?" Amanda said angrily. The dejected dog dropped her ears and sat in the grass.

'Can we play? Run? Frisbee?' Her thoughts were cautious but they easily pierced the blast wave that enveloped Amanda. Sydney and her little sister Tasman were Amanda's occasional running mates. They had obviously been left behind when their masters were evacuated from the apartment complex, and had been running free ever since, a situation that was all too common.

"Where's your little sister?" Amanda asked Sydney, who immediately jumped to her feet, tail wagging her whole back end. She looked to a dark hedge of manicured bushes and then took off, disappearing into the darkness. She barked several times and Tasman's higher-pitched bark answered. In less than a minute Sydney reappeared with the salt and pepper Tasman in tow. The younger dog spotted Amanda, dropped the tree branch she was carrying, and sprinted to her human friend. She jumped the curb and flew into Amanda's arms.

"Play. Play. Run. Frisbee." Taz was incessant. Sydney, not to be outdone, circled Amanda, whining an excited tune. Tasman squirmed out of Amanda's arms and jumped onto the back of her sister and the two dogs began to wrestle. For a moment Amanda simply watched the two dogs roll over each other and breathed in the purest form of joy which poured from her two friends.

Amanda finally looked up and found that Captain Reese had been distracted by the spectacle as well. They made eye contact and the air around Amanda began to reform. "Good night, Captain," she said after studying him for several seconds. "Go home to your family." She turned back to her car. Sydney and Tasman led the way, and when they saw the open door, they sprinted for the car and took up their usual spots in the back of the Jeep. Lister was standing by the passenger door.

"Friends of yours?" he asked.

"Best friends," she said tersely, and then climbed into the driver's seat.

Lister opened the passenger door. "I need to go with you. I can get you out of here safely. You can drop me and your friends off once we're clear."

Amanda stared at him, her blood still near the boiling point. "Why?" She asked pointedly.

"Firstly, I don't want to see anyone hurt, and that includes you." He cautiously sat in the leather seat. "Secondly …" He was interrupted as Tasman nuzzled his neck and demanded to be petted. "I saw what happened to you, and I saw what you did. Not just in Washington." He rubbed the dog. "They will never let you go. Ever. There will be no due process, you will simply disappear, and a lot of people will die as they try to hold you. And then you will die." Sydney forced her way under Tasman and displaced her little sister. "I don't know how to feel about what you've done. Maybe if I found myself in your shoes I might have done the same thing. Hell, I probably would have done a lot more." He paused for a moment. "I don't want to see you die because of it. But you need to get your head straight before you can be around people again."

Amanda stared at him, debating how to respond. The fires within her were burning out, and his last line echoed in her mind. "All right, Special Agent, you can come along. But I'm keeping these guys—they should never have been kept in an apartment anyway. So how do we get out of here?"

A note from the author

Amanda's Story is the prequel to *Hybrid*. Set seven years after Amanda disappears into the night *Hybrid* finds her living a quiet, anonymous life. Greg has recently retired but struggles with idleness as a strange flu and an even stranger outbreak of violent crime sweep through Colorado Springs. Amanda begins to sense the presence of another survivor of the Hybrid virus, as both Greg and Lisa notice a tall, dark man has been following them.

Something compels Klaus Reisch to find Amanda Flynn. She is Eve to his Adam, the only two survivors of the Hybrid virus, and nothing, not even his mission to spread a mutated version of the virus through the population of Colorado, will distract him. Only she has disappeared.

Phillip Rucker, the socially awkward coroner who spends more time in his own mind than he does in the real world, knows that something is wrong. He's convinced that the unexplained violence and flu are somehow related, and he has it very nearly worked out when he becomes infected.

Hybrid weaves its way through the corridors of the CDC to the streets of New York and LA as Reisch and his masters attempt to fulfill the Hybrid virus's full potential as the ultimate weapon of mass destruction.

About the Author

Amanda's Story is Brian O'Grady's second novel after his best-selling debut with *Hybrid*. He is a practicing neurologic surgeon and, when he is not writing or performing brain surgery, he struggles with Ironman triathlons. He lives with his wife in Washington state.